THE LOOSE RACK

AND OTHER STORIES

BY TERRY TALLENT

SILVER SPUR PUBLISHING
2015

ISBN: 13 978-0985842420
ISBN: 10 0985842423

LCCN: 2737896001

Silver Spur Publishing
Ojai, California

Front cover photo by Chris Ritke. Taken at 'The Hub' in the Ojai Arcade, 2015.

For Tom

"There is nothing that says more about its creator than the work itself."

Akira Kurosawa

The Loose Rack
& Other Stories

Contents

The Loose Rack

1993

I'm in this murky pool hall in Kailua, Kona sweating like the main course at a *luau*. I'm sweating because I'm in the middle of a best-out-of-seven match for the Kincaid Pool Cup and losing big-time – three games to none. My opponent is my older brother, Jake, who turned fifty years old today. I flew over from the mainland yesterday to help him celebrate.

We have this pool tournament every time he and I get together. I won the last time we hooked up, which was in Ventura about five years ago. Whoever holds the cup always brings it along whenever we plan to meet, and right now it's sitting over there on a ledge next to the pool cues. The trophy looks like gold but it's really only a cheap plastic thing. It has a brass plaque on its wooden base that reads "THE KINCAID POOL CUP." And underneath that, in smaller letters, it says: "Current Champion." It ain't much, but we both covet it just the same.

Coming into the pool hall this afternoon I figured he'd be a pushover because Jake's been drinking beer all day. But his hands are steady and his eyes are icy with concentration. My heart's pounding and I'm feeling a little weak in the knees because I'm in real danger of being swept here.

Even though I'm half in shock, I have enough sense left to realize I've got to stop giving him such a tight rack. So this time, while he's looking the other way, I rack 'em real loose so the balls won't go anywhere when he breaks. That's what you do when someone's shooting like he is. I'm determined not to let this guy sweep me, even if he is my brother and just turned fifty. I didn't come all the way over here to give him the Cup as a birthday present. And besides, if he sweeps me I'll never hear the end of it.

I haven't given up hope because the one thing I've got going for me, the thing I've always had going for me, is luck. Even when life knocked me down I'd look up and there'd be Lady Luck standing there with her hand out to help me up. But you

1

could never say the same thing for brother Jake. He had Irish luck: if it weren't for bad luck, he'd have no luck at all.

So I stand back and watch him sock the cue ball into the loose rack and only three or four balls skitter out and roll weakly towards the railings. The rest of the balls just sit there clustered loosely in the middle.

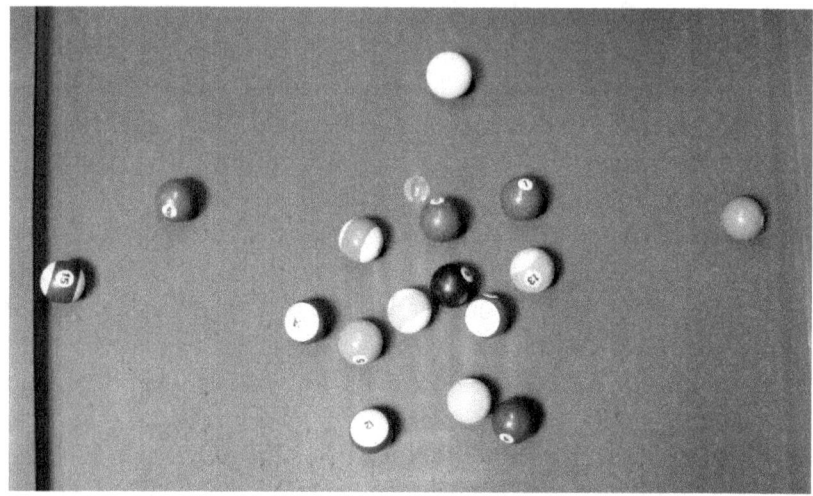

"Nice rack," says Jake, sarcastically.

"Sorry," I say, innocently.

Now we both know we'll have to select our shots carefully. We'll have to hunt and peck and look for openings and play defensively. No more of this slamming balls into the pockets left and right like he's been doing. Now it's a tactical game, a game that will be decided by strategy, and of course, luck.

My brother lives over here on the Big Island. He came here about ten years ago, and it was the best thing he ever did. He must have left most of his bad luck behind, because ever since he came here things have been going well for him. Back on the mainland he was about to go under.

All my brother's bad luck began when we were teenagers back in California. He got his first car when he was sixteen. It was an old beat up 1948 Dodge. He spent a lot of time tinkering with the engine, transmission and brakes; then he slapped some Bondo on the body dings, got a $50 Earl Scheib paint-job, and set the whole shebang down on a new set of retread tires. That old Dodge turned out *primo*. When winter came he decided to show off his new machine by taking a few of his buddies (and me) up into the mountains above Ojai to goof around in the snow. This turned out to be a very bad idea.

Once we got up there we stopped by the roadside and filled up a cardboard box with a bunch of snowballs and went barreling up the mountainside pelting road signs as we went. Pretty soon we started bombarding families building snowmen alongside the road, and then we started in on passing cars. We blasted one old guy's windshield, but then watched in alarm as he slammed on the brakes, turned his car around and started chasing after us with his windshield wipers working overtime.

So Jake put the pedal to the metal and zoomed up the mountainside bent on escape. He rounded a hairpin turn, spun out on a patch of ice, and slid sideways into a berm alongside the road. The car rolled over, like in slow motion, balancing momentarily on two wheels. I looked out the side window and saw we were hanging over a five hundred foot precipice. Oh, no!

The guy sitting shotgun opened the door as we went over and my brother and his two buddies fell out into the snow as the car rolled over them. But since they were in the doorway they didn't get crushed. The car started rolling down the slope sideways with me and my friend Deuce in the back seat. The car went airborne a couple of times, spinning like a high-speed lathe. One of those times it landed on the roof and the windows popped out. Deuce was catapulted out of the back window and into a tree where he got hung up in the branches. Unable to get out, I rode the tumbling car all the way to the bottom where it came to rest upside down. The roof was flattened down level with the body, both doors ripped off; the front seat was gone, as was the hood.

Everyone was all beat up, but no one was killed or seriously injured, and no one even got any stitches. The one who got hurt the most was my brother, of course. He broke his collar bone when the front seat of the car came flying out of the air and landed on his shoulder. So, my brother lost his car, not to mention nearly killing us all. Bad luck, you might say. I figure the only reason we lived through it was because I brought along my good luck.

Meanwhile, back in Kona, I hunt and peck and scratch and claw, and somehow luck my way to a win at that loose-racked game. My brother is stunned. He was on the verge of a great victory. Inconsolable, he turns and reaches instinctively for his beer. But there is no beer. Why? Because this place doesn't serve beer. It's a family billiards joint. It was the only place we could find to play. What a break for me. Now the game score is 3-1. Having escaped a sweep, I'm feeling more confident now. Under my close scrutiny Jake racks 'em up and I blast off into game five.

My brother's bad luck continued. He knocked up his girlfriend when he was nineteen years old. She was seventeen. Being a sincere, thoughtful boy (and not wanting to go to jail), he did what he thought was right. He married her. This was another idea that didn't work out like he planned.

To support his wife and child Jake got a job working for the state of California on a highway survey crew. He also started attending classes at Ventura College three nights a week so as to better himself. On the nights he wasn't at school he washed dishes in a local restaurant to help make ends meet. Not surprisingly, his pretty young wife got bored sitting around the house all the time, and took to cruising Main Street in his '56 Chevy. She met some cute guy and started playing around.

One night the owner of the restaurant where Jake worked had a heart attack and was taken to the hospital. The restaurant closed and Jake got home early that night. He walked in and found some stranger sitting on his couch with his feet on his coffee table, a can of his beer in his hand and an arm around his wife. My brother went ballistic, dragged the guy outside and began beating on him. His wife called the cops and when they pulled up to the rented house, there's my brother with the guy in a headlock, running him into a telephone pole. The cops arrested my brother for assault and handcuffed him. As they drove him off to the station Jake looked out the rear window and saw his wife with her arm around the guy, helping him back into the house.

Several months later he found out his wife was pregnant again. When the kid was born it looked like the guy with the big bump on top of his head. My brother got divorced and ended up paying alimony and child support for two kids.

Because I'm feeling confident now, kind of hitting my stride, I win game five going away. Game score is now 3-2. My concentration is getting sharper by the minute, while Jake's seems to be slipping. Grumbling, he racks 'em up for game six.

So my brother got a Harley Davidson and joined a motorcycle club called *Los Borrachos* (The Drunkards). He figured he'd start having all the wild fun he'd missed when he was married. About this time he met a foxy Asian lady in a bar and asked her out. Before long she was pregnant. So my brother wound up marrying her and they lived together until she got sick and tired of him being gone all the time – either working, going to school, or riding his motorcycle all over the county bar-hopping with his buddies. She divorced him, and so then he was paying alimony to two wives and child support for three kids.

I win game six easily. I'm sharp. I can't miss. Game score tied at three all. One game to go to decide the championship. One game to decide who goes home with the vaunted Kincaid Pool Cup. My brother is the one sweating now and after each missed shot he turns around looking for his beer. "Damn this place," he hisses. "What kind of pool hall is this, anyway?"

So my brother went downhill fast on the mainland. He quit school and his dishwashing job. He wrecked his bike on a weekend ride and got arrested for drunk driving. Then he lost his job with the state. When he got out of jail he met an ugly bar troll. But looking through a haze of alcohol and cheap pot he was convinced she looked like Cleopatra. He asked her to marry him, and she, seeing nothing but dollar signs, agreed. But it didn't take her long to realize that her meal ticket was all punched out because of Jake having to pay so much alimony and child support. So she asked for an annulment. She was willing to settle for a one-time pay-off of a thousand bucks. It was all he could scrounge up, but it was worth every penny. He was then broke and unemployed.

He eventually found a job humping lumber for some house-framing contractors. After he proved himself to be a hard worker they began teaching him some carpentry. After a year or so he thought he was getting pretty good at it. That is, until the day he inadvertently cut off the ends of three of his fingers with a circular saw. Oh, brother. So then he was maimed, unemployed, and on the dole until his hand healed.

While he waited he spent most of his time in bars. He got into fights – one-handed, one-sided fights. One sadistic bully took particular delight in beating him up every time they met. So Jake got one of his patented bright ideas: he bought himself a handgun. One night the bully ran into him in the parking lot of some honky-tonk, but before he could beat my brother up again, Jake ducked into his car and pulled out the pistol. He didn't shoot the guy, but began firing angry shots into the ground and into the air while yelling at the guy how he was sick of all this shit. Somebody in the bar called the cops and they came roaring into the lot and arrested Jake at gunpoint.

But then, against all reason, my brother's luck began to turn. After his hand healed and he got out of jail he joined the carpenters' union and started finding work. By some miracle, he met a fine, decent woman who saw something in him that nobody else did. They got married. The following Christmas they came out here to Hawaii to visit her parents who were retired on the Big Island. The island life and its distance from the source of all his trouble appealed to Jake, and they decided to move out here. In the meantime his first two wives remarried, and so he was off the hook for alimony and child support.

It took him awhile, but he eventually got a full-time job with the Big Island County Parks Department doing construction and repair work in beach parks all around the island. It was his dream job. Before long he was able to buy a house way out on the rugged Puna Coast, far away from all the bad memories and the people who had tortured his soul for all those years. And he was truly happy for the first time in his adult life.

Blam! I sink the eight ball and win game seven, thereby accomplishing one of the greatest comebacks of all time!

Maybe I should have let Jake win, seeing how it's his fiftieth birthday and all. If this had been the game of life I would have. But it ain't. This is pool, man.

The Ventura County Writers Club
Presents this

First Place Award, Adult Category

In this, the Fourteenth Annual Short Story Contest.

to

Terry Tallent

For his story titled, "The Loose Rock."

Presented January 14th, 2014

John B. Baerus, President

Stella Ricksen, Contest Chair

The Coast
2005

The coast of California wanders up from Mexico in a nonchalant sort of way. Traveling in a northwesterly direction it is sometimes caressed, sometimes pummeled by the mighty Pacific. But the coast pays little attention to such vicissitudes. It is in no special hurry to get anywhere, and cares not a whit for traveling in a straight line. It pauses occasionally to embrace tranquil bays or lean an elbow out into the sea to form rugged, windswept promontories. Sometimes it just lays itself out in long, lazy stretches of sandy shore.

When the coast rises from the water's edge it often climbs into steep crumbling bluffs or cliffs from whose heights it casually casts earth and stone down into the sea. At other times it simply shrugs itself up into dunes, or soft, rolling hills. The coast meanders along with this devil-may-care attitude for 1,100 miles before stumbling across the Oregon border.

There is one distinctive stretch of California's coast that deviates from the generally northwesterly heading. It lies in the southern part of the state between Santa Monica Bay and Point Conception. Here the coast bends into a peculiar east-to-west alignment. As a result, if you stand on the beach here and look out to sea you find yourself facing south. This seems odd. Since you're on the West Coast, it seems reasonable to expect the sea to lie to the west. But as you stand on this contrary stretch of shore you are confounded by a southern sea. Hence, this region of California is sometimes referred to as the South Coast.

If the day is clear when you stand here you will see a string of dry, mountainous islands paralleling the coast some twenty miles out to sea. These are the northernmost of the eight Channel Islands. They are so named for the hundred-mile-long channel they form between themselves and the coast. This relatively calm and protected body of water is in turn called the Santa Barbara Channel. It is renowned for its handsome countenance and bountiful marine life.

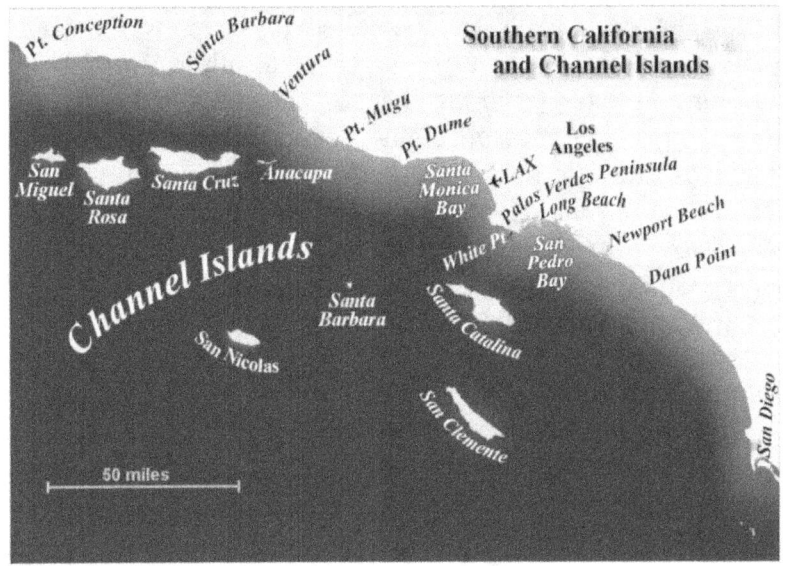

Despite the occasional storm that passes through the region, both the channel and the lands bordering it are blessed with some of the most beguiling weather in the hemisphere. It is a temperate realm of blue skies, brilliant sun, and gentle ocean breezes. Balmy days string themselves together like the pearls of a well-matched necklace. This idyllic Mediterranean-like weather is made possible by continental high pressure playing tag with the oceanic low pressure that ebbs and flows over southern California for much of the year.

Turn your head from the sea and you find that the land behind you is a dry place, a suntanned land of rolling brown hills blanketed by chaparral or covered in wild grasses dotted with oak trees. The hills roll back from the coast, growing higher and higher until they become the mountains of the Transverse ranges. These rugged mountains have long been an impediment to north-south travel in the state. Streams and small rivers flow south out of the mountains to the sea, carving fertile valleys as they go. Armatures of tule, cottonwood, and willow embrace the watercourses, while oak groves and stands of sycamore and alder grace the upland glens and valleys. It is a lovely and deceptively peaceful landscape.

But one should not be lulled to sleep by the benign weather and the South Coast's Arcadian allure, for they can both turn on you. Out in the channel, calm seas and no wind in the morning can presage eight foot swells and twenty knot winds by the afternoon – a perilous environment for small vessels and unwary beachgoers. Periods of dense fog are also a danger to anyone attempting to navigate coastal waters.

On the land, lack of rainfall is a constant threat to life in this arid region. Droughts can last for years. But whether or not in the midst of drought, brush fires are an annual scourge. When coupled with hot, dry east winds, the resulting conflagrations can consume everything in their path. Then, just when it seems destined the whole place will go up in smoke, or turn into a desert, the drought ends in a series of storms that sometimes bring rain of biblical proportions. Flooding and mud slides are the inevitable results. Add to these hazards earthquakes – these rock-rending temblors rumble up like mythical beasts from below terrifying all that live above, and devastating their puny constructions. So too consider the rare but inevitable visits of tsunamis and tempestuous Pacific storms.

But of course, these perils were a threat to life long before humankind came to the South Coast region. Before man appeared, deer, elk, and antelope roamed this tawny landscape unmolested but for the occasional predations of gray wolf, cougar, and Grizzly. Along mountain streams, burly black bears scoured the berry patches by day, while raccoons and other small animals slacked their thirst by night. On the hills and plains, rabbits, squirrels, mice and rats nibbled on the abundant seed and acorn resources. Small predators like fox, bobcat, and coyote found good hunting among the many rodents. So too did rattlesnakes and other serpents, as well as birds of prey like hawks, owls and eagles. The unattended remains of the dead became victual for hungry scavengers of all stripes, including the airborne ones – giant condors, vultures, buzzards, magpies, crows and ravens. Steelhead trout and other fish darted from pool to pool in the slow-moving streams that sauntered down to the sea.

Off shore, copious zooplankton provided a moving buffet for migrating whales. This same plankton offered up a seasonal feast for countless schools of sardines. These and other small pelagic species were in turn a roving banquet for the huge summer runs of bonito, yellowtail, albacore, tuna, and skipjack. Seals, sea lions and dolphins fed on these latter, and were in turn preyed upon by sharks and killer whales. Furry sea otters frolicked amid vast kelp beds and fed on flourishing colonies of shellfish. Sea birds in their multitudes soared and wheeled above the sparkling, wind-spanked sea.

Around the time of Christ this whole rich, dynamic region came to be peopled by a group of Native Americans known as the *Chumash*. They lived here in a benign, fine-tuned harmony with the sea, the land, and the offshore islands. The Chumash were a friendly and intelligent race. Journals kept by the first Europeans to come here describe them as being an industrious people, a people "well-formed and of good body," and that their women had "a neat and graceful appearance." By California Indian standards, they were a rich people, these Chumash. Their wealth came primarily from fishing and trading. They built fine sea worthy canoes in order to travel all along the South Coast and out to the distant islands. They frequently hosted land-bound neighbors from the interior who came to the coast to trade and escape the heat. But the Chumash were not only successful traders and fishermen – they were sophisticated hunters and gatherers as well, and among the finest craftsmen in California. They were indeed worthy occupants of this seemingly idyllic landscape. They lived and prospered here for several thousand years before the Spaniards came among them and changed their lives forever.

As of this writing there are seven cities dotting the South Coast. They are, from east to west: Malibu, Port Hueneme, Oxnard, Ventura, Carpenteria, Santa Barbara, and Goleta. There are numerous other small beachside communities scattered along this south-facing shore, but they are all unincorporated.

Of the cities mentioned above, Ventura is one of the oldest in California. It was formally established by the Franciscan missionary Padre Junipero Serra on Easter Sunday,

1782. He founded a mission there on that day, and the town eventually grew up around it. But it should be noted that even before Serra arrived, a Chumash village called Shisholop, near the mouth of the Ventura River, had been permanently inhabited for seven centuries.

Ventura, known officially as San Buenaventura, is wedged in between the sea and the steep hills that rise behind the town. It is further hemmed in by the Ventura River which empties into the sea just west of town. As Ventura grew, it did so in the only two directions it could – to the east, across a fertile alluvial plain that had once been covered in brush and trees, and to the west along the east side of the Ventura River basin. These areas were used as grazing and farmland during mission times. During the twentieth century they were overlaid by houses, roads, businesses, and eventually freeways.

Some of the stories in this volume are set in and around one particular area of Ventura: a spur of land that juts out into the sea at the mouth of the Ventura River. In the latter half of the nineteenth century, locals called it "The Breakers." When the sport of surfing became popular in the 1950s & '60s it was referred to as "The Point." Currently, it is officially named "Surfers' Point at Seaside Park."

The First Library Murder
2009

I had been re-reading Raymond Chandler's 1953 novel 'The Long Goodbye' and couldn't help notice that whenever Philip Marlowe and his friend Terry Lennox went out for a drink they always ordered Gimlets. And I remembered having read somewhere that the Gimlet was Chandler's favorite drink. So that Saturday night I went out to one of my favorite watering holes, the Village Jester, and tried one on for size. I had never had a Gimlet before. I discovered it is made with two ounces of gin and an ounce of Rose's Lime juice poured over ice and shaken well, then strained into a frosty martini glass rimmed with sugar and garnished with a wedge of lime. A Gimlet may also be served on the rocks. Sixty years ago it was the drink of choice in sunny southern California.

Gimlets go down pretty easy on a warm Saturday night at the Village Jester. I soon lost count of how many I'd had. I was more concerned about making time with the attractive Ojai divorcee I met there. She seemed to like Gimlets too, as long as I was buying. While not the most interesting conversationalist I'd ever met, she did seem to get younger and more charming and beautiful as the night progressed. Sometime around midnight she excused herself to go to the ladies' room, and never returned.

Not surprisingly, I awoke the next morning with a wicked hangover. My head felt like an overripe pumpkin that had been tossed from a speeding car. My throat felt like an abandoned gopher hole in a vacant lot. My stomach felt like something you might find squirming around at the bottom of a compost heap. And, unfortunately for me, I was scheduled to work that day at the Ojai Library.

Luckily, the library doesn't open until noon on Sundays. And I am eternally grateful that the library is a relatively quiet and serene workplace, and that the workload would probably not kill me even if I did have a hangover.

I worked the front desk that day. Traffic was thankfully slow, with only the usual ne'er-do-wells hogging the public computers and the occasional after-church patron wandering in to read newspapers or magazines, or to browse the stacks.

I was desultorily surfing the internet on the staff computer when a short, heavyset woman swung through the front door. She was clad in her Sunday worst – a green rainforest print dress with two red, yellow and blue macaws perched on a limb over her voluminous breasts. Her garb was a cruel assault on my tender rods and cones. The two birds pecked my eyes out, while her patent leather chartreuse purse and matching shoes only added to the pain. A voice twice as loud as it needed to be said, "I'm looking for a book."

"Well, you certainly came to the right place," I groused. "We have about forty thousand of them."

"There's no need to be flippant, young man."

I was vaguely flattered. I'm not that young any more. I tried to focus on the speaker. She would never see seventy again. Her face reminded me of Charles Laughton's in 'The Hunchback of Notre Dame.' I had to look away. The mere thought of swinging on ropes and ringing bells made me nauseous.

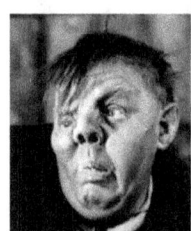
But I did my duty. I said, "I beg your pardon, madam. How can I help you?"

"My girlfriends were talking about a book they're reading. Something about tea. They said it was good. I want to read it."

"Oh, it *does* sound good. I want to read it too. What's it called?"

She glared at me. "If I knew what it was called I'd tell you, wouldn't I?"

"I was hoping you might."

She rolled her eyes. "You are impossible," she said.

"Someone suggested as much last night. Do you know who wrote the book?"

"Of course not." She was starting to steam.

The smell of frying old-lady perfume made me want to run to the men's room. But I stayed the course. I said, "So you don't know the title; you don't know who wrote it; but it had something to do with tea."

She sighed in exasperation. "Yes." She looked over my shoulder through the glass panes of the staff office behind me. "Is there a real librarian here?" she asked.

"Well, I thought *I* was a real librarian, but now I'm not so sure." I pinched myself.

She sighed again, and looked forlornly over at the aisles and aisles of books to her left.

I pressed on. "Was the book fiction or non-fiction?"

She looked worried, thought about it, checked her wrist watch, and then answered quite confidently, "Non-fiction. I think it was about a real man."

"I thought you said it was about tea?"

She held her breath and said nothing.

"So this book was about a real man, not a make-believe man. Was it a biography?"

"No, I don't think so."

I bit my thumb. "Is it a new book or an old book?"

"A new book. Well, maybe a few years old. Maybe more. My friends don't read *really* old books."

"Do you know what the book looks like?"

"Well, yes, I got a glimpse of the cover."

"And…?"

"Oh, I don't know. It was white, I think. It had a picture of some people on the front. Kids, I think."

The light from a cartoon light bulb went on inside my brain and nearly blinded me. I groped my way to the front desk computer and toggled over to the library catalogue. I typed in a name. I picked up a ballpoint pen and wrote "371.82209 Morte" on a Sticky Note pad. I peeled off the little yellow slip and handed it to her. "You'll find the book over there." I pointed towards the second aisle from the left in the non-fiction stacks. "Just find that number and you'll find your book."

She looked at me suspiciously. I deadpanned her.

"Oh," she said, brightening. "Well, alright." She turned and swung uncertainly across the blue carpet to the second aisle.

I sat down heavily on the rolling armchair behind the computer. I felt like I had just extracted a wisdom tooth. I massaged my temples and waited. About a minute passed. Then I heard her over-loud voice squeal in delight. "Oh, I found it! This is it!"

She returned to the desk limping and swinging her arms with that ghastly Laughton smile. She was holding a copy of Greg Mortenson's 'Three Cups of Tea.'

"Oh, my," she said. "You might be a librarian after all."

"There is a rumor to that effect."

"Are you always this impertinent?"

"Only on Sunday."

"Perhaps you should consider working some other day."

"Perhaps you should consider handing me your library card. I cannot check this book out to you without it."

She glared at me and plunked her chartreuse purse on the counter. To my credit I did not wince. After a period of tense searching she extracted her card. She flipped it down on the counter in front of me.

"What's your name, young man?" she said. "I have half a mind to report you."

"I have half a mind too. They call me Rex. Rex Libris. Ha-ha. That's a librarian joke."

She looked at me contemptuously as I scanned the barcode on her card under the red laser light. Her account came up on the screen. A window popped up over it asking me to verify her address. I scrolled down the window and said, "Mrs. Henderson. That's your name isn't it? Charlotte Henderson?"

"Y-yes." She was a little surprised.

"It's a pleasure to make your acquaintance, ma'am. The computer wants to know if you still live on McAndrew Road here in Ojai."

"Why…yes, I do. Warily she asked, "Why do you want to know… Rex?"

"*I* don't want to know. The computer does. It gets curious whenever a card hasn't been used for a long time. I guess you don't come to the library much."

"Well, no. I haven't been here for some time. And I certainly won't be coming in on Sundays anymore."

"That's a pity. I hope I don't miss you."

"You what?"

"I mean I'm pleased you will continue using your public library. And, luckily for you, I work several other days beside Sundays. I may have the pleasure of serving you again."

"I've had enough of your sarcasm for one day, young man. Who is the head librarian here? I want to talk to her about your rude behavior."

"*My* rude behavior? Mm-mm." I scanned the book's barcode and printed her receipt with the due date on it. I slipped the receipt in the book.

As I handed it to her I said, "I'm sorry, but the new head librarian is not in today. Her name is Ms. Grinch, but of course I affectionately call her The Old Bat. You can usually find her fluttering around here Monday through Friday."

"Well, I certainly will. And as for you, you so-called '*Rex*,' you had better start looking for a new job."

"I don't need a job, madam. I do this strictly for the entertainment value. Good day to you."

I felt bad about all this later. How was I to know that within a week Mrs. Henderson would be found murdered? Apparently someone had spiked her herb tea with hemlock.

I know what you're thinking, but it wasn't me.

The Waves

1955

I grew up in the small town of Ojai, California. It is nestled in a little valley inland from Ventura. We didn't have air conditioning back when I was a kid. Nobody did in the 1950s, at least as far as I knew. There may have been a few swamp coolers around, but we didn't have one.

During the months of July, August and September a withering heat settles into the Ojai Valley and squats there for what seems like forever. That's because Ojai is surrounded by steep-rising mountains and in the summertime hardly any breeze can get in to cool things off. Every once in a while, when it got so hot we couldn't even play outside, my mother would pile us kids into our woody station wagon and drive down to Ventura. Ventura was only fifteen miles away, but since it was on the coast it was at least twenty degrees cooler than Ojai. My mother would take us to the beach.

We loved going to the beach. It was so nice to get out of the heat. And we always looked forward to playing in the water. On the way to Ventura my brother and sister and I would be bouncing around in the back seat like so many white Mexican Jumping Beans. Our mother would have to keep telling us to settle down. If we ignored her she would threaten to turn right around and go back home. We would settle down a little, but we never took her threats seriously. She was as eager to get out of the heat as we were. Sometimes she bribed us by telling us that if we behaved she would take us to Mr. Top Hat and buy us all a chilidog. Mr. Top Hat was a little screened-in shack on the corner of Palm and Main Streets, and they made the best chilidogs in the whole world.

On the drive to the coast we would always have the windows down, and by the time we came to the outskirts of Ventura we could feel the cool air, and smell the wonderful tangy brine of the ocean. Sometimes my mother would drive a few miles west of town and pick a secluded spot along the old

18

Pacific Coast Highway, a place with a nice, sandy beach. But most of the time she drove right into Ventura and turned down California Street towards the water. She'd make a left on Beach Road, drive under the old wooden pier, and park in the lot just east of it. I think she liked to go there because they had lifeguards in the summertime.

We kids would tumble out of the car, chattering like so many excited seagulls, scoop up our gear, and race down to the sand. We could barely contain ourselves when we heard the deep rumbling of the breakers. We felt like running and jumping right out of our skins. My mother would choose a spot and have us help her spread out a blanket and set up her beach chair. Then we were on our own. We invariably sprinted down to the water, my little sister to wade in ankle-deep foam, and my brother and I to gallop into deeper water.

One of my early memories of the beach was of my brother and me getting into a wet-sand fight. We were out in the shore break, in water nearly up to our hips. We kept bending over in the water and scooping up handfuls of wet sand and chucking them at each other. We were concentrating on our game, having a blast, and not paying much attention to anything else. Suddenly a big wave came barreling in and knocked us both over. The wave rolled us up and sent us tumbling towards shore. When we finally stopped rolling we staggered to our feet gasping, and looked around with big eyes to see where we were. When we realized we weren't hurt, and no longer in danger, we laughed with delight. It was fun being scared as long as you didn't get hurt too bad.

I guess it was back then that I first fell in love with waves. They were noisy and scary and fun – an excellent combination for a kid.

On one of our excursions to the beach we learned how to body surf by watching the other kids. That was even more fun. We learned you had to wade or swim out to where the waves were just beginning to break. When you saw a good one coming, you turned around and started swimming towards shore. You could feel the wave draw you up and take you with it. Some waves were really quite powerful. Just when the wave folded over, you arched your back and kicked your feet. You could either put your arms in front of you like you were diving, or you could hold them against your sides. The wave would hurl you towards the beach like a missile and break all over and around you. It was so exhilarating. You could stay in the wave a long time if you did it right and kept kicking your legs. If you wanted to stop you just put your feet down and stood up in the water.

When we got tired or cold we would retreat to the beach and scamper up to where our mother was reading and sunning herself in her folding chair. We'd stretch out on towels in the sand. I liked to lie on my stomach facing the water. I'd rest my chin on stacked fists and stare at the waves rolling in off the Pacific. I loved to watch the sunlight sparkling along the face of them as they were about to break. And I would listen closely to the sound they made when they broke: either a soft boom, or a sharp clap, or sometimes a muffled roar. And they just kept on coming, one after another. From where I lay on the beach it was a distant, lonely, and peaceful kind of sound. It made me think that this is what heaven sounded like.

I was mesmerized by the brilliant turbulence of broken waves. It reminded me of puffy white clouds. And their rumblings reminded me of distant thunder. I would lie there for hours staring at the broken waves coming in. They looked a little like rolls of white carpet unrolling all the way up to the beach. I eagerly awaited the sucking sound they made as they were drawn back into the sea to meet the incoming surf. And all those sounds kept overlapping and repeating themselves, creating a soothing rhythm that sometimes put me to sleep right there on my towel.

I loved the waves. Each one was different from the one before and the one after. And each wave was beautiful in its own way, and no two were ever exactly alike. I liked the green ones best, although the blue ones were just as beautiful. Sometimes the waves looked almost purple when it was foggy. Sometimes they were the color of boxcars when a red tide was running, and sometimes they were tan when they were full of sand.

I thought that the waves must always have been there – since the beginning of time even – and that they would always be there. And they would always be the same, and yet never the same. They were like people, I guess. Each one was different, and had different moods.

I remember being surprised every time we made a trip to the beach because it was never the same as the last time we went. The sun would be at a different height or angle and that made the water take on a different look. The weather would be different too – mostly it was sunny, but sometimes it was foggy or cloudy. Sometimes the wind was blowing and it gave the water a rippled or choppy texture. I liked it best when the wind was so calm that it left the water as smooth and shiny as polished jade.

The shape of the waves was always different too. Sometimes they were long and stretched out like taffy, and at other times they were short and peaky like the top of a meringue pie. Sometimes a wave would break all at once, and sometimes in different sections at the same time, and sometimes it would start at one end and break in a smooth line all along its length like the falling of dominoes. Sometimes the waves were taller than I was, and sometimes they were no larger than the wake of a boat.

I noticed the waves seemed to come in towards the beach at slightly different angles depending on what part of the ocean they came from. Sometimes the current made the water feel really cold and at other times it felt as warm as a bath tub. And you couldn't tell if the tide would be high or low or somewhere in between. You just never knew what to expect till you got there.

One thing that was always the same was the delicious taste of chilidogs from Mr. Top Hat. We would stop there either before or after our excursions to the beach. The chilidogs were always served in little cardboard boats. The first few times we ate them we ended up with chili smeared all over our faces and hands and dribbled down the front of our clothes. After that, our mother always insisted we leave our chilidogs in the boats and eat them with plastic spoons. She always got each of us a small carton of milk to go with our chilidogs.

When we went home to Ojai at the end of the day I couldn't help thinking about the waves, how they would just keep on rolling in whether I was there or not. I thought about them sometimes as I lay in my bed at night. I could almost hear them then. It made me feel a little sad thinking about them. I thought it was a shame that no one would be there to watch over them, and to play in them if I wasn't there. I suppose I felt rather protective, or even possessive of them. It seemed as though they belonged to me somehow, or maybe it was me who belonged to them.

I think this is how a surfer is born.

In the Pines
1973

I took a summer job up in the mountains that year. But I was really just killing time until fall rolled around. November was when I was slated to enter America's own version of the French Foreign Legion – the Peace Corps. It wasn't like I was gung-ho to help people help themselves in some downtrodden corner of the world. I was just really fed up with life in the U.S. at the time.

And, well, if you want to know the truth, I was fed up with the way my life was going in general. I was tired of being a perpetual student and being broke all the time. And it didn't help that my live-in girlfriend of three years had evolved into a women's libber and decided she could no longer live with the male chauvinist pig that was oppressing her. And then there was that psychopathic Vietnam veteran I knew who couldn't make up his mind if I was his best friend or his worst enemy. I thought the best thing for me to do was to just get the hell out and get a fresh start somewhere.

But to get anywhere, even in the Peace Corps, you need some startup cash. So that summer I took a temporary job as a maintenance man at a campground way up in the mountains east of Redding. It was up above 4,000 feet, not far from Lassen Volcanic National Park. The camp had fourteen cabins, a dining hall, kitchen, showers, a boat dock, and other recreation facilities. It was nestled on the banks of Lake McCumber, a man-made lake. The dip-shits who created the lake hadn't bothered to clear the vegetation before they dammed up the stream. So there were all these dead trees poking their ugly heads up all over the lake. But the lake was surrounded by a vast, beautiful forest of ponderosa pine and Douglas fir. The nonprofit outfit that owned the campground rented it out to organizations like the YMCA, Boy Scouts, Girl Scouts, and groups of physically and mentally handicapped from around Northern California.

All I had to do was live up there all summer, keep the camp clean, fix broken stuff, and check the various camping groups in and out. I was also the town marshal so to speak. In return they paid me a decent salary, gave me a tent cabin to live in, and free food from the dining hall.

Well, it was a pretty sweet job. Mainly because I didn't have a boss. I had plenty of free time to clear my head. I never read a newspaper or listened to the radio, much less watched TV. The closest town was seven miles away. If I got bored, I'd take a hike, or pull out my trusty guitar and serenade myself. Sometimes I'd take a canoe out on the lake and paddle around.

Everything went along fine until one sultry night in August. I had strolled down to the boat docks to have a smoke and to check that all the rowboats and canoes were tied up. Well, as I was standing there on the dock looking across the water I saw a red glow coming from one of the dead trees out in the lake. I had no idea what it was. I wasn't worried about a fire, it coming from the middle of the lake and all. But I just couldn't figure out what that red glow was. It came and went, kind of like the beacon from a lighthouse. I decided to head on out there and get to the bottom of it.

So I climbed into a rowboat and pulled out across the lake. I kept looking over my shoulder as I rowed, using the red light as a guide. I remember it was very still and quiet out on the water. The only sound was the slap and whish of my oars dipping the glassy surface. There was no moon that night, but the stars of the Milky Way were brilliant in the clear mountain air.

When I got closer to the tree in question I saw a canoe tied up at its base. I looked up in the branches and saw somebody up there. They were perched on one of the lateral limbs smoking a cigarette. I pulled in close just as whoever it was launched the butt into a red arc over the water. I heard it hiss out.

I noticed that the canoe was a red one, which meant it wasn't one of ours. Ours were green. This one must belong to somebody from one of the other camps around the lake. So I figured whoever was up there could do whatever they pleased. It was none of my business.

I turned the rowboat around so I was facing the tree. Just out of curiosity I said, "Hi. What ya doing up there?"

"Smoking," came the reply. It was a woman's voice. Or maybe a girl's. I couldn't tell.

I looked around the silent, empty lake. "Mind if I join you?"

"Get your own tree, mister. If I wanted company I wouldn't be up in a tree in the middle of a lake in the middle of the night now would I?"

Fair enough, I thought. But I shipped my oars anyway. This was too intriguing to pass up. There was no wind and no current on the lake so I stayed pretty much in one spot.

I said, "Well, you don't mind if *I* have a smoke, do you?"

"Why should I? It's a free country."

So I pulled out my baggy of weed and proceeded to roll up a joint. I could tell by the way her head was tilted she was watching me.

"You roll your own, huh?"

"This is a special blend."

I licked the gummed edge, stuck the splif in my mouth and fired it up with my Zippo.

"You're young," she says. "I thought you were an old guy, a ranger or something."

I took a few puffs and held my breath. I was fairly close to the tree and I could see the smoke drifting up among the dead limbs.

"Hey," she said, "That's pot. Can I have some?"

"I thought you didn't want any company."

"Forget that noise," she said. "I'm coming down."

I could tell by the way she climbed that she was young, and that she descended with a good deal of confidence. She had a nice body, nice legs, bare feet. She wore tight shorts made of cut-off Levis and a skimpy top that showed her midriff. Seeing her made me think of Daisy Mae from the Lil' Abner comic strip. But as she got lower I saw she didn't have blond hair like Daisy. Hers was dark like Moonbeam McSwine's.

I unshipped my oars and back-paddled to the tree, puffing on my reefer. She stepped aboard nimbly and sat down on the stern seat. She looked at me expectantly. My eyes were glued to her. She was a lovely creature.

"Come on, buddy," she said. "Don't Bogart that joint."

We passed it back and forth. Between puffs I asked her name. She made a face and said it was Viola, after that hick town on the way to Lassen Park. She said everybody just called her Vee.

She asked me my name and I told her. We kept passing the joint back and forth until it was down to a roach. I tossed it overboard.

"So, what are you *really* doing out here, Vee?"

"Oh, God. I don't know how to explain it. But how about you? What are you doing here? You're not from around here. I can tell."

"I work over at Camp McCumber. I'm only here for the summer. "

"Where're you going after that?"

"The South Pacific."

"Wow. I can't even imagine that."

26

"You could if you tried."

"The only thing I can imagine is getting out of here. And I don't care where it is as long as it's far away."

"That's too bad. What's the problem? It seems like a nice enough place."

"Oh, God. You have no idea. I've been up here in these woods all my life. If you had spent eighteen years here you might feel different. It's these goddamn trees. They're everywhere. You can't ever get away from the trees. They're smothering me I tell you. Them and that son of a bitch old man of mine."

"You mean your father? What's his problem?"

"He says he's trying to protect me. From what, I don't know. But it's like he's always sticking his nose in my business. I can't go anywhere or talk to anybody without him checking up on me. I come out here sometimes where I know he can't find me. It drives him crazy."

"What about your mom?"

"Ah, she took off a long time ago. She couldn't stand him either. Hey, you got any beer or anything?"

"Naw. I'm kinda on the wagon."

"Boring. You gotta car or anything?"

"Yeah, I've got a car."

"Me too. It's my mom's old clunker. Hey, how about you and me driving down to Shingletown? We could go to the Ponderosa. I'll meet you there. They got drinks, and a jukebox. 'You like dancing?"

"Yeah, sure. But if you're only eighteen they won't let you in."

"Sheeut. I go there all the time. It's not just a bar, ya know. It's a restaurant too. They let anybody in. Besides, I know everybody who works there. They let me do what I want."

"I don't know. It's getting kind of late."

"Hell's bells, it's not even nine o'clock yet. Come on, man. Aren't you just bored out of your skull? I bet you haven't had any fun all summer. Come on and dance with me." Then she posed, thrusting out her chest and batting her eyes at me.

It was such a charming and blatant imitation of seduction that I had to laugh. I was warming up to this little scamp. The fact she was so attractive didn't hurt. Maybe I *had* been in the woods too long. So, I agreed to go. She clapped her hands in glee, and made to climb over into her red canoe. She made no attempt at modesty, but allowed me a clear, lingering view of her backside in the process.

I rowed back to the boat dock while she paddled across the lake to the other side. I went to my cabin and got my wallet and keys, then drove the seven miles of winding forest roads to Shingletown. I was eager to see Vee again. She looked good by starlight. But I wanted to see her in a brighter light. The little village was cloaked in darkness, all but the large rustic log structure that housed the Ponderosa. Red neon beer signs hung in the windows, and the sound of country music drifted out the wide-open front door.

I went inside and didn't see her anywhere. I ordered a mug of beer from the burly bartender. There weren't many patrons there that night. Just a few old guys in flannel shirts huddled up in a booth smoking cigarettes, telling lies and exchanging old hunting stories. A middle-aged couple and a family of campers were having late dinners in the restaurant.

Ten minutes passed, and then I heard the familiar but long-forgotten click of high heels on the floor. I turned to see Vee sashaying through the doorway. I nearly choked on my beer. She had changed into a whole new outfit: a short, red, form-fitting shift and red pumps. She looked terrific and she knew it. The effect was rendered even more charming when I noticed her wobble a bit on her high heels as she angled over to the bar area.

"Hi, handsome," she said, smiling impishly. She hooked her arm under mine. "Buy me a drink, will ya?" She turned to the bartender and said, "Hey, Dick, the usual."

Dick sighed, shrugged, and turned towards the shelves behind him.

"Man, this place is dead," said Vee. "Don't worry, we'll change that. Hey, John, you look better than I thought."

"So do you," I said. She reached over and squeezed my arm.

Dick served up something red and bubbly that had a maraschino cherry in it. I suspected it was something other than a Shirley Temple.

Vee took me by the hand and led me over to a corner booth. We talked for a while, getting to know each other. We had another round.

"Hey," she said to me, "you got any quarters?"

I handed her some. She got up and went to the now silent juke box. She plopped the coins in and started punching letters and numbers like a secretary typing a memo. A rock song came on with a heavy back beat. The next thing I know I'm out on the dance floor with Vee trying to keep up with her craziness. As she zigged and zagged and swayed and swirled she kept her eyes on me. I kept mine on hers. How could I not? She was incredible. After the third quarter the music turned slow. We danced slow and held each other close. I was a goner. The pot, the drinks, the altitude, the dancing. It all made me feel dizzy. I was weightless and floating. The only thing that held me to the earth was holding onto her.

We ended up in a deserted campground among the pines, in my van. I had a mattress in the back. As tacky as it might seem, we had the time of our lives. We might as well have been in the Waldorf Astoria. She was wonderful. And she didn't give a damn about anything.

The rest of the summer was a blur. I saw her almost every day or night. We were glued to one another. She seemed never to stop talking except when we were kissing. By night we were like octopuses. Our tentacle fingers were all over each other. We grasped, we caressed, we tickled, we kneaded. By day we were more like kittens. We arched and stretched, we wrestled and batted each other. We cuddled and groomed, and purred with delight.

But I have to admit that I never considered getting really serious about Vee; I was on my way out of the country. Yes, she was good-looking, and yes she was a fun and welcome diversion from my routine job. But we really didn't have much in common. She was a scatter-brained teenager, and I was ten years older and had three college degrees.

Regardless, my work suffered at Camp McCumber. I just could not be bothered with some of my mundane duties. I got a wakeup call at the end of August when the leader of the last camping group of the summer informed me that a man had come looking for me the previous evening. I asked who he was. He said he didn't know, but that he looked like a lumberjack… a big lumberjack. I couldn't understand who it might be. It couldn't have been my boss from down in Redding. He was a lawyer and always wore a shirt and tie and looked nothing like a lumberjack.

The following day I drove over to Vee's house as we had arranged the night before. She had invited me to lunch and had told me that no one would be home. I found the address and drove through a stand of trees to a clearing in the forest. A large log cabin stood in the center. Vee's old clunker was parked off to one side. She was sitting on a porch swing under the clapboard awning. She waved and rushed out to greet me.

We sat on the swing together and ate sandwiches and drank lemonade.

"Did you bring your guitar?" she asked. I had. I'm no great musician, but she seemed to enjoy listening and watching me play. I sing a little too. She liked that. And any musician worth his salt enjoys playing for an appreciative audience. So I walked out to my van to get my guitar. I slid open the side door and reached inside. Just then I heard a speeding vehicle out on the roadway. It slowed down rapidly, and turned into the driveway. It was a dark green pickup truck with a large bearded man behind the wheel.

"Oh, shit," said Vee. "That's my dad."

The man drove in quickly and parked next to my van. I stood by the open door with my guitar in my left hand. The man stared at me fixedly for a moment, and then glanced inside the van at my mattress. He did not look happy. He jerked at his hand brake and shut off the engine. I heard Vee hop off the porch and hurry towards us.

"Hi, Dad," she said nervously. "You're home early."

Her father never took his eyes off me. He got out of the pickup and slammed the door. He was at least a half a foot taller than me with broad shoulders, a powerful chest, and big meaty arms. He wore a baseball cap, a wool shirt, Levis, and work boots. I would put his age at about forty. A very fit forty. "Who's this?" he said.

"This is my friend, John. John this is my dad, Jim McBride."

"'Glad to meet you, sir," I said, and held out my hand. I watched it disappear into his big calloused paw. He tightened his grip until just before I started to squirm, and then eased up. Then he let go with a smirk.

"What are you doing here, John?"

"Well, Vee asked me to stop by for a bite to eat and to play a little guitar. But it's getting late and I think I better be going."

"No, no," he said. "Come on and play something. I'd like to see what you can do."

"No, I'd really rather not."

"Oh, but I insist. Come on, John. Let's go over and sit on the porch." He clapped his heavy arm across my shoulders and turned me towards the house.

The next twenty minutes were the most excruciating I ever spent. Poor Vee sat on one side of me on the porch swing. She looked pale and tense. Her father pulled up a chair next to me on the other side. He sat uncomfortably close to me. My nerves were shot.

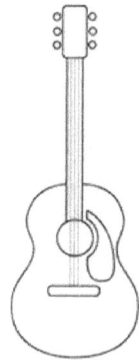

I strummed a chord. The guitar was a little out of tune. Mr. McBride grinned. I tried tuning up, but I was so nervous I couldn't seem to get it right. After a minute or so Mr. McBride started fidgeting. I decided to go ahead and play even though it was still not right.

I tried a couple of little instrumentals on for size. They sounded pretty pathetic. I couldn't find the rhythm. Mr. McBride interrupted and said, "Come on, John. Sing us a song. Come on, I want to hear you sing." All along he had been staring at me intently. I could feel his eyes boring into me even when I wasn't looking. He was the toughest audience I ever faced.

I sighed and without thinking began the song I should have avoided at all costs: 'Black Girl.' It's a folk ballad about an orphaned and disgraced black girl who spends her nights "in the pines, in the pines, where the sun never shines, and she shivers the whole night through." I guess I picked it because it was one of Vee's favorites. It's played in A minor with a standard three-chord progression with a little Am7 thrown in. I didn't remember until too late that there is a verse in it that no suitor in his right mind would play in front of his loved one's parent.

The verse goes like this: "Black girl, black girl, don't you lie to me. Tell me where did you get that dress of red?"

"I got it from miner who works in the hills, and I paid with my maidenhead."

When I sang that last line my voice cracked. I stopped playing. I glanced at Vee's father. His face was red and he looked like he was about ready to explode. I braced myself. I thought he was about to get up and crush me like a bug.

Instead he turned to Vee and said, "Why don't you stay here for a minute, honey. I want to talk to John inside."

Vee nodded solemnly.

Mr. McBride led me inside the house. He walked up to a gun cabinet standing against one wall. He unlocked it with a key. I almost soiled myself right then and there.

He reached inside and pulled out a bottle of Jack Daniels and two glasses. He poured a shot into each. He held one out to me and said, "I've got to hand it to you, John. You've got a lot of nerve."

We both took a drink. Then, looking me in the eye, he said, "Welcome to the family, son."

I started coughing, and Mr. McBride laughed and slapped me on the back a few times, harder than necessary I thought. I was pretty freaked out. I couldn't tell if he was putting me on or what.

After ten more minutes of agonizing awkwardness amid a profusion of excuses why I had to be leaving, I was finally able to extradite myself from the premises.

The summer camping season at Camp McCumber ended the following day. After I checked out the last group I was kept busy cleaning up the grounds, storing the boats and equipment, and prepping the buildings for the cold and snow of the coming winter. It took several days of hard work to get the campground all shipshape. When it was all done I left the mountain, and I never saw Vee or her father again.

A Letter from Samoa

1976

Dear Brother,

You must be surprised to hear from me after all these years. I wonder if you think of me now and then, and are perhaps curious about what became of me, the black sheep of the family. I sometimes think of you and our sister and our parents. I can still see your faces, although I suspect they have all aged some since I last saw you. I know you and I were never 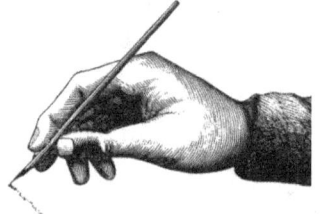 that close, but lately I've been thinking that since we *are* brothers, we ought to at least know where the other is and how we're getting along in life. I will understand if you choose not to answer this letter.

At present I am living in a secluded beach shack way out on the eastern tip of the island of Upolu. This island is part of the Samoan archipelago. Upolu is some forty-seven miles long and about twenty across, very tropical, mountainous, and primitive. There is an even larger, more primitive island to the west of us – Savai'i. Scattered around these two are a number of smaller, low-lying islands, most of them uninhabited. We are located just below the equator, about half way between Hawaii and New Zealand. In other words, out in the middle of nowhere.

My shack, with its paint-blistered, termite-riddled walls and its rusty corrugated iron roof, perches precariously on cement pylons just above the sand. It has no running water, no electricity and no phone. For domestic use, I collect rainwater off the roof by way of gutters and downspouts that empty into renovated fifty-gallon oil drums. There is no shortage of rainfall in these latitudes. I light the place at night with candles if there is no wind, or kerosene lanterns if there is. I cook my simple meals on a two-burner kerosene stove, or, if the weather is fine, over a wood fire under an open-sided shed next to the house.

This dilapidated abode of mine was originally constructed by New Zealanders some forty years ago, back when they governed this small island country. The house originally served as a district medical clinic. But after these islands gained their independence in 1962 the house was abandoned when the native government couldn't afford to staff and maintain it any longer. For years it sat here padlocked and empty, much battered by the elements.

Then a few years ago I came along and blew a little life back into the place. I cleaned it up and made what rudimentary repairs I could with borrowed tools and scavenged materials. Then I collected enough kitchenware and second-hand furniture to make the place habitable again, even comfortable if you're not too picky, which apparently I'm not. Living here is a little like camping out.

My furniture is of local manufacture, a little the worse for wear, but constructed of good native hardwood. I have two well-worn armchairs, a large writing table of variable leg-length (which I steady with cardboard shims), a settee and footrest with matching though somewhat tattered kapok cushions, an ample but almost humorously warped set of book shelves, a kitchen table of rich patina with matching bench, and a screened-in food safe (the legs of which are set in tuna tins half-filled with kerosene to keep the ants out). I built my own bed by nailing together reclaimed lumber, and then fitted it with a kapok mattress and pillow, and, of course, the obligatory mosquito net. My few clothes hang adjacent to my bed on an old broomstick suspended horizontally from the ceiling.

The screen door on the landward side of the house was so warped and out of alignment it refused to stay shut. Since keeping insects at bay is a priority here in the tropics, I had to find a way of keeping it closed. My solution was to attach a cord to a cup hook screwed into the top corner above the handle. The cord then runs over to a pulley which is attached to the ceiling near the side wall. The cord passes through the pulley and drops down near the floor where it is tied to the neck of an empty wine jug. When someone opens the door, the jug gets pulled up in the air. When the person passes through the door and lets it go, the weight of the jug pulls the door closed behind them. The jug bumps the wall going up and down, alerting the inhabitant that someone has opened the door.

As dilapidated and Spartan as my beach shack may be, its many louvered windows look out on a panorama of uncompromised beauty. Close in, the warm, amber-colored sand is lapped by a glistening expanse of turquoise lagoon. The glassy surface of this body of water reflects the wavering, ever-changing image of an inverted sky. Further out, the purple arm of a fringing reef lies across the shoulder of the lagoon, and beyond it tumultuous blue rollers pound themselves into a muffled white-foamed  oblivion. Half an indigo mile beyond the reef, amidst a jig-saw puzzle of submerged coral, lie a cluster of uninhabited, bush-covered, sand-circled islets where sea turtles go to lay their eggs on moonless nights like this one. Past those islets the South Pacific Ocean spreads out dark, vast, and empty all the way to the curving, star-crowned horizon.

A green river running down out of the lush volcanic mountains behind me empties into the lagoon just west of here. There is a V-shaped opening in the reef where the river flows into the sea. Sometimes I go surfing near that opening in the reef. (Yes, I brought my board with me.) But I have to be wary around that opening because it is a favorite haunt of the sharks. They wait there for refuse and dead things to come floating out with the current.

About a ten-minute walk to the east of my beach shack, right along the shore, sits the Samoan village of Lilo. It is the closest of about five primitive fishing villages spread along this part of the coast. Lilo is the home of perhaps twenty Samoan fishermen and their families. One of these fishermen has a beautiful daughter named *Masina*. She sometimes visits me in the middle of the night. Masina means "Moon" in Samoan. It is an appropriate name for her, for I rarely see her but by the light of the moon.

Because of the perpetual heat and humidity the people of these rural villages wear nothing but a rectangle of bright cotton cloth wrapped loosely around their bodies. This sarong or kilt-like garment is called a *lava lava*. The men wear it tucked in around their waist, the women wrap it around themselves from above the breasts to down about mid-thigh. Footwear consists of rubber thonged sandals.

The Samoans have made many adaptations to the tropical climate. The most obvious of these is the exclusion of walls in their houses. Their traditional thatch-roofed huts, called *fales* (faw-lays), provide shade from the scalding sun, shelter from torrential rain, yet allow ocean breezes to flow through unimpeded, thereby cooling and refreshing the inhabitants.

But for all a fale's airiness, there is a trade-off, for it provides no privacy to its occupants. Not surprisingly, the Samoans don't seem to care much. In fact, they behave as if living with no barriers between them and their neighbors is the most natural thing in the world. One might note, however, that the Samoans seem unduly fond of keeping track of their neighbor's business. Their constant scrutiny of one another provides an unending source of entertainment in these isolated villages, not to mention a perpetual supply of grist for the gossip mill. But then, this is part and parcel of how the culture regulates itself.

Be that as it may, a more certain drawback of residing in a house with no walls is that its denizens must be content to share their living space with an extravagant insect population – flies, nats, wasps and hornets by day; mosquitoes, beetles and thumb-sized cockroaches by night. One can add to this menagerie the infrequent but always disconcerting incursions of centipedes, scorpions, and rats. Although these last three are dealt with summarily, overall the Samoans demonstrate an abiding acceptance of the natural world. I suppose this comes from living close to the earth.

By tradition, each family owns a strip of land that runs from the seashore up into the mountains behind the village. On these long, narrow plantations they grow coconut, taro, breadfruit, and other tropical foodstuffs. The natives also keep pigs and chickens and cats and dogs, all of which roam free around the village. One must take care where one steps when walking in the village. When someone visits a local house, he or she always removes their sandals before entering.

I am something of an anachronism out here in the districts. It is not, as you might think, solely because I am a *palagi* (pah-long-ee), a white man. I am an anachronism because I don't have a family. I live alone. This is almost unheard of out here in the heart of Polynesia. To a Polynesian, family is everything. It is the basis of society and of the rich culture that has evolved here. Family is the well from which one's identity springs.

To choose to live alone, as I did, absolutely befuddles the Samoans. They look upon me like we Americans might look upon a visitor from another planet. Being somewhat superstitious, some of the villagers even fear me. They suspect I might be an *aitu* (ah-ee-too), a ghost. Accordingly, some give this shack a wide berth. Only Masina knows for sure I am no ghost.

It was not easy to explain myself to these people when I first came here. The villagers had been told before my arrival that I was a Marine Biologist who was coming to start a sea turtle conservation project. These facts did not enlighten them very much, for they did not know what a Marine Biologist was, nor did they understand the meaning of "conservation project." All they got out of it was "sea turtle." They knew they liked to eat sea turtles. Perhaps they thought I was going to help catch them. If that is what they thought they were mistaken, for part of my job is to keep them from doing just that... at least for the foreseeable future.

In old Samoa my job would have been superfluous, for by long-standing custom commoners were forbidden to eat sea turtles. Back then only chiefs were allowed to eat of its flesh or suck of its eggs. This strictly-held practice had inadvertently kept the sea turtles from being over-fished. But as the 18th century melted into the 19th, Samoa began to be visited by the human flotsam and jetsam of the Western world. First came the early explorers, then the whalers, and on their heels, the traders. Occasionally a deserter or escaped convict would find haven here, sailors continued to drop and raise anchor, beach combers came and went, wild-eyed hermits perhaps found refuge in the hills, and eventually, most regrettably, the missionaries came to stay.

With the wholesale conversion to Christianity, Samoan culture underwent a period of radical change. The powers of the chiefs were greatly diminished, and many of the old customs were abandoned, among them the taboo on eating sea turtles. The common people soon acquired a taste for them, and in their child-like fondness for excess, gorged themselves on these hapless, harmless, easily captured reptiles. Over the years the number of sea turtles declined until so few remained that their extinction in local waters seemed imminent.

Then, a few years ago, I appeared. I was just passing through, on my way to nowhere in particular, just a shell-shocked refugee reeling from the twentieth century. I was

39

staying a few days at Aggie Grey's Hotel over on the other side of the island, in the old ramshackle capital of Apia. One night in the hotel bar I struck up a conversation with a local man, a middle-aged German-Samoan fellow. I learned that he was the Director of the Fisheries Department for the newly formed and cash-strapped Samoan government. When I mentioned I had a degree in Marine Biology, his eyes lit up like a couple of Neon Tetras. He eagerly told me about the turtle conservation project that had been proposed, but not implemented because of the lack of a qualified person to run it. He had been dreading the thought of trying to recruit someone from overseas with the paltry salary they were offering. With hope and desperation in his eyes he asked me if I'd be interested in the position. He told me about this house and the friendly people nearby. It did not take me long to answer in the affirmative. Much to my surprise, he hired me on the spot, right there in the bar.

So here I came to rest. The pay is a joke, of course, but it is enough to keep me in food, candles, kerosene, and alcohol. And my job... what an utter joy! I wander the beaches of this lush island, and those lonely islets beyond the reef, beachcombing while searching for traces of sea turtle activity. I find some very interesting things on the beach. On certain rare occasions I come across a disturbed area in the sand. I know from experience that it is a sea turtle nesting site. I carefully dig down and locate the nest and then disinter the new-laid eggs. I bring them over here in my government-issued outrigger canoe, and re-bury them in front of the beach shack (known officially as The Aliepata Turtle Hatchery). I put chicken wire cages over the top of the nests so when the baby turtles hatch and dig up out of the sand, I can collect them and protect them from the birds, rats, dogs and fishes that would otherwise eat all or most of them.

I raise the hatchlings in rows of open coffin-like, concrete tanks of sea water that I built next to the shack. I feed my little charges on jellyfish and sea grass until they have outgrown most of their natural enemies. Eventually I take them out in my canoe and release them in the open ocean. Hopefully, they will come back in a few years to mate in local waters and lay their eggs on nearby beaches.

Sometimes I wonder if I'm wasting my time. I have no way of knowing at this point whether my efforts will have any impact at all on the turtle population. It will take years to determine that. And even if I am successful in re-establishing them here in viable numbers, who can say that the people will not just fish them back to the verge of extinction again. I suppose one just has to have faith that things will work out somehow, that things will get better. At least I am trying to do something. And if it turns out that I am wasting my time, I at least can think of no other place I'd rather do it.

The most difficult part of my job (other than keeping the sea and its creatures from swallowing me up) is to try to enforce the ban on the taking of turtles by local fishermen. The difficulty lies partly with the nature of the people and partly with their perception of me, an outsider and a white man.

The Samoans are a big people, and they have enormous appetites. They love to eat. While they consider variety in their diet important, it is a distant second to quantity. And in regards to quantity, it is common knowledge among the people here that a sea turtle can exceed even a large pig in size and weight. A full-grown green sea turtle (the prevalent variety here) can weigh as much as 200 pounds. The sea turtle has other advantages over a pig – you don't have to feed it all its life, and you don't have to worry about it plundering your (or your neighbor's) plantation. And what could be easier than to paddle up to a turtle dozing on the surface of the sea, grab it, and hoist it upside-down into your boat?

There are other factors at work. Samoans are known to be an extremely tough, war-like people with an over-abundance of pride. They would think little of breaking a head if that head was the source of an insult, whether intended or not. Add to the above trait the fact that the Samoans don't take kindly to a skinny (relatively speaking) white man telling them what to do on their own fishing grounds, and you can see why it takes a great deal of tact and a full measure of politeness to play "game warden" here.

And so it is that half of the people fear me because they think I am a ghost, and the other half resent me because I am a butt-in-ski and an ugly white man to boot. It is understandable then that I lead a somewhat lonely life here. But I don't mind. Really I don't. It is what I expected. It is in fact at the bottom of why I came out here in the first place. Still, it does get tiresome... being alone so much of the time I mean.

By the way, I have made arrangements with a local fisherman who owns a pickup truck to take this letter to Apia tomorrow. He and some of the others are out beyond the reef tonight fishing with torches. In the morning he will take their catch in the pickup to the open-air market in Apia, and promises to drop this letter off at the post office.

I am thinking Masina may come tonight. She will walk in the shadows alongside the dirt road that leads past my place. Masina no longer comes to me along the beach, because our secret was nearly discovered one morning when the village pastor awoke and noticed footprints in the sand. He saw one set

of tracks going away from the village, and one set returning. Being a fisherman himself, and knowing the rhythm of the tides, he knew the tracks had been made in the middle of the night. Luckily for me, the morning tide came in before he could finish his breakfast. The little wavelets from the lagoon washed away the footprints and left their destination undisclosed.

The pastor told the congregation of his finding during his sermon the following Sunday. He reminded the villagers that when they heard the pounding of the great hollow log at 10 PM, a strict curfew was in force. He informed them that it was in the dark of night that the Devil most often worked his mischief, and therefore all *good* Samoans should remain in their fales after the drumming sound. The pastor and the high-chief of the village would be watching, he told them, and woe be unto anyone caught "fale-creeping," as he called it. The pastor and the high-chief called upon the *aumaga* (ow-monga) to deliver a sound thrashing to anyone caught outside after curfew. (Loosely translated, aumaga means "the strength of the village." It is the organization of young untitled men which exists to serve the will of the village chiefs. In olden times, they were the warriors, but now they are the equivalent of public servants.) The pastor further stated that the council of chiefs would also levy a stiff fine against the family of the miscreant. The fine would consist of food.

Masina laughed about this later. She knows that the pastor and the high-chief are already the best fed people in the village. They would never be able to stay awake after the pounding of the hollow log. Their full stomachs make them sleep as if their heads had been pounded instead of the great hollow log. Her biggest worry is of running into one of the other young people from her village on their way to their own shadowy trysts. But then again, worrying is not something Masina spends a lot of time doing.

I am the one who should worry. As a government employee, I must keep good relations with the villages here in the districts. If Masina and I are discovered, there may be trouble. There may even be a scandal that rocks me right out of my job, my little beach shack, and even out of this country. I do not want that to happen for I have grown quite fond of Samoa, and of Masina.

I should perhaps mention that Masina chose me as her lover, rather than the other way around. And despite the fact that I have learned to speak a little Samoan, and Masina can speak a smattering of English, we seem to have little to talk about. What's more, we have no real interest in talking. Sometimes when she comes in the night, not a single word passes between us.

About the only thing we truly have in common is an incredibly strong desire to explore each other's bodies with our hands, our lips, our tongues, and our hungry loins. Sometimes she comes gliding out of the blackness like some kind of exotic, nocturnal feline. She makes a sound, like a panther, moaning with her need. I sense that she does not really trust me, the male cat. In some ways she even hates me, but when her desire rises in the night, she seeks me out, and she will not be denied. My neck knows the feel of her clinging bite.

I neither encourage nor discourage these nocturnal visits of Masina. She comes like a force of nature, like the wind, or the incoming tide, or the rising of the moon after which she is named. Who am I to attempt to change these vital surgings?

God only knows what Masina really is, or what she thinks of me. Perhaps she actually thinks I am an aitu. Perhaps by coupling with me she is making her own dark pact with the Devil. Or perhaps she is using the white knife of my maleness to cut herself free from the strictures of village life that bind her in a web of conformity.

I cannot fathom her mind, nor she mine. We come from different worlds. All we know is that we do this thing because of some undeniable compulsion that can only find its resolution under the cover of darkness. This is the way that all young Samoans make love, for the missionaries have done an exceedingly fine job in these islands. The days of open affection and guiltless sex have long since passed.

It is nearly 11 o'clock, and I have retired for the evening. I am finishing this letter while lying in my kapok bed. A warm breeze wafting through the louver windows sends ripples along the mosquito net. I watch the gossamer swells by the dim light of the kerosene lantern next to my bed. I love to watch these airy waves wash along the silvery gauze that envelopes me and protects me from those irksome winged stingers and crawling night things. I feel snug and safe within my tiffany womb.

It is good to take pleasure in this simple thing. As each day melts into the next I take greater and greater joy from such simple things. My life is so much better now. I feel a calm that I never felt before. There is a rhythm out here in the great Pacific, a rhythm that gets into your blood. It is like the ebb and flow of the tides. It is natural and as regular as the beating of your heart.

There is some mysterious, invisible force out here that somehow gets inside you. It changes you, brother. Perhaps it has something to do with the vast emptiness of the sea and sky. Somehow you feel smaller out here. Maybe it's the simple, non-mechanical sounds of the island, like now, the sounds I hear in the night: cicadas chittering in the trees across the deserted road, the murmur of waves breaking sporadically far out along the reef, the rasp of palm fronds whispering among themselves in the breeze beside the house, a lone dog barking far off in the distance...

As I lie in my bed, I try to think of how long I have been here in the islands. It has been several years now. I seem to be losing all track of time. I can feel by the gradual rise in the humidity that the rainy season will soon be with us again, and I know it is either late September or early October, but for the life of me I can't think of the date. I'll have to check my turtle calendar. Well, I suppose it doesn't really matter. What matters is that I'm here and not back in the hurley-burley of your modern world. I'd rather not even think about that world. What it has become only upsets me, saddens me.

Why I chose to live out in the middle of this great yawning sea, I'm not quite sure. Perhaps somewhere out here in the vast reaches of the earth's mightiest ocean there is a siren singing whom only lost souls can hear.

I knew when I first came out this way I was searching for something, but I didn't know what. A place perhaps. A place where I might lose my old self. A place where I might find something to do with the new self I felt growing up out of the ashes of my past. I wanted to do something with this new self that was more personally satisfying than anything I had ever done before. It would be something less artificial, something more closely connected to the earth and her great oceans. My soul was hungry for this change.

It is late, and I am feeling very sleepy now. But wait. I hear the whir of the pulley and the bump of the wine jug on the wall. I know of only one person who would walk unannounced into my house in the middle of the night.

Sorry, brother. I've got to go.

Moving to Ventura
1959

I would probably never have become a surfer if my family had stayed living in Ojai. The beach was too far away and I had no way of getting there on my own. I was lucky in a way – my family didn't stay in Ojai. In 1958, for reasons I have never understood, my parents decided they didn't like each other anymore. They decided to split up. At first I thought maybe it was something I did. I gave it a lot of thought, but I couldn't think of anything really bad that I had done. At least that they knew about.

I was thirteen when they sold the house in Ojai. My dad, who was a pharmacist, moved away to Long Beach. My mother took us kids out of school right after Christmas and we moved to Ventura. She got a job as a registered nurse at the county hospital, and with the proceeds from the sale of the house in Ojai, put the down payment on a brand-new tract house. It was located on a steep hill above Ventura High School.

From a kid's point of view we got a pretty raw deal. Our family broke up, we lost our dad and the fine old house we grew up in (not to mention the full-sized, antique Brunswick pool table we had inherited from grandpa), and we lost all our childhood friends. We ended up in new schools in a much bigger town where we didn't know anybody. And our mother was moody and weepy all the time. Sometimes she snapped or snarled at us. As you might imagine, we were not happy campers.

About the only good thing I could see coming out of the deal was that we were close to the beach. But in January of 1959, the month we moved to Ventura, the beach was not as pleasant as it had been in summertime. It was often cold and windy and cloudy. And the winter storms had washed away all the nice white sand and left a layer of beach rocks in its place. The air and the water were always cold, and the big waves and strong currents took all the fun out of swimming.

But still, on weekends my older brother Jake and I would pester my mother to take us down to the beach. If she didn't want to go, we'd ask her to just drop us off when she went to the market or whatever, and pick us up later. There were three good reasons we wanted to go down there: one, it was kind of depressing sitting around our new house on the hill with our mother moping around and drowning her sorrows; two, we didn't have a pool table anymore, which was our major form of recreation in Ojai; and three, we'd found something new and exciting going on at the beach — surfing!

We discovered a place about a quarter mile up the coast from the Ventura pier where surfers congregated. It was called The Point. The coastline juts out into the Santa Barbara Channel right there and creates a nice angle for waves to form. The waves at The Point are usually shaped in long, smooth lines that begin breaking out at the far end and continue along in a regular progression all along their length. That makes them perfect for surf riding.

In the early months of 1959 my brother Jake and I spent many blissful weekend hours watching the surfers at The Point. Sometimes winter storms would create massive waves. It was so thrilling to watch the young men who rode those waves. Every once in a while we would see a surfer get a spectacular ride that made us jump up and down with excitement. Sometimes it was frightening though, like when a huge swell would break on top of a surfer and he would get buried alive under a mountain of water. We would go "Oooh," and look at each other in alarm. We would anxiously watch until we saw the surfer come up and start swimming into the beach to retrieve his board. In those days nobody used ankle leashes like they have now. An ankle leash, usually six to eight feet long, tethers your board to your ankle so you don't lose it when you fall off. But back then if you lost your surfboard, you had to swim after it. A lot of times it would wash all the way in to the beach. Sometimes my brother and I, or someone else, would hurry down to the water's edge to keep a surfboard from slamming into the rocks along the shore. If the board hit the rocks it often got damaged, or *dinged* as they say in surfer parlance. Surfers appreciated it if you saved their boards.

We tried to inconspicuously hang around where they gathered when they weren't out in the water. They all seemed to congregate at the foot of Palm St. There was an old Victorian house on the west side of the street, and there were several older surfers who lived there. Quite a few of the local surfers would gather on the front lawn of the house, or around the low bluff at the end of the street.

Jake and I listened carefully to what they were saying, and we stole yearning glances at their surfboards laid out in a row on the wooden barricade at the foot of Palm. We learned some of the terminology of surfing by listening to them. We learned that the front of a surfboard was called the *nose*, the back was the *tail*, the sides were the *rails*, and the fin underneath was the *skeg*. We also learned that a *takeoff* was when you first caught a wave, and a *kick out* was what you did to exit a wave. When it was impossible to kick out, you had to *bail out,* which meant you jumped or dove into the water to keep from getting *wiped out,* which was when the wave broke on you and knocked you off your board. We learned that when you were riding a wave you could go faster by walking forward on the board and slower by walking back. We learned that *Gremlins* were young surfers, *Kooks* were beginners who thought they knew how to surf but didn't, and *Hodads* were guys who had surfboards and who dressed, talked, and acted like surfers but never went out in the water. They were fake surfers. Real surfers despised them.

We heard the surfers talk about all sorts of interesting things and we learned a lot – not to say we believed everything we heard. Sometimes they sounded like fishermen telling outlandish lies about the fish they caught. But we didn't care. We loved watching and listening to them. They were all so athletic, so strong and fit and sun-tanned. My brother and I decided that somehow, someway, we just had to become surfers too.

Jake and I had a couple of problems though. The first one was money. A new surfboard, we learned, cost almost a hundred dollars. That was a lot of money in 1959. You could get a good used surfboard for about half that. But my brother and I didn't have any money of our own. And our mother seemed to be a little hard pressed for cash right then. Jake and I decided to get part-time jobs and earn our own money. After school I went out and tried to get yard work from anybody who was willing to pay, and Jake got a job washing dishes at our new neighbor's German restaurant.

Our second problem was transportation. Although our mother tried to accommodate us as often as possible, sometimes she just couldn't. When she first went to work at the hospital she was put on the night shift. She was a nurse in the Emergency Room. In the evenings before work she would feed us our dinner and try to see that we did our homework. Then she would go and work all night at the hospital. She always came home tired. If she got home in time, she would take us to school. Otherwise, we walked. My mother would sleep all day. On weekends we had to be quiet so we didn't disturb her. She often told us she was too tired to give us a ride to the beach.

A few times my brother and I got so desperate we walked to The Point. But we found out that it wasn't as close as it looked from our panoramic view on the hill. In fact it was three and a half miles. That's seven miles round trip. Coming home was the hard part. Especially the last three or four blocks, which were up really steep streets. Right at the end, when our legs were screaming, it felt like we were climbing Mt. Everest.

We knew that when school got out for summer vacation we would want to go to the beach all the time. I couldn't see how in the world we could get there unless we walked. There wasn't any public transportation in those days. We were really in the dark ages.

My older brother, however, smugly pointed out to me that he would be turning sixteen in June. He would be getting his driver's license then. He envisioned borrowing Mom's car when she came home from work. She wouldn't need it anyway when she was sleeping. But we weren't sure she would agree to that. It would be much better if he had his own car.

So Jake sat down and wrote a long letter to our father in Long Beach. He reminded Pop that he was going to be turning sixteen in a few months and was wondering if it might be possible to get a car for his birthday. Jake knew he had always been Pop's favorite, so he figured he had a decent chance. We both waited and kept our fingers crossed. We just had to get some wheels somehow.

Poe, the Raven & Me (Part 1)
1994

Albert Einstein once said, "Our situation on this earth seems strange. Every one of us appears here involuntarily and uninvited, for a short stay, without knowing why. To me it is enough to wonder at the secrets."

And to me, the best month for wondering at such secrets is October. It is a month ripe with harvest, and yet a month tinged with regret over the loss of summer and of days past. As dark approaches on these October nights we feel a crispness in the air that was absent before. We see birds in flight and the turning of leaves. We sense the coming of winter. October reminds us that the sands of time are falling irrecoverably into the lower half of the hourglass. It foretells a time of cold and darkness to come. October is a time when our thoughts begin to turn inward. It is a time for wondering at the meaning of life, and for the contemplation of our own inevitable demise. Fittingly, October is also the month of Halloween.

Halloween is a time when we good-naturedly contemplate the images of our worst nightmares: monsters, witches, vampires, ghosts, axe murderers, horrifying demons of every description. It is a time when we playfully allow the dark images of our nightmares to come alive and dance before us. It is a time when our imaginations run wild. So, in the spirit of Halloween, let us talk of the secrets of the night, and of our nightmares.

We all have nightmares. They are just one of the many burdens visited upon us, we the current inheritors and progenitors of the human condition. Nightmares come to us unbidden and unwanted, and yet they come to us just the same. They contain secrets, these nightmares, and they hold a strange power over us, we who are both their creators and their victims. They are dark and mysterious, frightening, veiled in mist, invariably symbolic. But lest we forget, we humans are not the only creatures visited by nightmares. Any pet owner can tell you that dogs and cats have dreams and nightmares. Apes and birds and horses do too, I suppose, as do all other animals. Isn't it strange? But let us not dwell on the nightmares of animals, but on those of humankind.

One nightmare common to many people is that of falling from a great height. In your sleep you feel yourself involuntarily careening off some high precipice, and as you go over the edge you look down and see the yawning abyss below. The terror of it! Your body jerks reflexively trying to pull itself back to safety. But it is too late. You are falling. Your involuntary jerk awakens you and you find yourself lying in your own bed. Your heart is pounding. You are staring wide-eyed into the darkness. You are terrified, but safe, and thankful to be alive. This nightmare, though common, is at least short-lived.

Another common nightmare lasts somewhat longer: it is the one in which you are being chased by something frightening. Your pursuer is some evil person, or some snarling beast, or perhaps just a dark shadow, indistinct yet menacing. You try to run away from it, but your legs are so heavy or tired or mired down that you can barely move them. The monster of your dream descends on you. You cringe in prenatal fear as it prepares to deliver the deathblow. You wake up quivering there in your bed, unnerved down to the core of your being. You are afraid to move, lest it be real and lurking somewhere close by.

And then there's the nightmare about being trapped in some suffocating enclosure from which there is no escape. You feel so claustrophobic that you can't stand it. Maybe you are pinned under the rubble of a collapsed building and you smell smoke. Or you are alone and lost without a light in a labyrinth of caves deep underground. Or maybe you are naked and disoriented in a vast, impenetrable tangle of thorn bushes. Or you're tied to the railroad tracks and a train is coming. Or you are under the sea, with your foot clamped tightly in a giant clamshell. Or you are an innocent prisoner locked in a tiny cell in some foreign jail and no one knows your plight. Or a huge python has you wrapped up in its coils and is beginning to squeeze the breath out of you. In any case, you panic. You begin struggling. You struggle violently, but futilely. You become exhausted. You awaken in your bed, perspiring, your mouth agape, gasping for air. Your bed sheets are a moist and twisted mess.

Any of these nightmares will suffice. They are all capable of thrusting the icy blade of fear deep into your sense of wellbeing. And the blade sticks there until withdrawn by the agonizingly slow process of forgetfulness. But forever after the blade lies nearby awaiting the specter of a willful hand.

We have all had nightmares at some time in our lives, and there is no joy in the thought that we will have others in the future. They may be similar or altogether different from those outlined above. I must confess that I had a nightmare, many years ago, that haunts me to this day. I remember it vividly. It haunts me more than any other because this particular nightmare very nearly came true.

The seeds of my own particular worst nightmare were planted in me long ago by none other than that famous poet and storyteller, Edgar Allan Poe. I first became acquainted with his work as a schoolboy, and I have always admired it. I remember well The Pit & the Pendulum, The Black Cat, The Telltale Heart, The Premature Burial, The Cask of Amontillado, and many more.

But I was particularly fond of Poe's verse, especially his long narrative poem "The Raven." I was mesmerized by its unique rhythm, its alliteration and assonance, and its hypnotic rhyme scheme. To me, the sounds in The Raven tumble off the tongue like water cascading down a rocky gorge. I was enthralled by The Raven's bleak images, its somber tone, its dark and brooding atmosphere, its striking symbology. I was deeply moved by the exquisite theme of lonely anguish over the loss of a loved one. Put quite simply, I liked the poem because it was spooky. I read it many times as I was growing up. I did not know then that "The Raven" would cause me to have a nightmare, and that having that nightmare would ultimately lead me to my own near demise.

I should have known better. But no one ever told me: "Don't read Poe when you're alone on a cold October night when the wind blows through the barren trees and the waning moon plays hide and seek with the clouds."

No one ever told me: "Don't dwell on the dark images portrayed in the ramblings of a madman, no matter how poetic, for they are the stuff of nightmares."

No one ever told me: "Beware of what you dream, for what you dream may someday come true."

And since no one ever told me, I indulged in all that forbidden fruit. And that is why, many and many a year ago, in a little town by the sea, I had a dream, a terrible dream that one night summoned the Angel of Death to my very doorstep.

Before I tell you about my dream, I beg your indulgence while I digress and say a few words about Edgar Allan Poe and his famous poem "The Raven." After all, it is the source of my nightmare. Besides, I feel impelled to pay homage to Poe at this time of year. For the skies they are ashen and sober, the leaves they are withered and sere, and it is a night in the lonesome October of my most immemorial year.

Edgar Allan Poe (1809-1849) is one of the best known writers in American history. He was a "southern gentleman," brilliant, sensitive, and well educated. A poet. His personal life, however, was a shambles, and he lived almost his entire adult life in poverty. Though his writing gained him some notoriety in his own day, it did not bring him the wealth and distinction he so richly deserved. His tragic death under mysterious circumstances in Baltimore brought an end to a life punctuated at every turn by disappointment. He did, however, manage to write many memorable stories and poems along the way. Edgar Allan Poe is recognized for having founded the macabre as a literary genre, and for being the creator of the mystery story. His influence on other writers has been immense. He is rightfully considered one of the foremost figures in the history of American Literature.

Poe's work is almost invariably wrapped in gloom, which is a reflection of the misfortunes he met in life. And in one sense, his most famous work, "The Raven," prophesized the greatest tragedy of his life. When Poe was twenty-six years old he was already on the verge of both physical and mental collapse. It was then that he met his thirteen-year old first cousin, Virginia Clemm. She made him feel the surge of life again. They fell in love. Quickly and brashly they married.

But Poe's marriage was a good one. In it he found a long-absent source of happiness and solace. His marriage gave his writing new impetus too, a new urgency now that he had a wife to support. His finest works were written over the next ten years. But still he never seemed able to make ends meet. And then, in 1842, he learned his wife had contracted tuberculosis, a common disease at the time. Being poor, Poe cared for her at home as best he could. He was no stranger to TB. His mother, brother, and foster mother had all died of it.

In 1845 Poe penned his masterpiece, "The Raven." You no doubt read it in school. As you may recall, it is a long, narrative poem that tells the story of a man alone in his study late one night. The man, who is also the narrator, is trying to forget the recent loss of his loved one, "the rare and radiant maiden" Lenore. He tries to forget about her death by losing himself in his books. While dozing off around midnight, he is awakened by a tapping at his chamber door. He is frightened. Is it a visitor, or the ghost of Lenore? He asks who it is. There is no answer. He builds up his courage and goes to the door. He opens it, but is greeted only by darkness. He peers into that darkness "dreaming dreams no mortal ever dared to dream before."

He turns despondently back into the room. Suddenly he hears the tapping again, this time coming from his window. He goes and opens it, and to his surprise, in steps a raven. (In folklore, the raven has long been recognized as the messenger of death. This is because ravens are known to feed off carrion, among other things. Their presence often telegraphs that something dead is nearby.) The raven flies across the room and perches on a bust just above his chamber door, "upon the bust of Pallas." (Pallas is the name given to a famous bust of Athena, the Greek goddess of Wisdom.)

The man ponders the oddness of this development. He speaks to the bird, half-jokingly asking its name. To his surprise, the bird answers, "Nevermore." (Ravens, of course, along with parrots, parakeets and macaws, are capable of mimicking speech.) The narrator is amused at first. Who ever heard of a bird named Nevermore? Ha. But then the man turns melancholy. He muses aloud that the bird will no doubt leave him, as all his friends and his hopes have flown before. Then the bird says, "Nevermore."

The man comes to understand that the bird knows only that one word. So he sits down and begins asking the raven a series of questions. He knows full well what the answer will be. He asks the raven in a number of ways if he will ever see his beloved Lenore again. The answer is always the same, "Nevermore." Finally, tortured by his own questions and the inevitable reply, the man becomes furious. "Be that word our sign of parting…!" he shrieks, "…Take thy beak from out my heart, and take thy form from off my door!" But the bird only responds with the now predictable refrain, "Nevermore." The man realizes that the shadow of the raven will never be lifted from his life. The full realization of the death of his loved one stabs deep into his heart, driven there by the ominous word from the sharp, flesh-tearing beak of the raven. The truth and finality of his own personal loss is now inescapable.

This poem, as I mentioned, was prophetic. A mere two years after its publication Poe's beloved wife Virginia succumbed to tuberculosis. It is not difficult to see that the "lost" Lenore of the poem is the symbolic representation of his wife, Virginia. Predictably, Poe's life and career went into a tailspin after her death. There are tales of him visiting Virginia's gravesite, lying upon it and weeping at all hours of the day and night and in all kinds of weather. There are rumors of drug abuse and alcoholism.

Poe died under mysterious circumstances two years later. Some say his death was caused by alcohol poisoning, some say it was due to the abuse of laudanum, some say it was a simple case of pneumonia, while others are convinced he died of a broken heart. A new theory emerged some years ago. Dr. R. Michael Benitez of Baltimore, after examining Poe's medical records, believes he died of rabies! Now that is a theory I'd like to explore further. But not here.

Let us turn back to the subject at hand. The nightmare that Poe's poem inspired in me, as you might have guessed, revolves around a large, black bird. My nightmare went something like this: A huge black thing came swooping down out of the sky and aimed itself at me. I was scared. I ran. I could hear the wind whistling over its black wings as it approached. I couldn't seem to run fast enough. My legs felt heavy and numb. I heard a fluttering sound and felt a tingling at the back of my head and neck. I threw my arms up over my head. The beast fell upon me with flapping wings and grasping talons. The bird emitted terrible squawking sounds that deafened me. I tried to fight it off as it beat me about the arms and head with its wings. I couldn't see. I stumbled and fell. The thing landed on me. I tried to grab its flailing wings, but as I did so the raven lunged at me, stabbing me, burying its sharp beak in my chest. Ow! I felt pain there, and then I woke up. I found myself lying on my side, on top of the Poe anthology I'd been reading. The corner of the book was jammed up against my rib cage.

Wow! What a relief to be out of that dream!

I remember being disturbed by the dream, but that I eventually got over it. In fact, it wasn't long before I put the whole thing out of my mind. Years and years passed. It wasn't until I was nearly fifty years old that the raven paid me a second visit. And this visit was in the flesh, not in my dreams.

Apparently, the Harbinger of Death had been in no hurry to call on me. He had waited for over thirty years. But eventually he did come tapping, tapping at my chamber door. How he found me, what I did upon his arrival, and the dramatic conclusion of this strange tale, I will relate to you in future missives. Until then, I wish you peaceful nights and pleasant dreams. Enjoy them while you can.

The White Whale & the Red Baron
1959

Not long after we moved to Ventura I heard someone refer to our new town as Santa Barbara's ugly little sister. I didn't know what they meant by that. Ugly little sister or not, it was easy to see that Ventura had a lot more things than our old home town ever did. For one thing, it had a lot more people. There were only about 4,500 people living in the Ojai Valley when we moved. Ventura had nearly 30,000 at the time. And there were a lot of different kinds of people in Ventura too. Besides the usual white people, there were many more Mexicans than Ojai ever had. And Ventura had Negroes and Asians too, which we had had only glimpses of before. There were even refugees from the Dust Bowl who worked in the oil fields out on Ventura Avenue. Most of these people were poor and lived on the west side of town. We lived further east.

I saw right away that there were quite a few teenagers who liked to cruise up and down Main St. in their hotrods. There were so many more cars in Ventura, and the traffic along Thompson Blvd. was often bumper to bumper. This was in early 1959 before they put in the freeway. All the north-south traffic on the old Highway 101 came right through town on

Thompson Blvd. And all the cars and trucks had to pass through a dozen traffic lights along the way. Every morning and evening during the rush hour the traffic was backed up for miles. And unlike Ojai, Ventura seemed to be growing by leaps and bounds. New roads, houses, shopping malls, and schools were springing up all over the place.

We weren't used to all that commotion. Ojai was a sleepy little country town nestled in a secluded valley. Most of the people in Ojai were white, although there were a few Mexicans and maybe a few Chumash Indians running around. But everybody seemed to know each other there and nobody stepped on anybody's toes. There weren't that many cars in Ojai, and only one traffic light. People were friendly and helped each other if the need arose. People were decent for the most part, and went to church. They went to bed early and there was hardly any crime. By comparison, Ventura was a low-down, dog-eat-dog kind of town. My brother and I found that out the hard way.

After we had been working part-time for a month so as to earn money to buy surfboards, I met a kid named Rick in my eighth-grade class. Rick was a short, skinny, red-headed kid with freckles and buck teeth. He told me he had a surfboard for sale. And he only wanted twenty bucks for it!

The next day after school, my brother Jake and I went over to his house to take a look at it. Rick and *his* older brother Bill were waiting for us. Bill looked like a bigger version of Rick, only he had fewer freckles and no buck teeth. Rick and Bill had the surfboard laid out on sawhorses in the front yard. The thing looked more like a beat up paddle board than anything else. It was a home-made job, fashioned from quarter-inch marine plywood. It was shaped like a rocket ship, with a sharp nose and a flat tail. It was about eight feet long and two inches thick. It was hollow inside, painted white on the outside, and had a round hole near the tail that held a plug like the kind they used to have in thermos bottles. Rick told us that was so you could drain the inside in case it leaked. The board had a funny little wooden fin attached to the bottom, near the tail.

Jake and I put our heads together. We were concerned that this so-called surfboard didn't look anything like the ones we'd seen down at The Point. Most of the ones down there were either made out of solid balsawood, or out of Styrofoam with strips of redwood down the middle for strength. They were made waterproof by layers of fiberglass and resin. But the shapes we'd seen at The Point were totally different – more streamlined, like boats or skies. And as far as we could tell there wasn't one of them that was hollow.

We sort of hemmed and hawed, shifting from one foot to the other, standing there before our hosts. I finally plucked up enough courage to tell Rick, "Gee, uh, we don't know. This isn't exactly what we had in mind. This doesn't look like any surfboard we've seen before."

I have to hand it to the two boys though; they were pretty glib. Rick said, "Well, what do you expect for twenty bucks? This is a custom-made surfboard. And besides, you don't want to get a good board to learn on anyway. You'll just bash it all up. This is a perfect board to learn on."

My brother and I excused ourselves and stepped over behind the magnolia tree that grew in their front yard. We talked it over. What the kid said seemed to make sense. But we still didn't like the looks of it. We were both thinking it was kind of dorky-looking. We could never show up at The Point with that thing. We decided we'd better pass on it.

We went back to where Rick and Bill were waiting. Brother Jake tried to be diplomatic. He said, "Well, um, I, uh, we don't think this board is just right for us…"

"Well, hell," said Bill, scrunching up his face in disgust. But then it seemed as though he got a bright idea. He snapped his fingers and said, "O.K. You two seem like a couple of nice guys to me, and it's obvious you want a surfboard real bad. I'll tell you what we're going to do. We're going to give you this here surfboard for only ten bucks. You can't beat that. Ten dollars! Come on, what do you say?"

Had we been older and wiser we might have smelled a rat. But we weren't and we didn't. My brother and I figured for only five bucks apiece we could at least have something to ride the waves with, even if it was as ugly as sin. We could share it until we got enough money to buy real surfboards.

So we plunked down our hard earned cash on the top of the White Whale, as we came to call it. I grabbed the nose and my brother took hold of the tail and we carried it off. We walked all the way home, which was a good two miles and uphill much of the way. The damn thing was heavy as a tree trunk, but our hearts were light because we were dreaming of the day when we'd be sailing along on those big, beautiful waves. As we wearily trudged up the last steep block to our new house on the hill, we looked up and saw our mother standing at the picture glass window. She looked down at us, and then slowly put her hand to her forehead.

The following weekend we cajoled her into giving us a ride to the beach to try out the White Whale. We directed her to park down by the cove between the pier and The Point. We were too ashamed of our new purchase to be seen among real surfers. We also remembered the guys at The Point talking derogatorily about novice surfers. They called them *Gremlins*. Real surfers looked down on them because they were young, dumb, clumsy, and always got in the way. We were definitely Gremlins.

Claiming seniority because he was older, my brother took the White Whale out into the water first. He set it down in the shallows, pushed it forward, and leaped onto it in a prone position like we'd seen the surfers do at The Point. Jake started paddling. At first everything seemed to be going great. Several small waves broke over the board as he was paddling out. Then I noticed that the board seemed to be riding lower in the water than it had before. My brother started having to paddle really hard to make it move. Before long our new surfboard was under water and sinking fast. Jake swam ashore, pulling it behind him like a drowning victim. He dragged the White Whale ashore, straining mightily against its great weight.

With my help, we were just able to stand it up on its flat stern on the sand. We worked the lever on the top of the plug that made it get smaller, and then pulled the plug out of the hole. It took about five minutes to drain all the sea water out. Then we replaced the plug.

After some debate, we decided that I should make the next attempt. I paddled our great white surfboard out to sea once again, whereupon it immediately began to sink. Jake had to swim out and help me drag it ashore. We turned and saw our mother sitting in the station wagon with her hand over her mouth trying not to laugh.

We were disappointed, of course, but being young, determined, and hopelessly optimistic we were not discouraged. As we drained out the seawater once again, we took some comfort in calling Rick and Bill every foul name we could think of. We knew now why they had sold it to us so cheap. We carried the water-logged, so-called surfboard back to the car.

We decided that the only thing we could do was take the White Whale home and patch it up. Which we did. We discovered a bunch of places where it leaked. They were located in the joints where the top and bottom met the sides. We suspected that the plug leaked too. So my brother and I got some wood putty and plugged up all the cracks and holes. Then we sanded the whole thing down. We decided to paint it, which we did – a bright fire engine red. We positioned a square of wax paper in between the plug and the hole. We re-christened our surfboard *The Red Baron*.

The following weekend, despite it being cold and cloudy, we inveigled our mother into taking us down for another try. Once we got there we flipped a coin to see who went first. I was not surprised when I won. My brother was notorious for having bad luck. The surf looked to be about two or three feet high. I waded out in the chilly water with the board, and when I was waist-deep I sprang aboard The Red Baron and started paddling. The further out I got the bigger the waves seemed to get. I then discovered one of the elemental truths of surfing: waves always look bigger when you're out among them than they do from shore.

I was aware that the waves here in the cove by the pier didn't break the same way as the ones out at The Point. The ones over there broke gradually from one end to the other because of the angle of the shoreline, but here the waves came in parallel to the beach and broke more or less all at once. I figured the best thing for me to do was ride straight in.

It took a while, but I finally managed to paddle out beyond the waves and turn the board around facing the beach. The Red Baron seemed to be floating O.K., but I kept sliding all over the place on top of it. It was slippery as hell. Maybe we shouldn't have used that high gloss enamel paint. I had to hang on to the railings just to keep from sliding off. But I was thrilled to be out in the water, even though it seemed like I was at the South Pole or something. I started shivering like crazy. I don't know if it was the cold or the excitement of waiting for my first wave.

After a few minutes a nice one came along, and I started paddling towards the beach. I looked behind me and saw that somehow the wave seemed to have doubled in size and was about to break right on top of me. I was paralyzed by fear. I grabbed hold of the railings and hung on for dear life. I felt the three-foot high monster pick me up and hurl me forward with tremendous speed. It broke over me, and, after momentarily being buried in whitewater, I was jettisoned free and found myself speeding along towards the beach. It was absolutely thrilling. It was so thrilling I even forgot to try to stand up.

When the wave subsided I slid off the board and looked over at my brother to see if he had seen. Jake was standing at the water's edge beckoning me in. He'd seen it alright, and now he wanted his turn. Begrudgingly, I pushed the board ashore and turned it over to him. In a way, I was glad to be out of the water. It was freezing out there. I grabbed my beach towel and wrapped it around me.

"Hey," Jake said in disgust when he tried to pick up The Red Baron. "This damn thing still leaks." He tilted the thing from side to side and we heard water sloshing around inside. Together we raised it up and pulled the plug. About two gallons of seawater came gurgling out. Mumbling, Jake put the soggy wax paper back in place and stuck in the plug. Then he headed out into the surf.

Jake paddled out as I had done. He turned around just beyond the break-line. I could see he was having trouble staying on The Red Baron too. The top was just too slippery. We'd forgotten all about the fact that the surfers over at The Point rubbed blocks of paraffin wax on the top of their surfboards to make them less slippery.

A good-sized wave came along. Jake started paddling. The wave picked The Red Baron up by the rear. My brother, who wasn't holding on, slid forward on the slippery board. The nose pointed straight down into the water and dove for the bottom. The wave broke, flipping The Red Baron end over end, and sending my brother plunging face first into the shallow water.

I held my breath for a moment until I saw Jake surface once the wave had passed. My brother's luck hadn't changed. I half expected him to come up with all of his front teeth knocked out. But he didn't. He started swimming. I could tell he was angry by the way he was slapping at the water. Meanwhile, the Red Baron came gliding lazily in, belly up, towards the beach. It seemed to be riding kind of low in the water.

66

I waited on the beach until it washed all the way in. My brother arrived about the same time it did. He was using all those words our mother used to wash our mouths out with soap for saying. He was hopping mad. He grabbed at the board, determined to go out again. But he realized right away that The Red Barron weighed about a ton. It was full of water.

We dragged it up onto the sand and stood it up. It took about five minutes to drain it. We inspected The Red Baron and discovered that the nose was all bashed in from hitting the bottom, and that two long cracks had opened up along the seam between the bottom and sides. There was no way she could float again that day. We looked back at our mother who was sitting in the car holding a magazine in front of her face as if she'd been busy reading and hadn't seen.

Release

1972

The Earth tilted her soft, blue belly towards the sun, and the great South Seas basked in its brilliant light. As the sun baked the vast teeming reaches of the ocean, water vapor steamed up and formed ponderous masses of cumulonimbus. These then began a slow march across the wide Pacific and bore down on the Samoan archipelago. From the eastern tip of the island of Upolu, the clouds could be seen lined up across the whole curving stretch of the horizon, poised there like some invading army of shadowy gargantuans. The sun, rising behind them, outlined their monstrous, billowing forms in halos of silver light.

A young white man sat cross-legged on the roof of a catamaran as it motored towards the southeast. His long, flowing hair streamed back behind him in the warm morning air. His broad, bare chest was deeply tanned, and his baggy green swim trunks, worn and faded, hung loosely about his slim hips. Bare feet peeked out from under his folded legs.

As the vessel neared a tiny, crescent-shaped islet that lay just off the port bow, the young man, marine-biologist Allan Turner, studied its sandy beaches for turtle tracks. He could see none. Either there had been no nesting activity on this side of the islet, or the torrential rains that had been falling off and on for the past week had washed away all traces. It was the middle of the rainy season and the sea was calm now for the first time in days. Allan, seeing that the latest storm system had finally broken up, had taken advantage of this window of clear weather to put out to sea.

The catamaran, or *alia* as it is known in Samoa, was modeled after the double-hulled crafts of the ancient Polynesians. A platform connected the twin aluminum hulls, and upon it stood a low, open-ended cabin. The flat roof of the cabin offered protection from the tropic sun and the frequent rain squalls that swept through the region. The craft was designed for fishing beyond the reef, and was very seaworthy. It had the added advantage of being shallow-drafted so that it could easily navigate the shallow lagoons, and could even be drawn right up onto the sandy beaches. The alia was powered by a large outboard motor fixed to the rear of the platform.

Allan shaded his eyes with one hand as the early morning sun broke clear of the bulbous clouds. Below him, sitting cross-legged on the platform, was the sixteen year-old Samoan boy named Tavita. The boy was bare-chested like his mentor, but about his waist he wore the typical dress of the Samoans: a brightly colored kilt or sarong known as the *lava lava*. His right hand rested on the throttle of the engine, and his dark eyes scanned the sea ahead. It was not often that Tavita had the opportunity to handle the tiller, and he was eager to prove himself worthy of the responsibility. Tavita's bearing demonstrated this, and hinted at the intelligence and pride so common to his people.

Suddenly, high above the approaching clouds, a golden streak of light seared silently through the morning air.

"Wow!" shouted Allan, catching sight of it. He pointed and said, "Look, Tavita! Do you see it?"

"*Oka, oka*! I see it, *Aleni*," said Tavita, calling him by his Samoan name. "But what is it? A falling star?"

"No. It is the American astronauts returning from the moon. Wow! Look at them burn!"

"*Oi!* (Oh-ee) Why you telling to me a lie, Aleni?"

"I'm not lying to you, Tavita," said Allan, as they watched the golden line of light disappear behind a towering cloud.

"That was Apollo 17, with three *palagi* on board. They will land in the ocean between Pago Pago and the Cook Islands. Large ships wait there to pluck them from the sea. You must have heard this on the radio."

"Yes. I remember now. But I still cannot believe it, Aleni. How could those palagi do such a thing? And I do not understand why they would want to go to such a place. Is it not cold on the moon?"

"It is only cold on the far side. It is very hot on the near side."

"Oka! Then why do they go there?"

Allan sighed. "You always find a way to ask me difficult questions, Tavita. It will be very hard for me to explain these things to you."

The burning line briefly reappeared as it streaked from behind one cloud and then disappeared again behind another.

"Oi. Sorry, Aleni. But you are always knowing the answers. My father, he is telling to me you are a very educated man and I should be listening to your words. But even if I do not always understand your words, I like to listen to them anyway."

"That is nice of you to say, Tavita, but while you are listening to my words you are drifting off course."

"Oi! Sorry," said Tavita, looking ahead and quickly adjusting the tiller to take them clear of the brush-covered, crescent-shaped islet that the natives called *Nu'ulua*.

Allan smiled over his shoulder at the boy. "Tell me, Tavita, do you remember the first time you went to Apia?"

"Yes. I remember it well. I was very frightened to be going there."

"But if you were frightened, why did you go?"

"Because my father offered to take me one time when he went to visit our relatives there. I was too ashamed to tell him I was afraid. I was also wanting to see if what I heard about Apia was true. I heard it was a very big and dirty place, with many people, and that some of them had white skin like you, Aleni. This was the thing that frightened me the most, because I heard as a child that you *palagi* are very dangerous and that you sometimes are eating small Samoan children when they are being bad. I also heard that there were many cars and buses in Apia and it is very dangerous to be crossing the road."

Tavita noticed Aleni had turned back to the front and was watching the sea and the sky.

"But I also knew that there were many shops in Apia where a person could see all sorts of beautiful things, and even buy them if that someone had money. I was curious about the very large houses  called "theaters" where someone could see "movies" about cowboys and kung fu boys. The older children in our village even bragged to me that they had eaten a very good thing, a sweet and cold thing called *aisa kalimi*. I wished to eat it too."

Allan nodded and said, "Ice cream. So you went with your father?"

"Yes. We took the bus from our village and rode for a very long time along the coast. We passed by so many villages that I lost count, and then we went up over the mountain into the clouds and rain and down to the coast again, and we finally came to Apia. I was very excited for being there."

Allan looked over his shoulder and said, "And now do you know why the American astronauts went to the moon?"

Tavita looked at him, puzzled. "What have they to do with me going to Apia?"

Allan smiled at him again, "You think about it, and we will talk of it again. But for now, how are the baby turtles doing? Do they need to be wet? They should not be allowed to get too hot."

"They ride well, Aleni. I poured them with a bucket of ocean not long ago. But they seem to want out of their wire cages. Perhaps they smell their home in the sea."

"They will be free soon enough, Tavita. Take us out about a mile beyond Nu'ulua."

Tavita was not sure what a mile was, but he knew it was far. He did not worry because he knew Aleni would tell him when they had gone far enough. These palagi were strange people, and were often difficult to understand. But they knew many things, and if one were patient, one might learn those things from them.

Allan continued to gaze towards where he had seen the command ship 'America' blazing through the atmosphere. It was gone now. He wondered if the three souls on board were on course and if they would be picked up all right. What a tremendous achievement, he thought. It was almost enough to make him proud of being an American.

As the alia chugged beyond the lee of the islet and out into the rolling ocean, Allan wondered how he could explain the concept behind the space program to the boy. For that matter, how could he explain the war in Southeast Asia to him? The boy had been pestering him with questions about that as well, ever since the news of the renewed bombings came over the one and only radio station they could get in Samoa. The kid seemed to think that just because he was an American he should know everything about what his country did.

Allan loved the Samoans, but sometimes they truly exasperated him. Their curiosity was insatiable. Whenever he sat down to talk with someone new, he inevitably faced the same barrage of naive and forward questions: Where is your family? What are the names of your mother and father? How many sisters and how many brothers do you have? Why did you come to live so far from home? Are you not lonely? How can you live here without a family? Do you not miss your own country? What is it like there? Is it as dangerous as they say? Are you rich like the rest of the Americans? Why do you not take a Samoan wife and have many babies? The list of these inevitable, predictable questions went on and on. Allan had grown weary of fielding them from each new acquaintance.

He supposed that their curiosity was healthy. It enabled these primitive people to come to know something of the outside world through him. And the outside world was new to them. For centuries they had lived in isolation, but with the coming of independence from the protection of New Zealand in 1962, this tiny island country had thrown open its doors to the outside world. He was one of the first palagi these district villagers had ever known. Over on the other side of the island, in the capital of Apia, things were different. But out here, the people might as well still be in the stone age. They lived much the same as they had for thousands of years, but for the addition of mission churches and a few other modern trappings.

Allan tolerated their questions and tried to give them answers they could understand. But it was not easy. They had difficulty grasping Western abstractions. Even though he had learned their language reasonably well, it was difficult to explain things to them in their own tongue because they had few words that he could use to explain the many complexities of the modern world.

The morning sun shone strong into Allan's face through the miles wide crevice between two towering thunder heads. Its low reflection off the ocean was too bright for his eyes. He put his two palms down on the roof and scooted his rump around until his back faced the sun. He looked behind the alia to the tiny islet they had just passed, and beyond it about a mile to the reef around Upolu, the main island of Western Samoa.

There was a strip of turquoise that marked the lagoon, and beyond that he could just make out the thatched roofs of Samoan *fales* peeking from under the coconut trees along the shore. The emerald green of the plantations rising up the slopes glowed luminescent in the low sunlight. Jungle-clad extinct volcanoes then climbed haphazardly into the misty, cloud-embraced regions above. From his point of view, off the eastern tip of the island, Allan could see old ridges of verdured lava sliding down to sea-level all along the south shore of the island, each succeeding ridge a different shade of green. Spirals of smoke rising here and there along the coastline marked the location of villages.

He had been here in Samoa for over two years now, but the natural beauty of the place still enthralled him. It was such a strong and rugged beauty. And the light! The light was the thing that turned the trick – that incredible ever-changing quality that sparkled through the pristine mid-ocean air to electrify the tones, textures and colors of the land. Blue and green dominated everything.

Allan sat on the roof and mused, wondering what it must have been like when the first Polynesians came upon this scene. God knows what brutality or hardship drove them to seek new islands, or how much suffering they endured to get here. He wondered what their reaction to a scene like this must have been after so many days or weeks on the open sea. It must have really blown their minds.

Allan noticed that the color of the ocean was changing. What had been a clear, light blue tinged with green, was now turning a deeper, darker blue. They were getting out beyond the submerged foundation of the island and into deep water. Allan imagined the sloping sides of the extinct volcano plunging down into the clear, dark depths thousands of feet below their dwarfed little vessel. It made him tingle with wonder, and he felt a sudden kinship with the astronauts he had just seen returning from outer space. He sensed the vastness of the universe extending below and above his own inconsequential being.

The alia rode up and down the ocean rollers. Allan let Tavita take them out a little further and then motioned to him to cut the engine. A sudden silence descended on their world.

Allan stood up on the roof with his knees slightly bent, balancing himself against the gentle rocking of the boat, and scanned the immediate area of the alia for signs of sharks or other large predators. When he was satisfied there were none, he climbed down off the roof and dropped lightly to the platform.

"Let us release them quickly," he said. "We did not feed and care for these baby turtles for the past year just to see them end up as breakfast for some hungry fish."

Together they carried the two chicken-wire cages over to the stern and unhooked the hinged lids. Inside were thirty yearling green sea turtles. The man and the boy eased the cages down into the clear, warm water and watched the turtles float to the surface and begin swimming. Some needed a little coaxing, almost as if they were reluctant to leave the safety of the cages.

But for the most part the turtles seemed happy to be in their natural habitat for the first time. They sported about the boat for a while, several of them even trying to clamber up the sides of the pontoons, but eventually they began to wander off in the current. The man and the boy could see them paddling now and then, and diving playfully under the surface as they drifted off to wherever sea turtles go to grow up.

Allan felt a little sad to see them go. They were like children to him. He was relieved though to see that they had started their new life safely. They had outgrown most of their natural predators by now – all but the largest fish and, of course, the sharks. But with any luck, most of these yearlings would survive now and come back as adults to mate in local waters and lay their eggs in the sand of local beaches.

A far away rumble from within the army of approaching clouds drew his attention. A breeze was picking up, and the monstrous clouds, heavy with rain, were bearing down on their vessel. It was time to return to the island. Allan pulled life into the outboard motor and swung the alia about. He set the throttle on full and raced the clouds back towards his home on the shores of Upolu.

Subject: Der Faderland
Date: Sunday, 22 March 1998

Dear Comrades,

A cold Scandinavian wind blows out of the north stirring the dust of a thousand construction sites here in Berlin. Night still brings freezing temperatures, while cloudy daylight begrudgingly hauls the mercury up into the low forties. Thank God for long johns, gloves, and me faithful "Tam O'Shanter."

By the way, Saint Patrick's Day came off in Berlin with only a slight hitch. I did manage to spend several lovely hours in an Irish pub in the Ku'damm listening to live music and exchanging lies with a fine Irish lad who went by the name of Shamus. His lively banter may have set my mind to spinning a bit, for when I finally boarded the U-bahn to return to the hotel, I somehow managed to get myself perfectly lost. As you might imagine, knowing little of the local lingo, I had a fair time of it getting home. You might further imagine my wife, Gretchen, greeting me at the door with what amounted to a verbal rolling pin.

We are still comfortably ensconced in the Westin Grand Hotel in what used to be East Berlin, but are growing increasingly anxious to be done with living out of suitcases and eating hotel food every day. So far, we have been unable to locate an apartment that will suit us. We had one nice possibility, but it fell through when the owner insisted we sign a five-year lease. We were obliged to decline. It is not uncommon for Berliners to spend the greater part of their whole adult lives in the same apartment. This makes it a hard lot for a couple of transients like ourselves.

Berlin is truly a great city, rich in history and culture, but still plagued by some of the same problems that brought it to ruin half a century ago. But it is an exciting place to be right now. We are here in time to see it in the final stages of its phoenix-like rise from the ashes. The new capitol complex will be absolutely stunning when it finally encompasses the old Reichstag on Unter den Linden (Under the Lime Trees).

Surprisingly, though Berlin has 3.5 million residents, it contains a good many parks (which they call "forests") and abounds in lakes, streams, and rivers. It has a great rail, bus and subway system, and the drivers of automobiles seem sensible, safe, and slow on city streets. A couple of downsides are that breathing the air here is like sucking on an exhaust pipe, and everybody seems to smoke cigarettes everywhere all the time. The museums, concert halls and art galleries are astounding in their architecture, their number and their content. And by God, if you love pork, this place is hog heaven.

We are planning a quick trip to Paris next Friday. Just a hop, skip, and a jump from here. (After all, Hitler did it in no time.) We will be staying at the Westin Hotel at Versailles where Gretchen has a business meeting. We hope to ride bikes on the weekend in warmer weather around the park-like stomping grounds of old Louie The What's-His-Name. It will be the first of what we hope will be many trips around Europe during our stay here in der Faderland.

Auf wiedersehen.

Deuce

1959

In January of 1959 I was a mid-year, eighth-grade transfer student, and my new school was Cabrillo Junior High School in Ventura. It wasn't much fun. All the kids there had their own friends which they'd known since grammar school. I was the new kid in school without a friend in the world. I was the hick from the sticks of Ojai. A real nobody.

The first week was the roughest. Girls in my home class whispered about me behind my back and giggled into their hands when I looked around. There were a couple of bullies in my class too. Since I was new, and not too big, they tried to pick on me. One day one of the bullies followed me after class and as I was walking down the corridor he soccer-kicked the back of my foot so that it slammed into the back of my other leg and I stumbled. When I turned around he said, "You sure are clumsy, kid. Why don't you learn how to walk?" Other kids who saw and heard him laughed.

I could feel my face flush with embarrassment and anger. I said, "How's about I practice by walking on your face?" He got mad at that and pushed me into a row of lockers. That's when I punched him in the nose. I'd never punched anybody in the nose before. I don't know what came over me. I guess I was upset about having to move and all. The kid got a bloody nose.

Our teacher, Mr. Benson, came out of the classroom just then and saw what was going on. He told us to stop fighting. He looked at the bully's nose, and told him to go see the school nurse. Then Mr. Benson took me to the principal's office. I was scared. Here it was my first week of school and I was already in trouble. The principal, Mr. Taggert, turned out to be a nice guy though. He didn't telephone my Mom or send me home. He just gave me a lecture about getting along with the other kids. I guess he didn't understand what a jungle it was out there.

Word of my punching that fellow in the nose spread around school. The girls still whispered about me, but they didn't giggle so much. Some of the boys avoided me. I guess they were scared or something. But if I thought my trouble with bullies was over, I was wrong. Some of the big guys wanted to kick my ass to show that they were tougher than me. I got into a couple of more fights in the weeks to come, but none of the teachers caught us so I didn't get into any more trouble with the principal.

Surprisingly, I never lost a fight. I don't know why. The guys I fought were always bigger than me. I guess I was lucky. And I was always scared. I used to go kind of nuts when some bully tried to pick on me. I'd start yelling and cussing and acting crazy. My arms and fists would start spinning like Popeye the Sailor's. I found that landing the first punch worked out pretty well, especially if it caught them in the nose or the mouth. People generally don't like the feel of that. Me fighting like a mad dog must have surprised the bullies, especially since I was only of average size, and kind of skinny. I didn't look anything like a tough guy. But after a while the bullies left me alone.

I never did mention these things at home, especially not to my mother. I figured she had enough to worry about without being concerned about me. I figured that what she didn't know wouldn't hurt her. At the dinner table I did my best to conceal my scraped and scabbed knuckles from her. If she happened to notice anything, I would just say I hurt my hand surfing.

I used to walk home from Cabrillo when school let out. That was because my Mom was still sleeping at three o'clock. It was a couple of miles, and, as usual, the last few blocks were like hiking up the Himalayas.

One afternoon in late February, around the time I turned fourteen, I was trudging up the hill when I heard someone call out from behind me, "Hey, soldier, pick up the pace! Come on, double-time." I looked back and saw this short, nerdy kid gaining on me rapidly. His arms were swinging like he was on the parade ground or something. He was a pudgy little guy with a buzz haircut. I recognized him from around school.

He kept on talking as he drew abreast of me: "Get that head up, soldier. Eyes forward. Shoulders back. Now march! Hup, two, three, four." I noticed the kid had funny-looking eyes. They looked in two directions at once. I guess that's why they called him Deuce.

"I ain't no soldier," I said.

"I know. You're that new kid in school. What's yer name?"

"I'm John. You're Deuce, right?"

"That's what they call me, the sick bastards. You live in one of those new houses up on the hill, don't you?"

"Yeah."

"I watched 'em build those houses. I'm glad they're done. They made a hellava racket. Boy, they sure did carve up that hillside to put them in. You must be a rich kid to live up there."

"Ha! That's a good one. Where do you live?"

"Over here on Sunset. We're in that old two-story house right where the road curves. It's only a couple of blocks from where you live. We've been there forever. My Dad's a rocket scientist out at Point Mugu."

"Rocket scientist? You're lying, boy."

"I ain't lyin'. He really is. He works on guidance systems or something."

"Hmmph."

"What's your Dad do?"

"I ain't got no Dad. My mom's a nurse."

"What happened to your Dad? Did he croak or something?"

"Naw. He moved away to Long Beach."

"That's lousy. Why'd he do that?"

"Hell, I don't know. Maybe he got sick of us. Or maybe my mom threw him out. He likes to drink a lot. What difference does it make, anyway? He's gone."

We walked along in silence for a while. Finally, Deuce said, "Well, '*fuck it*' is what I always say."

"That's what I say too."

"Hey, John, ya wanna come over to my house? I got this bitchin' new guitar for my birthday. I'll let you play it."

"I guess so. But I don't know how to play a guitar."

"Ah, hell, it's easy. I'll show ya."

I followed him to his house and his Mom gave us lemonade and cookies. Then he showed me his new guitar. It was a nice one, even though it was made in Mexico. And he could even play a few chords on it. He played me this song called, "What are you gonna do with a drunken sailor?" It was pretty funny, especially the way Deuce sang it. One of the answers to the question is, "Shave his belly with a rusty razor." I laughed over that one. Another one was, "Put him to bed with the captain's daughter." Ha, ha.

I decided I liked Deuce. He was smart and funny. Since he wasn't a big guy, he didn't try to act tough around people, unless he was putting them on. I found out he was forever joking around and laughing it up. He was a happy kid. And he always seemed to look on the bright side of things. I guess he was one of those eternal optimists. I didn't always agree with him, but he did cheer me up some.

Deuce and I ended up walking home from school together quite a lot after that. It was nice having someone to talk to. It wasn't long before we became fast friends. And through him I met a number of other boys. As it turned out, Deuce and some of his friends wanted to be surfers too.

By May of that year my brother and I were still trying to save enough money to buy real surfboards. It wasn't easy though. We discovered there were all kinds of other things in Ventura to spend money on. Things like 45 rpm records of the latest hits, and movies, and snacks and soda pop and stuff like that. It was hard to sacrifice those things for a hypothetical surfboard. But we really did have the surfing bug, and we tried to be strong. It was hard to be patient though because it was taking a lot longer than we expected.

And here it was almost summertime and we still didn't have enough money. I was finding that people were really cheap when it came to paying a fourteen-year-old to do yard work. Sometimes I had to work all day on Saturday just to earn five bucks. A lot of times I didn't even make that much. Sometimes I didn't make anything at all because nobody would give me any work. Some of those bastards did their own yard work.

Jake wasn't doing much better. Our mother would only let him wash dishes at the restaurant on weekends. And he couldn't even do that unless he finished his homework first. During the week he was a sophomore at Ventura High School, which was right down the hill from our house.

Sometime towards the end of May, my mother dropped a bombshell at the dinner table. She announced that she and our Dad had been talking on the telephone and decided that my brother would go to live in Long Beach for the summer. Pop had arranged a job for Jake as a stock clerk and janitor at the drug store where he worked. Jake could earn a lot of money. And he would need it to pay the upkeep and insurance on his new car. New car?! Yes! Since Jake would turn sixteen in June, Pop was going to get him a car! It would be a used car, a cheap car, but who cared?

Jake was ecstatic. He was finally going to make some real money, and, he was going to get some wheels. Jake left for Long Beach on a Greyhound bus a couple of days after school let out.

I was happy for him, I guess. But I was jealous that he would be earning money and getting a car. I tried to get his old dishwashing job, but the owner said I was too young, so I was stuck slogging away at my lousy yard work.

I spent a lot of time with my new friend Deuce that summer. He had his new guitar and was getting better and better at playing it. He knew a bunch of three-chord progressions and could play songs. He could even do a little 'pickin' an' grinnin.' Folk music was starting to be popular, thanks to the Kingston Trio and other groups. Deuce taught me where to put my fingers to make chords, and showed me how to strum. His friend, Dremel, also had a guitar. Sometimes we would get together and have what they called a Hootenanny. That was when people got together and sang folk songs.

I couldn't afford a guitar because I was trying to save my money for a surfboard. But I did spend the ten dollars my mom gave me for my fourteenth birthday on a cheap ukulele. It was better than nothing. You tuned it up by humming "my dog has fleas."

Every chance I got, however, I would ask my Mom to take me down to the beach with The Red Baron. Jake and I had repaired it several more times during April and May, and it would actually stay afloat for fifteen or twenty minutes at a stretch. I would take it out in the surf near the Ventura pier. I would rub the top with a block of paraffin wax like the guys at The Point did. After numerous applications, the wax built up into a bunch of little beads about the size of your fingerprint. The beads made the board rough and gave you traction.

It was a disappointment to discover that Ventura gets a lot of fog during the month of June. I never realized that before because it was never that hot in Ojai in June and so we rarely went to the beach then. But now that we lived here it was obvious that a thick fog covered the sea and shoreline almost every day. The fog doesn't affect the size of the waves, however, and it tends to make the water smooth and glassy. Those are good things. But fog also makes surfing a rather chilly proposition. I didn't let the cold stop me though. I'd do

anything to get out of the house and be on my own. When I was surfing I could forget about everything else. When I was at the beach I stopped missing my Dad and my brother and my friends in Ojai. And I didn't have time to think about how sad my mother was, or even to feel sorry for myself. I didn't even think about what a heartless, lonely town Ventura was. Surfing takes a lot of concentration. It's fun, but you still have to concentrate on what you're doing. That keeps your mind off other things.

One typically foggy day towards the end of June, I was actually able to stand up on The Red Baron. I rode a wave for four or five seconds before I lost my balance and fell off. It was a momentous occasion for me. For the first time I could actually feel what it was like to ride a wave while standing up. I was really excited about it. Surfers would say that I got *stoked,* which means the same thing.

I learned that you don't stand facing straight forward on your board. You have to stand sideways with one foot ahead of the other. Most surfers stand with their left foot forward so that they're facing the wave when they're riding. You can see the wave ahead of you better. If, on the other hand, you stood with your right foot forward you were called a *goofy-foot.* That was because your back would be towards a right-breaking wave, which most of them are along the south-facing beaches in California. I was a regular foot, although they didn't have a name for that.

I also learned you had to stand up really fast during the takeoff. If you took too long, the chances were you would lose your balance and fall off. Also, when you stood up, you had to center your weight on the board. If you were too far forward the nose would dip under water and you would go *pearl-diving.* If you were too far back, the board would slow down too much and you would *stall out.* Then the wave would leave you behind.

After that first time, I was able to stand up and ride the whitewater on a regular basis. Then I started trying to maneuver the board to the left or right. You have to be able to steer your board if you want to ride real waves. You do it by shifting your weight to the rear foot and leaning to one side or the other.

Turning The Red Baron was not easy. The shape of it was all wrong for surfing, and I usually ended up falling off. Every once in a while though, I actually made the ungainly beast do what I wanted.

Surfing was a lot of fun, but I found out that you spent most of your time paddling, or waiting for the right wave, or swimming after your board after you lost it. It seemed like the rides didn't last long at all. But the thrill of it was worth all the effort. Especially the takeoff – that part when the wave first grabs you and propels you forward. The acceleration is exhilarating, and you can really feel the power of the wave. It's like having your finger on the pulse of the ocean.

I felt from the beginning that there was something really special about surfing. It was special because you were actually interacting with a force of nature: a wave that had traveled thousands of miles to get to where you were. And then you met it and tried to become a part of it. If your timing was off, or you made a mistake, the wave would leave you behind, or wipe you out. But if you were able to synchronize with it, if your location and paddling speed matched the wave, and you did everything else right, you could actually catch it, stand up, and ride on it. It was so glorious to be standing up there, flying along with the air streaming over your bare skin. It made you feel so free, so alive. You felt like some kind of Greek god racing along on a water-borne chariot.

My mother once asked me why I always wanted to go surfing. She wanted to know what it was that I found so fascinating about it. I didn't know how to answer her. I didn't know how to describe what the surfing experience meant to me. I wish I would have had a better vocabulary back then. I would have told her it was like a mystical experience. That it was like communing with God, or with the universe. All I managed to tell her was that I thought it was a blast.

It wasn't long before my friend Deuce started going to the beach with me. He was helping me learn how to make music, and now I was showing him what I had learned about surfing. I would let him take The Red Baron out in the waves and try it himself. It turned out he really liked surfing too.

Despite his appearance, he was a pretty good athlete. It didn't take him long to learn how to do the same things I did. I wasn't surprised when Deuce turned out to be a goofy-foot though. He was a goofy kind of guy.

Deuce and I were forever cursing The Red Baron. We kept having to drag it ashore, tilt it on end, pull the friggin' plug, and stand around for a half hour while it drained. And that ugly piece of crap wouldn't turn worth a damn when it was in a wave. The rails were square, and not designed for turning. It really limited what you could do.

By the middle of July, however, Deuce had come up with a brilliant idea. He knew this young man named Ted who lived across the street from his parent's house. Ted was a house-framer by trade, and he owned a real surfboard. Since Ted worked most of the time, he didn't have much of a chance to go surfing, except on weekends. Sometimes he didn't even go on the weekends because he had a girlfriend who took up a lot of his time. Deuce asked him if there was any chance he could borrow his surfboard when he wasn't using it. Deuce assured him he would be extra careful with it. Apparently Ted liked Deuce and he trusted him enough to agree to let him use it. Deuce and I were really happy about that, although I don't think Ted knew I was part of the deal. The board was nine feet, six-inches long and had been made by Reynolds Yater of the Santa Barbara Surf Shop. It was constructed of Styrofoam with a redwood stringer down the center. The fiberglass and resin finish gave the board a nice light green color. It was a good surfboard. From that day on The Red Baron was retired to my garage.

Subject: Versailles
Date: Saturday, 4 April 1998

Mes Amis,

We flew Air France out of Berlin, dined on bread, cheese and red wine, touched down at Charles Degaulle, bypassed not-so-gay Paris, and hopped a train to Versailles. Checked into a top floor suite at the Trianon Palace Hotel with a view of the Chateau de Versailles.

Old Louis XIII used to like to hang out around here and hunt god-knows-what in the surrounding forests. He built a "modest" hunting lodge here on a rise overlooking the long, verdant valley. When he eventually waltzed off into that great ballroom in the sky, his son, Louis XIV (a long-haired, noble-nosed stud in tights) started adding on to the hunting lodge and ended up building the most opulent palace in Europe. Louis XIV was a big strapping fellow, an excellent horseman and avid hunter. He had an eye for the ladies, and exquisite taste in art, music, and all the sensual delights. He also happened to be the king of the richest nation in Europe at the time. He was no slouch when it came to spreading the francs around either. He was a mover and a shaker... he had the seat of government in Paris moved out

here to his house so he could keep an eye on his shifty ministers and make sure there were no plots afoot.

The Chateau he built is shaped like a giant U with wings. The two to three-story

87

building complex covers an area equal to several football fields! No lie. And the architecture, the furnishings, the art work... my God! As I wandered through rooms, room after endless room, each seemingly more beautiful than the last, I had to keep reminding myself to close my gaping yap. By the end of the day I had a kink in my neck from gazing up at the decorated ceilings, many of which had paintings that rival that of the Sistine Chapel. And then came the famous Hall of Mirrors with its panoramic view of fountains, statuary, lakes, and the surrounding countryside. Holy Christ!

I now have a fair idea of what fabulous wealth means, what it can do, how it can be used to build something incredible, even if it does end up being an empty pleasure dome that has no real meaning other than a testament to personal vanity. And yet at the same time, it cannot be denied that what has been created here is a lasting temple for the display of some of the finest art of which man is capable.

The hotel where we were staying had a stable of bicycles for the use of its guests. We bagged a couple of them and went for a three-hour ride through the formal gardens and stands of woods that surround the chateau. (There is a ten-foot stone wall around the whole complex. The wall is about ten miles in length and has fourteen gates.) We rode around the man-made lakes (all perfectly geometrical and lined up to provide fabulous vistas to the chateau up on the hill). Avenues of trees were so perfectly straight they looked as though they'd been drawn with a T-square. It was a warm, sunny Sunday, with literally thousands of Parisian day-trippers there who'd taken the half-hour train ride out from town. Many carried picnic baskets, while others toted just a couple of long baguettes and a bottle or two of wine. Many brought their dogs, everything from poodles to Russian Wolf Hounds. Many of the women mistook a stroll in the park for a stroll down some fashion runway. I didn't complain.

After such a feast for the eyes, I was glad to get back to dreary Berlin in the rain. Absorbing too much beauty is like too rich a diet, or drinking too much wine. It turns the stomach.

Adieu for now.

Leana

1972

A pretty half-caste girl sat behind the front desk of The Strand Hotel in the islands' capital and feverishly worked the adding machine. She had to get the totals done before she left. God knows what the Samoan clerk, Eta, would do with the day's receipts if Leana didn't cover herself. Even though she was part Samoan herself, she did not trust them.

The watchman, Fa'avale, who had been sitting gossiping with several taxi drivers on the benches outside the hotel, stuck his head in the front door. He was a big bronze man, tall and powerfully built. He had been hired as watchman because the riff-raff of the town feared him, and would therefore stay away from the hotel and not bother the guests. It was well known around Apia that Fa'avale had once beaten a man to death in a fit of rage. He had been arrested, tried and convicted. His sentence had been to serve a whole year in *gaol*. By Samoan standards it had been a harsh penalty, for in Polynesia, confinement, with the resulting isolation from one's family, is the worst punishment imaginable.

Fa'avale said in Samoan, "*Ia*, Leana, your father, the doctor, he has arrived and sits in the car waiting for you."

"Oi! Thank you Fa'avale," she said, shifting nervously in her seat. She attacked the keys with even more urgency now. She wasn't afraid of Fa'avale. To her he was a big teddy bear. It was her father she was concerned about. She did not want to keep him waiting. She knew he had just gotten off duty from the government hospital and would want to hurry home so he could change clothes and head for the golf course.

The telephone rang and she snatched it up irritably. "Talofa," she said. "Strand Hotel. This is Leana."

"Hello, luv, this is your favorite Kiwi bloke calling," said a male voice. "How's it today?"

"Oh, hi Peter," she said. "I'm very busy, and my father is waiting to fetch me home."

"Yea, yea. I won't keep you then. I'm just ringing up to see how you are, and to thank you for the date last night. I hope you're not mad at me."

"Oh," she said, rolling her eyes. It had been another boring night at the Surfside Club. Peter drank too much, spent half the night talking to his mates, and when he did dance with her he had done so in an ungainly manner. It was embarrassing. And then, to top things off, he had tried to get fresh with her on the way home. She despised men who couldn't hold their liquor.

"That's all right, it was fun," she said lamely. She bit her lip as she caught herself doing just what the Samoans so often did: tell the palagis what they wanted to hear... never mind what the truth might be. God, she hated it when she did that.

"Did you really have a good time?" he asked, surprised, but unconvinced.

She stiffened slightly, "Yeah, sure I did." She couldn't seem to stop herself. She cradled the phone between her head and shoulder and tried working the adding machine, one hand on it, the other turning the receipts.

"Bang on! In that case, would you like to go out again tonight? Some of the blokes and I are heading down to the Mt. Vaea Club tonight. I know it's a bit on the rough side there, but don't worry. I'll protect you from the bloody coconut heads. Won't you come along?"

The thought of another boring night surrounded by drunken Kiwis, and even worse, drunken Samoans, made her cringe. She wished there was more to do at night other than go to the clubs. "No," she said, "Not tonight. I'm busy. I have to finish making my gifts for Christmas, and get the last of the invitations to our New Year's Eve party ready."

"Oh, a party?" he said, "Am I invited?"

"Of course you're invited, you rummy Kiwi. Don't you remember me telling you last week?" she said. She was unable to keep her exasperation at bay.

"Ah hell, I must ha' been bloody pissed or somethin'."

"Listen Peter, I really can't talk now."

"Alright then, I'll call you tomorrow or come by. Are you working?"

"Yes. Aren't I always?"

"Yeah. You are. Maybe I'll stop by with me mate, Henry."

"You know that Sadie doesn't like boys coming around and bothering the help."

"I'm not coming around to bother her bloody help. I'm coming in to sop up a bit of the old piss, that's all."

"Goodbye, Peter."

"Goodbye. Bloody hell," he mumbled as he rang off.

Leana used to like going out with men. Her parents had let her start dating at 15. She found it amusing the way men reacted to her. She liked teasing them and leading them on. It was kind of a game, or contest between her and some of the other half-caste girls in town... to see who could attract the cutest palagi men. But lately all the fun seemed to go out of it. All the men she knew only wanted two things: to get pissed and grope young ladies. She was sick of it. There had to be more to dating than that.

Leana finally got the totals right and put everything in an envelope and sealed it. She gave it to one of the girls to carry to Sadie, the owner, who lived next door. She quickly tidied the desk and smoothed out her uniform. Grabbing her purse, she hurried out the door.

It had begun to rain again, not a gentle, temperate rain, but a punishing tropical downpour. Torrents from this latest squall swept over Apia harbor across the street from the hotel, battering the cargo ship tied up at the wharf. At least the rain was a relief from the oppressive heat and humidity that had hung heavily over the day.

Leana's father, Dr. Gunther Dietrich, was parked in front of the awning by the sidewalk. Leana quickly got in and said, "Hi, Dad. Thanks for waiting. I had to finish up." She spoke in English, it being the lingua franca in Apia, although her family sometimes used German at home.

"Ya, I understand," he said good-naturedly in his heavy German accent. "You must finish your job before you can go." He was a ruggedly handsome man of fifty-nine, somewhat portly now, and bald except for a thick fringe of dark hair around the sides. His skin was swarthy and brown, inherited from his German-Samoan mother. His nose and lips, however, could be no other than pure Teutonic, garnered from his full-German father. Dueling scars, called "schmiss," slashed across his cheeks during his university days in Berlin, would have made his face look fierce had it not been for his almost perpetual sunny disposition.

Dr. Dietrich turned the yellow Datsun around and drove along Beach Road through the heavy downpour, the wipers working at their maximum. He clicked his tongue in the manner in which Samoans demonstrate disapproval and said, "*Ach*, with this rain, I'm afraid my golf game with Malietoa will have to be put off."

"I'm sure that won't disappoint Mum," said Leana.

Dr. Dietrich continued along the curving road that bordered the harbor, heading for the east side of the old port town. The dreary, gray sky painted somber tones on Victorian-era government buildings, white-washed churches, and the rag-tag collection of shops that hung along the inland side of the road. Leana stared out her window on the ocean side. She watched the droning rain play across the flat, grassy, reclaimed area. The shallow east end of the bay had been filled in some years ago and was slated for development someday. It would not happen soon, however, for the struggling young government of this newly independent country had little money to spare. Leana turned her head back towards her father when she noticed that he had passed Ifiifi Street, the road that led up the hill to their home.

"Where are we going, Dad?" she asked.

"Oh, your Mum wants some watercress for a salad tonight. We go to the New Market." He deftly maneuvered around and between the stop-and-go puzzle of taxis, trucks and buses that plied this rain-swept, seaside town, the only town in the country. Shortly, he pulled up in front of the open, shed-like structure known as the New Market.

"The parking lot is awfully muddy, Dad," said Leana. "Just drop me off here. I won't be a minute."

"Here. Take my coin purse, Leana."

"No, no. I'm old enough to start helping out. I've got money," she said, jumping out of the car and racing for the shelter of the corrugated iron roof.

The large, open-air marketplace was crowded with Samoans, many of whom had just come in to get out of the rain. Vendors, their fresh produce displayed on mats on the cement floor, sat or reclined or even slept in that innate indolence that is characteristically Polynesian. Great bunches of green bananas rested alongside rows of brown-skinned taro stacked like logs. Breadfruit and coconut arranged in pyramids like cannon balls stood next to live pigs and chickens which lay on their sides, their legs bound, eyes warily watching the passers-by. Old men proffered carved wooden kava bowls or balls of sennit woven from coconut fiber, while old women hawked cowry shell necklaces and jewelry crafted from polished coconut shell. A fish market and adjacent food stalls in the rear of the building added their savory and unsavory aromas to the noise and bustle of the crowd.

Leana wasted little time in finding a portly, salt and pepper-haired Samoan women who sold watercress bundled in thin strips of pandanus. The woman sat cross-legged on a mat, her wares spread out around her.

As Leana approached, she bent her knees slightly and stooped forward, thereby showing respect, for it is impolite to stand upright over someone in Samoa. Pointing at the watercress, Leana said in Samoan, "How much is that thing?"

"Thirty *sene*," came the reply.

"*Ia*, that is good. Give me two, please," said Leana, digging into her purse.

"Yes, it is good," said the matronly Samoan smiling and handing her the bundles.

"*Ia, fa'a fetai tele*," said Leana handing her a one *tala* note. The women gave her two twenty-*sene* silver coins change. Leana hurried to the street where her father was waiting.

"How much were they?" her father asked after she had darted through the downpour and into the car.

"Thirty *sene* each."

"Whaaat? That's too much," he said. "The last time I paid only twenty *sene*."

"Oh, Dad. Don't sweat it. If we were living in the States, watercress would cost five times as much."

"But this is not the States. And what you mean 'Don't sweat it'?"

"It's just a saying they have in the U.S. It means don't worry about it."

"How do you know this? You have not been there."

"I listen to the radio, you know the Top 100 Countdown with Casey Casem, every Saturday morning. 2AP monitors it from that station in Pago Pago. Elke and Gaby and I listen to it every week. We learn a lot from it."

"You learn about the cost of watercress on the radio?"

"No, silly. Maggie told me that the last time she came home from Hawaii. We learn about pop culture on the radio."

"But what is the use of this pop culture information," asked her father as he swerved the car around several cavernous, water-filled pot-holes.

"It's not just information, Dad. It's the latest music. And we find out what's happening in the U.S. and in England, and in Australia."

"Don't we get the world news every morning on 2AP when they monitor Radio Australia?"

"Yes, of course. But I'm not talking about news. I'm talking about what's hip. We want to know what's really happening."

"What is this 'hip'?"

"Oh, Dad, you're so cute, even though you're square."

"'Square'?" he said shaking his head. He turned the car up Ifiifi Street and ascended the hill above Apia. Hibiscus hedges lined the sides of the road and a hodgepodge of European-style houses and Samoan fales peaked from behind the foliage. The car passed the graveyard and then the compound of Teacher's Training College.

"I do not understand these modern sayings," said Dr. Dietrich, "and I do not understand why the boys wear long hair and I cannot understand the words to this rock and roll music."

The rain had stopped now and the sun emerged from behind a massive cloud.

"Oh, Dad, it's just the style. The girls and I, we just don't want to be old fashioned, that's all."

"And what is wrong with old fashioned? You do not like old fashioned?"

"It's not that I don't like old fashioned, it's just that I want to know about things that are new. And you know how backward things are here, Dad. We are so behind the times, it's not even funny. Here it is almost 1973, and the most modern stuff we have is from the 1960s. You can't get stylish clothes here, or new music, or anything. Why, if it weren't for the magazines we get from overseas, and the radio show once a week from Pago Pago, we'd be nowhere. We wouldn't even know what was going on in the outside world. Even the TV that Dr. Fisch gave you – it's black and white and so fuzzy you can hardly see the picture – and we only get one channel for a couple of hours each day. And the few programs we like are weeks old by the time we see them." Steam began to rise as the hot sun beat down on the wet roadway.

"Ach, you go on and on. Do we not have a good life here? You and your sisters and your Mum have things much better than most people here in Samoa."

"I know we do, Dad. And we're thankful. But it's just not enough for me. I want to get out of this place. I want to get out in the world and do something. I want to be somebody. I don't want to spend the rest of my life in this place. It's just too small and backward."

Dr. Dietrich scowled at his daughter. He did not like to hear her speak this way. Why couldn't she be a good little girl like she used to be? It seemed like only yesterday. But now look at her: a nearly grown up young woman with a lot of silly new ideas. How old is she now? he wondered. Nineteen, he thought. He could not remember for sure. He had never paid much attention to his four daughters. There were too many of them and he was too busy taking care of people at the hospital. There had always been a shortage of doctors in Samoa.

"Ach, you are getting upset over nothing," her father said, "just like your mother does sometimes. Don't be foolish."

Leana pursed her lips and put her head down. There was no use arguing with him. She knew from long experience just how stubborn he could be, and how distant and far away he always seemed.

Dr. Dietrich pulled the car into the grassy driveway in front of their home. The house was a relic from the German colonial period. Set in a lovely garden of flowering plants and spacious lawns, the wood-framed house was two-storied, with high ceilings and wide windows all around. The walls of the upper story extended out beyond the lower, thereby sheltering the glass-less, but screened lower windows. Windows on the upper story were fitted with louver panes that could be adjusted up or down to keep out the rain or direct the flow of air. The inevitable corrugated iron roof used in tropic regions was painted red, and the sides of the house had a fresh white coat. It was a fine old structure, a perfect adaptation of European architecture to the island environment. The house was government owned and maintained, and was provided free of charge to Dr. Dietrich, a customary benefit for the director of the hospital.

Leana had grown up in this house on the hill and she loved it. She and her three sisters, the half-caste daughters of the top medical officer in the country, had enjoyed a privileged childhood in this palatial house next door to the government hospital overlooking Apia.

Once inside the door, Dr. Dietrich carefully wiped off his leather shoes with a rag while Leana carelessly kicked off her wet sandals and ran in. "Hi everybody! We're home!" she called, loud enough to be heard over the blaring stereo.

"Ya, hello," her mother called from the kitchen. "Gunther, you don't go to golf today?"

"Do you think I am a duck that I can play in this weather? It will rain again soon."

"Good," said Clare Dietrich, a lively, though high-strung German lady. Clare had met her husband in Köln, during the war. He had been billeted in her parent's home while he recovered from shrapnel wounds. She had fallen in love with the handsome German soldier as she helped nurse him back to health.

"Then I will start dinner now," she said. "I want to get it over and done with. I'm starving. I had nothing for afternoon tea... no cake, no pie; just a cup of instant coffee and a few soda crackers with jam. Did you get the watercress?"

"Ya, sure," said her husband as he entered the kitchen. He hugged and kissed her and pressed the sopping wet watercress to her bare back.

"Ach! Stop it you idiot," she cried, in mock anger.

Leana skipped into the living room, happy to be home. There she found her younger sisters Elke and Gaby sprawled out on the floor, one reading a book, the other a four-month-old-magazine. A Jackson Five album thumped in the background.

"Hi you guys. What's going on?" said Leana.

"Nothing. We're bored," said seventeen year-old Elke, who had recently graduated from St. Mary's missionary school. "How was work?"

"Rather slow. There's not many tourists now that it's the rainy season. But I did talk with those two new United Nations guys. You know, the cute ones we saw in town the other day. They're staying at Sadie's until they can find a flat to rent."

"Oh yeah?" said Gaby, the baby of the family at sixteen. "What are they like?"

"They seem nice. They're Swedish. They didn't talk very much though. They just stood there staring and smiling and saying '*ya*' a lot."

The telephone rang and all three girls yelled "I'll get it!" but Leana was on her feet and had a head start. She snatched up the phone and answered, "Hello. Dr. Dietrich's residence."

"Hello. Leana?" said a female voice with a very nasal New Zealand accent.

"Yes." said Leana, then with her hand over the phone, "It's Lise," to her sisters. "Turn down the stereo."

"Lise here. I'm just calling to tell you how terribly sorry I am that I shan't be able to attend your little party on New Year's Eve."

"Oh, no," said Leana. She truly was disappointed. Lise had thrown a party of her own several months ago, and it had been a huge success. Leana wanted to show that she and her sisters could do just the same.

"Yes," said Lise. "I'm afraid I won't be in-country just then. My family and I are flying down to Auckland tomorrow to visit my uncle. You know, Uncle Manfred who owns the trading company there? He's having us all down to the ranch at Rotorua for the holidays. We're staying a fortnight."

"Oh," said Leana, "That's too bad. We'll miss you. There's sure to be a mob here, and we're putting on a feed, and there'll be plenty to drink, and we've got new music tapes from the States."

"Yes, I'm sure," said Lise. "It sounds lovely. I'm terribly sorry I shan't be there. Some other time, perhaps.

"Well, I really must run now. We have to drive out to Apia Park to arrange for the board and exercise of our horses while we're gone. I wish your family had horses so we could ride together sometime. Oh, well. Cheerio. I'll give you a ring when we get back to see how things went."

"Goodbye," said Leana, disheartened. "Bon voyage."

"What did she want?" asked Elke as Leana hung up.

"Oh, she's off to New Zealand and won't be coming to our party. I'm going up to change."

Leana climbed the stairs glumly. All the happiness at being home had drained away. She undressed before the full length mirror in her bedroom and threw her uniform on the floor in the corner. The Samoan house girl would pick it up tomorrow and wash and press it. Since domestic help was so inexpensive in Apia, she and her sisters had never had to worry about doing chores or picking up after themselves.

Leana glanced at herself in the mirror and frowned. She did not see the beautiful, newly-budded figure of a young woman standing there. She took no notice of the finely sculpted breasts, the thin waist, or the nicely flared and rounded hips. She was unconscious of her shapely legs. It never occurred to her that her skin was flawless and had that look of perpetual tan that often blessed the offspring of mixed families. Her eyes were a deep brown color, but she was unaware of just how expressive and attractive they were. Her face reflected the finest features of her Polynesian and European ancestry, and they were framed in a halo of long raven hair.

But this was not the image Leana saw when she looked in the mirror. She saw a poor little half-caste tramp, not as white as Lise, nor as beautiful. Though her father was an important and respected man, he had no money. Not really. Because the country had socialized medicine, her father only earned a few thousand a year. Not like Lise's family. They were wealthy, and they traveled. They always had nice clothes and things.

Leana hated herself for what she saw as her shortcomings. She didn't want to have the party anymore. She sighed heavily, because she knew she had to. Most of the invitations were already out, and people had accepted.

She went into the bathroom and turned on the shower. She was oblivious to the fact that a warm shower was a luxury in Samoa. Her family had always had one. Before stepping into the stall, she glanced down at the sink and noticed, to her horror and disgust, that someone had left the cap off the tube of toothpaste, and that a huge cockroach, as big as her father's thumb, had its head stuck into the opening and was feeding on its contents.

The Point Beckons

1959

Now that "The Red Baron" was retired and Deuce and I finally had a real surfboard to ride, our surfing skills began to improve rapidly. We were learning to ride the unbroken part of the wave. From watching accomplished surfers at The Point we knew that the object was to stay just ahead of the break. You try to stay as close to it as possible without letting it catch you. Just ahead of the breaking part of the wave is what surfers call the *curl*, which is where the swell curves over in the act of breaking. It is the fastest part of the wave, and that's where you want to be – in the curl. If you do it right, you "shoot the curl," which is a little like becoming the pea in a pea-shooter.

Deuce and I couldn't shoot the curl at the pier because the waves came over all at once and gave you no place to go. So we decided to move further to the west where the shoreline began to bend towards The Point. We found that the nearer we got to The Point, the better the waves were. By the end of July we were inching our way closer and closer to that hallowed ground. We weren't quite ready to go all the way though. Since we were both still Gremlins, neither one of us wanted to get into trouble with accomplished surfers. They were older and a lot bigger than us, and they were very possessive of The Point. We wanted to be good enough so that they didn't have an excuse to kick our asses.

The area known as The Point stretched from the fairgrounds in the west to near California St. in the east. Back in 1959 there were four streets that ran from old town Ventura down to The Point. They were Figueroa (which borders the fairgrounds), Palm, Oak, and California. When the 101 Freeway was constructed in 1961, Palm and Oak St. got cut off from The Point. You can still get there on Figueroa and California, however, on the former by way of an underpass and the latter via an overpass. There used to be a cross-street bisecting all four streets near The Point. It was called Beach St. It ran along the coast from the fairgrounds, under the pier, and all the way to the Pierpont beach area.

There was a block of old houses nestled in the very center of The Point. It was bordered by Figueroa, Palm, and Beach Road. We didn't know it then, but that block was smack dab in the middle of an ancient Chumash Indian village. But of course there was no sign of any Indians in 1959. The block had six or seven wood-frame houses on it, as well as several large oil storage tanks along the Figueroa side. These tanks held crude oil delivered there by pipeline from the oilfields in the Ventura river basin further inland. The oil was stored in these tanks while awaiting regular visits by tanker ships. A submarine pipeline ran from these tanks out to a mooring area about a mile offshore. The ships would hook up to the end of the pipeline, and then crude oil was pumped into their holds for transport to refineries in the San Francisco Bay Area and elsewhere.

The waves at The Point used to start breaking right about where that pipeline ran into the sea. Generally, the waves had a long, symmetrical shape, and, due to the angle of the shoreline, they broke in a smooth progression from one end to the other. Most of the good surfers went out in the water between Figueroa and Palm Streets where the waves were the best. Under the right conditions it was possible to ride for as long as a hundred yards. As the waves traveled further to the east they began to peter out. But they would often reform around Oak St, and sometimes these reborn waves had good shape too.

We spent a lot of time down at the beach during the summer of '59. Sometimes one of Deuce's parents would give us a ride. Other times my mother was recruited. Usually, whoever gave us a ride didn't want to hang around for hours on end while we were surfing. So they would leave us there and pick us up later in the day. We asked to be dropped off, along with our borrowed surfboard, between Oak and California St., which was kind of the butt-end of The Point. We were less noticeable there, and the waves, even though they were left-overs, were rideable. There was hardly anybody else in the water where we were. And the waves were much better than by the pier.

I remember there used to be a beautiful old Queen Ann Victorian right on the corner of California and Beach Road. It was a two-story house, painted white, with a steep, green-shingled roof. The house had one of those round, turret-like corners with a pointy roof. The turret was on the west side of the house and looked out towards The Point. The yard was one giant succulent garden surrounded by a white picket fence. We used to admire the house when we were out in the water. I would have sold my soul to live there. The city of Ventura, in its vast wisdom, tore the house down about five years later in a frenzy of urban renewal. A tacky, multi-story Holiday Inn hotel was erected in its place.

One thing we learned about surfing in Ventura was that there is a perpetual current that runs parallel to the beach. It moves like a slow-moving river from west to east. When you're sitting on your board waiting for a good wave to come along, the current is constantly pushing you to the east. In order to maintain your position relative to the shore, you have to keep paddling against the current. The best way to maintain your position is to pick out a landmark on the shore and paddle just enough to stay abreast of it. We often would use the turret of that old Victorian as a landmark.

As the summer wore on, Deuce and I started seeing other boys starting to surf. There were even a couple of girl-Gremlins. These new surfers were mostly our age, and usually started out down by the pier like we had. Deuce and I figured they got interested in surfing because of that stupid movie "Gidget" which came out the same year. Deuce and I had seen Gidget at that old art-deco theater, the Mayfair, and we thought it was dumb as hell. It was just a corn-ball romance starring Bobby Darren, whose screen name was "Moon-Doggy." He was a surfer, but he kept singing these goofy songs to Sandra Dee, who was Gidget. Sometimes she sang back. It was horrible. And the surfing scenes were really fake too. I mean, what self-respecting surfer takes off on a wave at the same time as six other guys just so they can be together? And Gidget kept getting tangled up in seaweed and Moon-Doggie kept having to save her. And that older character, the guy they called "Kahuna" – he turned out to be nothing but a big phony. The movie was an embarrassment.

But everybody else who saw it seemed to swallow "Gidget" hook, line and sinker. And they all decided they wanted to be beach bums just like in the movie. Some of these new Gremlins tried going directly to The Point to surf. But before long we would see them down at the pier where we'd been. I guess the real surfers ran them off and told them where to go.

We didn't welcome these new Gremlins either. Sometimes they would come out in the water where we were by Oak St. They invariably got in our way. You'd be riding along on a wave and all of a sudden, there'd they be: sitting on their boards right in your path looking at you with this dumb, surprised, and then scared look on their face. You had to steer around them to avoid running them over, and that usually caused you to lose the wave or get wiped out. Sometimes these new guys tried to catch waves right in front of you so they could ride with you. That was the last thing we wanted. They invariably fell off, and their boards would go flying every which way. That scared us and made us mad. We were scared because we didn't want to run into their boards and put a ding in Ted's surfboard, not to mention our bodies. We were afraid if we got a ding in Ted's board he wouldn't let us use it anymore. We started to realize why the guys at The Point didn't like Gremlins. They were a hazard to navigation.

Sometimes when we saw a new Gremlin show up at the beach, Deuce would saunter over there and start talking. He'd say, "Hey, buddy, are you trying to learn how to surf?" When the guy admitted it, Deuce would tell him, "Well, listen here pal, I've got news for ya. These waves here are only for advanced surfers like John and I. The waves are much better for learning over there at The Point." Deuce would point to where he meant. He'd say, "You ought to head on over there." He liked seeing how long they would last with the big boys. Deuce got a kick out of putting them on like that. He was a real joker.

Another reason we didn't like new surfers was that some of them were low-down dirty thieves. Deuce and I usually packed sack lunches when we went to the beach. You get awfully hungry when you surf, what with all the exercise, the excitement, and the fresh salt air. One time somebody stole our lunches when we weren't looking. Another time they made off with my beach towel. After that, one of us would always have to keep an eye on our stuff while the other one was out in the water.

We observed that it wasn't only dog-eat-dog on the beach, but out in the water as well. Sometimes guys would get in altercations over whose wave was whose. Several times we saw guys paddle into the beach and get in fist fights over something that happened in the water. Surfing etiquette dictates that you don't take off on a wave that somebody else was already riding. These new surfers were oblivious to anything like etiquette. They were just doing what Moon-Doggie and Kahuna did. They didn't even realize they were cutting you off. Sometimes older surfers would get pissed off and run the interloper over. Sometimes the guy who got cut off would kick out really hard trying to hit the Gremlin. Big guys tried to intimidate smaller guys. Surfing, we learned, was not all fun and games. Deuce and I tried to stay out of trouble as much as possible because we were trying to protect Ted's board.

By the middle of August, Deuce and I decided we were ready to leave these low-life Gremlins behind and head for the Promised Land. One day when Deuce's rocket scientist Dad gave us a ride to the beach, we noticed there was nobody out at The Point, so we had him drop us off right at the foot of Palm St. This was indeed sacred ground.

He dropped us off right in front of the barricade that blocked off the end of the street. It looked like a wooden fence for livestock. It was placed there by the city to keep drunks from driving down Palm St. and plunging over the low bluff into the water. The barricade was painted white and had triangular reflector lights nailed to it so you could see it at night. Along the east side of Palm St. was a block-long dirt parking lot, and along the west side were three old houses. They looked out across the parking lot towards the Ventura pier. They must have been nice white houses at one time, but age, fog, and the salt air had turned them all gray. They looked kind of rundown, and the bushes around them were all crooked and hoary with age. Each house had a little front porch, and a tiny patch of weedy lawn that nobody ever watered. There were similar houses all around the neighborhood, all of them equally run down and in need of repair. But right at the foot of Palm St. was the crowning glory of The Point: a wonderful old, two-story Victorian with a red roof. Although it wasn't in any better condition than the others, it towered over them, and was the grand dame of the block.

It wasn't nearly as nice as the one down at the foot of California St., but it had the perfect location. Surfers called it The Point House. We knew that it was split up into rental apartments. We could tell that the people who lived there were not rich by their cheap clothes and beat up cars. They were mostly working people with low-paying jobs. We'd seen some older surfers going in and out of The Point House from time to time. A couple of them must have lived there.

Our inaugural day of surfing at The Point was a memorable one. It was a foggy day with a thick red tide running along the coast. The sea was the color of ox-blood soup due to all the plankton, and it left your skin feeling kind of sticky. But we had the water to ourselves most of the day. I think the reason for that was that the county fair was on just then. All the regular surfers were either working at their jobs or had gone to the fair.

The parking lot between Palm and Oak Streets was full of empty cars. Since the parking was free, fair-goers left their cars there rather than pay for parking at the fairgrounds.

The surf was only about two or three feet high, but it had great shape. As usual, we took turns riding Ted's board and we both got some nice, long rides. We were amazed at how much better the waves were at The Point. It was like the Garden of Eden compared to where we had been for the last two months. We decided that this would be our new spot. To hell with the hot-doggers, the bullies, and the wave hogs. It was a free country and it was a free beach. Besides, we were starting to get pretty good at this sport. At least that's what we thought at the time. We didn't know it but we had only graduated from being Gremlins to being Kooks. A Kook is somebody who has a higher opinion of his surfing abilities than is warranted.

Waves during the summertime are generally small at The Point. That was good for Deuce and me. They were good to practice on. The waves weren't scary because they weren't big enough to really hurt you. Sometimes one of us would fall on top of the board, and that hurt a little. Sometimes when you got wiped out, the wave would grab the board and slam it into you. That could hurt big-time if it caught you just right. But that summer nothing really bad happened to us, verbal threats notwithstanding.

Deuce and I surfed The Point almost every day after that. At first some of the regulars gave us the old stink eye. Some of them said stuff when we were out in the water. Stuff like, "Hey kid, I hear your mother calling you," or "Gee, I hope it don't hurt too bad when I kick out on your head, or "Hey, Kook, don't take off in front of me or I'll run you over like a toad on the road."

But we didn't have as much trouble with the regular surfers as we had imagined. Once they saw we could at least stand up and ride waves they didn't bother us so much. One time, though, I saw an older guy ride up behind Deuce when he was on a wave, and give him a big shove. Deuce, being a goofy-foot, went flying backwards head over heels and hit the water with a big splash. The older guy kept riding like nothing had happened. Deuce's board washed all the way into the beach. Deuce cussed a lot, but the older guy just laughed it off when he heard him.

I did learn something about surfing in red tides on that memorable first day at The Point: you need to wash yourself off real well after doing it. And that goes for your swim trunks too. I always showered after surfing anyway, but that day I forgot to rinse out my trunks. That night I went into the bathroom where I'd hung them over the shower curtain and discovered that they were glowing in the dark. I found out all those little organisms are phosphorescent. If you ever go to the beach at night when there's a red tide running, you can see broken waves glowing in this beautiful, light blue color. If you're a surfer, you wonder how many of those little critters are swimming around in your orifices.

Another thing Deuce and I noticed as the summer drew to a close was that our knees and the tops of our feet had taken a lot of wear and tear. All the surfers back then paddled from a kneeling position on the board, which was a trick in itself. You had to balance yourself perfectly in the middle of the board – not too far forward or too far back, and definitely not to one side or the other.

Deuce and I found out that when you spend a lot of time paddling on your knees with your feet laid out behind you, they eventually get rubbed raw on the board. After a while all the skin got worn off and you actually started to bleed. You had to get out of the water then so you didn't attract sharks. Eventually, you'd end up with scabs on your knees, or on the top of your feet, or even on your big toes, and they wouldn't heal until you stopped surfing for a while. If you tried to surf too soon, the scabs would get soft in the seawater and come off. Then you'd have these big, open wounds about the size of dimes or even nickels, and it was too painful to kneel on them. The only way to keep surfing was to paddle lying down.

When we weren't at the beach, we always had to wear Band-Aids on our knees and the top of our feet. If you didn't, your trousers or your socks and shoes would rub on them when you walked. That was painful, and kept them from healing. And sometimes the wounds would ooze and your pant legs or your socks would end up sticking to them. Even if you wore short pants you had to keep Band-Aids on, otherwise you attracted flies. Sometimes when you took the Band-Aid off, it pulled the scab off with it. Sometimes I would sit around the house barefoot and in short pants trying to let the wounds dry out so they wouldn't get infected. That really grossed out my twelve-year old sister, Jane. My mother used to put hydrogen peroxide on them, because iodine was too painful. My surf-sores never completely healed until about a month after school started.

After several years I developed what they call "surf knots" (or "surf bumps"). I got them on my knees and on the top of my feet. In pre-surfing days those knots on the knees were called "nun's knee." Nuns and priests and altar boys got them from kneeling in prayer for hours every day. Doctors call the condition *Osgood-Schlatter*. It is the medical term (named for the two doctors who studied it first) for a buildup of calcium caused by the repeated and prolonged pressure of your body's weight on your knee bones. Young people undergoing rapid growth are usually the ones to get them. In my case it certainly wasn't from prolonged praying. About the only praying I did back then was to pray for good surf. I guess my penance is that I still have those bumps to this day.

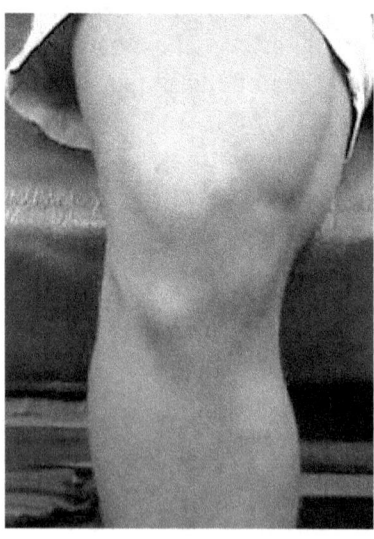

Poe, the Raven & Me (Part 2)
1994

The winter of 1994-95 was about as friendly as a pit bull with a sour stomach. Torrential rain, cold, tempestuous winds, and terrible flooding shredded Southern California. Your humble scribe and the redoubtable Gretchen were residing on the coast at the time, in a condominium in Marina Del Rey. The gloomy weather lent an appropriate backdrop to the strange events that were about to unfold. Although I was unaware of it, my nightmare was about to come true. The bird was on the wing. So, gentle reader, I invite you to do as F. Scott Fitzgerald once suggested: "Draw your chair up close to the edge of the precipice, and I'll tell you a story."

A bitter gray light gummed the dawn like a toothless wolf. Dawn barely noticed. It had been bitten by a lot of wolves before, but this one was a pretty sorry excuse for a wolf. I awoke alone in my bed. My corporate wife was out of town on a week-long business trip down Mexico way. I had spent the last three days by myself, cooped up in the house by the worst storm of the winter. But overnight it had left town too, and was now ravaging the Sierras. The next storm, according to the forecast, was right on its heels. But in that gray dawn I felt myself strangely enclosed in an eerie window of calm.

After a solitary breakfast I retired to our small patio to check the weather and to sip a second cup of coffee. The skies were ashen and still, but showed no sign of impending rain. I was entertaining a serious case of cabin fever and felt a strong urge to get out of the house. I was considering taking a long overdue trip sixty miles up the coast to Ventura. I owned a small rental house there and needed to confer with my tenant. Also, my father had not been well of late and I wanted to pay him a visit. There were other reasons as well.

As I stood debating the advisability of such a trip, a dark movement in the sky caught my eye. I saw three birds flying rapidly across my field of vision. The one in the lead was large and black. It was probably a crow. I glimpsed something dangling from its beak. The other two birds were much smaller. They chased the bigger one, diving and swooping and pecking at it. I assumed the crow had plundered their nest. The thing dangling from its beak was no doubt a hatchling. I shuddered. Life can be so cruel. I followed their dismal flight until they disappeared towards the northwest.

Now, let me say before we go on that I have never thought of myself as a superstitious person. Nor have I ever been one to seriously consider such things as evil omens or portends of disaster. And it was no different in this instance. It was only later that I lent to this small vignette of the birds a deeper significance, a decidedly more ominous interpretation.

Standing there on the patio, having watched their flight, I found myself facing northwest. This drew my attention back to my proposed trip, for I was facing my destination.

What the heck, I decided, I might as well go. What's a little foul weather anyway? What are you, a sissy or something? I'll just drive up to Ventura for a few days. Get out of the house. Even if another storm comes along, I always have places to stay in the benevolent environs of my youth. I can wait a storm out there just as easily as here, and find pleasant company as well.

So I made some phone calls. Then I tidied up the condo, and packed an overnight bag. I left a note for my wife in case she returned before I did. I checked my car: tires, gas, oil, etc. It wouldn't do to break down with another storm on the way. I checked the weather report on TV. The next storm was heading in from the south, just like the previous one. It was laden with warm, moist, tropical air and it was headed right at the cold front that hovered over Southern California.

The storm was expected to hit the mainland that evening. I also learned that the Pacific Coast Highway had been cleared of the latest mudslide and was open to through traffic (a courtesy provided, at taxpayer expense, to wealthy Hollywood-types who have expensive homes in Malibu). I decided to take the PCH and ride with the rich. There is always less traffic on that route anyway, and it is a much more scenic ride.

On my way out of town I passed the neighborhood pub: The Harp & Crown. From a recent foray there I had learned that this humble Irish pub held a once-a-month poetry night wherein local nutcases could gather to air their compositions. In a blinding flash of devilment I had decided to subject them to my recital of "The Raven." But I couldn't do it at the time for the simple reason that I couldn't remember it. It had been twenty years since I had committed the poem to memory. But I decided to work on it for the following month's meeting. By this point in time, I had nearly mastered it again.

As I drove along the coast heading towards Malibu and the rugged coast beyond, I was struck by the gloom that pervaded the usually sunny landscape. A dank, moldy blanket covered the sea. Muddy waves lurched along the battered beaches looking sick and sluggish. They'd been poisoned by the tremendous runoff from the canyons. The sea beyond was the color of a nasty bruise. Dark, evil-looking clouds lurked like Blackbeard's minions far out on the horizon. They seemed only to be waiting for darkness to fall before barging ashore and having their way with the landscape.

I thought, now here is a setting fit for Poe! Driving alone, as I was, it was a perfect opportunity, in a most fitting atmosphere, to practice my recital of "The Raven." Granted, the other motorists might think me a bit daft driving along talking and gesturing to myself. I didn't care. I had the words memorized already, but I needed a lot of work on the delivery. I wanted it to be just right. I fully intended to knock the denizens of the Harp & Crown off their barstools.

So, driving along that dismal shore, I began again the familiar lines, "Once upon a midnight dreary, while I pondered weak and weary over many a quaint and curious volume of forgotten lore…"

I remember the first time I decided to commit the poem to memory. It was when I was teaching high school English in Western Samoa back in 1974-75. My syllabus called for me to cover a section on poetry in each of my five classes. I had several reasons for spending the inordinate amount of time it took to memorize the thing:

ONE: The Samoans, like all Polynesians, have a long oral tradition. They can recite many old legends from memory. They can recite their lineage going back hundreds of years. They like to quote old adages and wise sayings. They are capable of beautiful, extemporaneous speeches. They are natural-born orators. I thought it would be appropriate to recite "The Raven" rather than just read it. I thought they'd like it too, because for some odd reason Samoans love the sound of Shakespeare. They are enthralled by the sound of his words even if they don't understand them. I figured they'd feel the same about Poe.

TWO: The Raven is a wonderful poem for teaching all the tenets of poetry. It contains almost all the literary cranks, gears and levers that pick words up off the page and make them fly. The poem was challenging, long and complex, richly textured, and full of symbology and historical allusions. It was a perfect tool for instruction.

THREE: After nearly a year in Samoa I was bored stiff. I was beginning to think tropical islands are not all they're cracked up to be. I needed some diversion, something to occupy my mind. I was facing a three-week break between the second and third school terms. I had no money and there was no place to go. I counted the stanzas of "The Raven." There were eighteen. I had twenty-one days to learn it. I figured: learn one stanza a day for eighteen days, and you have three extra days before school starts to polish it up. I wanted to give a really bang up, dramatic rendition. And that's what I did.

If the Samoans had worn socks I would have blown them off. About two weeks into the third term I had developed into something of a celebrity around Samoa College. The word spread throughout the campus that the new "palagi" teacher was putting on a show in his classes. It had to be witnessed to be believed. The other teachers heard rumors and gave me long curious glances in the staff room. The students took to calling me "Mr. Nevermore" behind my back. (Maybe I was as much a joke as I was a celebrity.) However, whenever I substituted in absentee teacher's classes, the students invariably demanded a recitation. I always obliged. And they always listened with rapt attention. I may have made a fool of myself but at least I did it whole hog. And I believe I managed to teach them something about poetry along the way.

For a few years after committing "The Raven" to memory I used to recite it at Halloween parties and other appropriate and inappropriate venues. I left Samoa and returned to the U.S., and after a time I left teaching. I grew bored with the poem and it gradually slipped from my memory. I took up other work and new interests. Years came and went. I moved many times and left Poe far behind me. Or so I thought.

But now, here I was twenty years later, in February of 1995, driving along the edge of a storm-tossed Pacific Ocean, once again reciting "The Raven." This second learning of the poem had been much easier. Instead of it taking me three weeks, it had only taken two. I finished my practice recital about the time I rounded Point Mugu. I aimed my car towards my destination.

I arrived safely in Ventura and drove immediately to my little rental house. I met my tenant there and we discussed some work that needed to be done on the place. My tenant was a nice, clean, single young man of the Yuppie variety. At one point we walked out into the back yard to look at some trees that needed pruning. We were standing on the back lawn facing each other talking when I noticed that his attention had wandered. He was looking over my shoulder at something behind me. His face melted from one expression into another. First it was surprise, then puzzlement, and finally a look of growing concern. He never took his eyes off whatever it was behind me.

"What?" I asked. His fixed stare was beginning to worry me, and the look on his face made me feel threatened. I quickly turned around. And that's when I saw it! I still cannot believe it to this day. But there it was. It was a raven! It was perched on the six-foot high cinderblock wall that surrounds the property. It was staring at me. I felt a chill pass through me. The bird was huge, black, beautiful, evil-looking. Its eyes bore into me. I gasped, and my hands went reflexively to my chest.

The raven seemed startled by my sudden movement. It spread its great wings and lifted off the wall. It turned in profile, drew itself higher in the air, and flew over the top of the house where it disappeared  from view. I stood there stunned. My heart was pounding. I felt faint. This can't be real, I thought. I stared after the bird, but it was gone.

"What was that?" said my wide-eyed tenant. He looked frightened too.

"That was a raven," I croaked.

"Are you sure?" he said. "It looked like a crow or something. God, but it *was* big."

"That was no crow." I felt woozy. "Let's go inside."

114

We went inside. I asked to sit down.

How could this be? I thought. I'd just finished reciting the poem about this ominous messenger of death. And the next thing I know it pays me a visit. And in all the years I had lived in Ventura County I could never remember having seen a raven before. I'd seen plenty of crows, but no ravens. And for it to appear just now! It was unbelievable. This had to be some kind of bizarre coincidence. Only this, I hoped, and nothing more.

My tenant seemed quite concerned about me. "Say, are you OK? You look kinda pale, like you've just seen a ghost." I laughed at this, a little too loud I'm afraid, and with a hint of hysteria in it.

I tried to explain to him about the poem. How I'd just recited it. He confessed he'd never read it. Oh Lord, I thought, "What on earth is going on in the schools these days?" I tried to explain about the raven. How there has always been this superstition that it was the messenger of death. Since the days of the ancient Greeks and Romans, ravens have been known to follow armies. They seemed to know that where armies go death follows. Ravens knew there would be plenty of slashed and bleeding bodies to pick, and plenty of staring eyeballs to pluck. The legend grew that they knew beforehand when death was close.

I told him about how, even in the Bible, the raven is mentioned as a messenger of desolation. Do you remember the Old Testament story of the Great Flood, and of Noah and the Ark? (Genesis, Chapters 6-9.) After forty days and forty nights of riding out the flood Noah opened the window and released a raven. But the raven never returned to the ark. Seven days later Noah released a dove. The dove did return, carrying in its beak an olive sprig, and by that sign Noah knew the flood was subsiding. But what, you might wonder, happened to the raven? My guess is that it was probably hungry after forty days and forty nights on the ark. I might even venture to say that it was "ravenous." It no doubt found plenty of floating bodies to feed on — rather like edible life rafts — and it therefore saw no reason to return to the ark.

115

All this stuff went, ssssfffttt, right over my tenant's head. I noticed he was starting to look askance at me. Like maybe I was a mite touched in the head. I decided I'd better leave before his suspicions were confirmed.

As I drove away I couldn't get the raven out of my mind. It couldn't have been a crow. It was too big. And that beak. It was massive. And those talons. No. It was no crow.

It was so strange, it showing up there, I mean. It made me feel weird, uneasy, a little bit frightened. As I said before, I never considered myself a superstitious person. But the coincidences here were just too striking. I wondered if there was any truth to the stories I'd heard. What if the bird had really come to tell me of some impending death? It was then that I had a chilling thought. I thought of my father.

My father had recently undergone a leg amputation. In fact, it had been his second amputation in three years. He was now legless and wheelchair-bound, living in a care facility in Ventura. My sister had informed me by telephone that he had come down with pneumonia after the second operation. I felt a sudden, urgent concern. What if the raven had come to tell me of *his* imminent demise? I drove with a vague foreboding through the soggy streets of Ventura towards the rest home where my father was sequestered.

To be continued…

Dispatch from Berlin #3
1998

Subject: Home Sweet Home
Date: Tuesday, 9 June 1998

Greetings from Sausageland,

We are comfortably ensconced in our new rooftop apartment here in Berlin. And, at long last, we are back on the mighty Internet at home. But because of a few bugs in the system I am continuing to use my Hotmail address until we and our carrier get ourselves sorted out. I can't tell you what a hassle it was to even get a phone line installed. The phone company here in Germany is owned by the government, and brother, do their employees have a bad attitude. They act as if they are doing you a favor just by showing up for work. Talk about rude and arrogant. Now I know why our government broke up AT&T's monopoly.

We have been getting some very hot weather in Berlin lately, with temperatures in the nineties. This makes it a little uncomfortable at times in our rooftop apartment. But we will take that over the big freeze of winter any day.

Our apartment is located in a neighborhood called Charlottenburg in West Berlin. More specifically, we live in an area known as the Kurfurstendamm, or Ku'damm for short. It is a very densely populated neighborhood and has been called, by some, the showcase of West Berlin. On its wide boulevards one can find some of the finest hotels, restaurants, nightclubs, shops and department stores in the city. Among the latter is the largest department store in Europe, the famous KaDeWe.

I have heard the Ku'damm referred to as the Fifth Avenue of Berlin. I would say it's a bit more like the Times Square of Berlin. There's a fair amount of grit and sleaze to go along with the glitz and glamor.

Our street is a perfect example. At the end of the block sits the Europa-Center, a well-known multi-storied shopping mall.

All of the buildings along our street are six stories high. Two of these buildings are hotels. The others are either apartment houses or office buildings. The ground floors of these buildings are commercial. They contain, among other things, five restaurants, four bars, a couple of sidewalk cafes, a sausage and fresh-fruit drink emporium, an expensive jewelry store, a couple of dress shops, a gambling casino, a transvestite cabaret, and, get this, a sex-change clinic! (So, if you ever come to visit us and would like to make a dramatic difference in your life, just stroll a few doors down from us and they'll fix you right up.)

Our neighborhood is also famous for its zoo and aquarium. (I might inject here that not all the animals are in the zoo. Some of them wander the streets in the form of runaway German teenagers, vagrants, aging hippies, and the occasional murderous-looking skinhead.) The neighborhood is bordered by a huge urban park (the Tiergarten), and also contains a high-speed, inter-city train depot.

With all the activity going on around us you might expect that there's a fair amount of noise. You are correct. But being up on the sixth floor helps, as this puts us above most of it. It's a little like living in an eagle's nest. We can step out on our balcony and check out what's going on in the neighborhood.

One sound we can't avoid is the frequent "ah-eee, ah-eee, ah-eee" of emergency vehicles rushing here and there. (Whenever I hear them I can't help but think of bumbling Inspector Clouseau being whisked off by the gendarmes.) Judging from the frequency of these sirens, a lot of people must be coming to grief around here.

Another sound we hear frequently, although it's not nearly as disturbing, is that of chimes. About a block from here are the ruins of the Kaiser-Wilhelm Gedachtniskirche. It is an old cathedral that was heavily damaged by bombs during WWII.

Only the spire and part of its base remains. The spire is hollow and open to the sky. It was left that way as a reminder of the war. Berliners call it "the hollow tooth." But somehow, the chimes still work. They play a pretty little melody and then chime the passing of each hour. We can see the spire over the rooftops from our front windows. It stands in stark contrast to the modern buildings all around it.

For quieter repose we retire to the patio in the rear of the apartment that overlooks the open courtyard of our building. A huge elm grows from the square and sticks its head high in the air over the rooftop. Swallows dip and dart around the square to the sound of pigeons cooing from the eaves. Occasionally, crows will perch in the elm and scold us for being up so high. I think they caw in German.

Our apartment is much larger than anything we were led to believe was affordable in Berlin. The living room itself is forty feet long by eighteen feet wide. It's like a bloody bowling alley. We now kick ourselves for only shipping half our furniture over here. We sit at opposite ends of the living room and say, "Hello down there." The echo comes back, "Hello, hello, hello."

We have two bedrooms, one and a half baths, a modern kitchen and an office. Plenty of room for visitors. One nice feature of the building we live in is that it has an elevator. It is a rarity here in Berlin, and a godsend. I, at my advanced age, am not prepared to be humping those six flights of stairs every time I go out.

If you ever want to drop us a line, or perhaps drop in, here's our address:

Marburger Strasse 16
10789 Berlin
Germany

The Spawning of Groupers

1972

It was just before midnight, and a full moon shone down on the open sea. From time to time a cumulus cloud would glide in front of the moon and turn the sea obsidian. Tavita stood on the aft deck of the alia, next to the silent outboard motor, pointing a flashlight down into the water. Aleni was down there somewhere.

Tavita was frightened. He did not like being out at night, especially out here on the rolling ocean alone on the alia. It was of little comfort to him that most of the village fishermen were afloat in their outriggers, and in the vicinity. He could see their lanterns here and there, spread out for a mile to the north and south along the coast. He knew their fishing lines would be down in the water. Tavita glanced nervously over at the reef, about a hundred yards to the west, checking to be sure the alia wasn't drifting that way. He had little to fear from that quarter, however, for the tide was ebbing now.

Aleni had taught him that the spawning of groupers takes place during the first full-moon tides of the year in this part of the Pacific, and that it is an excellent time to catch them if one could just find them. Aleni had described to him how the groupers swarm just at the edge of the drop-off where the reef meets the deep sea. They gather down there by the thousands,  drawn by the light of the moon. The female grouper's eggs are fertilized in the water, and then are swept into the open ocean by the receding tide. There is a reason for this Aleni had told him: if the eggs remained near shore they would be eaten by all the fish living along the reef.

It was Aleni who had organized the villagers for tonight's fishing, and it was he who had arranged for the trucks of ice to be brought over from Apia. A successful night of fishing would bring much needed cash into the village.

Tavita's attention was suddenly drawn to the little rectangle of water between the twin pontoons behind the deck. Bubbles were rising there and breaking open on the surface. Aleni was coming up.

Tavita kept his flashlight trained on the bubbles, and shortly, he saw a dark figure rising into the circle of green light. The reef fish which had been attracted by the light scattered as Aleni surfaced. Aleni was wearing his black farmer-john wet suit, the one with short sleeves and legs, and on his back were strapped two cylinders of compressed air. When his head was out of the water he tilted his diving mask back and removed the mouth-piece.

"*Malo*, Aleni," said Tavita. He was relieved to see his friend again. He had been deathly afraid for him. He could not believe Aleni would go down there alone at night. It was something Tavita would never consider doing himself.

"*Malo lava*," said Allan. "I have found the groupers. They are just below us and drifting slowly to the north along the reef. Give the signal for the other fishermen to come. I will go down one more time to keep track of the school. In ten minutes I will return. Tell the fishermen to have their long lines ready. Keep your torch pointed into the water so that I can find you."

"*Ia, ua lelei*. I will do it."

Allan pulled on his mask and put his mouth-piece in place. Then he rolled forward and his flippers glistened in the air briefly as he dove straight down. Tavita saw Aleni's underwater flashlight come to life, and watched the glow shrinking down into the depths with the dark body of Aleni descended above it. The eerie sight made Tavita shiver involuntarily.

Tavita stepped quickly under the cabin roof and retrieved his Triton shell. He returned aft and placed the little hole near the base of the shell to his lips. Then he blew a long, trumpet-like blast across the waters. He turned to the side and blew again, turned again and blew. Then he took up the flashlight and blinked it on and off, first one way along the reef and then the other. He saw little lights blinking back at him.

Allan felt the pressure on his ears increase as he went down. He took time to relieve the pressure by holding his nose and blowing softly. For the first twenty or thirty feet the clear water was dimly lit by the moon and stars. But the deeper he got, the darker it became, and soon he could see nothing but that which lay in the small tunnel of light from his flashlight.

At forty feet, pointing the light straight down, he could make out a swarm of thirty or forty groupers below. They would be the spawners that periodically rose above the great mass of groupers below. Allan watched as a big twenty-pound female pelted out a stream of eggs. A male then swam over the eggs shooting out a cloud of *milk*.

Allan continued his descent, feeling the pressure mounting and the water growing chill. He brought his light up to check his depth gauge. It showed sixty feet. When he flashed his light downward again he saw a great mass of fish swarming like bees. He wanted to get a better idea of their numbers, so he descended another twenty feet and began to circle the giant school. His flashlight played across their teeming numbers as they cruised around in a tight circle, sometimes darting up and down, or to the side. The school seemed to be drifting along in the current. Allan noted they did not have the normal grouper coloring: white and brown banding with a dark stripe through the eye. When spawning, groupers take on all kinds of colorations. He could see that some were stark white, rising up like ghost fish. Others were all black or all brown. Some were white on one side and black checked on the other, and a few even had a red hue.

Allan also noted that the school was not the usual ball-shape, but had formed itself into a huge cone-shaped configuration. The tip of the cone pointed up towards the surface. Allan's flashlight followed the widening cone downwards into the depths as far as the light would reach, and still could not see the base of it. But what he did see down there sent a chill up his spine. He was not the only creature circling the school.

Through his torch light some twenty feet below him passed the broad, striped back of an enormous shark. Allan knew immediately that it was a tiger shark, a man-eater. Judging from the length of time it took to pass through the light, Allan estimated it to be over fifteen feet long – a tremendous specimen.

This animal was nothing like the timid white or black-tipped sharks that were common on the reef. Allan's light followed it until it was out of sight, moving closer to the reef on the opposite side of the swarming groupers.

His first impulse was to swim after it. It might be a good idea to keep it in sight. At least he would know where it was. That would be better than having it appear out of nowhere all of a sudden. But more than that, Allan was curious. He'd never seen one that size before. It was beautiful, in a fascinatingly deadly sort of way. It was such an exquisite, proficient, stream-lined killer, and it operated in this dark world without an enemy that could threaten it. Being a marine biologist, Allan wanted to watch it operate.

But then for some strange reason he thought of Leana. Her image materialized out of nowhere, seemingly unbidden, and it gave him pause. For the first time in years, it seemed to him, he had something to lose by taking this chance. Perhaps if he had not met that lovely young woman two weeks ago in

Apia, he would already be on the trail of this shark. But now the scales had tilted somehow. Tilted just enough for him to realize that he had something more to live for, something to cherish.

Almost unconsciously he began to move his legs, stirring his fins, propelling himself slowly upwards towards Tavita's beckoning light. He played his own light over the swarming groupers below. They seemed agitated now. Perhaps they sensed the danger.

Allan continued his ascent, nervously shining the light all around him, searching the cavernous dark for the shark, expecting any moment to see it rushing at him out of some unexpected quarter. And, as he rose slowly towards the surface in that great pool of liquid night, his sense of the preciousness of life was brought home to him as it never had before.

South Swell

1959

One evening towards the end of August, I was sitting at home watching the Huntley & Brinkley news on our old black and white Motorola. There was a story about a big hurricane off the coast of Mexico. Apparently, the hurricane had sunk some fishing boats and was now spinning around like an out-of-control egg-beater off the coast of Baja. I didn't think much of it at the time, but the next morning when my Mom took Deuce and me down to The Point we found that a six-foot swell was breaking. The waves were long, crisp, and clean under the bright morning sun. When they broke they did so with a solid boom that we could almost feel sitting there in the car. They changed the whole atmosphere of the beach. What had been a calm bay with tame little waves breaking along the shore was transformed into a wild ocean with man-sized waves breaking out in deep water. It dawned on me then that this swell had been spawned by the hurricane.

Deuce and I sat there in the car with our mouths open and our eyes glued to the first big south swell of the summer. These were the largest waves we'd seen since we started surfing. We could hardly wait to get out in the water. The sun was bright, the day was balmy with a light breeze, and the waves were perfect: big enough to be exciting, but not so big as to scare the living bejesus out of you.

Deuce dug a quarter out of his coin pocket and positioned it over his thumb in preparation for flipping it, which was our usual custom. He and I had a ritual of flipping a coin to see who would take Ted's board out first. Just as he was about to flip the coin, my mother, who had been staring out the windshield with us, said, "Oh, my goodness. Those waves are so big. I don't know if it's safe for you boys to go out there. I think we'd better go back home."

"Mom!" I said, thunderstruck. "You've got to be kidding! It's not *that* big out there. Come on. We're not afraid."

(This wasn't exactly true, but these waves were too good to pass up.) "Really, Mom," I pleaded. "You can't do this to us. We just *have* to go out there. We can handle it. Really."

"I don't know," she said, unconvinced. "I'd feel a lot better if there were some lifeguards here." She was talking like the mother from hell, the nightmare nurse from Hades.

"But look over there," I said, pointing. "There's at least a dozen surfers out in the water. They're all good swimmers, just like us. And they all have boards and if anyone gets in trouble, they'll help out. That's what surfers do. You just have to let us go out. This is the best surf we've seen all summer."

Mom chewed on her thumb, staring out the windshield as the big blue swells came streaming in like an accident in a giant roller pin factory.

"That's right, ma'am," piped in Deuce. "John and I are getting to be old pros at this sport. You needn't worry. And you know we can both swim like fish. We'll be just fine, ma'am." What a con artist.

She was out-gunned and she knew it. She caved in. "Oh, alright," she said. "But I'm staying right here in case anything happens. You boys better be careful."

I rolled my eyes, but Deuce just grinned and gave me a wink. Then he flipped the coin. I called heads, and it came up heads. I was glad, but a little nervous as I pulled Ted's board out of the back of the station wagon. I could hear the surf booming as I lay the board down on the dirt parking lot. My hands shook a little as I gave the top a fresh coat of paraffin wax. I picked the board up under one arm and walked down a narrow path in the bluff to the shore. The beach had a nice layer of summer sand, and it was easy walking out into the water. When I was about waist deep I sprang onto the board and knelt down. I started paddling.

In small surf it is easy to paddle out through whitewater and breaking waves. But I found out that it's a different story when you're in bigger surf. After I had paddled out a little way, I saw a big wall of whitewater bearing down on me. It was taller than I was, kneeling there on my board, and I could hear it rumbling angrily as it came on. I paddled harder as it got closer.

I figured I could just punch right through it the way I was used to doing. You lean forward and grab hold of the rails and stretch your legs out behind you on the board. You kind of do a pushup with your arms. That lets the wave pass between your body and the board. When it passes, you kneel back down and start paddling again.

But this wave surprised me with its speed and power. It grabbed the nose of the board and flipped it up and backwards in the blink of an eye. The board smacked me hard right in the face. I was stunned, but managed to keep my grip on the rails as I went over backwards. I found myself buried upside-down in the avalanche and being pummeled and dragged back towards the beach.

When I finally managed to get myself and the board back to the surface and in calmer water, the wave had passed on. I had lost about twenty yards. I was too proud to give up, even though my face was throbbing with pain. Since my mother was watching from the car, I couldn't let her see I was hurt. I was afraid to look back at her in case she might be beckoning me in. She would take us home for sure. Straddling the board with my legs, I twirled my legs under water and turned the board out to sea. I got back on my knees and started paddling again. Another big wave came rumbling in. And I could see another big one breaking just beyond it. This was downright scary. My heart was pounding. I had to do something or the same thing would happen again.

When the next mountain of whitewater reached me I decided to try a maneuver I had seen other surfers use during last winter's storms. Just before the wave gets to you, you lean forward and grab the rails on either side just behind the nose. You take a deep breath, and then you roll over sideways into the water. You position yourself underneath your upside-down board and grab the rails near the front. They call this the Turtle Roll. You hang below your board like a sea anchor. Hold on tight and brace yourself. That's what I did.

The wave roared over the top of my upturned board with furious energy. But since it didn't have much to grab hold of, it quickly buried the board and hurtled on. It was frightening being under there and feeling and hearing the power of tons of rushing water over the top of me. I held my breath for what seemed a long time. But soon the surge subsided and I felt the board bob to the surface. As quickly as I could I flipped the board back over and scrambled onto it. I hadn't lost nearly as much ground this time, and I immediately started paddling. I was breathing hard.

Within a matter of seconds, however, the next wave came roaring down on me. Again I did the grab-and-roll maneuver. I had to do it a third and a fourth time as well. When I came up after that last one I was gasping for air. I hoped I wasn't getting an asthma attack. I'd had problems with asthma for as long as I could remember. I didn't know if I had the strength, or the air, to take on another wave.

But, as usual, my luck changed for the better. It seemed that a lull in the waves had settled in. Waves usually come into the beach in a series. They number from anywhere between seven and eleven swells – sometimes more. Surfers call these series of waves *sets*. Between sets there is usually a lull. That's the best time to paddle out. Had I been more experienced, I would have waited till the set was almost finished before stepping into the water to begin my paddle out. But on this particular day I got my baptism by fire, and learned a hard lesson. As it turned out, it wasn't the only lesson I would learn that day.

Because of the lull, I was able to paddle out into deep water beyond the break line. Once out there I got a chance to catch my breath. I felt like I'd just run the gauntlet, and even though I'd taken a beating, I was still alive and kicking. I angled the board towards the oil pipeline where the waves first start to break, and started paddling. I looked back and saw my mother standing by the side of the car, shading her eyes with one hand, and looking in my direction. Deuce was down on the beach, pacing back and forth. I knew he wished he was out here too.

I was lucky in that most of the surfers in the water had ridden waves in the previous sets and were in the process of making their way back out. There was only a few of them out where I was. I looked out to sea and saw a new set forming. A couple of the older surfers started paddling out deeper to meet it. I followed suit. Those guys kept paddling as they rose over the first swell. I did too. But then I saw the second wave. It was a nice big one, and it didn't look like any of the other guys were going to grab it. So I stopped paddling and turned my board towards shore. I looked behind me and saw the blue wall rising up, cutting off the horizon. I thought I was in just the right position to catch it. When it got close I started paddling harder because it seemed to be moving pretty fast. I then learned another basic principle of surfing: bigger waves travel a lot faster than smaller ones.

Even though I was paddling as hard as I could when the swell picked me up, I didn't have enough speed, or maybe I was too far out, because the wave passed me by and I dropped down in the trough behind it. Damn. I'd missed it. I looked behind me and said, "Oh, shit." The remaining waves of the set were coming on. They were bigger and therefore breaking further out than the previous one. I spun my board around and paddled for my life. I didn't want to be caught inside. Nobody wants to be caught inside when a set's coming in.

I climbed up the face of the first wave, which seemed to be about six feet high, and saw the lip just curling over in the act of breaking. I had just enough momentum that I burst through the thin layer of water at the top as it went over. My board went airborne momentarily before slapping down flat on the surface behind it. My arms dug into the water desperately as I saw another big wave behind it.

The next one was even bigger than the one before, and I stroked like a madman, trying to avoid it breaking right on top of me. I rose up the vertical face, but by the time I was about half-way up I realized I wasn't going to make it. I was too late. The wave curled over and I discovered I was no longer going straight up, but was starting to bend over backwards. I was about to experience one of the worst things that can happen to a surfer: going *over the falls* backwards. First I saw the sky, and then everything went dark. Fear gripped my heart in an iron grip.

The crest of the wave broke on me with a resounding crash, filling my eyes and nose and mouth with water, and then drove me backwards and downwards with the board right on top of me. Tons of rushing water collapsed on me and I found myself tumbling and being jerked all around. I felt something hard hit me in the ribs. It must have been the surfboard. Then I was somersaulting with my arms and legs going every which way. Everything was white and noisy with rushing water and bubbles. I was holding my breath, but I didn't know how much longer I could. I thought that if the wave didn't let me go soon I just might die.

But eventually the wave passed on and I was able to make it to the surface by following the bubbles. I tread water, gasping for breath. Then another wave came crashing down just beyond me and I had to dive down in the water to keep the whitewater from drawing me up into it. And then another wave came, and another. Between waves I looked around for Ted's board. It was nowhere to be seen.

When the set subsided, I started swimming for shore. Looking in, I could see Deuce pulling Ted's surfboard up onto the sand. As I got closer I saw he was busy putting a fresh layer of wax on it. He certainly wasn't wasting any time. Deuce and I had a regular arrangement. The guy's whose turn it was could stay out and ride five waves or until he got wiped out and lost his board, whatever happened first. Then it was the other guy's turn. Even though I hadn't ridden any waves, I got wiped out and lost my board. So now it was Deuce's turn.

My mother was standing next to the car looking very tense. As I got into the shallows and stood up, I saw she had her arms crossed over her chest. Deuce sprinted for the water with the board under his arm. He wanted to get out there before she did anything rash, like make us leave.

The ribs on my right side were throbbing with pain, but I resisted the temptation of rubbing them with my hand. I didn't want her to know I was hurt. There was no way I was going to give her the satisfaction of saying "I told you so." As I walked up onto dry land I gave her a big smile and waved my hand at her. She seemed to relax a little bit.

I climbed up the bluff to the car to towel off. My mother walked around to the front of the car and said, "Are you all right, John?"

I laughed carelessly. "Oh, yeah. No problem. I sure did get wiped out though. Ha, ha." I went to the car and got my towel and buried my face in it.

I wished she wasn't standing out there in plain view like that. It was embarrassing having your mother hovering around.

"Gosh, I thought you might have gotten hurt when I saw that big wave come down on you."

"Naw. That stuff happens all the time," I lied. "Hardly anybody ever gets hurt."

I dried my scrawny fourteen year old body off and suggested we sit in the car. I folded up my towel to sit on.

When we were both back in the car my mother said, "Your face looks awfully red, John. Are you sure you're O.K.?"

"Oh, look!" I said, pointing. "There's Deuce. He's going for a wave."

Deuce was paddling like a crazed monkey and just barely managed to catch the top of a steep wave. It was curling over just as he tried to stand up. He and Ted's board went airborne as they dropped down the vertical face, and when he hit the bottom the jolt sent him tumbling off sideways. The wave collapsed on top of him, and as we watched, Ted's surfboard was ejected out of the whitewater and flew high into the air, spiraling like a cork screw.

"Oh, my!" my mother exclaimed.

"I've got to save the board!" I shouted, bounding out of the car before she could say another word. I scurried down to the beach as Ted's board came gliding in on the shore break. I could see Deuce swimming after it like this was the Olympics and he was Johnny Weissmuller. He didn't get there in time to keep the board from reaching shore. Now it was my turn again.

I didn't even bother waxing up, but headed straight into the water. I passed Deuce on the way out. "Man, what a pisser," he shouted as I went by him.

"John! Oh, John!" I heard my mother calling from the car. I pretended I didn't hear her. Man, this was just like what that guy said to me when we first started coming to The Point: "Hey, kid. I hear your mother calling you." What a complete drag.

As luck would have it I managed to get out into deep water without having to run another gauntlet of broken waves. I guess I hit it just right in the lull between sets. I was determined not to let these waves get the best of me. I was mad. Mad that they had beat me up so bad the first time. Mad that my mother was being such a worry wart. Mad that I didn't have my own board. Mad that if I got wiped out again I would have to turn the board over to Deuce.

I had to wait awhile to catch the right wave. At first I was too far out, being somewhat gun-shy from earlier. Then when I moved further in, more experienced surfers beat me to the punch and caught the waves ahead of me. But finally I was alone with a beautiful blue swell walling up in front of me. I knew this was the one.

I turned towards shore and paddled hard. I made sure I had plenty of momentum as the wave drew up behind me. I could feel my heart thudding in my chest as the wave picked me up and propelled me forward. I sprang to my feet. As I dropped down into the wave I turned the board ever so gently to the right. I did not want to make a mistake. I completed the turn, the wave curled over my head, and my board sprang forward the way a horse does when you lay on the quirt. It is impossible to describe the thrill that I felt just then. I was racing along as fast as a horse could gallop, but I was enveloped in a beautiful blue-green curl that hung above me like a crystalline umbrella. I felt a joy so keen it hurt. But it was not just joy, it was a joy married to fear; it was exhilaration, and it was lust – lust for speed, power, grace, grandeur, honor, passion, peace, everything all rolled into one. It was "the absolute ultimate," as that moron Gidget used to say.

Subject: The Toilets of Berlin
Date: Saturday, 20 June 1998

During the Cold War, a special bureau of the German Democratic Republic must have designed the toilets of East Berlin for the express purpose of further depressing and humiliating the populace so that it might be more easily controlled. Brilliant! How ingenious of the state to intrude on one of the most private moments in its citizen's lives – the trip to the toilet. The beauty of this sinister psychological stratagem is that its creators were able to make such intrusions on a daily basis, seven days a week, 365 days a year. By the simple act of redesigning the throne on which the poor souls sat, they could bend their minds to the point of breaking, and bring their eyes nearly to tears. A classic move! (Or should I say "movement.")

The toilets of East Berlin are the most diabolical objects Socialism ever dreamed up. The lip of the bowl is deceptively normal, having the familiar oval shape. The design of the inside of the bowl is where they worked their demented magic. Instead of the inside of the bowl tapering down gently in a civilized manner into the usually ample pool of water, the fiends created a nearly horizontal porcelain shelf that stretches from the rear of the bowl up to near the front. There, the shelf descends abruptly into a four-inch diameter hole, at the bottom of which lies a pathetically shallow pool of water. The cold, heartless shelf sits like a glaring white paddle, a bare six inches from your bum.

But here is where the real psychology comes in: whatever business you are able to produce sitting over this intimidating shelf lands perilously close to your person. If what you produce is what we euphemistically refer to as No. 1, you are in danger of giving yourself a golden shower (albeit localized). If what you produce is No. 2, and that product is of the loose variety, you stand a good chance of being splattered. If, on the other hand, your No. 2 is solid and extremely voluminous, you stand a good chance of it piling up to within reach of your quivering loins. The best strategy here, I have found, is to try to coil it up like a snake. At any rate, the result is prolonged fear and trepidation at the threat of being soiled.

By far the most unpleasant aspect of the whole No. 2 scenario is the sight and smell of what you have produced. True, you don't have to look, thereby solving the first problem. Avoidance, after all, is something oppressed people are adept at anyway. The second problem is not so easily dealt with – i.e., the smell. This is especially true if you are the type of person who likes to linger over his or her ablutions. I'm not one of you by the way. But then, you never know. Should one find oneself somewhat constipated by the unhealthy and unbalanced diet of the typical German, then one must needs be longer about one's business than is normal or comfortable.

It should be understood that with a normal, humanely designed commode, the product of your No. 2 slides easily into a generous bowl of water, and lies for the most part submerged. This vastly decreases the amount and the power of the resultant aromas. But, as the GDR was fully aware, when your product is lying on a porcelain shelf, open to every vagrant breeze, steaming and noxious, the baseness of your existence is brought home to you, and to anyone else in that part of the building, in no uncertain terms. This weakens you psychologically, making you much more amenable to manipulation and control.

Well, back to the matter at hand. The only logical thing you can do, if your reign on the throne is to be a long one, is to flush intermittently, thereby clearing the shelf of the current offending object. Unfortunately, another clever aspect of the GDR design now comes into play: the water comes rushing down from the giant egg-shaped tank behind you with overwhelming force. The water surges over the porcelain shelf like a tidal wave sweeping across some seaside parking lot. Your product, an abandoned brown car, is caught up in it and hurled forward at near-supersonic speed until it slams headlong into the front of the bowl, whereupon it disintegrates into a million pieces. It is not a pretty sight, and the back of your legs stand a good chance of taking shrapnel hits. (Additional warning: it is suggested that one avoids spreading one's legs and bending forward to look when the flush is executed.)

About the only good I can see in this demented shelf is that it comes in handy when your physician wants you to provide him or her with a stool sample.

You can understand that after years of daily exposure to such toilet-trauma, the glory of the human spirit has been much diminished in East Berlin. The GDR's nefarious psychology was too successful, however, and in the end it backfired on them. It broke the people's spirit. As a result, the whole Eastern Block collapsed, and The Wall came tumbling down. All this for want of a decent toilet.

But, then again, I can't say that the toilets of West Berlin are much better. The bowls of these commodes don't have the notorious shelf, but conversely, their sides taper down at an alarmingly steep angle. At the terminus there is, once again, a pathetically small pool of water. Sitting on one of these contraptions is something akin to sitting on an upturned traffic cone. You try to aim for the miniscule hole in the bottom. If your aim is not perfect, your No. 2 paints some rather interesting patterns down the sides of the bowl. Pondering them is something like taking a Rorschach test. (I wonder if that eminent psychologist had something to do with the design.)

But no matter whether you do your business in East Berlin or West Berlin, you end up spending an inordinate amount of time cleaning your toilet. It is only logical that time spent in this fashion draws away from your productivity in other areas. No wonder the German economy is struggling. One would think that a society able to design and produce the wonder that is the Mercedes Benz automobile could put a little more effort into a much simpler device at home, a device you use every day.

And while we're on the subject of trips to the loo I feel impelled to say a word or two about German toilet paper. It is not soft and cottony; it is not as white as the fresh driven snow; it is not gentle to the touch like lamb's wool. Americans are in for a rude awakening the first time they complete their business and struggle to tear off their first uneven strip of this wicked product. Their most tender areas are in for another unwelcome surprise. The feel of recycled cardboard comes to mind, or maybe emery paper. Heaven help you if you have hemorrhoids or a urinary tract infection. This slightly brown, papyrus-like substance will make you wish you could go back home and squeeze the Charmin one more time.

But back to the subject of toilets, allow me to briefly describe another strange anomaly in the field of commode-design here in Berlin. There are hundreds of "platz," or plazas, scattered around the city: Alexander Platz, Wittenburg Platz, Nollendorf Platz, etc. They are often located at crossroads to main traffic arteries. They are wide-open areas containing statuary, fountains, or perhaps trees and plants. Berliners like to stroll around these platzes, or sit calmly in them smoking and contemplating their lot. Frequently these platzes are equipped with pay toilet facilities.

These facilities are odd metal-walled structures shaped like an extremely large can of ham. There is a slot on the outside where you insert your 50-*pfennig* piece. A whirring sound ensues, and a large door swings open revealing the Spartan interior. You step in and pull the door shut behind you, hoping like hell this isn't some new-fangled gas chamber designed especially for tourists. You settle down to business. If you are lucky enough to read German, you will be informed by the sign in front of you that after twenty minutes the door will open automatically.

Consider your fate if, a.) you don't read German; b.) you are somewhat constipated; c.) you figure this is a good time to study that street map so you can find your way back to the hotel; and d.) your twenty minutes expires. You guessed it. The door automatically swings open exposing you in full-frontal view to hordes of pedestrians and passing motorists!

Ah, such is the low-life here in the future capital of the Fourth Reich.

Deus Ex Machina
1978

It was two-thirty in the morning as I walked along Market Street in San Francisco. Restored antique street lights cast a mythical golden glow over the deserted sidewalks. No traffic moved along San Francisco's premier boulevard, but along its dim edges random parked cars brooded in silence. Occasionally, I could hear the echo of a vehicle moving up the long corridors that branched off Market, but it was eerily quiet downtown. At each intersection wisps of fog swirled around the corners and fluttered my thin jacket. I was still five blocks from the corner of Van Ness where I planned to catch the "Night Owl" bus home.

I had just gotten off work from my temporary job stuffing envelopes at a bank in the financial district. It was a lousy job with lousy hours and lousy pay, but I was new in San Francisco and it was all I could get on short notice.

As I walked, I noticed two dark figures moving along the sidewalk up ahead. They were heading my way. I felt a tinge of unease. It was late at night, and but for them, the streets were empty. As the figures drew nearer, I made out that they were young men dressed in baggy clothing. One of them seemed to notice me for the first time and hesitated. He put his hand on his companion's arm and spoke to him out of the side of his mouth. They both looked in my direction. Then there was a verbal exchange between the two men. Because they were still a block away, I couldn't hear what they were saying.

My unease grew. I was certain they were talking about me. The larger of the two seemed to be the leader. He said something to the smaller man, who nodded in agreement. Then they began walking forward with a more deliberate gait, their attention riveted on me.

I was afraid now. My eyes darted back and forth along the dim, cavernous blocks. There was not another soul in sight. I realized that at this pace I would come together with the two men at the next intersection. I considered turning back, or perhaps crossing over to the other side of the street. But if I did I was sure they would know I was afraid. Maybe they would follow me. Maybe they would *run* after me.

I didn't think I could outrun them. They looked young and tough. I wasn't old by any means, but I knew I was woefully out of shape. I knew that if I ran I would be winded after only a block or two. And if they chased me down, I would have to face them out of breath.

I laughed nervously to myself. I was being silly, of course. These men weren't out to get me. But I chastised myself nonetheless for letting myself go the way I had. I had been sedentary for several years now, working at desk jobs and getting no exercise at all. I ate too much, and drank and smoked too. I was terribly unfit and I knew it.

I hadn't always been this way. When I was young I played sports. I'd been a good athlete and led an active life. I'd even been in a number of fist fights as a teenager, and had never lost. But that was a long time ago. I had never been a big man. I was of average height, but of slim build, and had never been what you would call strong. Now, my muscles were soft, and I had a pot belly. I knew I would be an easy target if these two were up to no good.

As the two men drew nearer, I became more and more convinced they were planning to mug me. Their eyes were glued on me, and they kept murmuring to one another. Occasionally, they would glance around, no doubt checking to see if there were any witnesses. As the distance between us diminished, the question of running away was rendered moot. I would never make it now. I thought the only thing I could do was to try to bluff my way past them.

But in my heart I knew it was hopeless. I hadn't the size to intimidate them. And I knew my body language had already telegraphed my weakness. I slowed my pace, hoping to put off the inevitable, hoping for a miracle.

I thought about the contents of my pockets. My wallet held only about twenty dollars in cash. But there was also a bank card and a couple of credit cards. I guessed I could afford the cash loss. I would try to give them the cash only. But what if they demanded my wallet? And what if they made me go to an ATM machine and withdraw more cash with my bank card? I didn't have much money left after the expense of moving to the city and I couldn't afford to lose any. And what about my credit cards, driver's license, and my little address book? I didn't want to lose those.

Then I had a worse thought: the keys to my apartment were in my pocket. What if they took them and went to my home? I thought of my young wife lying alone in our bed. *Oh, Jesus.*

I considered the idea of resisting. I used to be able to handle himself pretty well. Maybe I could fight them off. But what if I couldn't? Maybe they would get really pissed off. Maybe they would beat the crap out of me, or maybe even kill me. Maybe I should just hand over my wallet and be done with it. But that was no guarantee that they would leave me alone. Maybe they would despise me for being such a wimp and decide to rough me up. I hated to think about that.

There was a traffic signal at the intersection just ahead, and the light was green. The two men got there first and stepped down into the crosswalk. They avoided looking at me now, pretending as though they were unaware of me. They looked cunning and mean. As they crossed the street, the two separated and angled to opposite sides of the sidewalk. The bigger one, the leader, stopped next to the traffic light pole. The other man took up a position with his back against the building on the corner. I saw that I would have to pass between them.

I was very close now. My legs felt weak, and the blood pounding in my ears nearly deafened me. My emotions ricocheted between fear, hate, self-loathing, and despair. My only hope was that I was wrong about these two. I prayed that they were just having a little fun with me.

Just then, the traffic light changed from green to amber. In that same instant I heard a loud noise rising behind me. It was the roar of a car – a big car with a powerful engine racing up Market Street. Then I heard it decelerate rapidly as the light changed from amber to red. The car came to a screeching halt a mere ten feet from where the three of us had come together. I turned my head and looked. Two young, beefy white boys sat in a souped up GTO. They had crew cuts and wore military fatigues. Their windows were down and they were smoking cigarettes. Rock music blared from the stereo. They were obviously on their way back to the base after a night on the town.

The two recruits turned their heads idly as they waited for the light to change and gazed over at the three of us standing on the corner. It didn't take them long to sense that something was wrong. They sat and stared. The three of us on the sidewalk stared back in a frozen tableau.

It was a moment that I would remember for the rest of my life. I would remember it every time I went to the gym to lift weights, or to swim laps in the Olympic-sized pool. I would remember it every time I played tennis or rode my bike across the Golden Gate Bridge. I would remember it when I hiked the steep hills above San Francisco Bay or jogged along its fog bound shores.

The leader of the two muggers on the sidewalk hissed, "Shit," and with a jerk of his head, motioned down the street to his companion. Grudgingly, they moved off. Over his shoulder, the big one spat back, "You're lucky, punk," and kept on walking. I turned to the army guys in the car and smiled my relief and gratitude.

With a knowing grin, the passenger nodded and said, "'You all right, man?"

"I am now," said I, wiping my forehead.

"Hop in. We'll give you a lift."

The Dodge

1959

My sixteen year-old brother showed up at the end of August. He'd been in Long Beach all summer working in the same drugstore as my dad. I was out watering the lawn when he pulled up in front of our house on the hill. He was driving a beat up old 1948 Dodge. It was the color of a rotten fig, with numerous dents and scratches in the body. The tires were old retreads. It had a cheap seat cover over the front seat to hide the upholstery, which was torn and faded. But Jake was all smiles and his blue jeans were bulging with the money he'd earned that summer.

Not having seen him for almost three months, I was struck by how much he resembled me. He was of average height for a boy of his age, with a medium frame, but definitely on the thin side. The main difference between him and me, other than being a little older and a little taller, was that he had black hair and brown eyes like my mother. My little sister Jane and I have fair hair and blue eyes like our father. My mother thought Jake was handsome, and I once heard a teenage girl call him cute, but I didn't know as either one of them could be trusted. Jake seemed to have grown since I'd last seen him, both in size and maturity. And he exuded a new-found confidence.

After my mother and sister had finished fawning all over him, they went down to the market to get the fixings for a special welcome home dinner they were going to prepare that night. After they had gone, Jake and I sat down in the living room to get reacquainted.

Jake said, "Well, Johnny-boy, you look like you're sprouting like a bean stalk. And you look pretty fit. Your arms and shoulders are bigger, and, man, you sure are tanned. You must have spent a lot of time doing yard work this summer."

"Naw. I've been surfing, mostly."

"Surfing? How could you surf on a piece of shit like The Red Baron? I thought you were going to be working this summer like me... so we could buy real surfboards."

"My friend Deuce borrowed a nice board from his neighbor. We spent most of our time riding it at the beach. I did make a little money doing yard work though. But damn, these people around here are cheap. Most of them take care of their yards themselves. I tried to get your old job washing dishes at the German restaurant but they said I was too young. Hell, I'm only two years younger than you."

Jake said, "Well, I've been working my tail off all summer, and I've got almost three hundred dollars saved up."

"Three hundred dollars?! How'd you do that?"

"Well, thanks to Pop, who's a friend of the owner, I was making ten cents over minimum wage."

"What's 'minimum wage'?"

"That's the least amount the government says employers have to pay you. Minimum wage right now is one dollar an hour. I was making a dollar ten."

"Wow. You're lucky."

"I know. And not only that – Pop bought me that fine old Dodge out there for my birthday. The first thing I'm going to do is fix it up, and then I'm gonna get a surfboard."

"Oh, really? Deuce and I have been surfing at The Point."

"The Point! Wow. You guys must be getting good."

"We're O.K. We're still learning though. But we did get some fabulous rides the other day. You shoulda been there. The surf was about six feet. It was really bitchin'."

My brother stood up and looked out the picture window towards The Point. You could see it from our house even though it was over three miles away. "I wonder what it's like today," he said. "It doesn't look very big."

"Why don't we take a ride in your new car and we'll check it out?"

So we went out to his bomb and headed down the hill. I was relieved that his brakes were in decent shape because the hill was very steep. Once we were down in the flatlands I noticed that Jake's clutch work was a little jerky, but for the most part he could drive all right. At least I didn't feel like I was going to die any minute. As we turned onto Main St., Jake flicked on the radio. It actually worked. When it warmed up we heard Johnny Horton singing 'The Battle of New Orleans.' Above the banjo picking, I asked Jake how Pop was doing.

"Oh, he's about the same," he said. "But he's put on quite a bit of weight. I think it's because of all the booze he drinks. That guy Al who owns the pharmacy where Pop works is a real lush. He keeps an open bottle of scotch on his desk all day long. I used to see Pop sneak into his office a couple of times a day to have a little nip with him. They're drinking buddies. Sometimes they go out to the bars after work. The drugstore sells liquor too, along with all the other stuff pharmacies sell. Pop brought a bottle of bourbon home almost every night after work. It was usually gone when I woke up in the morning."

"What kind of place does he live in?" I asked.

"It's a little one-bedroom apartment near the beach. The couch folds out into a bed. That's where I slept."

"Did you ever go to the beach?"

"Yeah, sure. But there wasn't any surf there. I used to go swimming though. But it wasn't much fun. I didn't know anybody at first. Sometimes I just went running for miles along the beach."

"What did you do at the drugstore?"

146

"Oh, I did a little bit of everything. Every morning I'd vacuum the store and clean the windows. Then I'd clean the bathroom and empty the trash and all that. I spent a lot of time during the day opening boxes and shelving merchandise. Sometimes I was sent to deliver prescriptions to old people around Long Beach. I got lost a lot in the beginning. I washed dishes at the soda fountain when they piled up. I did everything that nobody else wanted to do. Everybody there used to boss me around. But I didn't care. They were paying me good money, son."

"I ain't your friggin' son."

"Oh, don't get your dander up. It's only an expression."

"So what'd ya do when you weren't working? What did you do at night?"

"Usually I just watched TV. Sometimes I did sit ups and pushups while I was watching. I even did chin ups out on the clothesline crossbar. Once in a while I'd go out to a movie. By the way, did you see 'Gidget'?"

I rolled my eyes. "Don't even mention it." Jake smiled and nodded. Johnny Horton got done and Bobby Darin came on and started singing '*Dream Lover.*'

"Once I got my car running I went out on a few dates," said Jake. "After a month or so I kinda had this girlfriend down there. Her name was Mona. Wanna know what else?"

"What?"

"Mona was a negro."

"A negro?!"

"That's right. She was beautiful. She was a sales clerk at the drugstore. She and I went out a few times."

I was shocked. Growing up we'd never even seen a negro until we moved to Ventura. And we didn't know any of them. I don't think I ever even talked to one. All I knew about them was what I'd seen on TV.

"Did you ever kiss her?" I asked.

"Yeah, a bunch of times. She had nice lips. Big juicy ones."

"What did Pop think about you going out with a negro?"

"He didn't seem to care, which kinda surprised me. You know how he can be. But Pop knew Mona from the drugstore and he thought she was a nice girl. And let me tell you something else, John – and this is just between you and me – Pop had a few girlfriends of his own."

"Girlfriends?! But, what about Mom? They're still married aren't they?"

"Yeah, sure. But Pop was telling me that things are different with a man. He said they need female companionship. He used to go to this bar in the neighborhood and meet women. A couple of times when I was there he didn't come home at night."

"Aw, jeez."

"Don't you dare say anything to Mom about this though. Pop was saying he was hoping to get back together with her sometime."

"Get back together?"

"Would you please stop repeating everything I say, for Christ's sake."

"But how can they get back together if he's going out and spending the night with other women."

"Well, it's like I say – she doesn't have to know about that."

"Well, to tell you the truth, Jake, I don't care if Pop ever comes back. I never did get along with him anyway. He was always mean to me. And he was always calling me names, like 'smart aleck.'"

"That's because you were always talking back to him."

"Yeah, and what if I did? It seems like the only time he ever talked to me was to order me around, or else to tell me how dumb I was because I screwed up somehow."

"Aw, he ain't all that bad."

"You just say that because you were always his favorite. And Jane was always his cute little baby girl. I'm nothing to him. And he's nothing to me."

"Aw, don't be that way. He probably won't be coming back anyway."

"Good."

Jake spit out the window. Buddy Holly, who died in a plane crash earlier that year, came on the radio and started singing his posthumous hit, '*It Doesn't Matter Any More.*' Jake said, "How's Mom been lately? She looks a little tired."

"Oh, she's O.K. She's still working the night shift at the hospital. But I've been noticing that she's been hitting the bottle more than usual. She drinks the same thing as Pop: bourbon and soda. She drinks when she comes home from work in the morning. Sometimes she gets to slurring her words and gets kind of wobbly. I try to get a ride to the beach out of her before she gets too bad. She's got a couple of nurse friends that come over on the weekends and they all drink together. One time one of her friends spent the night on the couch. In the morning there was a big spot on the cushion where she'd peed."

Jake grimaced and said, "Eww."

"Yeah. And Mom says she doesn't have time to do stuff around the house anymore since she's working, so Jane and I get stuck with it. We do all the dishes and the laundry and vacuuming and cleaning up around the house. I've been doing all the yard work too. I feel like a goddamn house drudge. About all Mom does anymore is go to the market and cook. Sometimes she doesn't even do that. Sometimes Jane cooks, which is kind of a hit or miss proposition. A lot of times Mom just goes out and picks up ready-made food. Either that or we eat TV dinners."

Jake spit out the window again and said, "I ain't been eating that good myself."

When we got to The Point, Jake parked the Dodge in the dirt lot. We were the only car there. That was unusual. It was late afternoon, the waves were small, and a strong northwest wind swept through the Santa Barbara Channel. The surf was 'blown out,' and there was nobody in the water. No surfers, no fishermen, no sailboats, no ships, no birds, no sign of life anywhere out there in the sea. It was eerie. We just sat there for a while looking at the empty ocean and let the wind stream through the open windows. The lowering sun glittered across the choppy expanses, and backlit the brooding Channel islands out there on the horizon.

We heard Paul Anka come on the radio singing that tear-jerker, '*I'm Just A Lonely Boy*.' Jake groaned and twirled the dial. He found another station and a new song came on, a song I'd never heard before. It was an instrumental called 'Sleepwalk' by Santo and Johnny. It sounded pretty good. It had this electric steel guitar that echoed as it wove its way through a haunting, dream-like melody. While it was playing I told Jake all about Deuce and my adventures that summer.

When '*Sleepwalk*' was over, Jake cranked up the engine and headed the old Dodge towards home. '*Stagger Lee*" by Lloyd Price was blaring as we rolled up California Street. Jake said, "I've been thinking about something all summer, John, and I've made up my mind. I'm going out for football this year."

"What? You've got to be kidding!" I stared at him in disbelief.

"I ain't kidding. I've been exercising and running on the beach. Can't you see what good shape I'm in? Feast your eyes, boy. You're looking at the next star halfback for the Ventura High School Cougars."

"Halfback? Half-ass is more like it. You're not big enough to play football."

Jake looked askance at me and said, "The hell, you say?"

"Come on, Jake. You only weigh about a hundred and thirty-five pounds. Those big guys will flatten you like a pancake."

"I don't care how big they are. They have to catch me first. I'm fast, boy. Real fast. I'm faster than any of those big guys. And I'm a lot faster than you'll ever be."

"Hey, I'd be fast too if a bunch of guys weighing fifty pounds more than me were after me."

Ignoring me, Jake said, "And you know what else I'm going to do? I'm going to fix up this old car so that you won't even recognize it. It'll look like a dream. And then I'm going to buy me a good ol' surfboard and start hitting the waves again. And I'm going to get my old dishwashing job back at the restaurant. I gotta keep making money. I'll need it to keep my car up. And I'm going to get me a new girlfriend when school starts. A real pretty one. She and I can cruise Main St. in my fine automobile."

"How in the world are you going to do all that, Jake? You can't go to school, play football, go surfing, get a girlfriend, cruise Main, and wash dishes. For one thing you have to wash dishes on weekend nights. And aren't high school football games on Friday night? How can you play football and go on dates with your girlfriend and wash dishes all the same time?"

"I'm only going out for the junior varsity team, you dolt. They play their games on Friday afternoon. I can still work on Friday nights."

"Not if you're in a body cast, Nimrod."

"I ain't going to be in no body cast, Dufus."

"Hmmph," I said, "Well, if you're busy doing all that stuff you're talking about, when are you going to do your homework, Einstein?"

"'The same as you, Dimwit – at night."

"You're crazy, Jake. You can't do all that stuff."

Jake looked over at me and smiled, "You watch me, junior. And by the way, what the hell are you gonna do with yourself?"

"Nothing. Hell, I'll only be in ninth grade. They don't have a football team, or any other kind of team. If I didn't have to, I wouldn't even go to school. I'd be surfing every day. Damn, pretty soon school starts and I'll only be able to go on weekends. I could surf after school if somebody would give me a ride. If you weren't going out for that stupid football team we could go every day after school."

"There are other things in life besides surfing," Jake said.

"Not for me there isn't. Surfing is the only thing I want to do. All I want is to be out there in the water where everything's clean, and everything's honest, you know, like fair and square. And I'm going to be the best surfer there ever was, Jake. There's nothing else I want to do. I don't want to go to school and I don't want a job and I don't want a girlfriend."

151

"No girlfriend? I always thought you were kind of a homo," said Jake, grinning.

"Gee, it's swell having you back, Jake."

When we got home we found Jane and my mother busy fixing up a big, delicious dinner for the returning hero: pigs in a blanket, mashed potatoes with gravy, and peas. It was Jake's favorite meal. I liked it too, except for the peas. I hate peas. I've hated them ever since my dad made me eat them when I didn't want to.

The following day Jake started pounding out the dents and sanding down the scratches on his '48 Dodge. I tried helping him, but he didn't like the way I was doing it and told me to flake off. When he had the dents out and sanded, he sprayed gray primer on them. The day after that he took the Dodge down to *Earl Scheib*'s and had it painted a bright turquoise-green color. He had them paint the tire rims the same color while they were at it. Jake polished up the hub caps and painted some kind of black stuff on the tires. He bought a shiny new brodie knob and fastened it to the steering wheel. Last of all, he bought a little jiggle-head doll that looked like a Chinese Cooley and set it up in the rear window where it looked out the back with its head bouncing up and down. Chinese stuff was "in" that year. When Jake was done, that old Dodge looked just like he said it would: like a dream.

I had tried helping him out with his various tinkerings, but he was always criticizing my work, just like Pop used to do. It was 'his' car and he wanted to do it his way, all by himself. Finally, I just said, "Fine," and walked off.

I was fed up. I was jealous. I felt like a real loser. All I had to show for my summer was twenty-four lousy hard-earned yard-work dollars in my bank account. And, big deal, I could play four or five stupid songs on my ukulele. I had open wounds on my knees and feet like Jesus Christ. And I had the dubious distinction of having been the substitute man of the house in the absence of my father and brother.

My twelve-year old sister, Jane, meanwhile, was on the cusp of becoming a budding and beautiful teenager with all the attendant interminable phone calls and god-awful giggling.

Personally, I didn't see what was so damned funny about everything. Jane and her friend Emily from down the street were forever talking. Talking, talking, talking. I don't know what they found to talk about. It drove me crazy. She used to be a sweet, quiet little girl. Now I hardly recognized her. She was like a different person. She even wore a training bra of all things.

Jake started going to two-a-day football practices at the high school. But amazingly, he still had enough energy left to want to go surfing when the weekend came. On Saturday morning I helped him take the back seat out of the Dodge so we could haul Ted's surfboard. We picked Deuce up at his house, and stuck the borrowed board in through the trunk and tucked the nose under the front seat. Jake tied down the trunk lid, leaving about a six inch gap where the tail of the board stuck out. The only problem with this setup was that as we drove down to The Point, the exhaust from the tailpipe got sucked up inside the car. The three of us just about passed out from the fumes. By the time we got to the beach we all had bloodshot eyes and were feeling kind of woozy.

"I guess I'm going to have to get a surf rack for the roof," mumbled Jake as he staggered out of the car. "It's like a friggin' gas chamber in there."

It was a real drag with all three of us trying to use one surfboard. You had to wait forever for your turn. When one of us was out in the water, the other two would sit in Jake's car and listen to the radio. We'd listen to people like The Platters, Guy Mitchell, Connie Francis, Pat Boone, Danny & The Juniors, Jimmy Rogers, Marty Robbins, and of course Elvis. There were plenty of other people making good music too.

I felt sorry for my brother when he was out surfing. Deuce and I were way ahead of him as far as skill went. Jake kept falling off, and he ended up doing a lot of swimming. He got frustrated when he saw what we could do. Then he'd get impatient while he waited for Deuce and me to take our turns. The next day, Sunday, Jake threw The Red Baron in the trunk along with Ted's board. But after it sunk on him a few times he decided 'to hell with it.' The following weekend, Jake bought his own board from a guy who wanted to sell his old one. Jake's first surfboard was a Velsey balsawood. He let me ride it a few times. It was a nice board, but I thought it was a little on the heavy side.

Unfortunately, school started up about then. Surfing, which had been the only joy in my life, slowly began to fade like a summer dream.

A Postcard from Grandma

1961

When my future surfing buddy, Billy, was fourteen-years old he found himself enrolled at the Arizona Ranch School for Boys. It was located about fifteen miles northwest of Tucson. The ARSFB was a boarding school for troubled teens, and by most accounts Billy was fully qualified.

Despite the strict regimentation of boarding school life and the usual tedious classes, the main emphasis at ARSFB was on outdoor activities: riding, camping, hunting, boy-scout-style survival training, and so on. In addition, each boy was assigned his own horse. Billy's horse was an aging mare named *Nellie*. He was responsible for feeding her, brushing her down, and riding her on a daily basis. He also mucked out her stall, gave her fresh hay to sleep on, and told her his troubles if he had a mind to.

The ARSFB was out in the desert, of course, but it was also in the vicinity of multiple washes and dry riverbeds. The locals call them arroyos. Flash flooding is a common occurrence along these dry watercourses during the fall and winter months in Arizona. Not long after one of these seasonal gully washers, one of Billy's teachers, a Mr. Garrett, took about fifteen kids out on a horseback ride. Billy and Nellie were included.

Mr. Garrett was a large, gruff man who looked and acted more like an old-time cowboy than a teacher. He led them out about a mile from the school, and then down into a likely-looking arroyo. The water had all washed away by then and the sand was dry. It was a sunny day and Mr. Garrett foresaw no problem at all. He had led his students out there in search of fossils and any other artifacts that may have washed down in the flood. As it turned out, fossils were not the only thing they found.

They were all riding along single-file, with Billy, being the youngest, bringing up the rear. He was looking from side to

155

side when he noticed a slight movement in the brush that grew along the side of the arroyo. It was then that he uttered those fateful words. He said, "Whoa, Nellie."

She stopped. Billy dismounted and went to investigate. What he discovered amidst the bush was a large black lizard with big orange bands along its back and sides. It was lazily digging in the sand. Billy was shocked. He had discovered a Gila Monster!

He called out to the other riders who were by then leaving him behind. His message was slowly passed up to Mr. Garrett at the front of the column. The teacher quickly rode back and as he approached, he yelled out, "Be careful there, young fella!"

Well, Duh, Billy thought. He had learned about Gila Monsters in school. It is one of the few venomous lizards in all the world. It lives in the southwestern deserts of the United States. The Gila Monster spends most of its time under rocks or in shallow burrows. Though it is a rather rotund and generally slow-moving creature, it is capable of quick thrusts and is equipped with powerful jaws. It is also very cranky and poisonous. It has the tenacity of a bulldog, so once it latches onto its prey it will not let go. Although it feeds mainly on eggs, it also catches and eats small birds, mammals, lizards, frogs and insects, not to mention consuming carrion. The Gila can grow as long as twenty inches and weigh up to five pounds, although the one Billy discovered that day was only about half that size. The Gila Monster produces its poison in glands in his lower jaws. As the Gila gnaws on its prey, its saliva transmits the poison into its victim's flesh, slowly killing it.

Mr. Garrett's face lit up. "Jeepers, that's a nice specimen. Let's take it back to the lab, boy. We have an empty terrarium

there. We can study it."

Then he looked at Billy and said, "Well, go on, young fella. Pick it up like you learned in biology class."

No freaking way, thought Billy. But when he looked up and noticed all the other kids looking down at him from their horses, he said, "Yeah, sure. No problem." So he put his thumb and forefinger around the sides of the Gila's upper neck and took a firm grip just below its jaw so that it had no chance of biting him. Then he picked it up. He was surprised at how heavy it was – at least a couple of pounds. The lizard didn't like being picked up and started squirming around and flicking its forked tongue. To keep from losing his grip, Billy had to use his other hand to grab hold of its fat body. The lizard had sharp claws that pawed the air. It was then that Billy noticed its smell. It smelled really bad – like something dead.

Mr. Garrett called out to one of the kids to get him a gunny sack. Several of the kids had them for collecting fossils. When he got his hands on a sack he dismounted and held it open and told Billy to drop the Gila Monster in it. So Billy did. Then the teacher told one of the other boys to give him a piece of leather strapping off his saddle. The strap was about a foot long and a quarter inch wide. He wrapped the strap around the top of the sack a few times and tied it firmly in place.

When he was done, Mr. Garrett turned to Billy and said, "Well, since you caught it, partner, you get to carry it." He handed Billy the gunny sack with a benign smile, then remounted and rode back to the head of the column. Billy supposed they were going to keep on searching for fossils or whatever.

Grumbling, he climbed back on Nellie with the cumbersome gunny sack. By the time he got situated he found himself at the rear of the pack again. He had the reins in his right hand and the sack in his left. He clucked his tongue to Nellie and followed the riders along the arroyo.

After a couple of minutes riding Billy felt a nudge at the top of the sack. He wondered what it was. He found out rather quickly. Using its claws, the Gila Monster had crawled up the inside of the gunny sack and found Billy's hand holding it. From inside the sack it lunged up and bit down hard on the meaty part of the boy's left hand.

Holy crap! It hurt like hell. Billy yelled and tried to drop the sack, but the whole thing just clung to him. The Gila had a really strong grip on his hand.

Billy yelled out to the group again, "Help! Help! He's got me!"

Then the lizard started chewing on him: chomp, chomp, chomp. Billy's hand felt like it was on fire. He grabbed ahold of the Gila's body from outside the bag and tried to pull it off, but it just clamped down tighter. Then it started chewing on him again. Blood started soaking through the sack.

"Help! Help, goddamn it!"

Billy kept trying to pull the monster off but it just wouldn't let go. His cries for help were eventually passed up the column until they reached Mr. Garrett. He rode back with a frown on his face. He always knew Billy was a trouble-maker. He could tell that from the get-go.

While Billy waited for him he studied the rhythm of the Gila's bite. It would go: chomp, chomp, chomp, then relax. Chomp, chomp, chomp, then relax. Each cycle would last about five seconds. Billy waited until the exact "relax" moment and then jerked its fat body down and away from his hand. And, miracle of miracles, he managed to pull it off. He immediately dropped the sack on the ground. The lizard had been chewing on him for over a minute by that time.

Mr. Garrett finally arrived and looked at Billy's pale face and his bleeding hand, and then down at the bloody squirming sack. He pushed his Stetson back off his forehead and said, "Well damn, you don't look so good, partner. You better get down off your horse."

So Billy dismounted and backed away from the gunny sack. His body shook as he stared down at his hand. It was bleeding badly, and he was beginning to feel a little woozy. The Gila had taken a chunk out of his hand. Mr. Garrett got down off his horse and cut a piece of leather off Billy's reins to use as a tourniquet. He tied it around his left arm just above the elbow. Then he sent a rider back to the school and told him to bring the jeep and the school nurse. He told the boy to hurry. He probably knew it would take some time to get help… time Billy might not have.

Billy's knees felt weak and his legs began to wobble. Mr. Garrett suggested that he might want to sit down. Billy obliged him. The boy started feeling very strange. He was lightheaded and dizzy and a little bit nauseous. But at least the pain in his hand had subsided. Then he began to feel drowsy and alarmingly short of breath. But he didn't really care. He was just glad that burning pain was gone. It was right about then that Billy went into shock.

He vaguely remembered the jeep arriving, and the bumpy ten-mile ride into Tucson. They took him to St. Mary's Hospital which was the oldest hospital in town. By then he was totally witless. The only thing he later recalled was telling anyone who would listen that he was too young to die.

*   *   *   *

Billy woke up slowly. He found himself in a hospital bed in a small room. He had needles in his arms covered with tape. He had a bandage on his left hand. And he was very thirsty. He had never been so thirsty in all his life. A really nice nurse who looked like a nun brought him a glass of orange juice.

After he drank it and was able to speak, he said, "What happened?"

"You are a very lucky young man," she said "They tell me we haven't had a Gila Monster case here in twenty years, and that poor fellow didn't make it." She straightened and fluffed his pillows. He could smell her. She smelled good… and clean. "You've been unconscious for three days. We didn't have the right anti-venom here, so we made our own and hoped it worked."

Billy nodded, "I knew I was too young to die."

She smiled. "Just remember this: you've been given a second chance. God was looking out for you. He must have big plans for you when you grow up."

159

Then she left to go find the doctor. Billy thought that maybe the next time he got the chance he would ask her to renounce her vows and run away with him.

While he waited he looked around the room and noticed the late afternoon sun shining through the window. It cast a beam of light directly onto the bedside table. Two objects were illuminated there: one was a bouquet of flowers sent by his father, and the other was a postcard from his grandmother. The postcard read, "Dear Billy — If you can read this you're OK! Love, Nana." On the front of the postcard was a picture of – you guessed it – a Gila Monster. Grandma always did have a great sense of humor.

P.S. After a month of jail time in the classroom terrarium, the captured Gila was *very carefully* taken back to its old home in the arroyo and released unharmed.

The History Lesson
1959

It was with a good deal of regret and resentment that I returned to Cabrillo Junior High School in the fall of 1959. All I wanted to do was surf and continue to lead the life of a carefree beach bum. I was depressed at the prospect of spending the next nine months cooped up in some boring classroom. I resigned myself to having a perfectly rotten time at school. Despite my bad attitude, my negativism began to evaporate on the very first day back at school. This was due in large part to the charm of my home-room teacher, Mr. Gates.

Mr. Gates was a short, ruggedly handsome man of about forty. He had dark, thinning hair combed straight back, and a nose that took a nosedive towards the floor about half-way down the bridge. He volunteered that it had been broken when he was in the Navy during WWII. Mr. Gates, as we were to learn later, had been the middleweight boxing champ of the U.S. Pacific Fleet.

Despite his tough appearance and pugilistic background, Mr. Gates was a gentle and caring man. He had a lively, entertaining manner and would interrupt his lesson at the drop of a hat to tell an interesting story. On that first day of school he informed us that, among other things, he was a 'history buff.' He thought history was a fascinating subject, and he hoped that we did too. He told us that history could actually come alive if you let it. All you had to do was look around you. As an example, Mr. Gates asked us, "Did you know that this school is named after the first European ever to explore the coast of California?" Warily, a few of my ninth-grade classmates nodded their heads.

Mr. Gates grinned and said, "That European's name was Juan Rodriguez Cabrillo. He was a Portuguese navigator in the employ of Spain. He sailed up to California from Mexico in 1542. That was a long time ago, kids, over 400 years. The reason Cabrillo came here was that he was searching for something called 'the Straits of Anian.' That's what people in those days called a river they thought joined the Atlantic and Pacific oceans. They wanted to find it because it would have been a terrific shortcut between Europe and Asia. There was no such river, of course, but they didn't know that at the time. Cabrillo was also looking for cities and rich countries. Needless to say, he didn't find any of those things."

JUAN RODRIGUEZ CABRILLO.

About this time my attention began to wander. I had noticed a very pretty girl to my left who seemed to be gazing in my direction. I blushed involuntarily, and looked over my shoulder to the right to see if she was looking at someone behind me. She wasn't.

Mr. Gates continued. "But one of the things that Cabrillo did find was an Indian village right here in Ventura. The Indians were called Chumash. They lived down near the mouth of the Ventura River, near where the fairgrounds are now. Actually, the village was right where today's surfers go to ride waves."

My head jerked up on hearing that, and I was all ears.

Mr. Gates went on to say, "Do you know the place I'm talking about? My son tells me it's called 'The Point.'"

Vigorous nods peppered the classroom.

"The Chumash village was on a low bluff right above the beach between what is now Palm and Figueroa Streets. The village had many large, dome-shaped houses scattered right along the shore. The houses were thatched in *tule* gathered along the banks of the Ventura River. And, kids, that village didn't just spring up overnight. It had been there for five hundred years when Cabrillo came along in 1542. Can you imagine? The Chumash were living at The Point long before Columbus even discovered America."

I glanced over at the pretty girl to my left and noticed she had nice legs and really cute shoes.

"Like all the explorers of his time, Cabrillo had a penchant for claiming other people's lands, and for naming places that already had names. He called the village '*Pueblo de Las Canoas*,' the Village of the Canoes. He called it that because when his two ships anchored offshore, he saw many plank canoes lined up on the beach in front of the village. Some of the canoes entered the water and came out to visit Cabrillo's ships. The canoes were painted a dark red color and decorated with inlaid mother of pearl. They were light and buoyant, and could really fly over the water. Cabrillo, and the explorers that came after him, found the Chumash to be a friendly, hospitable and generous people. He stayed for four days before heading further up the coast."

I glanced over at the pretty girl to my left, and caught her looking at me again, but she quickly looked away.

"During his stay Cabrillo learned that the Chumash used their canoes for fishing and trading along the coast. They also made frequent trips out to the Channel Islands, twenty miles out to sea. Some of the canoes were quite large  – they could hold as many as a dozen paddlers – either that or fewer paddlers and a considerable amount of cargo. The Indians knelt in the canoes, one behind the other, and used these long, two-bladed paddles which they dug into the sea on either side. They would chant in unison so they could synchronize their paddling.

The way Mr. Gates was talking made my imagination run wild. I closed my eyes and forgot all about the pretty girl. I erased from my mind all the modern buildings and roads and cars in Ventura. Then I pretended I was on one of those ships anchored offshore. I could almost feel the ship lifting and falling as the blue swells rolled underneath. Looking towards the beach I could see prehistoric whitewater washing up on a cobbled shore. I saw the sloping beach, and the red canoes waiting. Above the earthen ledge the village spread, and I could see smoke rising from the many domed houses. Beyond, the verdant river valley spread out between empty brown hills, and, looming in the background, the purple mountains of the Maricopa. I felt a gentle breeze, and listened to the lonely sound of waves breaking in the distance.

That made me think about surfing again, and I began to wonder if those Indians ever caught waves in those red canoes. I figured they must have, at least when they were coming into the shore. Maybe there were even Chumash surfers. I thought that if those Indians could build something as complicated as a canoe they ought to be able to make something as simple as a surfboard.

"So, you see what I mean?" asked Mr. Gates. "History is all around you if you look for it. That's one of the subjects we're going to study this year."

He broke the spell he had created when he told us about all the other stuff we were going to learn that year. Mr. Gates was our social studies teacher. He told us he was a tough grader, so we had all better do our homework and be prepared for the tests he was going to give us. Mr. Gates added that he would give extra credit to kids who did special projects.

After class I went up to him and told him I wanted to find out more about those Indians that used to live down at the beach. He said he would lend me some books to read, and that I could earn extra credit if I wrote a report. I said O.K.

When I turned to leave I saw the pretty girl from before standing near the door looking through her purse.

Subject: Parades
Date: Friday, 17 July 1998

One time back in the 1980s, when Gretchen and I were living in Rockaway, New Jersey, we decided to spend Easter in New York City. We wanted to witness the famous Easter Parade down Fifth Avenue. So we checked into a hotel on the corner of that fabled boulevard, and about ten o'clock on Sunday morning we went down to the lobby and asked the concierge what time the parade started. The man shrugged and said, "Oh, any time." We said, "Uh, you mean there's no starting time?"

"Well, no, not really," he replied. He looked at us more closely, trying to determine if we were from outer space. "Hmm," we thought, "this is rather strange. Maybe this guy has been tipping the bottle, or maybe he just doesn't know what time it is and doesn't want to admit it. New York is so full of eccentrics." So we walked out onto Fifth Avenue to find out for ourselves.

It was a nice sunny spring day, but a bit on the cool side. There was no traffic on Fifth Avenue since both ends had been barricaded, as had the cross streets. We didn't hear any bands playing and there were no floats in sight. There were no spectators lining the sidewalks. "Hmm," we thought again, "maybe we're too early."

We did notice there were quite a few people walking in the middle of the empty street. The men, for the most part, wore suits, and some of them carried walking sticks; the women wore bright spring dresses, and many were sporting hats or bonnets. We assumed they had just come from church. They all seemed to be heading downtown. So, we figured, "What the heck, we might as well follow them. They must know something we don't. Maybe they're going down to where the parade starts."

So we started strolling along too. But pretty soon we noticed there were a lot of people walking in the opposite direction as well. "Hmm," we thought once more. "What in tarnation is going on here? We better ask somebody."

So we stopped a smartly dressed young couple and asked them, "When does the parade start?" They looked at each other and laughed. The woman turned to us and in a tone so typical of the New Yorker, a tone dripping with condescension and bemused disdain, said, "Why, this is the parade!"

"Oh," we said in unison. Then *we* had to laugh. Boy, did we ever feel like a couple of dummies. Just a couple of hicks down from the hills of New Jersey. Somewhat red-faced, we thanked them and quickly walked on.

The reason I relate this story is that we recently had a couple of similar parade experiences here in Berlin. The first of these was at the annual Christopher Street Gay Parade. Now, we had seen gay parades before, when we lived in San Francisco, so we thought we knew what to expect. There would be a gay marching band, maybe some Dikes on Bikes, and a curious collection of transvestites and assorted lesbians. Maybe a few banners claiming gay rights and advocating some political cause. We had seen it all before.

Well, we weren't too far off in those particulars, but we were completely blown away by the extraordinary diversity of the participants of the gay parade here in Berlin, the extreme oddities of their dress (or undress), and most of all, by their outrageous behavior. If that weren't enough, our minds were absolutely blown by the size of the parade. It was colossal.

Now in San Francisco, you have a relatively small city of about 800,000 people. Though the gay parade there draws on gay communities from throughout the Bay Area, the total number of marchers in S.F.'s gay parade numbers, perhaps, a few thousand.

In Berlin, on the other hand, you have a major metropolitan city numbering in excess of 3.5 million people. The annual parade here also draws on gay communities from all over Germany, and even from some of the neighboring countries. Add to this the fact that here in Berlin you don't actually have to be an official marcher to join the parade. You just walk out into the street and start struttin' your stuff. (Sort of like the Easter Parade in New York – the crowd becomes the parade.) I would say the participants of the gay parade here numbered in excess of one hundred thousand! No lie.

The parade started out in our neighborhood of the Ku'damm and marched about 4 miles east through the Tiergarten, passed under the Brandenburg Gate, rolled down Unter den Linden, and ended up at Alexander Platz where a huge street party ensued.

There weren't really any floats, per se. But there were a hundred or more flatbed diesel trucks and an assortment of odd-ball, jerry-rigged vehicles that were crazily decorated. These carried some of the official parade groups. Leading the phalanx was a truck sporting an erect, fifteen foot-long paper mache dong that pointed forward over the cab at a forty-five-degree angle. It looked like some weird pink rocket in Moscow's May Day Parade. Between the various trucks that followed, marched thousands upon thousands of gays and lesbians of every size, shape, color and description. Some of the trucks hauled bands or giant stereo systems that blared party music. Some trucks carried specialized riders, like the deaf-mute gay organization that rode along, happily signing to the crowd as they went. Another hauled handicapped gays. Some trucks carried gays or lesbians from other cities or countries. The most colorful one was from Nigeria. About every tenth truck was a rolling bar. You could buy beer, or sausages, or even mixed drinks as they passed by.

Gretchen and I were not too taken aback by all the same-sex kissing going on. We'd seen it before. We were surprised, though, that the paramedics weren't called in to untangle some of those tongues. We did get a shock by what was happening on one passing truck. We saw one guy on his knees giving another guy head! Now that's something you don't see every day. Later, on another truck, we saw a guy giving his all to another guy from behind. They were both naked and standing up. Now I never expected to see men having sex, much less in broad daylight on the back of a flat-bed truck rolling down Unter den Linden in front of thousands of other spectators! Hooeee!

There were quite a few naked or partially naked people in the parade. Many of them wore body paint. It's amazing the number of variations one can paint on breasts. The preferred mode of dress for most though, was leather, and plenty of it. Latex and rubber were also popular. There were hundreds of transvestites in the parade; many of them walked the whole way in spiked heels. Roller blades transported hundreds of flitting fairies hither and thither. Many of the marchers carried cups of beer or open bottles of champagne.

All along the parade route, polizie stood on every corner. But the crowd was happy and gay and the cops seemed to have very little to do but watch. They didn't seem to think anything of the nudity, the public sex, the drinking in the streets, the cacophony of sounds, the humping of the dancers, or the smell of marijuana floating in great clouds through the air. It was as if it was tacitly understood that for one day a year the denizens of Sodom and Gomora were allowed to take over the streets of Berlin.

A few weeks later, in what I guess was the "straights" answer to the gay parade was an event heralded as "The Love Parade." It is an annual event, I guess. We heard it was all about wild women and horny men marching and raving to techno music. We heard there was a million people coming to Berlin to participate. Oh boy, that's all we needed, a few more people. The public transit authority advertised a special offer on subway fares. They knew from past experience that surface transport would be totally gridlocked in Berlin. So they offered special passes on the underground for ten *marks* (about $5.70) for unlimited riding from Friday through Sunday. As a bonus, they gave out a box of condoms for each pass purchased. Apparently they knew a few other things from past experience.

The parade was to take place on Saturday, and on Friday people started arriving from all over der hinterland. We barely got any sleep Friday night because several carloads of teenagers from out of town parked on our block. They partied all night with their car stereos going full blast (Eurotech – yikes), and they didn't pass out in their cars until almost dawn. They got a couple of hours sleep before the parade started.

Again the parade started in our neighborhood and followed the same route as the gays. But the numbers! My god! I've never seen so many people in one place in all my life. Our neighborhood was an absolute zoo. Teutonic hordes of teenagers were milling around with open containers, smoking joints and acting as crazy as possible waiting for the parade to start. On top of this, dozens of mad vendors were selling whistles. These whistles were like police whistles, with those little balls that spin around in the chamber. Everyone had one. Hey, what a great idea: supply a bunch of turned-on teenagers with shrill whistles. (My ears! Oh, my poor ears!) We dodged, bumped and bounced off people all the way to the underground. We got the hell out of there. We took the jam-packed train to a stop out in the Tiergarten where the crowds weren't so swollen.

We found a spot under a tree beside that wide boulevard and settled down to see what we could see. What we saw was a vast river of people passing before us. The now familiar flatbed trucks accompanied them. But there were no bands in this pageant. Instead the trucks carried mammoth sound systems broadcasting techno music full blast. It was so loud the ground actually vibrated under our feet. We saw a guy walking ahead of one of these trucks with a big grin on his face. He was carrying a large sign that read, "Kiss your fucking ears goodbye."

Stunned and deafened, we watched as the living river flowed before us. It was a crowd that local newspapers estimated afterwards to be in excess of 750,000 people! And they were all part of the parade!

And what a colorful crowd. It was a cavalcade of the young, for the most part, rebellious and yet paradoxically conforming to some unwritten code of dress and comportment. Many wore costumes... or maybe they were uniforms (you never can be sure about the Germans). At any rate they were outlandish, sex-crazed costumes. Hell, the parade was a combination Halloween party and Bacchanalian revel. There were punk rockers, cheap tarts, wanton trollops, hard-assed skin-heads, grungy long-hairs, leathered-out Michael Jacksons holding their crotches, swinging disco babes, styled out rich dudes, funky bell-bottomed hipsters, disheveled floozies, and technicolor-haired, T-shirted pubescent teenagers popping zits as they went. They were sex-starved, music hungry, boisterous, happy, eager, and frustrated.

There were beautiful people, and there were ugly people. There was a Who's Who of every brand of Euro-trash you'd ever want to meet. Some were so bad they looked like genetic experiments gone haywire. One guy who looked like some kind of perverted computer nerd with a really gross body paraded buck-naked except for his horn-rimmed glasses and his day pack. (The cops made him put on a plastic raincoat he was so ugly.)

But these Germans, they do know how to party. They drank, they smoked, they dropped acid, they French kissed, they howled, they gyrated to the music, they hooted in falsetto voices, and dry-humped their way on down the street. 750,000 of them. Some ran off in the bushes to couple in the bushes of the Tiergarten, and then rejoined the parade ten thousand people later.

And they had an attitude. It seemed to say, "Hey, this is us and this is what we do. Get into it. If you can't get into it, well, fuck off."

After about three hours of this, I decided to fuck off.

I have subsequently determined that I've had enough parades to last me for a good long while.

Poe, the Raven & Me (Part 3)
1994

It was with no small amount of trepidation that I entered the old folk's home where my father lived. I had no idea in what condition I would find him. The appearance of the raven had changed everything. I paused at the door that led to the wards and took a deep breath. When I opened it I was greeted once again by the vague but pervasive smell of human decay. Evident too was the powerful smell of disinfectant. As strong as the disinfectant was, it could not completely mask the odor of old age, nor the melancholy scent of the slow ebbing away of life. A heaviness settled over my spirit, as it always did when I visited that place.

I walked down a long gleaming corridor with Spartan two-person rooms off to either side. Overhead florescent lights gave off an institutional glow, a timeless, changeless illumination that sought to ban all shadows from both sight and mind. It seemed to me that the light's ultimate purpose was to exile the shadow of death from the confines of those white, sterile walls. But for all that perpetual luminescence, the light could not keep the Angel of Death at bay if he chose to enter, for the Angel casts no shadow.

Ghost-like aides in white uniforms moved about with unsmiling faces. A handful of elderly residents sat in wheelchairs along the hallway. Some of them looked up as I passed. Their eyes showed fear, or resignation, or a mild curiosity at my passing. One old gentleman's eyes came into focus as I passed, as if he were coming back from far, far away. He appraised me with the wise old eyes of a patriarch. He seemed bemused at what he saw. Further on, an old woman grasped at my arm. "Help me," she begged, "Help me." An aide appeared out of nowhere and trundled her away. Other old-timers sat in their rooms staring at TVs. Some lay in their beds with mouths agape, as still as fallen statues. Some lay moaning from the pain of some real or imagined ill. I walked on, seeing more than I wanted of Time's unkind handiwork.

I made my way down near the end of the hall, to my father's door. I screwed up what courage I possessed and entered the room. I saw my father slumped in his wheelchair facing the window, his back to the room. His chin was resting on his chest. He was absolutely motionless. "Pop?" I said. "Hey, Pop! Wake up. You have a visitor." There was no response. Filled with dread, I crossed the room. I lifted my hand to him, but hesitated. I was almost afraid to touch him. He might be cold. I put my hand on his shoulder and found him still warm. I shook him gently. "Hey, Pop," I said. "Wake up. It's me, John."

He snorted, and lifted his hoary head. He adjusted his glasses on the bridge of his nose and looked up at me with rheumy, sleep-filled eyes. "Oh, son. It's you. Well, this is a surprise." I breathed a sigh of relief. What a fool I'd been. The raven. Ha! What a joke.

So I sat down with the old goat and we had a nice long chat. He was as crusty as ever, and in surprisingly good spirits. The last time I had seen him he was quite depressed, as might be expected of a man in poor health and with both legs lopped off above the knee. During my last visit he was very unhappy about living in this place. He wanted to go home. But it was not to be. He was no longer capable of living on his own.

I asked him how he was doing now, how he was adjusting to the place. To my surprise, he actually seemed to have grown to like it there. He had made friends with another old gent, the former mayor of Santa Paula. And he was fond of some of the staff members, particularly a pretty Mexican girl who changed the sheets. He liked the food too, which I found pretty amazing.

However, at one point in our conversation, he said to me, "There's only one thing I can't get used to."

"What's that?"

"I can't get used to the idea that I'm going to die here."

That one sent a chill down my spine. I was troubled by it because I knew what he said was true. He probably would die here, or in the hospital. I struggled to think of something appropriate to say. I couldn't think of anything. What I eventually came up with was rather flippant and trite. I said, "Well, gee, you have to die somewhere. What difference does it make where?"

He looked at me sharply and said, "What do you know about dying?" I felt the hair rise on the back of my neck. "Not much," I mumbled. (In fact, I knew all I wanted to know.)

Our conversation then moved on to other, lighter topics. I spend a long time there that afternoon, and overall, it was the best visit I'd ever had with him. Eventually, I took my leave, promising to visit again before I departed for home.

In what remained of the afternoon I took care of some business in Ventura, and did my best to forget about how silly all this raven business had been. As evening approached, the coming storm entered the Santa Barbara Channel and bore down on the coast. I drove over to Surfer's Point and watched gargantuan dark clouds scudding across the sky. In the foreground, tortured brown waves pounding along the littered shore. I turned tail in my car and fled inland along the swollen Ventura River as dark and the storm descended.

I had made arrangements to spend the night with friends in Ojai. I met my friends as planned and we went out to dinner. Over Thai food, I told them of the strange occurrences of my day, of the three birds in Marina Del Rey, of my recitation in the car, and of the appearance of the raven in Ventura. I told them I was concerned because the raven was known to be a bearer of ill tidings and of pestilence. My friends were amused, but I could tell they were skeptical. They suspected me of telling a tall tale, of laying on the malarkey, or maybe of just being a little more nuts than usual. But I wasn't. I wasn't then, and I'm not now.

As we left the restaurant and were returning to my friends' home, the black lips of the storm closed over us. High, gusty winds and strong rain licked the mountain-clad valley like a giant tongue. Then the storm swallowed Ojai in one giant gulp.

We settled comfortably in front of my friends' fireplace and enjoyed some relaxed conversation over a glass of wine. About ten o'clock, it being a weeknight, we decided to call it an evening. I retired to the small cottage behind the main house where I was to stay. I unpacked my few belongings and reclined on the bed to read and listen to the rain beating on the roof, and the wind thrashing among the trees.

I must have dozed off, but sometime later I awoke feeling very hot. I couldn't understand it because it was cold and I didn't have the heater turned on. I took off all my clothes and lay on top of the bed. I tried to read, but my vision became blurred and I couldn't focus on the words. I started to get a really bad headache. Pretty soon I began to feel nauseous. The feeling quickly escalated. Eventually I had to rush into the bathroom where I was immediately and violently ill.

This was most unusual. I'd had a few drinks that evening, but not nearly enough to cause this reaction. And I hadn't been feeling sick that day. I returned to the bed and lay down. I felt a little better, except for my headache, which got worse. My skull felt like it had a hatchet buried in the top of it. All too soon the nausea returned, and again I had to rush into the bathroom and vomit in the toilet. This time it was much more violent than before. I vomited over and over until I thought there was nothing left to heave. But I was wrong. I knew now that there was something seriously wrong with me. I flushed the toilet and watched the vile stuff spinning down in the whirlpool.

I could hear the storm howling outside. The cottage seemed to shudder with each new blast. Yea, though I walk through valley of the shadow of death…

I tried to navigate back to the bed, but before I could even get out of the bathroom a vicious new pain doubled me over. It was like an ice pick stabbing into my guts. I crumbled to the floor and lay there in the prenatal position until it eased somewhat. As I tried to rise I was seized by an overwhelming need to void myself. Desperately I crawled back to the toilet and somehow managed to drag myself up onto it. I sat down just in time. A terrible, swift explosion of diarrhea followed. I sat there and shit as though there was no end to it. The smell was awful, offensive even to me in my consummate misery. My bowels felt like a bowl of salted, squirming worms, alive and extremely unhappy at being so. Then, a new wave of nausea swept over me. I had to vomit again! But how could I vomit when I was in the middle of having diarrhea? I'll tell you how. I doubled over, spread my legs, and aimed between my legs. My aim was not perfect. I liberally soiled my legs, the toilet and the floor. Oh, God, the misery. I was erupting from both ends at once!

I knew now for certain that what I had was food poisoning. It must have been that Shrimp Pad Thai I had with dinner. I knew it was food poisoning because I'd had it twice before, once back in college, and again when I ate tainted fish in Samoa. Had this been my first go-round with it, I may have panicked, as I had nearly done those other two times years ago. But back then, at least someone had been there to comfort and watch over me. This time, however, I was alone.

There was some measure of comfort in knowing what was wrong with me, if such a thing as comfort was possible in my tortured condition. I realized, however, that people *do* die of food poisoning. I was beginning to wonder if I might be one of them. It wouldn't have surprised me.

When I was young I was pretty crazy and reckless, and I never thought I'd live to see thirty, much less forty. And I didn't care if I did or not. But at this point in time I was only a few weeks shy of turning fifty. Old enough to die, that's for sure. Well past due, I reckoned.

As I languished there on my sullied throne, I experienced a fleeting vision of the three birds I'd seen that morning, the crow with a hatchling in its mouth, and the two frantic parent birds. I felt as if they had directed me here. They were somehow involved in this.

I continued having wave after wave of convulsions. They went on for a long time, till well after midnight. Talk about "Once upon a midnight dreary..." Sheesh! Finally, my retching turned into the dry heaves. They wracked my body repeatedly. Suddenly, unbelievably, I felt a brand new pain. It started out as a strong burning sensation in my chest. It quickly grew in intensity. It felt like a hot, sharp-tipped blade was being slowly thrust into my heart.

I believed I might be having a heart attack. The pain grew to a point where it was almost unbearable. I knew then that I was mistaken when I thought the raven had come that day to warn me of my father's impending death. He had come to warn me of my own. And here it was!

I experienced a horrifying slice of déjà vu. My dream of thirty some years ago flashed before my pain-clenched eyes. You know, the dream where I was chased by the big black bird, where I wrestled with it, and then it stabbed me in the chest with its sharp beak. It was obvious to me that the dream was coming true. I remembered with growing horror the line from The Raven, "take thy beak from out my heart..."

"Oh no!" I thought, "I'm dying of a heart attack right here on the toilet. I'll probably keel over and crack my head open in the process. Somebody will find me here buck naked, splattered with shit and vomit with my brains splayed out on the floor." Oh, what an ignoble end! But, to tell you the truth, at that point I really didn't care. I was in so much pain that I would have welcomed death. At least it would have put an end to the torture I was undergoing.

As I was thinking these thoughts I began to absent-mindedly massage the terrible pain in my chest. It felt good to do so. And oddly enough, the more I massaged the pain, the more it subsided. I rubbed the painful area for a long time and eventually, to my great relief, it went away.

I finally figured out what had happened. I wasn't having a heart attack, I was experiencing a major muscle cramp in my chest and abdomen from all the convulsions I'd been having. It was gone now. Exhausted, I slid down off the toilet and lay on the floor. I let the cold concrete suck the heat out of me while I caught my breath.

It was then, staring up at a bare light bulb on the ceiling, that I realized I was going to survive this. I had turned some kind of corner, a corner of mortal reckoning, here in the wee hours of the morning. I was starting to feel better. The nausea was subsiding, as was my headache. I had voided all the poison that had made me so desperately ill. Granted, I'd been put through the ringer, and I was as weak as a kitten, but I felt like I was over the worst of it.

I had a raging thirst. Taking small doses, I was able to keep some water down. I rested for a while longer on the bathroom floor. When I felt up to it, I took a shower and then fell onto the bed and pulled the blankets over me. I went to sleep immediately and slept through the night. When I woke up the next morning I felt almost human again. I was still very weak, I had a sore throat, and was seriously dehydrated, but damn, for having nearly died I felt pretty good. Outside, the storm had dissolved into a gentle rain that pattered soothingly on the cottage roof.

The night before had been a tempest, both for Southern California and for me. I had worked myself into a frenzy when I thought I might die. I had actually terrorized myself with a piece of literature! In hindsight, I find that fairly amusing. If I'd had a weak heart I might have scared myself to death. Edgar Allan Poe would have been gratified, I'm sure.

So, after all that had happened I was left to wonder what all that stuff about Poe and The Raven and the three birds meant. The explanation would have been obvious if I had died. But I didn't. So what was I to make of it all? I can't tell you. I can only leave you "to wonder at the secrets," as Albert Einstein said at the very beginning of Part One.

Well, I may not have many answers to the secrets, but I know one thing: I know that the Grim Reaper came after me that stormy night. And that he took a giant swipe at me with that wicked-looking scythe of his. But the big oaf missed! Ha, ha. Nice try, dude. Better luck next time.

Fall Into Winter
1959

I never did rewrite that paper for Mr. Casey, and I never did get any extra credit. I had other things on my mind. One of them was that pretty fourteen year-old girl in my home-room class. Her name was Amber. She had these beautiful honey-brown eyes. I noticed them right away when I caught her looking at me a couple of times. Once we got to know each other, she told me her eyes were the color of amber, like her name.

Amber had a perfect nose too. It was the nicest nose I ever saw on a girl, or anyone else for that matter. I could go on about her flawless complexion and her auburn hair, but I won't. Sometimes when Social Studies got over in the morning I would walk Amber to her next class. Sometimes I even carried her books for her.

Deuce and his buddy Dremel gave me a hard time about that. They said I was pussy-whipped. I told them they could both go to hell. I knew they were just jealous. Unlike a lot of girls her age, Amber had these pert little breasts that showed up real nice when she wore a sweater. She wore sweaters quite a lot as winter came on. Deuce said he bet they were falsies. I said I bet they weren't.

After a month or so Amber and I started going to the movies together on the weekends. Since neither one of us was old enough to drive, we walked. I'd meet her downtown in front of either the Mayfair or the Ventura Theater. We went to the bargain matinees. The first movie we saw together was a French film called 'Breathless' with Jean-Paul Belmondo and Jean Seberg. It seemed kind of crudely made, and was filmed in black & white. I guess it was supposed to be artistic or something. It was about a handsome Parisian crook and his beautiful American girlfriend. Amber and I thought it was kind of weird, but very romantic. Despite the fact that we didn't follow the plot very well, we held hands during the movie, and shared our first kiss.

The next time we went to the movies we saw 'North By Northwest' by Alfred Hitchcock. Amber got scared during that one. She grabbed hold of me and practically crawled into my lap. She ended up watching the movie with the side of her face pressed right up against mine. Pretty soon we started kissing like mad. It was during that movie I discovered Amber didn't need to wear falsies. I would have loved to inform Deuce of that fact, but I never did because he had such a big mouth.

Amber generally liked to go to sucky movies like 'Pillow Talk' and 'The Diary of Anne Frank.' I liked stuff like 'Ben Hur' and 'Suddenly Last Summer.' I was jazzed when 'Pyscho' came out the following year. But when I tried to get Amber to go with me, she absolutely refused. She'd heard all about it.

Despite my infatuation with Amber, my obsession with surfing held me up like a hammock. Every weekend morning when we woke up, Jake and I would look out our picture window and look over at The Point, over three miles away, to see if it was breaking. If it wasn't foggy when we looked we could see whether or not a swell was running. We'd grab a quick breakfast and then pick up Deuce and the borrowed board in Jake's car. Then we'd haul ass down to The Point.

Sometimes Jake didn't go out in the water because he was too banged up from taking too many hits playing football. He had made the JV team and was one of the first-string half-backs. The other half-back was bigger and stronger, and they used him and the full-back to run inside and off-tackle. They'd use Jake by pitching out to him outside, or tossing a screen pass, so he could use his speed in the open. The defenses generally got wise to this gambit as the game progressed, and started lying in wait for him. He'd go zooming around the corner only to find a couple of linebackers waiting for him. They'd put the hammer on him if they could. Jake was quick and slippery, but that didn't help him if they caught him. He took a lot of hard hits.

As the weeks passed we noticed the water was getting colder and colder and the weather more and more unpredictable. But sometimes there were warm offshore winds that came down the Ventura River valley and blew straight out to sea. We called them Santa Anas. We found out it was a whole different experience surfing in offshore wind. On the plus side, it was a lot easier to paddle out into the surf with the wind at your back. And when you caught a wave you could feel the power of the wind sweep in under the curls and hold them up. While riding you found you could make sections that you wouldn't normally have been able to because the wind kept them from breaking just long enough for you to sneak through. On the down side, it was harder to catch waves paddling into the wind. Also, when waves curled over, the wind blows the tops off of them and sends a curtain of spray sailing out behind. If you missed a wave you got rewarded by a slap in the face from a blast of salt spray. It stung the eyes.

We discovered another spectacular thing too: when you kicked out, the wind caught your board and flung it out of the wave like it was shot from a cannon. Sometimes your board would spiral for ten or twenty feet through the air. Guys straddling their boards outside and not paying attention would sometimes get whacked by them.

Deuce and I started seeing a few kids we knew from school at The Point. One of them was our friend Dremel. He couldn't surf worth a damn in the beginning, but he got better as time went on. He eventually became a pretty good surfer, as did we all. I knew Dremel from Cabrillo Jr. High, and from having played music at his house. Deuce and I would often go there on Friday nights and have Hootenannies.

Dremel was a funny guy. He had this rubber face that he could twist into all kinds of hilarious expressions. He often acted like a fool and played these funny, weird songs. And, if anything, he was an even bigger bull-shitter than Deuce. I met his parents at his house, and I liked them immediately. They were friendly and normal, and they didn't drink. They always seemed interested in what we kids were doing, and no matter what it was, they seemed to find it extremely funny. And when I went there they always remembered my name, and seemed happy to see me. Going there was like a breath of fresh air compared to the way things were around my house.

Dremel had worked for his Dad's construction business during the summer and had earned enough money to buy his own board. We started picking him up on our way to The Point. In exchange for the ride, we told him he had to share his board, which he reluctantly did.

Dremel was a skinny kid like most of us, but he had a terrible complexion. I guess that was from him squeezing his pimples all the time. He always had these big red blotches on his face and neck. Sometimes they got big whiteheads on them. Dremel used to gross us out every once in a while by popping them at us. We'd have to dodge those pus missiles. I used to slug him on the arm for that.

By the time November rolled around we were starting to get some stormy weather, with periods of rain sweeping in off the Pacific. Sometimes the surf was all chopped up at The Point and unrideable. Once in a while we heard from other guys that it was better at The Overhead or at Rincon, or at other beaches. It all depended on the weather and the tide and the direction of the swell. So, Jake and the rest of us started driving up and down the coast looking for the best surfing conditions. Jake had to get a rack for the roof of the car because on long trips we couldn't take the exhaust coming in through the open trunk. Sometimes the fumes got so bad you felt like puking.

A few times that fall we woke up to rain pattering on the roof. If the surf looked good we'd go surfing anyway. That was a new experience for us. It didn't really matter that much since you're always wet when you surf anyway. As long as the surf was worthwhile we didn't really mind the rain. It did make you feel a little colder than usual, but we were starting to think that enduring the cold was part of the machismo, and therefore, part of the appeal of surfing. The only bad thing about surfing in the rain is that sometimes it gets in your eyes and you can't see very well. Once in a while you got wiped out because you couldn't see a section folding over in front of you because of raindrops hitting you in the eyes.

We were getting used to surfing no matter what the weather, which was challenging because none of us had wetsuits. Hardly anybody did in those days. It was particularly hard when a cold front would move through. I still remember that first step into the icy water on a cloudy and windy day. It sent a shiver through your whole body. And then when you were paddling out and a wave broke in front of you and drenched your whole body it was a shock, I can tell you. But strangely, the thrill of catching waves under adverse conditions had an attraction all its own. I guess we felt a little like cave men hunting wooly mammoths in the snow. It was the thrill of the hunt. But our hunts didn't last too long. We found that you couldn't stay out in the water as long as we had in the summertime. We just got too cold.

About this time some of the surfers started building bonfires on the beach. The early surfers, the dawn patrol, would gather up a bunch of driftwood and pile it up in a circle of stones. They'd jam wadded up newspapers underneath and set it

burning. Then they'd go out to catch some waves. When they couldn't stand the cold anymore they'd come in to a nice, hearty bonfire.

But I found that if there was a wind blowing, or if it was raining, it was still cold by the fire. You could only get half your body warm at a time, either your front or your back. You had to keep turning around in a circle like you were a chicken on the rotisserie. Also, if the wind was blowing, you had to stand upwind of the fire or all the smoke would blow right in your face. Sometimes it got pretty crowded on the upwind side of the fire. Occasionally, there was more than one bonfire burning.

Finally, I got a bright idea. I went to a thrift shop in downtown Ventura and bought a second-hand overcoat. I would take it with me when I went surfing. When I got out of the water, covered in goose bumps and shivering like a madman, I'd towel off and put on my overcoat. Then I could stand in front of the fire with my back to the wind and open the front of my coat. The coat protected me from the cold wind and formed a nice, warm little cave in front that trapped the heat. Pretty soon other guys started getting overcoats too. It kind of became our uniform, along with our wet, baggy swim trunks. The overcoats added to our non-conformist hooligan image too, which we thought was kind of cool.

Although there was a sprinkling of new surfers like us there, most of the guys who hung out at The Point had been surfing for years. We tried to make friends with the old guys, with varying degrees of success. But we, by participating regularly in the sport, had joined the fraternity of surfers whether the old-timers liked it or not. We shared the same goal, which was to get the best possible ride under whatever conditions we found on any given day. We shared the same thrills, the same successes, the same disappointments and discomforts as them. Eventually, they grudgingly came to accept us. Finally, we were real surfers.

At fourteen, I didn't know why they made it so hard on us beginners until I became one of the old boys too. I eventually concluded that surfers are generally a selfish group. Every one of them wants the best waves for them self. The more surfers there are, the more competition there is, the harder it is to claim the best wave for yourself. Somebody is always trying to steal it from under your nose. In the coming years this would be a growing problem.

Speaking of problems, on Thanksgiving we got a surprise visit from my father. It was the first time I'd seen him since my parents split up. About three o'clock that afternoon I was standing by the kitchen window when he pulled into the driveway. Fittingly, my mother was just pulling the turkey out of the oven.

"Hey!" I said, "It's Pop!" My brother and sister and mother all came to the window and looked out.

Pop had on one of those knit British driving caps and was driving a brand-new Austin-Healy Sprite with the top down. The car was shiny and white and had those little frog-eye headlights. Pop was a tall, clean-shaven man, with a red, pudgy face. His pug nose held up a pair of heavy, horn-rimmed glasses. As he was struggling up out of the little car I could see his prominent belly. He must have put on twenty pounds since the last time I saw him. He used to be quite thin when he was young, but now he must have weighed in at over two hundred pounds. The way he walked up to the front of the house kind of reminded me of W.C. Fields. He was carrying a bottle of wine in one hand and a store-bought pie in the other. I half expected him to start juggling them.

It was strange to see him standing there on our front doorstep. He had trouble trying to ring the doorbell with his hands full. He finally managed to do it with the top of the wine bottle. Nobody knew what to do. We all just looked at one another. I didn't want to answer the door. I wouldn't have known what to say to him. Finally, Mom told Jake to open the door and let him in. I followed Jake to the door. Jane followed me, but ducked down behind me out of sight. She was giggling with nervousness.

Pop seemed kind of sheepish when Jake opened the door, but he tried to act happy-go-lucky. First off, he says "Hi, everybody." Then he came into the house. He turned to me and said, "Take these, will you son?" and handed me the bottle and the pie. I took them into the kitchen. Pop gave Jake a big hug, followed by my sister, Jane. Jane seemed happy to see him, but kind of confused and shy. She kept looking at him to see if he was really her father, or just some stranger doing an imitation. Pop repeated several times how much he had missed us all. Then he went over and kissed our mother and whispered something to her while he held her.

My mother didn't seem all that surprised to see him. She took his arrival right in stride. I think she must have known he was coming. I noticed she kept sneaking looks at us kids to see how we were taking it.

She turned to Pop and said, "I thought you might have shown up earlier. We're just about to sit down to dinner."

"'Sorry. I got a late start," he said. "But, man oh man o'shevats, it sure smells great in here." Gazing over at the counter he said, "Why don't you let me carve up that turkey, Jewel." That's what he always called my Mom when he was being all lovey-dovey. Then he said to me, "Hey, John, open that bottle of wine, will you?"

While I was wrestling with the cork, Jake and Jane helped my Mom put the side dishes into bowls and platters and set them steaming on the table. We were all pretty quiet, except for Pop. He seemed to want to fill up the silence with talk while he was carving. He told us about how he slept in this morning because he was tired from working so hard, and how he got a late start and drove up the coastal route, which took longer. I was thinking he probably slept in because he was hung over, and then stopped at a bar on the way here for a cocktail.

When everything was ready we all sat down at the round table in the dining room. My mother had laid out the white tablecloth earlier and set it with our dead grandma's best china and silver. I hadn't noticed that she set an extra place. When we were all settled, we kids looked at Mom, not knowing who was going to say grace. Usually it was Jake or me. My Mom looked at Pop and said, "Would you like to say grace, Frank?"

"Why, yes. Thank you, Jewel."

186

He clasped his hands together and bowed his head. "Heavenly father," he began, "thank you for bringing us all together, and for keeping us well, and in your good graces. We beseech you to help us forget old wrongs, and to let bygones be bygones. Let us live with charity and goodwill, and let our hearts be filled with love and forgiveness as you have commanded. We thank you for this fine meal in which we are about to partake, and we pray that our family will be happy and whole again someday soon. Amen."

I noticed my mother getting a little teary-eyed. Personally, I felt like puking. We started dishing up the food after that. Pop poured out two glasses of wine, and handed one to my mother.

He held up his glass and said, "Here's to you, Jewel. You look beautiful. And you did such a wonderful job with the dinner."

"Thank you, Frank."

As we ate, Pop went off on a big explanation about his new car... how he'd always wanted a sports car and now that he was making more money, he couldn't resist the temptation of getting one. Yeah, I thought, and that's not the only temptation you couldn't resist. Pop went on to tell us how busy the drugstore was, and how many prescriptions he filled every day. When Pop ran out of wind, he asked my Mom how things were going with her job.

"Oh, it's going O.K." she said. "I'm getting tired of working the graveyard shift though. I was talking to my supervisor about it the other morning and he said that they might be putting me on the day shift come January."

"That's nice," said Pop, as he gnawed on a drumstick. "I think it's good you're using your education. Nursing is a fine profession."

After that, nobody had much to say. We kids didn't have a thing to say. There were long stretches when the only sound we heard was the clinking and scraping of silverware on the plates. Pop decided to try to get chummy with us kids. He took a swig of wine, and started with Jake.

"So, Jake, what have you been up to since you left Long Beach?"

Jake sat up straight in his chair like the obedient son he was. "Oh, well, for one thing I've been playing JV football, sir. I'm the starting half-back. But I've been doing well in school too. I think I'll be getting some good grades this semester. And you probably saw the Dodge out front. I got it painted and have been fixing it up. I got my job back washing dishes at the Bavarian Inn. And I bought a surfboard and Jake and I have been hitting the waves."

"Well, well" said my Dad, smiling. "It sounds like you're doing real well, Jake. I'm proud of you."

"And how about you, little lady?" he said, turning to my little sister.

Jane put her head down and blushed. In a low, shy voice she said, "I'm in seventh grade now, Daddy. This is my first year in public school. I don't go to St. Mary's anymore. I go to the same school as Jake. But he's in ninth grade, so I don't see him very often. I'm in the Girl Scouts too. Mommy takes me to the meetings. We sold Girl Scout cookies last month. And, well, I've been helping Mommy around the house. That's all, I guess."

Pop was beaming. "You're such a good little girl. You always were. And you're getting prettier all the time."

Jane blushed again and kept her head down.

Pop took another drink of wine and turned the old evil eye on me. "Well, John, what do you have to say for yourself?"

"Not much."

"Well, what have you been up to?" he asked.

"I've been going surfing and going to school."

After a long pause, Pop said, "That's it?"

"Well, whadya expect?"

Mom interrupted and said, "Don't be rude, John."

"Well, what do you expect me to say? I'm fourteen and I've got nothing. I don't have a car or a job or a surfboard. And I don't belong to the Girl Scouts. All I do is take care of the yard and clean the house and do laundry and boring stuff like that."

"I think you have a bad attitude, young man," said my father.

"Well, I think you…"

"That's enough, John," said my mother. She turned to my father and said, "I don't know why John is so modest, Frank. He is such a big help around the house. I don't know how I'd manage without him. Especially last summer when Jake was gone. And he's really turning into quite a gardener. He keeps the yard looking so nice. He's learning to cook too. I'm so proud of him. And you should see him surf. He's really quite good."

I was glad she said those things right then, although it was the first time I'd heard them myself.

Pop seemed satisfied with her explanation and let me off the hook. I'm sure he still thought I was the same old smart-aleck, but he didn't want to go after me right then. I was relieved about that. I was a little afraid of him. He was a lot bigger than me, and I knew he wasn't above taking his belt to me like he'd done before.

After we finished dinner Pop poured what was left of the wine into his glass and retired to the living room. Jake went with him and turned on the TV. The rest of us cleared the table

189

and started putting the leftover food in the fridge. After the dishes were done I went down the hall to the bedroom that Jake and I shared. I didn't feel like being sociable. I picked up the latest Mad Magazine and started reading.

About an hour later I heard my mother calling me. I went out to the living room and saw that Pop was getting ready to drive back to Long Beach. He had to work the next day. I felt kind of guilty about not spending any time with him, but like I said before, he and I never did get along that well.

Pop said, "Well, I guess I better be hitting the road before it gets too late. It's been wonderful seeing you all again. You have such a nice house. And the view is terrific. I wish I could live here too." He looked at my Mom, but she wouldn't meet his eyes. She didn't say anything.

"I hope you all know how much I love you," he said. "I really miss you. Do you think it might be alright if I come visit you for Christmas?"

My mother flushed. She looked from one to the other of us kids. I guess most of us looked kind of expectant. "That might be nice," she said. "What do you think, kids?"

We all looked at one another, and, I for one, didn't have an answer. I think we all had mixed emotions. We all remembered how nice Christmas had been in the past when we lived in Ojai. But we didn't know what it would feel like here in Ventura, especially with things being so strange and tense between our parents.

Pop said, "Well, why don't you all think about it. Jewel, maybe you can write to me and let me know if it's O.K. to visit." He glanced at us kids briefly and added, "And why don't you guys send me your Christmas Wish List while you're at it?" He smiled.

My brother and sister brightened up when they heard that. I had to work hard to keep my lip from curling into a sneer.

Dispatch from Berlin #6
1998

Subject: To market, to market, to buy a fat pig.
Date: Sunday, 26 July, 1998

    The typical German refrigerator is about half the size of those you find in the American household. Most of these mini-refrigerators have a tiny freezer section too, which further reduces the amount of refrigerator space you have. This creates a number of problems, the most obvious of which is – Where do you put the food after you stock up on beer? I guess Germans don't have this particular problem, as they don't mind drinking their beer at room temperature. Regardless of your beer drinking propensities, the fact remains that it is impossible to "stock up" on perishable food items. There is simply not enough room in the fridge. This means you have to go to the market almost daily to keep yourself fed. Either that or eat out a lot, which gets expensive.

    A trip to the market is something of an adventure here in Berlin. First of all, there are very few supermarkets. Mostly you find small to medium-sized neighborhood markets. They are usually on the ground floor of six story buildings.

    Almost all of the buildings in Berlin are six stories high. Don't ask me why. I guess it's because twelve flights of stairs are all the normal human can climb on a regular basis. Elevators are found only in the most modern buildings, or in older ones that have been renovated. In our apartment building, a tiny elevator has been bolted onto the wall out in the courtyard. I make the sign of the cross every time I climb into it. Most neighborhood markets don't have parking lots, so even if we had a car, parking would be dicey. Most people walk to the market and carry their groceries home.

    Markets in Berlin, and throughout Europe for that matter, do not provide their customers with grocery bags. You bring your own. A lot of people, including myself, use a backpack. This, of course, limits your purchases to what will fit in your pack. I see where some of the grandmas and hausfraus take along those little two-wheeled wire baskets when they go to market. They hold more and are easier to handle – you just pull them along behind you. I considered getting one, but decided against it. I figured it would be bad for my image.

When you walk into your average market here one of the first things you see are lines of grocery carts nosed into one another just like in any U.S. market. The difference, you discover upon closer examination, is that they are all chained together. There is a locking mechanism on each cart which can only be opened by inserting a one-mark coin. (Heaven help you if you have a lot of shopping to do and you don't have the right coin.)

I was rather miffed the first time I went to the market. I thought it was pretty low of them to charge people for the use of their grocery carts. So I kind of abused the cart. You know, I popped a couple of wheelies, pulled a brodie or two, spun a few donuts, accidentally bashed into a few counters. It was only when I was through shopping that I found out you get your one-mark coin back by reinserting the end of the chain into your lock. But then that made me wonder, why do they even bother locking them up in the first place? If you were going to rip one off, wouldn't it be worth one mark (about 58 cents) to get one? Even the homeless can afford that.

Another thing I found out the hard way about shopping here is that you have to weigh your own produce. Heck, I just grabbed a few bananas, a handful of tomatoes, a couple of apples, and a bag of spuds and threw them into the cart. When I got to the check-out stand the lady looked at the produce and then looked at me with kind of a tired, disappointed look on her face. She said something to me in her native tongue, the meaning of which I hadn't a clue. What she was no doubt telling me was that there were no scales at the check-out stand, that I had to take all the stuff back to the produce section, weigh it separately on the scales there, press the appropriate icon button on the face of the scale for each type, pull out the printed price tag for each, and attach it to the fruit or whatever.

When she was done telling me this I said, "Huh?" She sighed and got up to do it herself. I followed her, scratching my head as she wheeled my cart away. I watched her weigh & tag them and that's how I learned how to do it. When we got back to the checkout stand all the other customers in line had their arms crossed and were tapping their feet. While I was finishing being checked out they amused themselves by giving me the old stink-eye. Germans are not noted for their subtlety.

The markets here don't have bag-boys either. You put your own stuff in your own bag. And you better be quick about it too, boy. And you better pay up quick. Cash only. No credit cards. No checks. No funny business. Mach Schnell!

The markets open up at 0900 hours and close at 1600 hours. (Yeah, that's how they tell time here. Military time. Given the facts of local history, it is not surprising.) A few of the more contemporary markets stay open till 2000 hours. All the markets, like most shops and stores in Germany, are open Monday through Saturday. But when 1600 hours rolls around on Saturday, everything, and I mean everything, shuts down like a bunker under attack. They don't open again until Monday morning. Don't run out of milk on Sunday, buster, or you're S.O.L. No cereal for you, Dufus. And you better like your coffee black.

One of the biggest differences between American markets and German markets can be found at the meat counter. Let's just say the meat counter is, oh, twenty feet long. About fifteen feet of it will be loaded with every kind of pork product you could imagine: pork butt, pork roast, pork chops, pork loin, pork tongue, about twenty different kinds of pork sausage, pig's feet, pig's head, liver pate, and a bunch of weird stuff I

193

never heard of before.

The other five feet of counter space can be broken down this way: Give about half the space to whole chickens. (And these are pretty gnarly chickens. They give the term "free-range chickens" a whole new meaning. Where American chickens look a little like Danny DeVito, German chickens look more like Don Knotts.) Then you have about a foot of space devoted to lamb products. Whatever space is left over is given over to what passes for beef.

Beef is not very popular here, and it is expensive. Britain's recent spate of Mad Cow Disease certainly hasn't helped matters. What beef can be found here is either local German bovine, or suspicious horned specimens from Spain. Maybe we get our shipments the day after the Sunday bullfights. I find the quality of beef in Germany to be generally poor. It is somewhat tough and stringy; it is not well marbled, not very juicy, and not very tasty. Also, German butchers seem to be at a loss as to how to carve up the beasts. You find some really weird cuts. And if you want to buy a couple of steaks, you will be hard pressed to find two of equal thickness. The ground beef is suspect. It either exists without a morsel of fat, or it is oozing with it.

Some markets have a fresh seafood counter as well, and these seem to do a brisk trade. I don't know where the fish come from and I am a little uneasy about buying it. I'm not real sure about the state of the oceans around Europe, but I suspect the worst. I know that the rivers and lakes are heavily polluted, and I wouldn't want to eat fresh-water fish. I feel uneasy about the mollusks too, what with oil spills, sunken Soviet nuclear submarines, and chemical run-off from the rivers. By now you may be getting an idea of why Gretchen and I have both lost weight here.

Some Germans are health conscious, but not many. There are a fair number of vegetarians in Germany, and many of the markets here have fine fresh produce. What they lack in variety, they make up for in quality. They have the best tomatoes I've ever eaten from a store. They have great potatoes (of course) and wonderful fruit. Luscious pineapples, peaches, apples, cherries, etc. Funny about bananas though. They seem to be considered something of a delicacy, and are pretty expensive. You can find fantastic artichokes here. During the winter months we get a lot of fresh produce from Israel. (By the way, I read somewhere recently that the Jewish population in Berlin is one of the fastest growing segments of the city. I find that pretty amazing. Shows a lot of chutzpah.)

Most markets here have a deli section where you can buy all kinds of German delicacies. They make about ten different kinds of potato salad, and probably half that number of varieties of sauerkraut. They seem to like pickled food a lot: pickled cabbage, olives, cucumbers, cauliflower & carrots, pickled peppers, pig's feet, etc. They also sell great gobs of what looks like (and is) bacon grease. Apparently it is used instead of cooking oil.

Most markets also have a bakery section where everything is baked fresh every day. Anything from bread to rolls to cakes and pies. They don't use any preservatives here so the baked goods do not keep well. If you want fresh baked goods you have to buy them and eat them on the same day.

Cheese is really big here. Some of the markets have a cheese section nearly as large as their meat section. You can usually tell when you're getting close to the cheese section. You get a very strong whiff of what smells like the locker room after a basketball game. The cheese comes from all over Europe, and the variety is amazing. They even have orange cheddar cheese, which seems to be a great source of amusement to the Germans. "Orange cheese? Ha. It must be an American thing." (Actually, the cheddar cheese available here comes from Ireland, as does the butter.)

Milk is kind of a trip. It only comes in two versions: whole milk and 1.5 percent fat milk. And what about skim milk? You gotta to be kidding! Don't mess with a German's fat intake, Dude. In fact, don't even bother with the milk. Germans prefer cream.

All the markets here sell beer, wine and spirits (unlike Washington State from whence we recently hailed). The beer is good and cheap and plentiful. It comes in many different sizes and types of containers, including a one gallon can that looks like a keg with its own miniature tap. I usually buy mine in one-pint cans for about sixty cents a pop. The beers here, overwhelmingly pilsners, are generally 4.8 to 5.0 percent alcohol, about twice as strong as American beer. Wines from all over Europe are readily available here. They are generally cheaper than American wines, the exception being French wine. American wine is expensive here too. (Owing to shipping costs, I assume.) Spirits are generally cheaper here, but not as popular as in the States. Germans seem to like sweet liqueurs and sweet wines for the most part. (Barf out.) But beer and champagne are their mainstays.

Speaking of booze, many of the larger markets have beer & wine bars, most often located near the front of the store by the grocery carts. And they do a brisk trade. As a result, stressed-out shoppers are rare here. Germans shop a little, have a beer or a glass of champagne, shop a little more, have another glass, shop… Heck, this ain't half bad. (And by the way, yes, McDonald's and Burger King do serve beer here.)

One can see the influence of American food tastes here in Berlin. In fact, quite a number of canned goods from America appear on shelves here: beans, sauces, vegetables, soups, Coca-Cola Co. canned drinks, etc. Generally, they are more expensive than similar German products. The Germans seem especially enamored of canned goods. I guess it goes back to WWII, the Berlin Airlift of 1948-49, the Cold War days and all that. They like to stock up. You never know when those pesky Ruskies might come swarming out of the east again.

Germany has created many "knock-off" varieties of foodstuffs from America. Among their numerous attempts is their version of ketchup. It is awful: very watery with a strong vinegary taste, sweetened with sugar. Yuck! The only thing going for it is that it is red. They have failed monumentally in many other so-called American-food items. However, they have outdone the Amis in some respects. Although mustard is not of American origin, the Germans have a long history of it, and they are expert mustard makers. They call it Senf, and it is better than most American mustards. They love it on sausage and ham, and so do I.

One American product available here is the all-in-one-box Mexican Taco Dinners made by some outfit called Casa Fiesta. They are an abomination. Being a dyed-in-the-wool Southern Californian, the thing I miss most is good old-fashioned Mexican food. Luckily for us, our in-laws just came over for a visit from California and provided a mini-Berlin Airlift of their own: corn tortillas, beans, salsa, taco sauce, etc.

Gee, all this talk about food has made me hungry. And since it's about lunchtime I think I'll put the wraps on this edition of the Dispatches from Berlin.

Until next time, Guten appetit.

Kava

1973

The old Samoan with elephantiasis called to his grand-daughter late in the morning. He ordered her to pound him some *kava* root when she had finished her chores. In the old days, the chief's daughters used to chew it and spit the juices into the many-legged wooden kava bowl, there to be mixed with water. The damned missionaries and health officials had put an end to that, however. Another good tradition down the *pu*. But it did not matter in the end. The people adapted as they always did, and found a way to please the *palagi* and themselves at the same time.

Now they pounded the kava root with mallets and soaked the pieces in water and achieved the same result, except of course for the fact that the girls did not get high from the juice as they had done before.

The old man had grown very fond of kava over the years. It was always served at important functions, but like some of the other chiefs, Manu liked it for itself outside of its ceremonial function. He liked the taste. It tasted like the good muddy earth of Samoa. It was also good when your teeth were hurting you, as his often were. Kava numbs your mouth. It numbs your mouth and makes your head feel fuzzy. And if you have a pain in your stomach or somewhere else, it takes most of it away. Sometimes, if you have enough of it, it makes your mind travel to far places in the mountains or far out on the ocean and makes your eyes see more clearly.

When Matalena finally brought him his drink in his favorite kava bowl, Manu was relieved, for on this day he was feeling very much like a fishing net that is beyond repair. He needed the soothing drink. He resisted the temptation to scold the girl for taking so long to bring it. It did not matter. Young people did not care so much for the old, and they were careless in their manner to him sometimes. But he could not blame them too much. He had been the same when he was young.

198

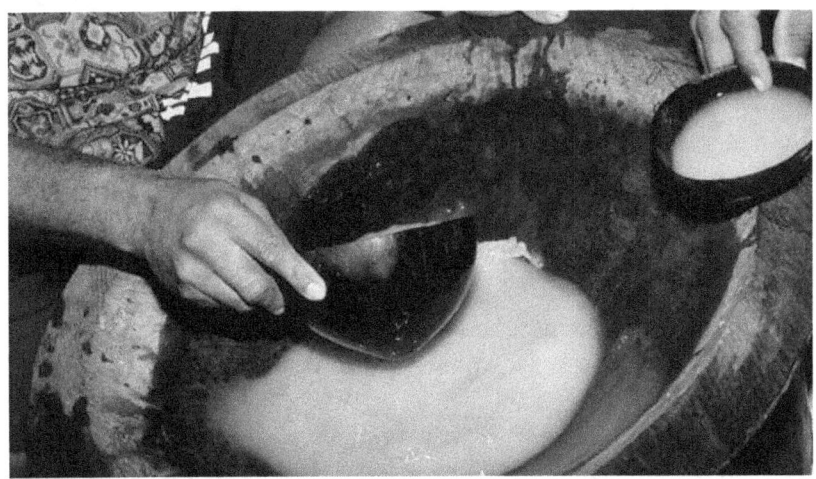

He dipped his half coconut shell into the mixture, poured a small libation onto the fale floor, as is the custom, and said, "*Manuia*." He took a sip. It was good and strong, the way he liked it. He continued to sip, slowly, taking only a little, letting it settle down there in his belly. Not too fast must one drink the kava, for it will make the greedy sick.

After a while, when the sun began to bend its path and its fiery head descended slightly towards the sea, the effects of the kava began to come over Manu. The pains in his joints began to dissipate, and a pleasant glow pervaded his consciousness. He watched the foolish hens scratching around the edge of the fale. He laughed when he saw the neighbor's dog being mounted by one of his own family's scrawny curs.

Manu rolled a cigarette and blew smoke at the flies that buzzed around the remnants of the potion in his bowl. He felt good, but he was tired. His body told him it was time to sleep. But he felt uneasy. There was something wrong in the village. He sensed it. He could not tell exactly what it was, but something was not right. He had been concerned with the well-being of the village for so long as a chief that he could always tell when something bad was about to happen. He could feel something, an undercurrent, something intangible.

If he could only concentrate long enough, he could perhaps discern it. But he was tired now. He flicked the cigarette butt away and lay his head down on the miniature wooden stool that was his pillow. He listened for a short time to the sounds of the village, and to the little waves washing up along the shore of the lagoon, and then, just before he closed his eyes, he saw a most unusual sight: a black *Tropic* bird flying over the village.

This was not a good sign. Most Tropic birds are white with only small black markings. His father had told him a long time ago if you ever saw a black one, you were seeing an *aitu*, a ghost. Manu was frightened and would have arisen, only he was too tired now. The kava was strong and he was weak. He closed his eyes and fell asleep.

Manu dreamed an evil wind was blowing down on the land. It was a wind that only blew at night, so that the people did not even know it was there, for they were sleeping. Only Manu did not sleep. The wind came out of the *pu*s in the mountains, from out of those deep holes that Pele had carved in the dark places, the places in which lived the *aitu*. The evil wind was sent by the aitu to infect the people, to make them weak so that their enemies could conquer them.

How could Manu stop these evil winds from blowing through his village? He did not know. Maybe they not only blew through the village, but throughout the whole district of Aliepata, maybe even throughout all of Samoa. He moaned as he lay on his mat with his head on his wooden pillow. His body twitched, like a dog's does sometimes when it dreams. If Manu could only find these *pu*s in the mountains he could stop up the holes with large stones and trap the evil wind inside. But his legs were no good to him now. They were as big around as a coconut tree. They would not carry him as they once did.

He must find a young person to do the work. It must be someone strong and trustworthy. It must be someone who believes, and is obedient. If they were doubtful they would certainly fail. Who could it be? Who in the village could he trust with this secret? Not his sons, nor even his grandsons. They would not believe him. He had to find someone who would listen to him. But who? There was no one, no one to stop the evil wind that blew from the mountains.

When Manu awoke, the sun stood low in the sky and a fresh breeze blew in from the sea, cooling his body. He sat up slowly and rubbed his face with both hands. He looked around him, and there, walking along the shore near the *fale* was the palagi fisherman, Aleni. He was carrying his snorkeling gear.

"*Malo*, Manu," said the young white-skinned man with the flowing hair like a woman.

"Malo lava," replied Manu groggily. The kava had been strong.

"I hope that you have had a good sleep," said Allan.

"A good sleep, yes, but I did not dream of good things."

"Would you like to talk?"

"Yes. Come into the fale. We will talk, but first I must make water."

Allan helped Manu to his feet, and waited while the old man made his way slowly out to the rocks along the shore, his huge legs helped along by his wooden cane. Manu faced the sea and reached between the flaps of his *lava lava*. It is not customary in Samoa to make water in plain view of the village, but exceptions were made for an old man with elephantiasis. Out of respect, everyone looked the other way.

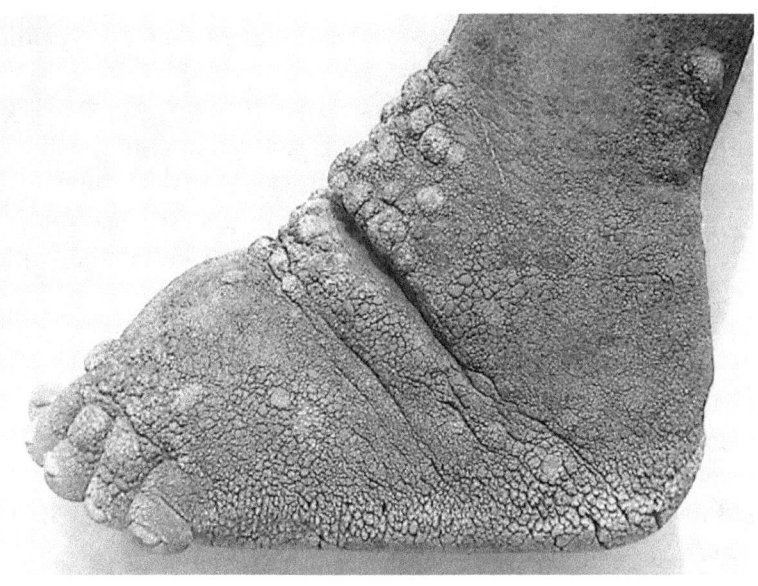

When he returned and had seated himself, Manu called to Matalena again. When she appeared at the edge of the fale he said, "Girl, *fa'amolemole*, bring some tea for myself and my visitor." Then he turned to Allan, who sat cross-legged on the floor, and looked at him with sad, tired eyes.

Allan could see that the old man was troubled. "The sea is rough?" Allan said.

"It is very rough," said Manu, "and there is a headwind."

Allan paused, and then replied, "Although I am only a man standing on the outrigger to keep the canoe from capsizing, I will take the helm if you need me."

Manu looked away across the lagoon towards the sea. After a time, he said, "When I was a boy, all I could think about was the future, of what I would become. When I grew up and had the tattoo hammered into my flesh, all my thoughts were of the present, of how to live my life. When I became a chief in my middle life, I spent many hours thinking about the past, seeking guidance. Then I got to be an old man and I started to think about the future again, mainly about how little time I had remaining. Now that I am nearing my grave I see things differently again."

"And how do things look to you now?"

"It is hard for me to say. I see things that I never did before. And what I see, I fear."

"Tell me what frightens you."

"I cannot say for sure. But things are changing much too fast now. I fear the mountain has cracked. Inside things are coming out. They are bad things. Bad for us all. And bad for our way of life. Once they come, things will never be the same again."

"I do not know what you mean."

"I cannot explain it. All I know is that the people here in Samoa are like children. They are no match for those dark winds that blow while they sleep. I feel the power of an evil ghost approaching. Do not ask me what form these forces truly take. I do not know. All I know is that they are evil. They carry the smell of dead things. Do you feel it too?"

"I feel something," said Allan. "I feel that something is not right. When I first came to Samoa I thought these islands held everything I could ever want. Samoa seemed better than my own country in almost every way. But now I have come to understand that Samoa is no better or no worse than any other place. People are basically the same wherever you go. I came here looking for something that wasn't here. I was looking in the wrong place. Although Samoa has helped me, she cannot give me what I want."

"What is it that you want?"

"I cannot explain it."

"So, you feel something is wrong too?"

"Yes. Something is wrong."

Matalena came back to the fale carrying a pot of tea and a dish of arrowroot cookies from New Zealand. The men waited until she was gone.

Manu said, "We are like the two helmsmen of a double canoe. But are we not steering in different directions? Are we not speaking of two different things?"

"Perhaps. How can I help you? What would you have me do?"

Manu looked at the young man. "I do not think you are strong enough yet to do anything. You do not fully understand the *fa'a Samoa*, the Samoan way. How can you defend something you do not understand?"

"It is true what you say. I do not understand, and I am not as strong as I might be. But I am only a man, and a man without a family at that. All I can hope to do is try and to understand as much as possible."

"Understanding is not enough. You must do something. We must all do something or our vessel will sink and we shall all be swimming. And I do not have to remind you, Aleni, of the dangers of swimming. Even the best swimmer will eventually feed the fishes."

Coyote Wind

1963

On a warm fall night I lay awake on my bed feeling so frightened and alone that I could hardly stand it. It was after midnight and I had lain there for two interminable hours tossing and turning and staring into the darkness. Outside, a warm Santa Ana wind blew like the harsh breath of some half-starved coyote. I listened to it rake over the roof shingles and rasp along the stucco walls. I heard it snuff under the eaves and pant against my bedroom window. That desperate coyote embodied every demon haunting my teenage soul.

It was the middle of September, and I had just graduated from high school the previous June. It wasn't the wind that kept me awake that night; it was the turmoil going on inside my mind. I was agonizing over the future. Quite frankly, I was unnerved at the prospect of adulthood. I knew that my childhood was over, but I knew I was not even close to being grown up. I had no idea what I was going to do with the rest of my life. I had no passion for anything except surfing, and I felt like I didn't know enough about anything to be useful to anyone. The thought of taking some meaningless, low-paying job and working at it for the rest of my life appalled me.

In desperation I had enrolled at the local community college. Classes were set to begin the following week. It wasn't ambition or the thirst for knowledge that made me enroll. Continuing my education was just a way of buying time. Going to school was just a place to go, someplace to be. I really didn't know what else to do with myself.

The Vietnam War was just beginning to turn nasty, and the prospect of me being drafted into the military was very real. I thought that if I was in college I might get a deferment. I didn't think I could handle the military, and I certainly didn't want to go to Vietnam to kill people and maybe get myself killed while I was at it.

That summer I had a girlfriend named Nicole. She had just turned seventeen. She would be a senior when high school started later that month. Nicole was a very pretty girl, and had a great body. Nicole and I had had sex two or three times over the past few months, and I was very much in love with her.

On that fall night, as I lay awake in my bed, I thought about all the things that were wrong with me and my life. I was really concerned about what would become of me. I had no real hope for the future. Things had gotten so bad I thought I might just be going insane. I had to do something. It was after midnight and my parents were sleeping off their bourbon and pills across the hall. My sister was asleep in the room next to mine. My brother had gotten married the year before and moved out. I climbed over on top of my brother's empty bed under the window and sat on it cross-legged. I drew open the curtains and looked down at the city spread out below me.

My family lived in a middle-class tract home on a hillside above Ventura High School. We had a fine view of the city, and during the day, you could see the Santa Barbara Channel and Anacapa and Santa Cruz Islands out in the distance. Down to my left I could make out a dark stand of Eucalyptus trees. Behind those trees was my girlfriend's house. Nicole lived less than a mile away. I started thinking about her, and I couldn't help thinking how beautiful she was, and about the times that we had had sex. I shouldn't have started thinking about that.

The more I thought about her the more I wanted to be with her. I was so lonely and miserable, and I thought she was the only one in the world who understood me. It seemed I only felt comfortable and happy when I was with her. I decided to go down there and visit her.

As quietly as possible I got dressed and then opened the sliding glass window and pulled off the outside screen. I climbed out of the window and closed it behind me. The warm coyote wind whipped around corner of the house and tore at my hair and clothing. I made my way past my parents' bedroom window to the front of the house. My '56 Ford was parked in front. I was too afraid to drive it though. I thought my parents might hear me start the engine, or, they might hear me driving up the hill when I came home. I decided to walk. It was safer.

All the houses along the way were dark and silent. The only sound was the wind gusting down off the hill. Debris, running before the wind, skittered along the roadways. It only took me about fifteen minutes to get to Nicole's house. Nicole's father was in the construction business. He had remodeled his own house, transforming the garage into a bedroom for his daughter. Where the big garage door had been he built a waist-high brick wall and installed paned windows above it. My heart was pounding as I walked up next to those windows.

I took a deep breath and rapped softly. I held my breath. At first there was no answer. I knocked again, a little louder. I heard a stirring inside, and then the curtain was pulled aside and I saw Nicole standing there. She looked half asleep and a little scared. Her hair was a mess, but she looked wonderful. I gave her a shy wave and a forlorn smile. She beamed back at me. She seemed happy to see me. She glanced over her shoulder, and held her finger up to her lips for quiet. Then she motioned to me to go around to the side door.

The wind was really gusting along the dark, narrow passage beside the garage. It took Nicole a minute or so to open the door. I think she must have been brushing her hair or something. When she finally did open the door she took one look at my face and pulled me inside. The next instant we were in each other's arms. I think she knew something was wrong. It felt wonderful to have her body pressed against mine. We stopped hugging long enough to look at each other. She started to ask me a question, but I stopped her with a kiss. Then we kissed again, longer and deeper.

It wasn't long before we were running our hands over each other's bodies. I lifted up her nightie, and she raised her arms as I pulled it off. She only wore a pair of white panties underneath. She was breathing deeply now.

Before long we were both naked on top of her bed. We kissed and fondled each other for a while, and then I mounted her. The second I entered her all my problems and worries faded into nothingness.

We had only been making love for about a minute when all of a sudden the room was filled with a blinding light, and I heard a woman's voice say, "Nicole!" It was her mother. She was standing in the doorway with her hand on the light switch. I'll never forget the look on her face and the sound of her voice. Her face was a mask of shock, her voice a keen of horror and disappointment.

Nicole went rigid under me. "Mother!" she cried. She shoved me aside and scrambled away. I quickly pulled the rumpled sheet in front of me to cover my nakedness.

"What are you doing?" her mother. "Oh, Nic, how could you?"

"Oh, mother! I'm sorry. I'm so sorry."

"Get dressed – both of you." Her mother turned her back and said, "I want to see you in the kitchen. "Now!"

Nicole found her nightie which was crumpled on the floor, while I hurriedly pulled on my clothes. We didn't say a word or even look at each other. My mind screamed, "No, oh no, no. no."

We both entered the kitchen. I was in shock. My whole body trembled. I looked around the lighted kitchen, hoping to God that Nicole's father wasn't there. He wasn't. If my face looked anything like Nicole's, it was beet red. Nicole looked shaken, ashamed, humiliated.

Nicole's mother said, "I can't believe what I just saw in there. Nicole, how could you let this boy into our house? And John, just who do you think you are to come sneaking in here in the middle of the night? I have half a mind to call up your parents right now and tell them."

"Oh, no, please don't," I croaked.

"You're just lucky my husband is still asleep. If he knew you were in here and doing what you did, I hate to think what he might do."

"I'm sorry," I said. "I'm really sorry. It will never happen again. I promise."

"I know it won't, because I don't want you to ever see my daughter again. And I thought you were such a nice boy. Was I ever wrong. Now get out of my house and don't you ever come back here again. And I don't want you telephoning either. You two are finished. If I ever catch you seeing or talking to Nicole again, I'll tell my husband, and I can guarantee you he'll come after you. And I'll call your parents too. Now, get out."

All I could do was look at her helplessly. I could tell she was really upset. I was afraid to beg or to argue with her in case she got even madder and started yelling. I knew if her husband woke up he'd kill me for sure. I looked at Nicole. She wouldn't meet my eyes. Her head was down and she was crying. Her face was still very red. I could tell she was just barely holding herself upright. I looked beseechingly at her mother.

"Go," she said, pointing at the front door. I could tell from the look on her face that she hated me now.

In a daze I went to the door, unlocked it and stepped out into the darkness. The coyote wind grabbed me again and pummeled me like a ball of fur. I hurried out of the yard. I didn't know where to go, but I knew I had to get away from that house. I headed back along the sidewalk the way I had come. My legs were shaking so badly I could hardly walk.

Over and over again I moaned, "No, no, no." I stumbled along the sidewalk as if in a dream, or more accurately, a nightmare. I was in shock. Everything had happened so fast. I wished it had been a dream, but my surroundings and the wind told me that I was really here and it really had happened.

It took a while for the reality of it all to sink in, and when it did my anguish, my wretchedness, my self-loathing, and my fear were utterly complete. The east wind grabbed at me as if it would carry me away, and I wished that it would. Anyplace would be better than this place – any place at all. I thought I would rather be dead than face the reality that was my life. No matter how bad things had been before, at least I had Nicole. Now I had nothing. I was alone in my misery, and I could see no end to it. A vast emptiness stretched out before me into eternity as the wind howled through the Eucalyptus trees.

I walked zombie-like back the way I had come. I didn't know where I should go or what I should do. If there had been a cliff nearby I probably would have jumped off it. By now it was probably two o'clock in the morning. The wind whipped around me like a screaming banshee.

The images of what had just occurred kept replaying before my eyes in an endless loop: Nicole arching in the darkness towards me; the shocking bright light; Nicole's mother standing there in the doorway; the silent, panicky rush to dress; and then the nightmarish scene in the kitchen. Echoing in my ears were her mother's wrathful words, sounding like the pronouncements of some vengeful god, driving me out of Eden and back into the windy night.

As I walked through the darkness I recalled her threatening to phone my parents. I wondered if she might decide to call them after all. I imagined what it would be like to hike up the hill to my house only to find all the lights on inside and my parents waiting for me. I knew I couldn't bear to face them. Not tonight. I was too broken to face anyone. I would rather die.

The thought of Nicole's mother calling my parents forced me to quicken my steps. I knew I had to go home immediately. Maybe, if I got there in time, I could intercept the call. Maybe they wouldn't hear the phone ring. Maybe, if I got there in time, I could just take the phone off the hook so Nicole's mother couldn't get through. I started running. I ran until the hill got too steep and I couldn't run any more. I could feel my chest tightening up. I felt like I was having an asthmatic attack. I had to slow down.

When I rounded the last corner just below the final block, I looked up and was unimaginably relieved to see that the house was still dark. I climbed the last steep street as quickly as

I could. I paused in front of my house just long enough to catch my breath. The gusting wind whipped around me as I stood there gasping with my hands on my knees. Then I went around to the back and as quietly as possible slid open my bedroom window. I climbed in. I stood in the room, my heart pounding, listening intently. Blessedly, the house was silent.

I quickly took off my shoes and socks and jeans. Dressed only in my underwear I silently twisted the doorknob to my room and ever so slowly, like the murderer in Poe's *The Tell-Tale Heart*, I opened the door. Nothing was stirring. I tiptoed down the hall and out to the kitchen where our single telephone was located. I picked up the receiver and held it to my ear. The sound of the dial tone was a relief, but it sounded very loud to me. I placed the receiver face down on the counter and retreated to the living room. My heart was still pounding. I sat on the couch and stared into the dark.

I wondered what would happen in the morning. I would have to hang up the phone before my parents got up and went out to the kitchen. If the phone rang before they left for work I would have to be there to answer it before they did. I could pretend it was a wrong number.

When my heartbeat returned to normal, I felt exhausted, totally done in. But I knew sleep was impossible. I realized too that I was very thirsty. I went back out into the kitchen and drew a glass of water from the tap. As I drank, I noticed the phone's dial tone had been replaced by a loud rhythmic screeching. I quickly wrapped the receiver in a kitchen towel. Then I crept back into my bedroom. I didn't want to take the chance that one of my parents would get up in the middle of the night and find me skulking around the darkened house. I silently closed the door behind me.

I lay down on my bed. I had been disturbed the last time I lay here, but that was nothing compared to what I felt now. The demons crawled over my flesh like so many evil little creatures. They burrowed through my eyes and ears and ate into my brain. My face was a tortured mask.

The guilt I felt was not nearly as painful as the thought of never seeing Nicole again. I wanted to see her so badly that I wanted to scream. I wanted to hold her in my arms and comfort her. I wanted to apologize to her for getting her into so much trouble. I wished I could call her, but I couldn't see how I could ever do that again. Her mother would be hovering around the phone like a hawk. If she answered and I hung up she would know it was me. She might call my parents if she thought I was trying to reach Nicole. It was hopeless.

I wished I could crawl into a deep hole and never see anybody again. I couldn't face them if they knew what I had done. Even God would turn his back on me. He probably already had. I thought about the Catholic religion, the one I had been raised in, and I wondered what kind of sin I had just committed. Was it a mortal sin? Or maybe one of the lesser ones? Either way, I knew that if I died right then I would go straight to hell. And I knew it would be that goddamn coyote wind that carried me there.

The Chilidog Run
1985

As I pull the rented car into the driveway I see that my old man's front yard looks more like the gates of hell than ever. The plants are all overgrown and hoary looking, the lawn is brown and sparse from lack of water, and there are dead leaves scattered all over the place. Huge, grizzled Junipers sprawl every which way across the front of the house, their upper branches drooping onto the roof. His corner lot is outlined by a row of gnarled and stunted pines that border the sidewalk. Their sap-oozing limbs jut out into the walkway. I can see where some fed-up neighbor has lopped off a few limbs here and there to clear the walk – not at the trunk or any logical spot on the branch – but just sawed them off any old place leaving ugly stumps that remind me of war-time amputations.

Through the dusty lace curtains of the front window I see the profile of the old codger sitting in his favorite chair reading the newspaper. Since he didn't hear me drive in, or even slam the car door, I suppose his hearing is catching up with his failing eyesight. I do a quick calculation and figure he must be about seventy now.

I knock on the door and then open it and step into the house. I figure there's no need to make the old buzzard get up and answer the door. After all, it's only me, his long lost son, home after three years living on the East Coast. I guess it is about as far as I could get without leaving the country. My brother probably made the better choice by moving to Hawaii. *One flew East, one flew West, one flew over the Cuckoo's Nest.*

As I walk into the closed up house the stench of dirty old man and urine hits me in the face like a fetid wash cloth and I almost lose my breakfast right then and there.

Pop looks up from his ugly brown chair with a look of consternation edged with fear. Then he recognizes me and puts down the newspaper.

"Well, well," he says with a yellow-toothed grin, "What do you know?" He struggles to his feet using both hands to help push himself out of that raunchy recliner chair that he's had forever, and I see how much he's aged since the last time I saw him.

If you were to see a photograph of him as a young man, you would never recognize the stooped and grotesquely obese creature that stands here now. He looks worse than I've ever seen him before, and that's saying something.

His bloated face, red and heavily veined, glows from under an unholy halo of thin, silver hair that sprawls, wild and unkempt about his scaly scalp, and hangs down nearly to his shoulders. His bearded jaw is slack and I expect a line of drool to ooze out of his gaping mouth at any moment. Long neglected teeth caked with plaque still manage to cling somehow inside that wet, quivering hole. Blue, cataract-plucked eyes peer unsteadily at me through grungy, mega-thick glasses. He's wearing filthy pajamas with food stains all down the front and a greasy looking robe. He is barefoot. His blotchy, scarlet feet stick out from under frayed cuffs and blossom with long, yellowish toenails that curl and split in all directions.

God knows how long it's been since he's had a bath, shaved, combed his hair, brushed his teeth or changed those odoriferous bed clothes. He looks like someone's worst nightmare, or one of those twisted Hollywood creations for a Class B horror film.

He walks unsteadily towards me with an idiot's grin on his face and starts to spread out his arms to embrace me, his long lost, second most favorite son. But I can't bear the thought of being drawn in to smother against his stinking hulk. I quickly extend my hand for him to shake instead. He stops just in time and takes my hand in his.

"Hello...uh, son," he says with a slight slur. "It's good to see you again." I am immediately suspicious that he can't remember my name. He obviously doesn't remember me calling him last week to tell him I was coming. But I know, unless he's really blown a fuse this time, it will come to him. We shake and I'm surprised at the strength the old reprobate still possesses.

"Well, it's good to see you too," I hear myself saying, although what I'm thinking is: "I wish I could say the same for you, you odiferous degenerate. You look worse than Charles Laughton on his worst day." But of course it's too early for that kind of talk.

I guess he figures the social formalities are over with, either that or he's tired of standing up, because he abruptly turns away from me and totters back to his chair. I see a brown stain has soaked through the back of his robe where he's soiled himself. He slumps down ungracefully into his naugahyde recliner, bumping his head in the process, and lets out a sigh. I can see that he's a bit confused about what to do next, and is debating whether or not to pick up the newspaper again. But he decides that I might think it's bad manners, so he looks up at me and says, "'Have a seat, son. How long are you here for this time?"

I look around for a place to sit. I eschew the chairs with the grease stains where your head would rest and the suspicious discolorations on the seat cushions, and decide that the sofa is the safest bet. He rarely sits there. I just have to move aside a slew of well-thumbed magazines and newspapers.

"Oh, I don't know," I say in answer to his question. "A day or two, maybe."

Before I sit down I ask, "'You got any beer, Pop?"

"Naw," he says with a scoff. "Just the usual – Early Times and soda. Help yourself if you want. It's out in the kitchen. You know where it is."

I don't really like bourbon and I'd much rather have a beer, but I need a drink to brace me against the smell, and for what is to come. So I tell him "OK," and head for the kitchen. I hear him pick up the newspaper as I round the corner.

The kitchen is in worse shape than the living room. Dirty dishes and glasses are piled high in the sink, some of them half-filled with water, on top of which floats round green rafts of mold. The smell is horrible. Open packages of nuts, cookies and candy line the counters, along with sundry abandoned left-overs, half-eaten sandwiches, sagging yellow globs in butter dishes, and a bunch of untouched, rotting bananas. The stove is caked with multicolored, splattered messes and the sticky floor tries to pull off my shoes with each step I take. A big green bottle-fly buzzes up out of the trash can in the corner, angry at me for interrupting its feast, or maggot laying, or whatever it was doing down in there.

The only clear space on the counter-tops is way down at the end where Pop's half-gallon plastic bottle of bourbon sits next to his shot glass, and, to one side, a plastic bottle of club soda and a couple of empty ice cube trays. I manage to find a clean glass way in the back of the top shelf of the cupboard. I get some ice out of the upper freezer section of the fridge, but don't dare open the refrigerator for fear of what I might find there. I mix myself a stiff one and get out of there as quick as I can.

I follow the discolored path and the trail of food crumbs across the olive-green carpet around the corner and back to the living room. I guess that I've given him enough time to get used to the idea that someone besides himself is in the house again.

Ever since his second wife, my step-mother Marge, died some five years ago he's lived alone in this house. Since he doesn't have anyone to wait on him hand and foot anymore he's gone into a long, steady decline. He rarely goes out, and he hardly ever has visitors. And believe me, what visitors do venture in, don't stay long. I don't know if it's the sight of him, or the smell and squalor of the place that gets to them. But regardless, they don't stay long. Pity the poor door-to-door salesman who stumbles in here and has to make a pitch to my old man.

Back in the living room, I sit down on the couch and take a drink of the poison that has created the monster squatting to my left in his groaning chair. He becomes aware of my presence again and begrudgingly folds and puts aside the newspaper. Although he is probably glad to see me, he doesn't like having people around much. They get on his nerves.

"So, how have you been, Pop?" I ask. I'm trying to be 'hail-fellow-well-met' at this point, trying to fight off that old sinking feeling that's dragging me down.

"Oh, I'm fine," he says. "I was sick as a dog last week, but I'm OK now."

I'm thinking, God, if he's fine now I would hate to have seen him last week. I continue trying to engage him in small talk, trying to draw him out.

"So what have you been up to lately? Have you done anything interesting? 'Gone anyplace?" I pretty much know the answers already.

"Are you nuts?" he asks. "You know better than that. I haven't been out of this house in a year at least. Well, that's not altogether true. I step outside twice a day. Once to pick up the morning paper, and again later to get the evening paper. The paperboys throw them on the porch so I don't have to go out into the yard. Other than that, I go from here to the bathroom, to the bedroom, to the kitchen. That's it."

"Sounds pretty exciting," I say. I can't resist sticking him with a little sarcasm.

"Am I going to have trouble with you so soon?" he says to me, turning his sagging neck so he can eye me through his goggles. Although he's never said so, I think he always did get a kick out of our little verbal duels, and now he knows he's in for another one. "Crime-a-ninny," he says, "you've only been here a few minutes and already you start with the smart talk."

"Well, what do you do with yourself all day?" I thrust.

"Well, I sleep most of the day," he parries, looking at me as if I really ought to know better than to ask such a stupid question. "After all, I don't usually go to bed until four or five in the morning. I can't sleep at night."

"What?! You've got to be kidding. Well, what do you do all night, then?"

"Why, drink and watch television. What else? Then when it starts to get light I go to bed and sleep till about one or two in the afternoon. As a matter of fact, I just got up about a half-hour ago."

"I can't believe this," I say. He has never been this bad before. Apparently he's afraid of the dark now.

"Then what do you do during the afternoon or evening?" I ask. "You obviously don't spend much time housekeeping or doing yard work."

"Are you crazy?" he says. "I'm retired! I don't do menial labor. Never have. After all, young man, as you well know, I was a pharmacist for forty years. And, I might remind you, a graduate of the greatest university there ever was: the University of Southern California! You see, son, we professionals don't do house work. And yard work? Forget it. That's why we have Mexicans." He's getting cranked up now and looking very smug. I don't want to get him started on pharmacy, or USC, or race. If I do he'll blather on all day.

He lifts his glass, which was hidden between a stack of "National Geographic" and "Sports Illustrated" magazines and expertly drains the last two inches.

"Is that your breakfast, then?" I ask.

"I don't eat breakfast. You know that."

"When do you eat?"

"When I get hungry. Want another drink?"

"I just started this one."

The bloated old fogey struggles up out of his chair. He peers out the curtained window, his attention caught by the gleam of the car.

"Hey," he says, looking completely baffled. "Somebody parked their car in my driveway." Maybe he thinks I got beamed down here by Captain Kirk or something.

"That's mine. I rented it at LAX."

"Oh? What kind is it?"

"It's a Ford Taurus. It's a luxury car."

"Oh yeah, I've seen those advertised on TV. How are they?"

"Not bad. Wanna go for a ride?"

"Hmmm." He seems uncertain, maybe even a little frightened at the idea. For a guy who must think of everything pretty much in the abstract now, he has to struggle with the idea of doing something in the real world. Finally he says, "Yeah, that might be nice. I haven't been out of this house for so long... It might be nice for a change."

217

"Well, I'd be happy to take you out, but you can't go looking like that."

"What's wrong with the way I look?" he says, nonplussed.

"Have you seen yourself in the mirror lately, Pop?"

"No. What's wrong?" He looks down at himself, mystified.

"You're dirty," I tell him. "You look like hell."

He seems not to have heard that. He has a way of only hearing what he wants to. He turns and heads for the kitchen holding his empty glass down at his side. "I don't know what you're talking about," he mumbles as he weaves out of the room.

"Why do you keep this place so closed up for?" I call after him. "It smells bad in here."

"Well, open the goddamn door if you want to," he shouts from the kitchen. I'm starting to get on his nerves alright. He doesn't like people much.

While he's out mixing himself another drink I open the front door and let the fresh air filter through the dusty screen door. Then I go over to the other side of the living room and open another window to get a draft going. It really does stink in here. I turn to see the old man holding a fresh drink and squinting disapproval at me.

"You'll make it cold in here," he says shaking his head.

"It's seventy-five degrees outside. You won't freeze, believe me. The fresh air will do you good. You shouldn't keep this place closed up all the time. It's bad for you."

"Bullshit," is his one and only word on the subject. He grunts down into his chair and pulls his robe closed in the front against the elements. Then he takes a swig of what looks like a double.

"I still don't understand what you do with yourself day in and day out," I say, wanting to get a better idea of what his life is like now.

"Oh, you know, I sleep a lot. Then I get up and have a drink and read the papers. I get a lot of magazines too. 'Really more than I can read now. And I watch TV and fix myself

218

another drink and maybe some food when I get hungry. By the way, would you like something to eat, uh, Slim?" (There, he's getting warmer. At least he remembers my nickname.)

He continues, "I have plenty to eat out there. Your sister just went to the market for me. I make up a list every couple of weeks and give her a blank check and she gets everything I want. She's such a wonderful person, that sister of yours. I know she's kept awfully busy with that family of hers, so I don't really blame her for not coming around much." He sighs, and sniffles a little, and takes another drink.

"The only thing that bothers me is that she won't bring me any booze. I don't know how many times I've asked her to pick me up a bottle when she's out. But she just won't do it. She used to. But ever since that damn doctor told me if I kept drinking I'd be dead within a year, she refuses to bring me anymore. She says she doesn't want to bring me the bottle that kills me."

"The doctor told you that you had one year to live?"

"Yeah," he says with a sly grin. "That was four years ago. Ha, ha. I guess I showed him. I'll show all of you. I'm going to live to be a hundred. You just watch me. Ha, ha. I'll show them all. I know for a fact that I'll outlive you, you little twerp."

The man is a lunatic. "No way, Pop. Look at me. I'm in great shape. But just look at you. You're falling apart. And you're overweight. God, are you overweight. I've never seen you this heavy before. What the heck have you been doing to get so heavy."

"Nothing."

"What have you been eating?"

"Oh, a lot of good stuff."

"Yeah, I saw all the cookies and candy in there."

"Did you see the soft drinks? If you get thirsty, you'll find all kinds them in the refrigerator. Sometimes I'm really thirsty when I wake up. There must be two cases of different kinds in there."

"More sugar. That's just great. I thought you were a pharmacist. Don't you know what all that sugar does to you?"

219

"Aw, what do you know? It doesn't hurt me any. And I love butter too. I must go through a pound of it a week. My favorite sandwich is to take two nice, fresh slices of Wonder Bread and spread about a half an inch of butter between 'em. 'Maybe sprinkle some sugar on it. Man, is that great."

"You're even crazier than I thought." I'm getting bolder. He's starting to get to *me* now. or is the bourbon? "Well, what else do you eat? I don't suppose you ever heard of fresh fruits and vegetables."

He ignores that last comment and says, "Oh, I've got a whole freezer compartment full of microwave dinners and burgers and fries and stuff. Your sister gave me a microwave oven last Christmas because she said she doesn't want me to burn the house down when I cook. Sometimes I forget when I've got something on the stove. She says I make too big a mess anyway."

"I saw that much when I went in the kitchen. Don't you ever clean up after yourself?"

"I told you I don't do menial labor. I've got a couple of gals who come in about every other week and clean up. And listen, you just better back off of me, buddy. I'm still big enough to kick your butt."

"Don't make me laugh." I take a swig of bourbon. The old goat is driving me to drink.

He rises up in his chair and shakes a scaly fist at me and goes, "Oooh, get over here boy and I'll box your ears. I'm not so old I can't take you down a peg or two."

"I'm glad I've got my boots on," I tell him. "It's getting awful thick in here. Can I use your bathroom?"

"Go ahead, smart aleck, you know where it is."

I make my way into the bathroom and brace myself. The smell of urine is almost overpowering. The old man's aim never was that good, and it's obviously getting worse as time goes on. I lift up the red and yellow toilet seat that's emblazoned with the USC logo and Tommy Trojan brandishing his sword and do my business in the dank pool. As I stand there I notice a rusty razor abandoned on the dusty shelf and a toothbrush that looks like it's been sitting there since the turn of the century. I manage to get water out of the corroded sink faucets and wash my hands. I stick my head into the shower stall and see cobwebs in all the corners and a couple of Daddy Longlegs mating in the tub.

As I walk back into the living room, the screen door suddenly opens and in flies a magazine and a couple of envelopes and some junk mail. The stuff hits the floor and then the door slams shut. I get a flash like this is feeding time at the zoo and the animal trainer has just thrown in a hunk of meat and slammed the door shut before he gets bitten. I see the postman's back receding rapidly past my rented car and down the driveway. I look at my old man. He's just sitting there matter-of-factly nursing his drink.

"Does he always deliver mail like that?" I ask.

"Yes. But usually the inside door is closed. He opens the screen door and sticks it through the slot in the main door."

"Throwing it in on the floor seems to be an odd way of delivering mail. What's his name?"

"I don't know. I've never spoken to the man."

"Really? How long has he been on this route?"

"Oh, I don't know, six or seven years I guess."

"And in all that time you've never found occasion to speak to the man?"

"What am I going to speak to him about?"

"Oh, for God's sake. Don't you have anything to say to anybody?"

"I don't talk to people unless they ask me questions."

"That's a hell of a way to be."

"I hardly ever see people anyway. When the Mexicans come to mow the lawn, I just go into the bedroom and watch TV until they're gone. I leave them a check stuck in the screen door. I do the same when the housekeepers come."

"I can't believe you live this way. Don't you ever get lonely?"

"Why sure I do, son. You bet I do. But... well, I don't know. I just never have gotten along very well with people. It's better if I just stick to myself and mind my own business."

"Boy, are you screwed up," I say. I take another drink of bourbon. "You know, it seems like every time I come here I

221

have to give you a good swift kick in the butt just to straighten you out for a while."

"I know you do, son. But listen here, don't start on me this time. I'm in no mood for that stuff. I'm getting too old for it."

"I was just in the bathroom. Holy Moley. It looks like the only thing you use it for is to take a leak. And it smells like half of it ends up on the floor. When's the last time you bathed yourself?"

He gives it some thought, and then says, "I don't know."

"Well, I was thinking about taking you for a ride in my new Ford Taurus. But if you want to go for a ride you're going to have to clean up your act first. Why don't you take a nice hot shower?" The old man squirms in his seat. Then he slowly shakes his head and finds something exceedingly interesting in his ice cubes.

"And why not wash that hair of yours while you're at it? I can't believe you. I remember when I was a teenager how you used to ride me about having long hair. And look at you now. What hair you have left is almost down to your shoulders. And that beard! I really can't believe it. Who do you think you are? Howard Hughes or something?"

"Ha, ha," he says. "What do you know about Howard Hughes?"

"Never mind what I know. Are you going to clean yourself up?"

"Not today. Maybe tomorrow."

"Oh, no you don't. I've heard that line before. Come on, get into that shower. Right now. I'll help you if you need it."

"No, I don't think so."

"Why not? I came all the way across the country to see you. The least you could do is make yourself presentable."

He hesitates, then he says timidly, "I...I...Well, I don't like to go in the shower because I'm afraid I might fall down. I'm afraid I might hit my head."

"Oh, come on. That's ridiculous. Is this your latest phobia or something? You're not going to fall down."

"I might."

"Bull. Not if you're careful. Maybe you'd feel better if I marched you out into the back yard and hosed you down with the garden hose."

"I'd almost prefer it, son. But it's too cold."

"Cold?! Pop this is Southern California in the summertime. It's not cold."

"I don't like going outside."

"Awww, for the love of Pete. You are really something else." I'm down to the last of my drink when I get a brilliant idea. I say, "'Tell you what, Pop. How about I take you downtown to Mr. Top Hat and we get us a couple of chilidogs. Remember them?"

"Oooh, yeah," he says, suddenly very alert. "I used to love those things. Mr. Top Hat makes the best chilidogs in the whole world. I tried to get them to give me their chili recipe once, but they just laughed. They wouldn't even tell me what brand of wieners they use." His mouth is watering and I can tell I've got the hook in him.

"OK," I say. "Let's go." He starts to struggle up out of his chair, but then I pull the plug. "But before we go, let's get you cleaned up."

He freezes, and then sinks slowly back down into his chair like a balloon losing all its air. "Damn," he says, suddenly looking very tired.

"Come on, come on," I say.

"Oh, alright. Just a minute," he says like a kid who's been told for the last time he has to go to bed. "I'll just finish my drink first, and then I'll go."

Man, oh man, anything to postpone the inevitable.

I know I'm going to have to help him, and the whole idea just grosses me out. But I figure it's worth it if I'm going to spend some time with him. He really does smell bad. I decide I'll need another drink to brace me for the task, and I go into the kitchen to make one.

When I come back in and sit on the couch and Pop bends my ear for half an hour telling me the same old stories I've heard a dozen times about how he was the president of his fraternity at USC and how he was a big man on campus and all that, and how he met my Mom and what a wonderful person she was and on and on, and then how she died. And then he starts bawling like he does every time he talks about her. I let him sob there in his chair for a while. Then I change the subject to the military and he tells me about how he was in the Navy in WWII in San Diego and everything else that I already know.

I sit and listen politely because I figure he must not get much of a chance to talk to anyone but himself. I watch as his drink slowly edges down towards the bottom. By now he's forgotten all about the fact that he's going to have to take a shower and that then we're going out for a ride and a chilidog.

Finally, his drink is empty and he starts to get up to make another one. By now he's loosened up and is feeling good again. Nothing like two doubles on an empty stomach to make him feel right. Then I drop the bombshell.

"O.K. Pop, strip! And get your sorry ass into the shower."

"What? Oh, no. I'm not ready yet."

"Oh, you're ready alright. Now get in there before I have to stick the boot to you."

"Don't get that way with me, you young punk. I'll get in there when I'm damn good and ready and not before. I want another drink first."

He goes into the kitchen and I stay on the couch listening. I don't hear a sound for about a minute, and then he comes back into the living room. His face is livid.

"Alright, you bastard," he fumes. "What the hell have you done with my bottle?"

"I hid it where you'll never find it in a million years."

"You son of a bitch!"

"I'll give it back to you after your shower."

"I'll kick your ass right here and now. I swear I will."

"Try it and you'll never get your bottle back. Now, go on. Get in that shower and wash yourself. And while you're at it, see what kind of job you can do drowning those spiders in the bathtub."

"I can't believe this!" he says. "My own son, pulling this crap on me. You rotten little ingrate, I'll get you for this."

"Ooooh, I'm really scared, old man. Get in there."

"Don't call me 'old man.' I'm twice the man you'll ever be. This just isn't fair. Here I am in my own house, minding my own business, and this spawn of cuttlefish comes in and starts ordering me around. You, you presumptuous guppy."

He moans and groans for another five minutes, but finally he resigns himself to the inevitable and gets undressed. I try not to look at the ugly rolls of fat and the flakey scales and red inflammations from his eczema and psoriasis. He takes off his coke-bottle glasses and gropes his way into the shower. He turns on the water and I hear him groaning in there at first because the water is too cold, and then too hot. He's really out of practice in there. Finally, he gets it right and I hear his groans turn to sighs of pleasure.

I call in to him, "Don't spare the soap, Pop. Make sure you clean out all the crevices. And wash your hair too."

"Mind your own business, you goddamn troublemaker," he calls back, sputtering like a drowning man.

While he's in the shower I scoop up the limp, dank pile of bedclothes that he was wearing and the incredibly soiled sheets and pillow cases off his bed and carry them at arm's length, trying not to breath, into the washroom and stuff them into the washing machine. I start it running with plenty of soap and bleach. I go back into the darkened, putrid bedroom and throw open the curtains and blinds and pull up the windows to air the place out. It's then that I notice his piss pot behind the chair, next to the bed. It's a plastic water jug with a handle on the side with the top crudely cut off. The thing is nearly full of stale, alcoholic piss. It reeks so bad I almost puke, but somehow manage to get it outside and dump it in the far corner of the back yard.

When I get back in the house the old man has finished his shower. I am pretty sure he hasn't been in there long enough to do a thorough job of it, but what the hell, I feel lucky to have gotten him in there in the first place.

He towels himself off and I direct him into the spare bedroom where he keeps his clothes. It's a struggle, but he manages to get himself into some underwear. He figures that's enough for now, but I persist and find a pair of pants with an expandable waistband that he can still fit into. Now he really figures he's done, but I manage to steer him back into the bathroom where I sit him down on the toilet seat. I start combing his hair back out of his face. His hair is full of knots and snarls from being unkempt for so long and he grunts and grimaces as I make order out of the chaos.

I figure while I've got him on a roll here, I might as well clean him up as best as possible before he absolutely calls it quits. I find a pair of scissors and trim his hair and beard, and the hoary stuff coming out his ears and nose. I leave him his moustache, but trim it so that it's up out of his mouth at least. I lather up the rest of his face, find a new razor blade and manage to get him shaved while only cutting him two or three times. All the while he sits there like some kid who knows he's being fussed over, not liking it much, but willing to put up with it because he's getting some attention. I slap a hot wash cloth across his mug when I'm done, and then have him dry himself off and splash on some aftershave. At last that rotten smell is gone.

He really needs his fingernails and toenails cleaned and cut, but I tell him he'll have to do it himself or get someone else because there ain't no way in hell I'm going to tackle that job. I know he won't do it, so we leave them.

I retreat to the living room and take a slug of my drink while he puts on a dress shirt and a tie and his blue blazer with the USC patch on the pocket. When he finally emerges from the back room he looks almost human again. He's carrying his goggle glasses and cleaning them with a tissue.

"You're looking good, sport," I tell him, "but you're a might overdressed. We're only going out for a chilidog, you know."

"I always look good," is his retort. "And besides, when I get dressed, I dress well, not like you, you over-the-hill hippie. Where's my goddamn booze?"

"Forget your booze. Let's go for a ride."

"I want a drink first."

"You can have one when you come back."

"Listen, you worthless excuse for a son. I'm not going anywhere until I get my drink. Now either you get in there and get me my jug, or you can get the hell out of my house right now and don't come back. Otherwise I'll just call up the taxi company like I always do and have them bring me a new bottle." He's feeling his oats. He would never admit it, but he feels a whole lot better when he's cleaned up.

"Alright, alright. Don't get your dander up." I go in and pull his half-gallon bottle out of the oven and plunk it down on the counter.

So he mixes himself another double and sits in a different chair over by the never used fireplace and starts talking. He's just recently got his latest issue of "Civil War Times" and this sets him off on a lecture, sans notes, about the vital contributions of General Lee's lieutenants during the war between the states. I try to pay attention as he goes on and on, showing off his encyclopedic knowledge. I'm not wild about the subject matter, but it's nice to see that he does still have moments when he's lucid and can remember things. But I wonder if he'll even remember I was here a week after I'm gone.

Finally, his drink is empty and he looks at me and says, "What's wrong with you, boy? Your dear old father is sitting here starving to death. Are you going to take me out for that chilidog, or not?"

Finally! I was beginning to think I'd never get him out of here. "Alright, old timer," I tell him, "don't lose your grip. But before we go anywhere I'd like to point something out to you."

"Oh, yeah? What?"

"Look at your feet."

No longer sitting in his recliner, he tries and fails to see far enough over his enormous belly to catch sight of his bare feet. But he finally manages to get a bead on them by straightening his legs out and lifting them up off the floor.

"Oh," he says. "I guess if we're going out, I better put on some shoes and socks."

"You're absolutely right, Ollie," I say in a Stan Laurel voice. Then I throw a verbal uppercut out of nowhere, "You might need them, because I may just decide to drop you off down by Hobo Jungle where the winos hang out, and you'll have to catch a freight train home."

"You always were a smart aleck, you know that, son?"

After a lengthy struggle with his socks and shoes that leaves him nearly exhausted, Pop and I are ready to leave. He gives me the keys to the house and we step out onto the porch. While I lock up, Pop clings to the awning roof post, looking around bewildered, like he's a stranger in a strange land. The sunshine nearly blinds him after the perpetual dimness of the house.

I step around him and get into the car. I sit and watch him build up his courage. He takes a big breath and then launches himself off the porch, and careens towards the passenger side. He puts one hand on the hood of the car to hold himself up as he goes around. He gets in and I feel the car tilting to the right under his weight.

I suggest he use the seat belt, but he's full of bravado after his success of making it to the car. He says, "No way. I'm no sissy. I'll take my chances without it."

So I start up the car and we begin our Chilidog Run. I check the traffic and then back quickly out of the driveway into the road. This speedy maneuver unnerves him immediately. The old geezer's eyeballs are ready to pop as I put it in drive and take off. He's not quite ready for this, I can tell. He grabs the arm rest with one hand and the seat with the other and holds on. He's having second and third thoughts about this whole excursion.

But after a few blocks of silent tenseness, unpunctuated by any bone-crushing collisions, he starts to relax a little. I guess he figures that if I was going to wrap us around a telephone pole I'd have done it by now.

"Want to go for a little ride first?" I say.

"Whatever, son."

So I turn down Seaward Boulevard, and head for the beach. It's one of those classic early August days along the Southern California coast. It's clear and calm, the sky an incredible blue, the air clean with a hint of salt off the ocean. I make a right onto Pierpont and cruise slow along the edge of the sand dunes towards the fishing pier. I roll down my window to let the sea breeze in.

At first the old man's head looks like one of those little bobble-head dolls people put in their car windows. Pop's taking in everything. There's so much to see! The way he looks, he reminds me of one of those flatland tourists when they first come out to California and see these dead brown hills diving down into the blue Pacific. They love it. Pop does too. You'd never guess he's lived in Southern California all his life.

His neck must be getting tired because pretty soon he leans back in his seat and just enjoys the feel of the ride and watches the sunlight dance off the water.

"Man, this is great," he says. "I'd forgotten just how nice it is down here."

"You should get out more often, Pop. There's a great big world out here waiting for you."

"How am I going to get out? After my third DUI they took my driver's license away, and I sold my car."

"Try walking. It might be good for you."

"Don't make me laugh. I have enough trouble just making it to the bathroom. How am I going to get anywhere walking?"

"Well, if you'd sober up once in a while you wouldn't find it so hard."

"Oh, boy. Here we go again. Why don't you just drive the car, son?"

So we cruise by the pier and over to Surfer's Point and I park the car in the crowded lot that faces the beach. There's a couple of tanned, young surfer chicks in the car just to the right of us blowing a joint, probably waiting for their boyfriends to come in from riding the waves. When I pull in next to them, they look over and take a gander at Pop. Their blood-shot eyes bulge and their mouths drop open, and then they start breaking up. They've never seen anything like him before. I'm thinking they're lucky they didn't see him a couple of hours ago. They'd probably keel over.

Pop is oblivious to them. He's watching the swells coming in, and the surfers in their glistening wet suits gliding and turning along the face of the waves. Out beyond them in the channel we can see sailboats from the marina, and it's so clear we can see way beyond them, all the way to the Channel Islands off the coast.

"I remember when you and your brother used to come down here to surf," he says, "and as I recall, you boys played hooky more than once to come down here, you rotten little truants."

"That was a long time ago. And look who's calling people 'truants.'"

"What do you mean? I never cut school in my life."

"Yeah, you just cut life."

But the old man doesn't hear me. He's discovered the two girls over to his right.

"Oooh. Mmmm. Slim, do you see what I see? Man, oh man. Would I like to get my hands on that stuff. Man, I would screw them like there's no tomorrow."

"Give me a break."

"Oooh. Look. They see us. They're smiling. They're laughing. Let's pick them up, boy."

"Are you kidding? Those kids can't be more than sixteen! Why, I'm old enough to be their father. And you, you dirty old man, what would you do if you did pick them up?"

"You just watch me." And before I can react, he's rolling down his window and smiling over at them with yellow teeth ablaze. Oh, Christ. He forgot to brush his teeth.

"Hi, girls," he calls out to them. "How are you today?"

The two stoney teenagers giggle, and the one behind the wheel winks at him and says, "Hi, handsome. How are you?"

"Pop, I think it's time we go get our chilidogs."

"Wait a minute, wait a minute... Hey girls, want to go for a ride in my son's new car? We're going to get some chilidogs."

I say to him, "Man, are you crazy?"

The girls start laughing their heads off.

The blond girl behind the wheel says, "Chilidogs? I thought guys like you were supposed to offer little girls candy."

Pop says, "You can have whatever you want if you go for a ride with us."

"Oh, Lord! Pop, shut up."

The girl looks at him, not so sure that this is a joke any more. She says "No thanks," and rolls up her window.

Pop turns to me disgustedly and says, "There. Are you satisfied? You just gypped us out of some feminine companionship. What are you, homo or something?"

"Oh, sure. Come on, let's get out of here."

I pull out and head the car downtown to Mr. Top Hat to get our chilidogs. Pop starts up with one of his old refrains, "Well, you did it again, son. You screwed me out of another piece of ass. I remember when you and I took that trip to Australia and New Zealand. Oh, man, how I could have scored on that trip! But, nooo. You were always there getting in the way. Man, oh man. I remember that one beautiful babe in Sydney. She really wanted it..."

"You really have a problem with reality, don't you, you old fart?"

"What do you mean?"

"You never even came close to scoring on that trip."

"Ha! That's what *you* think."

"You ought to thank me for going along. I kept you from getting punched out more than once by irate husbands. At the very least some woman would have slapped you silly if I hadn't stepped in."

"You're mad, do you know that son?"

"I'm mad alright. But not the way you mean. You squandered all the money you got from selling my dead mother's house on that trip. And you were so drunk and drugged out the whole time that you don't remember half of what we saw."

"I can't believe what I'm hearing. After your mother died I wanted... I just wanted to get away and forget about it. I was generous enough to take you along."

"Give me a break. You just wanted to take some protection along, someone to look out for you while you got wasted."

"That's not true. And besides, what do you mean by saying I was drugged out?"

"I saw those Dexedrine tabs you used during the day and those Tuinals you took at night. And it wasn't just on the trip either. I remember all the time when I was growing up I used to see all kinds of pills in your medicine cabinet: pain pills, muscle relaxants, tranquilizers, amphetamines, barbiturates. You name it, you had it. You must have just helped yourself to whatever you wanted in the pharmacy where you worked, right? I never realized you were so heavily into drugs until I moved away from home and found out not everybody's father lived like you do. I just don't understand how you could keep functioning with all the booze you drank along with the drugs."

"I've never heard you talk like this before, son."

"I guess it's just taken this long for me to get mad enough to say what I always felt."

"Why do you feel such resentment towards me? I never hurt you."

"You hurt me more than you'll ever know."

"How?"

"Well, just for starters, you never were any kind of a role model for a boy to have, or a girl for that matter. All you ever cared about was getting plastered. You destroyed my mother and you nearly destroyed your kids."

"Shut up!" he shouts. "Don't you ever say I hurt your mother."

"I'll say it. I'll scream it, you rotten slime ball. You killed her! You killed my mother!" At this point I'm starting to freak out and I have to pull over to the side of the road.

He says, "No. I never did." He starts to cry, and through his tears he blubbers, "She was the most wonderful, beautiful person I ever knew. I would never have hurt her."

"You goddamn hypocrite. Don't you dare say that. Have you been deluding yourself all this time about what really happened? Don't you know that you are responsible for her killing herself?"

"She didn't kill herself," he sobs. "She died of ulcerative colitis, in the hospital. You can read it on the Death Certificate."

"Yeah, that's what she died of all right. But you were the cause. All those years you drank away and made her life miserable. Finally, she left you and moved away and took us kids with her. That time away from you was the happiest, most stress-free time she and us kids ever had. But you couldn't leave us be, could you? You had to start calling her. You had to start coming around. Weaseling your way back in. She must have really loved you, or maybe she only loved what you once were. Either that or she just got lonely, or felt too weak to go on alone, because she took you back. She got tired of fighting your drinking and your drugs and so she started drinking and taking drugs right along with you."

He looks at me in horror. "No!"

"Yes, she did. But she wasn't strong like you were. She couldn't take that kind of life and she got sick. She was sick for years from the poison you fed her, and she suffered until the day she died. And that's why I say you killed her, you sleazy good-for-nothing degenerate." By now I'm slobbering too.

233

The old man covers his ears with his hands and cries out in anguish, "No. No. You don't understand."

"I understand more than I want. I swear, I really have to fight the urge to put a bullet through your sick, miserable brain. Especially when you're drunk and brag to me how you were unfaithful to my mother and were screwing that bitch who worked at the pharmacy. And on top of that, I know you probably killed your second wife too. Marge was under doctor's orders to take it easy because of her gall bladder, but she was so busy waiting on you hand and foot that she just wore herself out and died. Now just shut up, you miserable excuse for a human being, and let's go get our chilidog."

I put the car in gear and drove over to Mr. Top Hat at the corner of Palm and Main Streets. But the little corner stand that had been a landmark for years was all closed up. Plywood covered the windows, and we could see black scorch marks and blistered paint all around the exterior. It was obvious there'd been a fire inside and that the place had been gutted. Mr. Top Hat was no more.

So Pop and I drove back home and we never did get our chilidogs.

Curly
1964

A cold, foggy morning found me down at The Point, surfing as usual. I was dressed only in a pair of baggy swim trunks. The water was frigid, but I tried not to notice because the waves were overhead and had good shape. It was one of those classic surfing days at The Point. The water was glassed off and the waves broke clean and smooth with a hollow boom.

There must have been twenty surfers out in the water, and I wasn't thrilled about it. That was far too big a crowd for surf this size. Especially since half those guys didn't know what the hell they were doing. I wanted to separate myself from them, so I started paddling over towards the oil pipeline which was about a hundred yards to the west. The waves seemed to be peaking real nice over there.

We all had long boards in those days, and we used to paddle from a kneeling position. That kept us up out of the water for the most part, and marginally warmer. But you still couldn't help being wet all the time. I'd been out there for nearly an hour and was starting to feel the effects of hypothermia. So I didn't really mind paddling all the way to the pipeline. Paddling helps keep you warm.

Most of us regulars didn't have wetsuits. They were relatively new to the sport in 1964, and they were expensive. They were beyond most of our means. About the only people with wetsuits were older guys with jobs who were skin divers, and who occasionally surfed. They wore those thick, bulky, two-piece suits with the long flap in back that came up between your legs and snapped in front. We looked down on those guys as a bunch of sissies and interlopers. We called them Rubber Rats. I suspect we envied them, but we never would have admitted it back then.

When I got to the oil pipeline I raised myself up as high as I could on my knees and looked out to sea. It was hard to see waves approaching because the murky gray fog merged with the equally gray sea. But after a minute or so I could just barely make out the telltale undulations of an approaching set. It looked like a big one. I paddled out deeper to meet it. I was alone right then and had my pick of any wave in the set.

When I rose over the first one I marveled at its size. It must have been ten feet high. It was steep and smooth, and swept in like a wall of liquid slate. I could feel its power as I rose over the top. I glided over the next two as well. And then, there it was: the biggest wave of the set. Big, hell – it was huge! It was the biggest wave I'd seen all morning.

Desire and fear set my heart to racing as I quickly straddled my board and twirled my legs in the water to turn my longboard towards shore. I knelt on the board and started paddling. It only took a couple of strokes before the wave picked me up like an express elevator heading for the top floor.

I sprang to my feet. The takeoff was radical, and I almost went airborne, but somehow managed to maintain my balance as I dropped down into the maw of the wave. I turned the board to the right just as the wave curled high over my head in the instant of breaking. I streaked forward along the glassy tube just barely managing to stay ahead of the rolling break. I could hear its roar chasing me. I always loved the feeling of being locked in a big wave like that. It was so thrilling and scary. I raced along till I reached the shoulder of the wave, and then cut back  towards shore to let it build up again. When I turned into it again I saw the wave walling up in front of me, forming a high, straight, impossibly long section.

I knew then that I was in trouble. It was way too long a section. It was almost certain to fold over before I could make it through. I had to make a choice, and a quick one: either *kick out* now while I could, or take a long shot and try to squeak through.

I knew it was the wrong decision when I made it, but I went for it anyway. I was crazy as hell back then. As the wall got steep I walked forward on my board to gain speed. I angled down a little so as to position myself well below the center of the tube that was rapidly forming. As the thing curled over me I could see for certain that I wasn't going to make it. I ran to the nose and arched my back, sacrificing myself on the altar of the god of the sea – Kanaloa, Poseidon, Neptune, or whoever.

Then everything went dark and my heart nearly stopped as that huge wave came crashing down and gobbled me up. I was thrown off my board and sent tumbling. That wave pummeled me like an angry child with a rag doll, and did some pretty nasty things to me. Then she flushed me down an ice-cold toilet. I held my breath and curled in the prenatal position, hoping like hell I could hold my breath long enough, and that I wouldn't get slammed into something hard like my board or a big rock. Luckily, the water was still deep enough that I didn't hit bottom. After what seemed an eternity, the wave let me go and I somehow found my way to the surface.

I tread water, trying to catch my breath, looking around for my surfboard. It was nowhere to be seen. It was probably half way to the beach by now. We didn't use ankle leashes back then. We thought they would either rip your leg off or drown you somehow. Another huge wave came along and I had to dive deep down in the water to escape being sucked up into the turbulence again. Several more waves came, forcing me to dive each time. Finally, a lull settled in between sets. I was able to start the long, cold swim into the beach.

Despite the glassy aspect of the water, there was a strong current running parallel to the beach. As I swam towards shore I was drawn with the current towards the east. By the time I dragged my frozen carcass ashore I had drifted all the way to the foot of Palm St.

I looked up and down the beach for my board. Somebody must have dragged it out of the shore break, because I saw it perched up on a rock above the high water mark. I did the rock dance along the stony beach until I got to my board. I looked it over and was relieved to see that it had survived pretty much intact. It only had a few minor dings from hitting beach rocks.

I carried my board over to where I'd left my stuff on a rock below the low bluff. I toweled off, slipped into my second-hand trench coat, and made my way up to the bonfire. The bonfire, built with driftwood and surrounded by a concrete fire-circle, burned on the edge of the dirt parking lot. (The city had provided the circle to help keep us from burning the whole neighborhood down.) A handful of other young surfers were gathered around the fire warming themselves.

My toes were numb, my lips were blue, and my teeth were chattering like a pair of castanets. Hypothermia had numbed my brain too, and I felt as dumb as a donkey. I turned my back to the wind, and opened the front of my trench coat to the fire. The heat felt almost as good as sex.

My sometimes friend, Dremel, said to me, "Hey John, I saw you get wiped out. You really ate it, man. Why in the hell did you try to make that wave? It was impossible."

I tried to say "Fuck you, Dremel," but it came out all slurred. I was so cold I couldn't even talk.

But he got my drift. "Well, to hell with you then," he said, "See if I save your board again."

The boys around the bonfire had been talking about Vietnam when I first walked up. Now they started up again. My friend Deuce said he'd heard that Johnson was sending in more troops. The war was escalating. That meant more guys our age would be getting draft notices in the mail. A couple of the fellas said they were actually looking forward to it. They wanted to go. They thought it would be a blast. The rest of us just looked at one another. We didn't want any part of that action.

Most kids by the time they reach the age of nineteen, like I was then, have at least a general idea about what they want to do in life. Some, like those two idiots by the fire, want to go into the military. Some guys just want to find jobs, get a wife and start a family, some want to go away to college, and some just go looking for the fastest road to perdition. This last was the most likely route for me. In those days I didn't have any idea where I was going. I didn't know what I wanted out of life, or who I wanted to be. I only remember being frustrated and dissatisfied with just about everything. On top of that, I was angry. Angry with myself and angry at the world.

Just then I noticed an ancient panel truck turn off Beach Road. onto the last block of Palm St. It pulled up in front of The Point House. The truck had those old bug-eye headlights that hadn't been around since the 1940s. The van was an ugly maroon color, and along the side, painted in large black script, was the name "Rosinante."

I looked over at it wondering who was in it. I had never seen that panel truck down here before. I thought maybe it was a new surfer on the block. A bearded guy in his late 20s got out and slammed the door. He wore a greasy brown leather jacket, paint-splattered Levis, and army combat boots. His dishwater blond hair was long and wild and kinky. A lit cigarette dangled from his lips. Tucked under one arm was a large sketch pad, and slung over the opposite shoulder was an olive green daypack. He gave us all a look, and then stomped down the sidewalk towards the rear of The Point House.

"Who's that?" I asked. I didn't particularly like that look he gave us.

"Aw, that's Lenny's new roommate," said Deuce, who seemed to know everything that went on at The Point. "They call him Curly. He's some kind of artist or something."

I didn't realize it at the time, but I had just laid eyes on the man who would change my destiny.

Knockout at Foster's Freeze

1963

When I was eighteen I found myself deep in the throes of what I later learned was called teenage angst. I should have been over it by then, but I guess I was a late bloomer. I walked around most of the time with this really rotten feeling. I guess I was depressed or something. I found myself doing wild, unpredictable, almost suicidal things. Whenever I started feeling depressed it usually meant that trouble was not far off. And it certainly wasn't on one particular evening in early November.

On that night my surfer buddy, Moby, picked me up at my house in his turquoise 1954 Ford van. We called him Moby because his hair was so blond that it was nearly white. He was almost an albino, but not quite. Even though he had blue eyes his skin was normal and very suntanned from surfing. His nickname, Moby, was short for Moby Dick, the white whale. When we were mad at him we called him Dick Head.

That night Moby and I went down to a place on Ventura Avenue called The Friendly Market. It was friendly all right — they used to sell beer to minors if there was no one around. We bought a couple of six-packs of half-quarts of Brew 102, the cheapest beer you could buy. It was made in L.A., but it really didn't taste too bad. Then Moby and I drove down to the big dirt parking lot at The Point. We sat in the van and talked about surfing and drank beer until we got buzzed.

We saw a couple of other young surfers we knew doing the same thing down near the foot of Palm St. Moby and I took a leak off the bluff, and then went over to talk to them. Greg and Ron told us about a party they were going to out by Telegraph Tech. It was at the house of a girl they knew who was a senior at Buena High School. Her parents were out of town.

We followed Greg and Ron over there. The party was in full swing when we arrived. There must have been thirty or more kids there. About a dozen cars were parked along the street. Loud music came from the house, and we could hear everybody talking and laughing inside. We grabbed a couple of beers and followed Greg and Ron inside.

When we walked in the front door we saw a bunch of kids dancing in the living room. There were other boys and girls standing around talking and laughing or sitting on the couch or in chairs. It was noisy as hell. We went into the kitchen and were introduced to the girl who lived there. Her name was Ann. She was a pretty girl. There were about ten other kids crammed into the kitchen. I only recognized a couple of people at the party because most of the kids there were students at Buena High School. We four surfers had gone to Ventura High, Buena's cross-town rival.

Greg was talking to the girl, so the rest of us just sort of hung out in the kitchen. I saw that there were three guys wearing Buena letterman's jackets in the kitchen too. One of them was saying something about how they were going to kick Ventura High's ass this year in football. They all agreed. I couldn't help thinking his comments were directed at us. I took a drink of my beer and thought about it. I always seemed to take these things the wrong way back then. Instead of taking it as a joke, which is the way it was probably intended, I got mad instead. Instead of engaging them in a little friendly banter about the superiority of the Ventura High Cougars like I should have done, I just got sullen and didn't say anything.

The conversation changed after a little while, and I heard the big guy saying something about 'fucking surf rats.' Then they all laughed. Moby and my friends were not paying any attention. I guess they figured that these were just high school kids trying to mess with us. We were above all that. We had already graduated.

I couldn't overlook what he said, however. He was definitely referring to us. We were the only surfers in the kitchen. Now I knew there was going to be trouble. I stared at them with a sullen look on my face. The big guy, a guy who was obviously a football player, judging from his size and his letterman's jacket, said to me, "What are you looking at?" The kitchen suddenly became very quiet.

"A six-foot pile of shit," I said.

"Why you…" he said taking a step forward. I saw that he was actually more like 6'2" and weighed in at more than 200 pounds. I was 5'10" and about 150.

Then things got a little crazy. The football player and I tried to get at each other, while others in the kitchen tried to keep us apart. There was a lot of pushing and shoving and loud voices. Our hostess, Ann, had a terrified look on her face. "Oh, please," she begged, "Please don't fight. I don't want anything bad to happen. If my parents find out I'll be in big trouble."

"This guy is looking for trouble," I said. "I think he better leave."

"I'm not going anywhere, punk. I'll flatten you like a pancake." Again there was some pushing and shoving and yelling.

"You don't know who you're talking to," I said. "I'd kick your ass just as soon as look at you."

"Ha!" he said, "don't make me laugh, squirt."

This was all so typical. I'd been through this a dozen times before.

"I'll fight you anywhere, any time," I said.

"O.K." he said. "How about right now?"

"Oh, please," begged the girl. "If you have to fight, can't you please go somewhere else, Bob?" I guess the guy's name was Bob. I found out later he was an All-Channel League offensive tackle for the Buena football team.

"O.K., Annie," he said. "Hey you," he said, turning to me, "I'll meet you over at Foster's Freeze in ten minutes. That is if you're not too chicken." Foster's Freeze was a burger joint about a half a mile away.

"I'll be there," I said, "to attend your funeral."

"Ha," he said. He and three of his friends stalked out the front door and headed for their car.

I looked at my friends: Moby, Greg, and Ron. They were very quiet, and looked kind of pale. None of them were much bigger than I was.

I turned to Moby and said, "Hey, buddy, can you give me a ride over to Foster Freeze? I've got some Buena butt to kick." In my heart of hearts I was scared, but you would never have known it. I almost believed my own bravado. Apparently, my friends did too. They laughed and started chugging their beers in preparation for leaving.

We waited just long enough to give the football players time to drive off. Then we went out to our own cars. We decided that we would take one car and Moby would drive. Greg and Ron would ride with us, along with two or three other guys we knew at the party who decided to go along.

By this time Moby and I were about three-quarters drunk. I could tell he was happy and excited though. He had heard rumors of my fighting prowess but had never seen me in action. He was looking forward to it, especially because it was against such a big guy.

We all hurried out to his van and piled in. There were about seven of us. There were no seats in the back of the van, just an old mattress. This was Moby's surf wagon. Moby fired up the Ford and took off fast, burning rubber half-way down the block. He went around the corner going about forty. I guess he wasn't used to having so many people in his car. They added a lot of weight. As we went around the corner, centrifugal force swung the van out in a wide arc. Before we knew what was happening we skidded over next to the curb and slammed into the rear end of a parked car. Everybody in the back of the van went flying forward and ended up all scrunched up behind the front seats. Moby bashed his head on the steering wheel. I was sitting next to him, but I saw the accident coming and braced myself against the dash board.

Nobody got hurt very badly, just a few of bumps and bruises. Amid multiple groans and curses, we all piled out of the van to look at the damage. Porch lights went on all up and down the block. I guess the sound of the crash was pretty loud.

Moby's front end was all bashed in. We could tell the radiator was a goner because water and anti-freeze were leaking out onto the roadside. Both headlights were broken too and there was glass all over the place. The grill was smashed and the front bumper looked like a waffle. Moby groaned. He'd just had his van painted a couple of months before.

A couple of homeowners came out of their houses to see if anybody was hurt. One of them said, "Oh, no! That's my car." His back bumper and rear end were a crumpled mass mated to Moby's front end. The owner called to his wife standing back at their front door and told her to call the police.

I went into a huddle with Moby. I told him we had to get rid of all that beer in the van before the cops arrived. I told him I'd get Greg and Ron to help. The three of us made a subtle foray into the back of the van and scooped up the empties and the remainder of the full ones. While Moby was talking with the homeowner, we smuggled the full beers over to Greg's car which was parked a half a block away. We dumped the empties in somebody's bushes down the street. The cops arrived with flashing red lights just as we were heading back to the van.

I was getting pretty antsy by then. I was supposed to be at Foster Freeze right now duking it out with that beefy football player. I was obsessed with getting there as soon as possible. I didn't want that big jerk thinking I was a chicken. But now I was stuck.

I talked with Greg and Ron and the other guys while Moby was dealing with the cops. By then they were shining their flashlights around and inside his van. Greg said he could give me a ride in his car if I wanted. Ron was in too. They were eager to see the fight. But at the same time we wanted to stick with Moby until this mess was ironed out. After what seemed an eternity, the cops told us to push Moby's crippled van back to the closest parking spot. We did that, and then the cops left.

"God, I need a drink," said Moby, holding his hand to his bruised forehead.

"Come on," I said, "we've got the beer in Greg's car. Let's go. I've got a date at Foster's Freeze."

Greg had a little mini car and there was only room for four of us, so the other guys couldn't come. Greg drove and I sat shotgun. Moby and Ron sat in the back seat chugging beers on the way over to the burger joint.

When we first pulled into Foster's Freeze on Telegraph Ave. it looked like no one was there. By this time it was after eleven o'clock and the joint was closed. But as we pulled in we noticed there were a bunch of cars out in the back lot. There must have been twenty cars back there. They were parked in a semicircle right behind the burger joint, forming a kind of amphitheater. It reminded me of pictures I'd seen of ancient Greek amphitheaters, or maybe the Roman coliseum. I guess that made us gladiators.

Greg drove his car up next to the building and parked. "Oh, shit," he murmured as we saw about fifty kids all around those cars. All of Bob-the-football-player's friends were sitting on the hoods of their cars or standing between them talking to their girlfriends who sat inside. Some of them were smoking cigarettes and drinking cokes or beer. It was like a scene right out of that James Dean movie, "Rebel Without a Cause."

When we got out of the car, Bob stepped out of the semicircle and into the amphitheater. He said, "It's about time you got here, punk. We thought you chickened out."

"No such luck," I replied. I felt good now that I was there. I was pumped up. I knew he was a lot bigger than me, but that it didn't matter. I had fought a lot of big guys. In fact, I had never fought a guy my own size. They were always bigger. And they invariably underestimated me. They thought I would be a pushover. They took me for granted because I was small. Which was good for me. They didn't know how fast I was. Or how mean. I knew how to hurt people. Most big guys didn't know how to do that. They always relied on their size to intimidate people. Usually, they never even had to fight because their size scared most kids away.

Not that I wasn't scared. You're always scared going into a fight. You never know what the other guy is capable of until you mix it up with them.

My friends and I got out of the car. I stepped out into the amphitheater, leaving them behind.

I called out, "Let's get it on."

Bob quickly stripped off his letterman's jacket and handed it to one of his pals. He looked huge even without it. I was smaller of course, but I had big shoulders and pretty strong arms from all the paddling I'd been doing over the years. I was dressed that night in a white t-shirt, Levis, and boots.

We began the preliminary circle dance that is so common to these affairs.

"Let's make a few rules before we start," I said, circling to my left. "No hitting or kicking the other guy when he's down."

"O.K." said Bob, exuding supreme confidence.

"And when you've had enough," I said, "just let me know and I'll stop."

"Ha!" said Bob.

That's when I punched him in the mouth.

"Ow!"

The crowd started yelling and screaming. I could hear them cheering Bob on. Behind me I heard Moby yell, "Get him, John."

I managed to jab Bob a few more times before he got good and mad. People generally don't like getting hit in the face. He roared like a bull, and then lunged forward with his arms outstretched. It was almost comical. He really looked like a wild-eyed charging bull. I knew better than to let him get his hands on me. If he grabbed me and started punching me I was a goner. He was just too big and strong.

I ducked down and his arms closed over thin air. But he was leaning over the top of me now. I didn't like that. I had to be out in the open where I could use my speed. He tried to grab me but I wriggled free. But he swiveled like a good lineman and was bent over me again like King Kong or something. I threw a blind uppercut. Since I was crouched below him, I lifted with my legs and put all my weight behind the punch. I guess I got lucky. The uppercut caught him square on the chin.

I heard him grunt as his head snapped back. His body straightened up, and he keeled over backwards like a felled tree. I heard the back of his head hit the blacktop with a solid thud. It sounded like somebody just dropped a watermelon.

There was a sudden silence as everybody stopped cheering. They had heard the thud too. I stood there breathing heavily, looking down at Bob. He wasn't moving. I glanced over at Moby and my friends. They were looking down at him. I looked over at all of Bob's friends. They were looking too. I was probably more scared then than any of them. I thought I might have hurt him real bad, or killed him, and I didn't know what his friends might do.

"Hey, Bob," I said, talking down to his prone body. No response. Then, louder, "Hey, Bob!" Thankfully, he groaned, and began to roll his head weakly back and forth on the blacktop.

"That's it, Bob," I said. "It's all over now. Nice fight." I reached down and took hold of his right hand and helped him to his feet. Some of his friends came over to see if he really was all right. He stood there weaving and holding his head with both hands. I turned and walked back to my friends by the car.

"Let's get the hell out of here," I whispered.

We got into Greg's car. He started the engine. I looked back and saw about six of Bob's friends standing around him, comforting him.

"Drive," I said. Greg put it in gear and took off.

"Jesus, John," said Moby. "That was *so* fast. Sooo fast. I've never seen anything like it."

The other two guys were silent. I think they were just glad to get out of there in one piece.

Telegraph Tech
1964

About a week after that foggy surfing day at The Point, I walked into the Student Center at Telegraph Tech and saw the guy they called Curly for the second time. Telegraph Tech, by the way, was how we cynically referred to Ventura College, the local community college out on Telegraph Ave. Students who enrolled there fell into one of the following categories: they were either university rejects, young women looking for a husband, future tradesmen and secretaries, starry-eyed educational lifers, ambitious immigrants, soppy shmucks trying to better themselves, or young cannon fodder like me just killing time waiting to be drafted. Telegraph Tech had no entry requirements and was the cheapest and easiest two years of college you could buy.

As I walked towards the lunch counter, I noticed Curly sitting at a round table with two buxom girls and a young man. Curly was the strangest looking person I'd ever seen on campus. He had on a weird green and orange shirt that looked like it came from a thrift store. He had the sleeves rolled up and the front buttons opened down to his bellybutton showing off his hairy chest. A tarnished silver chain hung from his neck. Around his right wrist was a two-inch wide leather cuff that looked dark with age and long wear. He was drinking coffee from a foam cup and smoking a cigarette. His long kinky hair looked like he'd stuck his finger in a light socket. He had a moustache and kinky beard too.

As I walked by he turned to the very attractive girl sitting next to him and said, "That's the most ridiculous thing I've ever heard. If you weren't so ignorant you wouldn't go around saying stupid things like that. You don't know the first thing about Nietzsche. Do us all a favor – if you can't say something intelligent, don't say anything at all."

The girl's face turned bright red. She was so taken aback and humiliated that she immediately stood up and muttered something about having to go to class. Then she walked off with her nose in the air. Her girlfriend got up and went with her. I was sorry I'd missed what she'd said to bring all that on.

I went and bought myself a cheeseburger, fries, and a coke at the lunch counter. I flirted with the girl behind the  counter, and she gave me an extra helping of fries. The Student Center was crowded, it being noontime, and the only empty chairs I could find were at Curly's table. So I went over and asked if they'd mind if I joined them.

"It's a free country," said Curly, giving me a cursory glance. Then he went on talking to the other guy at the table. The guy turned out to be Lenny, his roommate, who I had seen a few times arriving or departing from The Point House in recent months. Lenny was a dark-haired boy in his early twenties, with beautiful blue Bambi-like eyes. Seeing Lenny up close for the first time made me think of a photograph I'd seen recently of that statue *David* by Michelangelo. He looked like he could have been David's twin.

"Listen here, Lenny," said Curly, leaning forward on his hairy forearms, "I know the rent is overdue, but I'm broke. Don't worry though, I know this woman who wants to buy one of my paintings. She's Deb's mother. You know Debbie... from our drawing class. Her mother's coming by the apartment tonight. I think I can get twenty-five bucks out of her. That will cover my half of the rent and the gas and electric bill. They'll even be some left over for food."

Lenny sighed with resignation. "What painting is she interested in?"

"The Only Girl I Ever Loved #23."

"That red one?"

"Of course."

"Can I ask you a favor?" said Lenny, looking worried. "Could you not be rude to her when she comes?"

"Who? Me?" Curly dismissively snuffed his cigarette out in the ashtray.

"I know your mother must have taught you good manners. Can't you at least try?"

"Leave my mother out of this. Don't worry, Lenny, I'll be on my best behavior."

"Speaking of behavior," said Lenny, "I wish you wouldn't use my bath towel anymore."

"Ahhh, man. Mine was so stiff it could stand up by itself."

"Take it to the laundromat. And your blankets and underwear while you're at it."

"I told you, I'm broke."

"Here," said Lenny, digging a dollar bill out of his pocket. "Go to the laundromat. I'm going up to the studio to do some painting." Lenny stood up. "I'll see you back at the house."

Curly pocketed the dollar bill. He sat back and crossed his arms with satisfaction. After about a minute he glanced down at my plate and said, "Mmm-mmm. They sure are generous with their fries around here. You can't possibly eat them all, can you, fella?"

"Probably not," I said. "Knock yourself out."

"What are you? A poet? Ha-ha." Curly picked up a big fat fry right off the top, dabbed it in my puddle of ketchup, and bit into it. I noticed his fingernails were very long and not all that clean.

Ignoring his flippancy, I asked, "So who's this Nietzsche I heard you talking about?"

Curly sighed. "Why am I surrounded by dunces?" he muttered. "For your information, Friedrich Nietzsche is probably the most important philosopher that ever lived, that's who. He not only challenged traditional morality, but Christianity as well. If you knew anything about anything you would know that he is the most influential thinker of modern times. All the philosophers of the twentieth century, all the psychologists, theologists, writers, critics, or whatever... they all owe him a huge debt. You, obviously, don't owe him anything."

I didn't like that last crack. "I may owe you a fat lip," I said, getting my Irish up. "Who in the hell do you think you're talking to? You don't know me."

"Thank God for small favors," he said. "You don't know me either. Let's keep it that way." He crossed his hairy arms and gazed out the floor-to-ceiling windows that looked out on the quad.

I was seriously considering standing up and smacking him one. But I figured I'd probably get kicked out of Telegraph Tech if I did. And, to tell you the real truth, I was more interested in eating my cheeseburger than in busting his head.

"That's fine with me," I said, taking a bite.

We continued to sit in silence for a few minutes – me chomping at my food, and Curly slurping his coffee – with a little more gusto than was warranted. Although I was a still a little miffed at him, I was amused by his outspoken directness, and I was a little bit curious. He seemed so much more self-assured than most of the young people I knew. He was obviously smart, and I imagined he was well-read too. And he didn't seem to feel threatened by me at all. I guess that was because he didn't know how crazy and volatile I was back then. I used to go around with this monumental chip on my shoulder, and I was ready to fight anybody at the slightest provocation.

Eventually my curiosity got the better of me and I decided to break our agreed upon silence.

"What did that girl say about Nietzsche that made you rank on her so bad?"

He turned his head imperially. "Oh, that. She had the nerve to say that she heard Hitler used Nietzsche's views to justify Nazism. She is not only ill-bred and ill-read, but woefully misinformed. Everyone knows the Nazis took a few of Nietzsche's aphorisms out of context and twisted them to justify the means by which they extended their power. She should have known better than to shoot her mouth off like that."

251

"Do you always talk to good-looking chicks that way?" I asked. "I never do."

He looked disdainfully at me and said, "I don't care what she looks like. She was wrong. All I did was set her straight."

After a pause, I said, "You live down at The Point, right?"

He gave me a questioning look and said, "Yes I do. How do you know that?"

"I saw you down there last week. I'm a surfer."

"Oh." He sounded bored.

"I saw your brown van down there too. It's pretty cool."

"Oh, yes. But she's not brown; she's burgundy. Her name is Rosinante." He smiled for the first time. "She's a classic isn't she?"

"What's this 'Rosinante' supposed to mean?"

Curly sighed and looked at my plate. "The answer to that will cost you another *pomme frite*, my friend." He reached across the table. "By the way," he said, picking up the best one and dipping it in ketchup, "you don't read much, do you?"

"What do you mean?"

"Have you ever read Cervantes?"

"Cervantes? I don't think so. But he sounds familiar."

"Ever hear of *Don Quixote*?"

"Oh, yeah. The guy who fought with windmills."

Curly nodded. "Well, at least you know that much. Cervantes was the guy who wrote it. Rosinante was Don Quixote's steed. And she's mine too. Ha-ha!" He absent-mindedly reached for another fry. I could tell he was hungry. But I wasn't sure I liked him being so forward with my fries. At that point in my life I didn't like much about people in general. I still had half a mind to kick his ass. But I have to admit, I kind of admired his attitude. It reminded me a little of my own, only mine was stupider.

Curly continued, "But I would be willing to bet that you never read Cervantes in your life. What in the world are you doing at Ventura College anyway?"

I considered his question carefully, and then answered quite truthfully, "I don't know. I guess you could say I don't know what else to do with myself. But you're wrong about me not being a reader. I like to read."

"Oh? You don't seem the type."

I shrugged. "Besides the reading I do for my classes, I read books."

"What kind of books?"

"Novels mostly. But right now I'm reading a collection of short stories by Jack London."

"Jack London? How quaint. London was one of those American Naturalists. He was a decent writer, I suppose, but I don't think he never wrote anything of lasting worth. Unless you want to count a couple of short stories and maybe that dog novel. I think he may have read Nietzsche though. You can see it in his Determinism, and his themes about the Will to Power. But I think he always stated the obvious: like 'The world is a bad place and if you're not careful it will crush you. And even if you are careful, it can still crush you.' So what else is new?"

"Well, I like him anyway. He's a good story teller."

"Why don't you tell me the story of how you got that shiner?"

"Oh, this?" I said, reaching for my eye. "I got in a fight last weekend. Some guy sucker punched me downtown. 'Just because I was out with his girlfriend. Hell, I didn't know she was his girlfriend. But if you think my eye looks bad, you should see what he looks like. He had to go to the hospital and get his face stitched up."

"So, you're a tough guy, huh?"

"I can be."

"You don't look the type."

"What do you mean by that?"

He looked me over. "Well, you're what... maybe 5'10", 150 pounds? You're too small and skinny to be a tough guy. You look like a middle-class pretty boy with your V-neck sweater and your creased pants. You don't even have a broken nose or cauliflower ears. Not yet anyway. Tough guys don't look like you."

"What are you, an expert?"

"I've been around the block a few times. And I've been around long enough to know that no matter how tough you are, someone tougher will come along sooner or later. There's no future in being a tough guy."

"Thanks for the advice."

I looked Curly over, sizing him up. I could tell he was out of shape. And I noticed that even though he was still in his twenties he was starting to get those little alcoholic spider veins on his nose and cheeks. I knew I could make short work of him. I think he knew it too. But he didn't seem to care. He grabbed another french fry.

"Your name's Curly, right?"

He looked at me again. "That's what some people call me."

"What's your real name?"

He crossed his arms and chewed for a while before answering, "You can call me Jason. What's yours?"

"John."

"'Pleased to meet you, I'm sure. Say, uh, John, are you going to eat all of that burger? It looks pretty appetizing."

"I draw the line at my burger, pal. I'm hungry too. Have another fry." And he did.

I said, "Jason, huh? That sounds Greek. Jason and the Argonauts and the Golden Fleece and all that, right?"

"You're not as ignorant as you look."

I laughed. "Gee, thanks," I said. His audacity was growing on me.

"But I'm not Greek," he said, "I'm Irish."

I told him the reason I knew about Jason was because I was taking a World History class that semester and we were reading about ancient Greece just then. I found it pretty interesting.

"You should read everything you can about the Greeks," he said in reply.

"Oh, yeah? Why's that?"

"Because they'll tell you everything you want to know. They developed most of the principles western civilization are based on. In more ways than not, we still think like the Greeks."

"Oh, yeah? Who do you think I should read?"

"Everybody. You've got to read Homer, of course. He wrote about the Greek gods, which were extremely important in their society, and in the way they saw the world. Then you've got to read the great philosophers: Socrates, Plato, and Aristotle. And while you're at it, read some of the tragic dramatists: Aeschylus, Sophocles, and Euripides. That should do for a start."

"That's a handful."

"Well, do you want to learn anything or not?"

"Yeah, sure I do. That's why I'm here, I guess."

"You better do more than guess, kid. I don't want to waste my time on you if you don't want to improve your mind. You seem like you've got a decent head on your shoulders. Either do something with it, or go out and get a job. Or if you're such a tough guy, why don't you join the army?"

"I'd rather do something with my mind. I want to do something good for a change. The way things are going, everything is turning to shit. I get into a lot of trouble. I want to learn something good. I need some answers. About life I mean. I'd like to figure out what it's all about."

"Ha. Good luck with that, kid."

I decided to ignore his wise cracks. "What makes you think the Greeks have anything to teach me anyway?" I said. "It doesn't seem that they would. I mean they were talking about things the way they were a long time ago. But I'm living now in the twentieth century. I need something that can help me now."

"If you want to learn anything worthwhile, you had better commit yourself to settling down and getting to work. You've got to start reading when you're young. Otherwise there won't be enough time. You'll get settled in your ignorance and your brain will turn to stone. There's too much to learn. More than you can ever learn anyway. How old are you, kid?"

"The name is John. I just turned nineteen."

"Oh, well, it's not too late. But you've got to buckle down and make up for lost time. And you've got to start with the Greeks."

"Come to think of it," he said, reaching into his daypack, "here's a book you can start with. It just came out this year. It gives a nice overview." Curly pulled out a book and held it out to me. It was called *Ancient Greece: The Triumph of a Culture* by somebody named Robert Paine.

I wiped my hands on my napkin, and took it. It was a hefty book, well over 400 pages.

"Wow," I said, "You're lending it to me?"

"Your grasp of the obvious is admirable. I'm finished with it, kid, and I'm tired of lugging it around. It's not a bad read, even though it only skims the surface. But you have to return it to me. It was a gift from a friend."

"But... but you don't even know me."

"Oh, I know you. I can read *you* like a book. I can tell you're too honorable not to return it." I couldn't be sure if he was being sarcastic or not.

I opened the book and thumbed through it. It looked like a history book. It had about thirty chapters, and had quite a few photo plates of Greek sculpture and architecture, along with some pen and ink drawings, and maps.

"This is great." I said. "I really appreciate you lending it to me."

"Bring it down to The Point when you're done and we'll talk. By the way, were you planning to drink the last of that coke?"

256

Dispatch from Berlin #7

1998

Subject: The Visitor
Date: Friday, 21 August, 1998

Wilkommen, stranger. It sure is nice having a visitor for a change. We don't get many of you these days. Now that you've had a chance to freshen up a bit, what would you like to do? Gretchen won't be home until about 1800 hours. It's a fine day for a walk, don't you think? Perhaps we should take a little stroll around the neighborhood. I can show you the sights. We can take the air, such as it is, and stretch our legs.

But before we go, I think you'd better change your shoes. Stilettos are not the best heels for the cobblestone sidewalks here in Berlin. You see, the Germans don't make their sidewalks out of concrete the way the Americans do. They don't pour slabs and make them all smooth and level. Those five-inch spiked heels of yours won't work very well here. I'd probably end up having to carry you home with a sprained ankle. My, but those *are* handsome boots you're wearing.

In Berlin, and all other German towns, they make their sidewalks by laying quarried stone down on a thick bed of sand. They use stone of assorted sizes, shapes and colors, and lay them down in various geometric patterns. Then they mortise them in place with more sand, run over them with a heavy roller, and then hose them off and sweep them clean. There's your sidewalk. One reason they make them this way is because all the utilities are underground, under the sidewalk. Placing them there is a good idea because then there are no unsightly utility poles and your infrastructure is spared the ravages of the harsh winters. And it is fairly easy to make repairs too. You just dig up the cobbles and the sand underneath. Then you make your repairs to the phone, power, water, or sewer lines. After that you just replace the sand and the stones, piece by piece. It requires some labor, yes, but then you don't have unemployment problems either. And you don't have to break up concrete, haul it off, and repour like the wasteful Americans.

One of the down sides of German sidewalks is that the crevices between the cobblestones make perfect nesting places for small bits of trash. They are especially suitable for cigarette butts. They get stuck down in there and nothing short of picking them out by hand will move them. I haven't seen anyone employed in this fashion so far. Another thing, cobblestone sidewalks are of absolutely no use to skate-boarders and in-line skaters. Ha-ha. And one last down side: it is not uncommon for clumsy or infirm pedestrians to trip, fall and go boom on the uneven surface.

So, stranger, while you change your shoes I'll just take a couple of hits off my asthma inhaler. It's not that I'm having an attack or anything, it's just that the air is a bit polluted out there. Well, if you insist on pressing me on the subject, O.K., the air is pretty bad. Well, O.K., it makes L.A.'s look good by comparison. Are you satisfied? But don't worry about me. I'll be all right. Just one more hit on my inhaler ought to keep my lungs open for a while.

Oh, and by the way, I hope you're not planning to change into waffle-soled shoes. I advise against it. They don't have Scoop Laws here in Berlin. I'm sure you've heard of doggy land mines. You might expect to encounter a few choice ones on our walk today. And I can tell you from experience that waffle-soled shoes are definitely not the best choice. Perhaps you have a pair of nice flat-soled shoes you could wear. They're easier to clean at any rate. Many, many Germans have dogs. As a general rule they like small lap dogs. But some like big dogs too. Our neighbor has an Afghan hound. The skinheads in Berlin like big dogs too: Dobermans and Rottweilers and huge pit bulls. They give them spiked collars and walk them around on chains looking for Arabs and Turks and other foreigners. But that's beside the point. All the people here like to walk their dogs. And dogs, being dogs, do what they do best on the sidewalks.

Oh, yeah, and you might wear a hat. There are a lot of pigeons out there that like to roost in the eaves six stories up.

258

There's always the chance that you might get bombed. The crows have a pretty good sense of humor when it comes to dive-bombing people too. Granted, the chances of you getting hit are slim, but I've seen it happen. I beg your pardon? You wonder if I'm going to wear a hat? You better believe it. I may be dumb but I'm no fool.

Doggonit, I just thought of something else too. When we get out there it would be best if you keep a close watch on the other pedestrians. I have found that the Germans aren't very adept at walking down a crowded sidewalk. They don't seem to watch where they're going. They seem to get distracted pretty easily. They just walk along looking in the shop windows or talking to one another or reading the graffiti that's scrawled on all the walls. The foot traffic doesn't seem to fall into a pattern either, you know, like keeping to the right, passing on the left, etc. There don't seem to be any right-of-way rules here at all. So people are forever bumping into one another. They wouldn't last five minutes on the streets of Manhattan. They would either be trampled underfoot or roundly cursed. Or both.

Many times I have seen Germans walk briskly out of stores directly into the path of foot traffic and run headlong into somebody. Wham! When it happens, they get this really surprised look on their faces. Like, How did this happen? I was just walking along minding my own business when ka-blam! Ach du liebe! And they never seem to learn anything from the experience. It is most frustrating. And it can be a little dangerous too. Two out of every three of them will be smoking a cigarette when they run into you. I'd hate to see that nice leather cat suit you're wearing get a burn in it.

And while we're on the subject of crowds: keep a good grip on that very large handbag of yours. There are plenty of pickpockets out there. That riding crop I saw in your handbag might come in handy. Or was it a quirt? If somebody tries to reach into your bag you could just give his hand a smack with it. Ha-ha. Just kidding. No, ma'am, I didn't mean to be impertinent.

By the way, do they have horses where you live? I saw what looked like spurs in your handbag too. Maybe we should go over to the Tiergarten. It's just across the Ku'damm from here. I think they have riding stables over there. Maybe we could rent a couple of nags and go for a ride. What? No, I'm not trying to be a smart-aleck. No, really. I'm just trying to be a good host.

Are you getting hungry? The reason I ask is that I thought we might stop at an Imbiss while we're out. An Imbiss is a sidewalk fast food stand here in Berlin. They sell mostly sausages with buns, and sometimes wienerschnitzel and pomme frites. You can also get canned sodas or beer or bottled water. Oh, by the way. I'd advise against drinking the tap water here. It is very hard, and full of chlorine. And it tastes pretty bad. Better stick to bottled water, or use a Brita filter like I do. At any rate, most of these Imbisses are Mom & Pop enterprises. Some of them are good and others not so good. You have to look sharp to see that they run a clean place. I got sick at an Imbiss over on the East Side once. Well, not really sick, but after I ate there it felt like some Nazi had kicked me in the stomach a couple of times with his jackboots.

I always feel kind of funny when I buy a rostbratwurst at an Imbiss anyway. The sausage is about sixteen inches long and they serve it to you in a bun that's about six inches long. They slather the sausage with mustard and send you on your way. Sometimes when I walk away from an Imbiss I feel like a real imbecile with this tiny bun in my hand and about five inches of curving dog sticking out on either end. The first time I bought one I was a little paranoid walking down the sidewalk. I thought everyone was looking at me funny because the guy had pulled a practical joke on me. But, no, they really are served like that. I guess the passersbys were just looking at me because maybe they wanted a bite. But I don't think I'll have any trouble with passersbys when I'm walking with the likes of you. You look pretty fit. You have big muscles for a woman. Incidentally, are you cold, or do you always wear those elbow length gloves? If we eat at an Imbiss I hope you don't get mustard on them. Ha-ha.

What? No I didn't mean anything by that either. I'm just kidding around. By the way, that's real kid leather isn't it? And such a nice shade of black.

Oh, I just thought of something else. I do hope you have a valid passport. Why? Because it's a good idea to carry it with you at all times. If for some strange reason while we're out walking we get stopped by the Polizei, you will certainly want to have proper identification on your person. I hate to think what might happen if your papers were not in order. This place is still pretty much a police state, you know.

What is that you say? I'm sorry I didn't hear you. My, I do prattle on, don't I? Now, what was that? You say you're not going for a walk with me? You don't walk much anyway? You usually take taxis? Oh, really? I do too sometimes. I find it kind of interesting that all the taxis in Berlin are Mercedes Benzes. It makes me feel regal when I ride in one.

What? You have no interest in taxis? And you have no interest in taking a walk around my funky neighborhood? Well, that's pretty stuffy of you I should think. It's really quite an interesting place. Come on, it'll be fun. Let's go out. Gretchen won't be back for a couple of hours yet.

What's that you say? You never heard of Gretchen? But I thought you were a colleague of hers from Copenhagen or London or somewhere? Isn't that why you rang our doorbell? No? Oh, no. This isn't apartment Five A. This is Six A. You must have rung the wrong doorbell. I've been expecting someone else altogether – her colleague. Oh, how stupid.

No, no. I don't mean you're stupid. Don't get mad. Yes, I did say something before about you being stuffy. I didn't mean that either. You're not stuffy, really. But my, you sure do have a temper, don't you? Alright. I'll shut up.

I didn't catch where you're from, ma'am? Berlin!? Oh, my god! I had no idea. Well, I should have figured it out by your appearance. You're so... so... stern-looking. And your garb, that's the Berlin Decadent Look, right? I might have guessed. But, I must say, your English is quite good. Much better than most Germans. And you have hardly any accent at all. I hope you weren't offended by some of the things I said about your hometown. You were? Well, I'm sorry. Really I am. Did anyone ever tell you how much you look like Marlene Dietrich?

Oops. No, please don't get offended. I didn't mean you looked old. Well, yes, I suppose I was a little out of line. Well, that too. But I don't agree with you. I don't really think I deserve to be punished for it. Can't we just be friends? No, huh? Gosh, you Berliners sure are a tough lot. No, I'm not saying I don't like it. No, not at all. It's an admirable quality I'm sure. What are you digging for in that voluminous bag of yours? Yeah, I know it's none of my business.

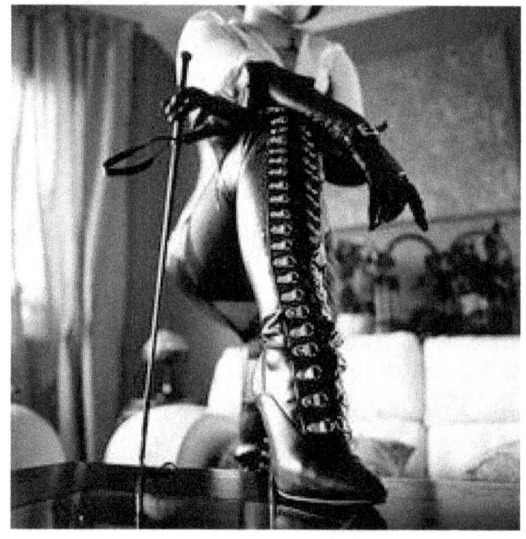

Gulp. Gee, how am I gonna get out of this one? While I do some fast figuring here, I had best bid you all a fond farewell from der Faderland.

My Dinner with Andrea

2005

Andrea invited me over to her place for dinner the other night. I brought along a few items that I thought might make the evening more gratifying. We began by uncorking my bottle of bubbly and getting to know each other better. I admired Andrea's luxurious walnut hair, her steamy blueberry eyes, and her plump raspberry lips. Her figure reminded me of a three-minute egg timer and her complexion was as clear as sifted flour. She had muffin written all over her. As the bottle got lighter I found myself working up quite an appetite for her.

Andrea seemed to be getting hungry too. She said she liked my spiky hair, which reminded her of meringue pie. She liked my gumball eyes too, as well as my caramel skin, my licorice-stick moustache and peppermint grin. I guess we both had a sweet tooth that night.

We decided to start cooking right away. Andrea spread her goods out on the kitchen table in a mouthwatering array of luscious shapes, colors and aromas. My stomach growled at the sight.

The first thing that caught my attention was her melons. I reached out and grabbed the two of them. I began fondling and juggling those succulent orbs with a dexterity that impressed even me. Indeed, they were so round, so firm, so perfectly formed that I couldn't take my hands off of them. Andrea seemed to be pleased with my admiration of them. Eventually, however, I was distracted by the two strawberries Andrea had playfully perched on top of them. They looked so nice and pointy, so ripe and juicy. I couldn't resist bending over and taking one in my mouth and sucking on it. There is nothing quite so enchanting as sipping champagne and then sucking on a sweet strawberry.

I was distracted again when Andrea opened my bag of goodies and pulled out the huge Polish sausage I'd brought along. She ran her hand up and down its gleaming length.

"What were you planning for dinner?" I croaked.

"Originally I thought of meatballs with noodle," she said, "but now that I've discovered this big Kielbasa of yours I'm thinking better of it."

"We could mash a few potatoes to go with it," I said, looking down at her white rounded loins and creamy thighs.

Distracted once more, I naively said, "Hey, what's that smell?"

"I'm steaming," she replied.

"You're steaming?"

"My sauerkraut is steaming."

"It smells inviting."

Andrea blushed and said, "I was famished so I started early."

"Why don't we have a little snack before we get down to the main course?" I suggested.

"What did you have in mind?" she asked, demurely.

"You could nibble on this nice crisp carrot I brought along. There are some plump cherry tomatoes too. Yes, they're down there in the sack. Meanwhile, I'll play around with your potatoes and sauerkraut and see what I can do."

"Ooh, sounds scrumptious."

While enjoying a few hors d'oeuvres we got down to some serious cooking. Andrea boiled my Polish till it was ready to burst. In the meantime I whipped up her mashed potatoes so they were nice and hot and frothy. I turned her feathery sauerkraut into a work of art: it was wet, warm, well-groomed and pungent.

I could see a desperate hunger in Andrea's eyes. Hoarsely she said, "Why don't you stick that Polish in there with the sauerkraut?"

"Alright then!" I said enthusiastically. "Here goes."

"Ooooh, dreamy," she crooned.

I plopped her mashed potatoes down, and then we fell to. My Polish disappeared in no time, enveloped in a fragrant mass of sauerkraut. The mashed potatoes vanished under the onslaught of our hunger. That little piggy Andrea gorged herself as though she hadn't been fed in a month. We didn't talk at all while we dined. We were too busy filling ourselves with pleasure.

When at last we both reached glorious satisfaction, and were, for a time, sated, Andrea sighed and looked up at me with those sloe, sleepy eyes of hers. She said, "My god, that was totally tubular! Where in the world did you get that Kielbasa?"

"It's an old family recipe, passed on from father to son."

"Are you ready for dessert?" she asked, timorously.

"Give me a little time to digest, won't you, love? But I am looking forward to something sweet. By the way, what's on the dessert menu?"

"Well, all I have on hand is a jelly-filled donut."

"That'll do for starters. But before we're finished I think we can manage a chocolate éclair."

"You are a decadent man," she said, licking her lips.

*   *   *   *   *   *   *   *   *

AWARD

FictionWeek's 2005 Western Hemispheric
Best Worst Sex Scene Writing Contest

Awarded for writing this year's
best worst sex scene by far

Presented to:

TERRENCE FRANCIS TALLENT

The Greeks

1964

One day after my last class at Telegraph Tech, I drove down to The Point to check out the surf. I had no back seat in my car and that allowed me to carry my board with me. I'd stick it in through the trunk with the nose resting on the folded down passenger-side front seat. That way I could keep it locked in the car while I was at school. I turned down Palm St. and pulled up to the wooden barricade at the end of the street. The rocky beach lay just beyond it. The wind was wailing, the tide was out, and the surf was small and choppy. The Point was obviously *blown out*. As I was backing up my Fairlane I noticed Curly sitting on a couch on the front porch of The Point House. He had an open book in one hand and held a ceramic coffee mug in the other. I pulled over and parked the car. I withdrew *Ancient Greece: The Triumph of a Culture* from the scatter of books under the folded down front seat, and made my way towards the house.

The wooden porch where Curly sat was on the east side of the house, so it was sheltered from the wind. As I climbed the steps, Curly looked up from his book.

"Well, well," he said, "if it ain't Rocky Marciano."

"Hey, Curly. I'm here to return your book."

"Ah, good. That was fast. How was it?"

"It was great," I said, holding it out to him. "I see what you meant when you said the Greeks were the basis of our civilization."

He put his mug on the arm of the couch and took the book. "Indubitably. Have a seat, lad."

I sat down on the couch, which had obviously seen better days. The Greeks probably put it here during the Golden Age. The springs were sprung, the covering was weather-beaten, and here and there stuffing stuck out of the cushions.

"We are indebted to the ancient Greeks for many things," said Curly. "But they are indebted to somebody too.

266

They owe a special thanks to their god Dionysus. He gave them wine." He held up his ceramic mug. "Here's to Dionysus and his great gift to the Greeks." He took a drink. He looked like he'd had a few already. He glanced over at me and said, "Would you like a drink?"

"Sure."

He pulled a gallon jug of Red Mountain Vin Rose from behind the couch. "Have you got something to pour it into? I don't bring glasses out here. They tend to break."

I went and got an empty paper cup from my car. He sloshed some of the cheap red wine into it, and then refilled his mug. "Here's to the Greeks," he said. We touched cups and drank. It tasted pretty bad. Red Mountain was a buck and a half a gallon back then. And if the truth were known, it wasn't even real wine; it was fortified with alcohol.

"I saw a picture of Dionysus in that book," I said. "He was a gnarly looking dude. Oh, and I saw your photograph in there too."

"What? What are you talking about? What photograph?" He looked at me suspiciously, and then at the book.

I said, "I was looking at the photo plates of some Greek busts. There's one in there of Euripides. He looked just like you, only older. Your face, your beard, your hair (although yours is kinkier), your nose, especially your nose."

"No. You're kidding me."

"Look for yourself. It's near the end."

He thumbed through the book and quickly found the photograph.

"Well, I'll be damned," he said. "I never noticed that before."

"I really loved that book," I said. I was excited about it and wanted to tell him everything. I told him that even though I

267

might have neglected my regular school work at Telegraph Tech, I read *Ancient Greece* in only a week. It was so great. It was one of those "I couldn't put it down" books. I knew some of that stuff from high school, and from my current World History class, but for the first time in my life I gained a real appreciation for the Greeks. The book gave me so much insight into their history, philosophy, art, government, and science.

I told Curly how fascinating it was reading about the different gods the Greeks worshiped. I was particularly taken with Dionysus. Everything Dionysus stood for appealed to me: he was the god of the erect phallus, the god of wine, the god of orgiastic and barbarian rituals, the god of physical pleasure. I was drawn to Apollo too, the terrible avenger who later became the god of healing.

I went on to tell him how jazzed I was by the military exploits of the ancient Greeks, and how cool I thought the Greek armaments were, especially their beautiful plumed helmets and embossed shields. I was amazed at all the battles they won at the very last moment, battles against seemingly insurmountable odds. They were so often blessed with incredible luck. But even so, they seemed to succeed primarily by sheer force of will. They also exhibited the utmost in daring, and their victories were punctuated by the ruthless slaughter of their enemies. Those qualities appealed to me. Reading about the Spartans, and later, Alexander the Great, had really brought home to me "the glory that was Greece."

It seemed miraculous to me that the Greeks managed to survive at all, I told him, much less prosper – especially since they were really nothing more than a loose confederation of city-states. Left to themselves, they could never seem to agree on anything. In fact, they often warred against each other. It was only at the last minute, facing ultimate defeat at the hand of their common enemies, that they somehow managed to work together just long enough to prevail. And then Greece flowered in what is called The Golden Age. What a glorious time that must have been, even though it lasted for less than fifty years. I loved the idea of the 'citizen soldier,' the one who was educated, physically fit, and fully engaged in political debate. The book left me full of wonder.

While I was telling him all this, Curly was grinning and quietly sipping his wine. When I was done, he said, "My word, you really got into it, didn't you, Rocky? Well, I'm glad you liked it, but that book only scratches the surface. You've got to dig a lot deeper than that to find their true essence. But I doubt that you ever will."

"Why do you say that?"

"Because you're a babe in the woods. You don't even know how. And besides, you need to look around a little and get your bearings. I think it's good that you at least have an idea of what the Greeks were all about though. That's more than most people have."

"What's that you're reading?" I asked, looking down at the two books by his side. One was a small paperback called "Has Man a Future?" by somebody named Bertrand Russell – an English philosopher. (I read some of his books a few months later.) Curly held up the other book for me to see. It was a trade paperback edition of *A Casebook on the Beat,* edited by Thomas Parkinson. "I'm revisiting the Beats right now," he said.

"What's the Beats?" I asked.

"Holy Jesus, Mary and Joseph," he said, shaking his head. You are such a square. You probably call them Beatniks. That's what those idiots in the press call them. I'm talking about great writers like Jack Kerouac, Allen Ginsberg, William Burroughs, Lawrence Ferlinghetti, Gregory Corso..."

"'Can't say as I know 'em. I've heard of Ginsberg though. Something about him being banned." I took a drink and grimaced at the taste.

"Ah, Jeez. What am I going to do with you, boy? Where in the hell have you been for the last ten years, you dumb puppy?"

"I ain't no puppy."

"Look here, Jack, or John or whatever. You have really got to start reading. You are like... nowhere, man."

"You kind of sound like a Beatnik."

"Shut up, will you? I'm serious." He took a drink. "Here's your next assignment, since you say you read novels. Read *On The Road* by Jack Kerouac. You can probably find a copy at the library.

"What's so important about these Beats, and this Kerouac guy?"

"You tell me after you've read it. I'll tell you this much: Kerouac is a great writer. He tells it exactly like it is. He doesn't disguise it, and he doesn't revise it. It's like stream-of-conscious writing. He's giving it to you straight. Do you dig, man?"

"I dig. You're getting weird on me, man."

"And when you go to the library, get a copy of *Howl, and Other Poems*, by Allen Ginsberg. That is if you can find a copy. Some of these damned libraries still won't carry it."

"Why's that?" I said.

"Because it's nasty. You'll like that."

"This wine is nasty, man."

"Have another glass and it won't taste so bad."

Subject: Spinning Wheels
Date: Thursday, 10 September, 1998

I was walking down the street one day, enjoying the sunny weather, when suddenly I heard the urgent jingle of a bell behind me. I stopped and was about to turn around when a bicyclist came zipping by me so close that it made me grateful I had shaved that morning. I was shocked, for I am unaccustomed to almost being run down on the sidewalk. The offending rider, without stopping, turned his head and rudely brought my ancestry into question. (At least that is what I think he was doing.) As I stood there with my mouth open, preparing to deliver some witty rejoinder, I almost got run over a second time by another bicyclist. He too turned and proffered several choice Teutonic slurs upon my character. Then he jabbed his index finger down at the sidewalk and rode off in a huff.

I looked down at the sidewalk and noticed something new and altogether novel to me. Whereas the greater part of the sidewalk was made up of gray cobblestones mortised in place with sand, there was also a one meter-wide strip of pink, interlocking bricks along the outer edge near the curb. A straight line of white bricks, placed end to end, separated this pink strip from the cobblestone. I have never been accused of being a genius, but I must say in my own defense that it didn't take me long to figure out that this was a bike path. I also figured out that I was standing right in the middle of it.

This revelation, the rudeness of its introduction notwithstanding, opened up a whole new world

for me. The bicycle! The bike path! Put them together and what do you have? Hey, a great way to get around. And, ooh so European.

For some time I had been frustrated because I wanted to see more of Berlin. Not having a car, the only way to get around was either by subway or bus or by walking. The subway is fast and far reaching, and you can see some interesting characters along the way, but you miss all the stuff aboveground when you use it. The bus routes are complicated, crowded, and not exactly my style. And walking is too slow and laborious for exploring large areas. Riding a bike, I decided, is the best way to get around Berlin. At least for my current purposes. You can see things close up, stop whenever you like, and still cover a fair amount of territory.

As luck would have it, Gretchen and I had our bicycles shipped over here with our other stuff when we moved here from Seattle. Up until recently we had limited our rides to the green expanses of the nearby Tiergarten. We had seen people riding bikes in the streets, but it looked kind of dicey to me. The streets are often narrow, and German drivers are a mite careless if you ask me. I mean, how careful can you be when you have a cigarette in one hand and a "handy" in the other? (A "handy" is the German term for a cellular phone. Everyone seems to have one here, even teenagers. It's kind of a status symbol.)

Up until my sudden revelation on the sidewalk that day, we had been blissfully unaware that Berlin is crisscrossed by miles and miles of relatively safe and creatively executed bike paths. Whenever possible, the paths here are laid out on the sidewalk rather than in the street. While this might put the occasional pedestrian at risk, the consequences of biking accidents occurring in the street are much more serious. In Berlin they try to keep the body count down whenever possible, which is not easy given the speed and the devil-may-care attitude with which German bicyclists travel. A large number of Berliners bicycle to work. The bike paths during commute hours are therefore a little like the *autobahn* in miniature. I try to avoid those hours.

I began to get serious about bike riding about a month ago. In the beginning, I just picked one of the cardinal points of the compass and headed out in that direction. I found that I can ride in any direction for more than an hour and still not come to the outskirts of Berlin. It is a big place. It is also a very flat place. There are no hills to speak of. I therefore have about 9 more gears on my 12-speed than I need.

I learned early on to take a compass and a map along on my rides. The first time I went out I didn't have either one, and, of course, I got stupendously lost. I had planned to ride south and then head east for a bit and then circle back north to home. I kinda scoped it out on the map before I left home. But after about an hour of riding, making innumerable turns, I couldn't for the life of me tell where I was or which direction I was heading. The sun was of no help because there wasn't one. The skies were the color of slate, with thick clouds stretching from horizon to horizon. The street signs were no help either. In the first place I couldn't pronounce their names (I've never seen such a collection of tongue twisters in all my life). And in the second place, even if I could pronounce them it wouldn't have done me any good. I had never seen or heard of them before.

I decided to try out my newly acquired language skills and seek directions from a couple of Germans I saw on the sidewalk. When I spoke to them they just looked at me with puzzled looks on their faces. It made me feel a little like Mark Twain when he was in Europe. He wrote how when he was "In Paris they simply stared when I spoke to them in French; I never did succeed in making those idiots understand their own language." I seem to be experiencing a similar lack of success here in Berlin.

What I eventually did was retrace my route. It was a long ride, but I got home O.K. My tongue was hanging down around my knees and looked like a rawhide belt, but I made it home. I learned on this inaugural ride that it might be a good idea to take a bottle of water along in future.

One of the reasons I had such a hard time was that the streets of Berlin, like most medieval cities, are not laid out in a grid like most American cities. Cities like Paris and London and

273

Berlin began as small trading villages on a river. The classic method by which medieval towns grow was repeated in each of them, and the evidence is still here today.

The earliest streets (if they still exist) weave in and out of the oldest part of town. These early streets are often quite crooked, meandering thusly either due to the whimsy of man, or by the dictates of topography. These early streets are usually quite narrow, some only wide enough for a couple of ox carts to pass abreast. As medieval towns grow, a few spoke-like boulevards may appear, radiating out from the center for ease of ingress and egress. As the town expands further the open spaces between the spokes are filled in by curving or slanting side streets. A few grid-like streets might appear, but generally there is no real plan. A medieval city evolves "organically."

Eventually, however, the complex tangle of streets that emerges makes it difficult for people and goods to get around. The streets become a maze and the neighborhoods become pieces in a jigsaw puzzle. So, usually what the government does is to direct a circular road to be built around the outskirts of town. Then, it is reasoned, you can travel around the perimeter until you get near your destination before plunging into the twisting streets again. As the town grows larger, a second circular road and even a third might be necessary. Berlin grew in such a fashion.

If you fly high over present-day Berlin you are struck by the fact that the borders of the town form an almost perfect circle. It is as though the town grew like a spore in a Petri dish. The surrounding flatlands are either farmland or forest. The city just abruptly ends, and *shazam*, you're in the country. No suburbs, no industrial zone, no nothin'.

Berlin is located on the great northeastern plain of Germany. It is a large area of very flat, sandy soil (good for farming) alternating with heavily forested tracts (some ancient, some recent – planted in rows for wood products). Both areas are broken up by a network of lakes, watercourses and low-lying marshes.

Berlin is no spring chicken. Carbon-dated artifacts indicate that this area was inhabited by humans as far back as

50,000 years ago. Berlin has been a permanent settlement for the last 2,800 years. It has been a "city" for the past 750 years. The tides of European history have swept over this area time and again. Conquerors came and went, governments rose and fell, the place was bombed and shelled almost into oblivion, and overrun by vengeful Russians, but somehow the city just kept plugging along. Berliners survived with a lot of pluck, some *savoir faire*, a little *panache*, and threw in some choice raspberries and thumbing of the noses at dictators and foreign potentates alike. Berlin has overcome isolation, a wrenching division, the Wall, and now an uneasy reunion. But once again it has become a world-class economic power, and the capital of Germany. Like most capitals in Europe, not only is the capital the government center, but also the center of commerce, transportation, architecture, art, music, fashion, you name it. People in Europe traditionally look to their capitals to see their own identity being formed and reformed. And it is no different here.

The first few bike rides I took had no real destination in mind. I was just out seeing what I could see and exploring different neighborhoods. But now I often pick out a destination on the map beforehand. I plot a route to it, and try to find a different route home. I ride to museums, art galleries, noteworthy landmarks, historical buildings, parks, lakes, and I might even squeeze in an imbiss or a pub along the way.

My most recent ride was rather an adventure. I decided to head southeast and check out Tempelhof Airport, the sight of the famous Berlin airlift. Tempelhof is one of three airports in Berlin. The others are Tegel (the main airport) and Schonefeld in East Berlin. But all three are unusual in that they are situated inside the city limits in built-up areas, and none of them are truly international airports. International travelers mostly have to fly into Frankfurt, some 300 miles to the west, and hop a commuter flight to Tegel.

Tempelhof is a regional airport used primarily for domestic flights by private planes and small commercial jets. Its location within the city makes it impossible to extend the runway for larger planes. Tempelhof's greatest claim to fame was its role in the great Allied airlift of 1948-49 when 1,300 planes a day landed there carrying food and other supplies. At peak times during the airlift, a plane landed every 90 seconds.

But the most memorable part of my ride had nothing much to do with history. Although I must say, I was impressed with massive structure of the terminal building. It was designed and construction initiated under the Nazis. It is shaped like a giant scythe, about four stories high, and built of really gnarly-looking stone slabs. It looks more like a fortress than an airline terminal. I rode along a bike path on the outskirts of the airport complex. I didn't feel like going into the terminal that day; I just wanted to see the runway and get a feel for the place.

I followed the curve of the scythe till I came to its tip. Just beyond the tip I saw an open gate leading to a long, narrow parking lot. Beyond the lot I could see the tarmac. I rode through the open gate hoping to get a closer look. I hadn't gone far when I saw a middle-aged couple emerge from their car and walk towards the gate. The woman, a rather fleshy, matronly lady, was leading a very small dog on a leash. The dog was about the size of a Chihuahua, but he had hair. When the dog caught sight of me it went absolutely berserk. It started barking hysterically and straining at its leash, trying to get at me. It was the tiniest attack dog I'd ever seen. I guess it wanted to rip off one of my toes or something. I had to laugh. I made a face at the dog, feigning deathly fear.

As I rode by the couple, the woman smiled conspiratorially at me and asked me a question. I didn't understand a word of what she said, but I assumed she was asking me if I was afraid of her vicious beast. I nodded agreement and said "Ja," and then rode on, chuckling.

I proceeded along the driveway until I came to an area free of cars where I had a fine view of the runway through the chain link fence. I stopped there and watched a twin-engine turbo prop take off. I noticed that the far end of the parking lot was closed off, so I couldn't go any further. The parking lot was maybe forty yards long and about half as wide. There was a driveway down the center and numbered parking slots along either side. I turned around and rode back the way I had come.

It was then that I made a rather disconcerting discovery. The gate through which I had entered was now closed, and the middle-aged couple and their dog were nowhere in sight.

When I approached the gate I realized, much to my chagrin, that not only was it closed, but that it was securely locked. The double-doored gate was made of chain-link, eight feet high, and equipped with an impressive-looking deadbolt lock that could only be opened with a key. Strung along the top of the gate were numerous strands of barbed wire. I looked around me. The whole parking lot was enclosed by an eight-foot high chain-link fence topped with concertina wire. Oh, my Lord! I was trapped like a rat.

But I had to laugh. Now I knew what that matronly lady was asking me back there. She wasn't asking me if I was afraid of her dog; she was asking me if I had a key to the gate. And I had said "Ja," like an idiot. This place was either an employee parking lot, or used by small-plane owners and pilots.

"Well, Idiot Stick," I thought, "here's another fine mess you've gotten yourself into." I peered around the immediate area. There were about 30 cars in the lot, but no people in them. There was no one in sight outside the lot either, and no buildings nearby. And the lot was screened off from the road by dense foliage. I was alone, a prisoner trapped behind barbed wire in the heart of Germany. Shades of Hogan's Heroes.

I had two choices: either wait for a flyer or employee to come along and open the gate, *or* try to toss my bike over the fence into the bushes and then try to climb over the concertina wire without emasculating myself. The first option seemed more attractive.

But after about ten minutes, I got impatient. It might be an hour or two or even longer before someone came along. It was about 6 P.M. at the time. Maybe no one would come along until the next shift change, maybe at 2 A.M. or whenever. Sweet Jesus, get me outa here!

But it was then that my Irish luck, my acute observational skills, and my brilliant intellect presented me with a third choice. I perceived that there was an iron rod attached to one of the swinging gates. The iron rod was about three feet long, and descended into a hole in the blacktop. The rod had a ninety-degree bend at the top, forming a handle

I lifted up on the handle of the bar and it emerged from the hole. With a little effort I managed to swing both doors inward just enough so that the deadbolt lock disengaged. Then the doors swung wide open just like St. Peter's Gate does for the innocent, the saintly, and the occasional repentant sinner. Hallelujah! I was free! Free at last. Oh, Lordy, free at last.

Curly's Pad

1964

After a few more flagons of Red Mountain on the front porch that day, Curly was looking rather blitzed, and I was not far behind.

He stubbed out his Camel in an old tuna tin and said, "I'm getting hungry. Hey Cassius, would you like to join me in a bite to eat?"

I hadn't eaten since that morning and my empty stomach was feeling poorly under the onslaught of cheap wine. "Yeah! What ya got?"

"I don't know. Let's go have a look."

So we gathered up the jug, the cups, and the books and headed around the north side of the old Victorian towards the back apartment. Neither one of us was walking that well. I was surprised at Curly's invitation. He had a reputation for being rather anti-social.

There was a sidewalk along that side of the house lined with forlorn succulents and water-deprived bushes struggling to survive. A set of creaky wooden steps led up to the door to his place. Actually, it was his friend's place. Lenny was an art student at Telegraph Tech too. Lenny was letting Curly stay there for whatever money he could scrape together. They were your typical starving artists.

The apartment door had windows in the top half that looked in on the kitchen. We walked in and found nobody home. The kitchen was small, narrow, and L-shaped. A gungy sink filled with dirty dishes stood on the right as you walked in. There was a linoleum counter beyond that angled around towards the left with cupboards above and below. Across the narrow kitchen from the cupboards was a greasy-looking gas stove with an old rattling refrigerator standing next to it.

"Have a look around," said my host as he plunked the jug of Red Mountain down on the counter. "I'll see what I can rustle up."

I squeezed past him as he opened the fridge door. I noticed a smallish room through a doorway off to the right. It was a combination bedroom and bathroom. A single bed, neatly-made, hunkered against one wall. Next to it stood a small wardrobe with a mirrored door. Wainscoting, painted white at least thirty years ago, lined the walls below dingy white plaster walls. There was no door to separate the bathroom which contained a shower, sink and toilet.

"That's Lenny's room," said Curly. "I crash in the other room, on the sofa."

The other room, the main room, was larger and lay beyond the kitchen. There was a bare lightbulb hanging from a cord in the ceiling, although the bulb was covered by a red paper Japanese lantern.

The walls were decorated with the two men's artwork. Lenny's included some fine-looking drawings in India ink, a couple of very nice portraits in oil, and a large well-rendered watercolor landscape. They all looked of professionally quality. Curly's were cruder, but more dramatic and outlandish, as I might have expected.

Below the artwork, the walls were again lined in painted wainscoting. Two beat up couches sat against opposite walls. One was larger than the other and was covered in a jumble of blankets. I guessed that was Curly's bed. There were several book shelves made of vegetable crates against the wall. The room was further cluttered with a mishmash of small garage-sale furniture, a table lamp, and an easel. On an old steamer trunk in the corner sat a dusty turntable, two small speakers, and a stack of LPs.

A large wooden table occupied the middle of the room. Half of it was covered with a red and yellow fringed shawl. The other half was stacked with all sorts of art materials: sketch pads, watercolor and oil pallets, brushes, cups of paint-tinted water, etc. There were two rickety-looking straight-back chairs at right angles alongside the table. Midway along the wall facing the ocean was a second door to the apartment. It had windows too, and led to stairs descending to the back lawn of the main house.

My guess was that this little apartment, which looked like an add-on to the main house, was originally intended as a residence for domestic help.

While I was checking out all these things I heard Curly shuffling and clunking around in the kitchen behind me. I walked back there and watched him put the finishing touches on a couple of very peculiar sandwiches. Four slices of bread arranged in a square rested on the not-overly clean counter. The two slices on the left were spread with a layer of cottage cheese over which was sprinkled chopped green onions and black pepper. The two on the right were covered with the remainder of the contents of a cold can of Campbell's pork and beans. He slapped the left and right halves together and handed me my sandwich with a flourish. Then he took up his own.

Standing there in the kitchen, we took simultaneous bites. The bread was slightly stale, but our eyes told each other the sandwiches were actually quite tasty. Of course, we were both famished.

"Pour yourself some more wine," he suggested, "and let's eat out there in the studio. There's something I want to talk to you about."

We moved out to the large table in the center of the room. He took the chair at one end. I put my wine down and pulled out the other chair. When I sat down my foot bumped up against something under the table. Whatever it was lay hidden behind the draping shawl. When I pulled up the shawl to see what was down there I let out an involuntary squawk. On the floor lay a grimy human skull wearing an army helmet staring up at me from what looked like a shallow box of mud. It turned out to be one of Curly's three dimensional art pieces. My reaction brought a snicker from its creator as he munched on his sandwich.

Upon further examination, I determined that the skull was made of paper mache, as was the mud surrounding it. A real army helmet had been cut in half and imbedded in the faux mud so that it looked as if a skull in a helmet was sticking up out of a shallow battlefield grave. The whole piece was smeared with muddy-brown paint so that it looked totally real.

"Sorry about that," said Curly. "Lenny wouldn't let me hang it on the wall. He says it's gross. Oh, well. It works better on the floor anyway."

I noticed that Curly had done several other outrageous pieces. One was hanging on the wall behind him. It had a thrift store antique gold leaf frame that was a lot worse for wear. The picture itself was made up of an actual mandolin that had been brutally crushed and splintered and imbedded in a bed of crimson paper mache gore surrounded by a flat black background.

Curly noticed me looking at it. "I call that one, '*Quiet!!!*' My musician friends hate it." He let out a fiendish cackle of delight, spraying curds of cottage cheese in the process.

"Don't get me wrong," he said. "I love music. I just like to stir things up. I found that mandolin in a dumpster."

I continued eating my strange sandwich. "What's that the painting next to it – that red, yellow and green one?" I asked. It looked like it had been painted on a rectangle of plywood.

Curly looked over his shoulder and said, "Oh, that's The Only Woman I Ever Loved #24."

"Number 24? That's how many you've painted?"

"Yeah. Sometimes I don't do any other work on the pretext of painting her portrait; and I paint her portrait so I have an excuse for not doing anything else."

I had no idea what he was talking about. And I couldn't make heads nor tails of the painting. It didn't look anything like a portrait. It had red, yellow and green lines slashing across it – some straight and some curving – all mixed up and crossing over each other. I guess if I studied it long enough I might have been able to discover a face in there somewhere. But I sure didn't see one just looking at it. It seemed like it had been painted either by a demented child or a drunk adult on the verge of passing out. I resisted the urge to shake my head.

Not knowing how to respond, I changed the subject. "You said you wanted to talk to me about something. What is it?"

Curly had finished his sandwich by then. He wiped his mustache and beard with the back of his hand and cleared his throat.

"Well, it's about Lenny, my roommate. It seems he has this rich girlfriend. He's been seeing her for the last few months. She's convinced he's a great artist. What a fool. Anyway, Lenny tells me she asked him to move into her apartment out by Ventura College. She told him he didn't even have to pay rent. She just wants to sit home and watch him sketch and paint. Personally, I think she's just horny."

"Well, he is a good-looking guy. And a really good artist," I added, looking over at his work.

Curly didn't seem to like either one of those comments. With a snarl he pulled the pack of Camels out of his shirt pocket and lit one up.

He tossed the matches aside and continued. "The point is, Lenny's moving out at the end of the month, and I don't have enough money to pay the rent here by myself. That's where you come in. How about you and I teaming up and sharing the rent? Aren't you getting a little tired of living at home with your parents?"

"You bet I am. I've wanted to move out for a while now. But it's not just that – this is a great old place – this house. I love it, and it's as close to The Point as you can get. Any surfer in his right mind would give his left nut to live here. You can wake up every morning and check out the waves just by looking out your own window. A few of my friends already live in the two downstairs apartments in the front."

Curly frowned. "O.K., Mr. Kahuna. Yeah, sure, it's a great place. But the question is: do you have any money? I don't suppose you're paying rent now.

"No I don't pay any rent. But, yes, I have money. I've got a part-time job as a box boy over at Mayfair Market. I have a car too." Then I started to get a little worried. I didn't have a clue what rents were like around here. "But hold on a minute. Just how much money are we talking about?"

"Well, the rent here is $40 a month. That includes utilities. Your half would be $20."

I did some fast figuring. I pulled in about $35 a month at my job. I also had a savings account with about $50 in it. I could use my savings to live on for a while, and then maybe take on some extra hours at the market while I continued taking classes at Ventura College.

The cost didn't matter to me at all. This was the chance of a lifetime and I was more than willing to pay whatever it cost.

Several weeks later I made my first faltering steps along the pot-holed road to manhood. I loaded all my worldly possessions into my baby blue Ford and bid my childhood farewell. It only took about fifteen minutes to drive from my parent's house to my new home at The Point, but it seemed like a million miles and a lifetime away.

My parents, of course, had their misgivings about my leaving. (They had gotten back together by then, and Pop had moved back in with us.) They weren't sure I was ready to be on my own. They thought I was too young, not to mention immature, and they worried about all the trouble I could get into down there at the beach. But at the same time I think my parents were relieved to have me gone from under their roof. I was not an easy person to get along with back then, and I suspect they considered me something of a loose cannon, and that they'd just as soon not have me going off in their house.

The events of the next few months are the stuff of legends. As a matter of fact, the whole history of the house and the land it stood on is the stuff of legends. But I had no real sense of history back in the summer of '64. All I knew was that it was a dream come true for a young surfer like me to be living right at the beach, at the best surfing spot in the county. The rent was affordable, and I had soul-mates in the other young surfers that lived in the house. And I was free from parental control and ready for whatever adventures might come my way.

It wasn't until several months after I moved in that I discovered that the rent for Curly's apartment was not $40 a month as he'd told me. It was only $20. He'd been screwing me for all the rent and living there for free. He made a little money of his own by selling his "art" to impressionable ignoramuses. He spent it all on cigarettes, alcohol, and gasoline for Rosinante. For food he sweet-talked sympathetic young coeds in the student center at Telegraph Tech into pillaging their parents' pantries for beans, rice, canned goods and anything else they might not miss. And those kids did it! They wanted to help this poor, struggling, charismatic artist. The proceeds ended up on his and my dinner plates. One time we even got a couple of frozen steaks.

When I found out he'd been cheating me on the rent we had a huge falling out. I immediately moved out of his place and into one of the front apartments. (There was a pretty high attrition rate among roommates up front. Those guys came and went at the drop of a hat depending on the current state of their meager finances.)

About this same time the city of Ventura condemned the house and all the houses around it. They called them substandard housing, which they were, I guess. The city called the neighborhood 'blighted' and earmarked the whole area for urban renewal.

During the months I lived with Curly I learned more about art, music, literature, philosophy, and personal attitude

285

than I had ever dreamed about. And those things made a permanent impression on my young mind. They were the foundation of what became a lifetime of reading and a lifelong appreciation for all the art forms, particularly painting. More importantly it awakened in me a strong desire to express myself creatively.

And along the way, Curly inadvertently taught me not to be such a sucker, such a sap. That conniving, lying, manipulating, egotistical prig showed me that there are all kinds of deceitful people in this world (he being one of the primary ones). He also taught me more than I needed to know about debauchery. He was a scoundrel, a fraud, a degenerate, a hustler, a lecher, a thief, and a thoroughly delightful rogue.

But despite his many shortcomings, Curly had a fine intellect, was extremely well read, and had a great sense of humor when he exercised it. And even though his art was often course, crude, and more-often-than-not rude, it was always amusingly creative. Who else would paint his own panel truck maroon with a broom, and then scrawl black lettering on the side panels naming it after Don Quixote's horse? Who else would paint endless numbers of abstract self-portraits and pictures of 'The Only Woman I Ever Loved'?

In hindsight, he was the funniest, most interesting, entertaining, and knowledgeable person I knew back then. He was not only a giant influence on me, but on many others who lived at or visited The Point House, or knew him from Ventura College. He changed the course of innumerable lives. There is a long list of people who knew him back then who, because of his influence, went on to become artists, musicians, writers, teachers, or psychologists. He inspired two people I know to become philosophy majors in college.

Curly and I remained friends despite him ripping me off. I saw him around every once in a while after the city bulldozed The Point House in the fall of 1964. But then around 1968 he seems to have dropped out of sight. No one knew where he'd gone. Years later I heard a rumor that he'd immigrated to Australia and married a beautiful blond and was now a father. Ha! That sounds like a rumor he might have started.

Dispatch from Berlin #9

1998

With typical German precision summer came to an end on August 31st. During much of August the weather had been sunny and warm, even downright hot on a few occasions. It allowed us our first outdoor swim since coming to this fair city. In the company of a local German psychologist and his schoolmarm girlfriend, we partook of the greenish waters of Krumme Lanke, a small lake in southwest Berlin. (I call it Crummy Lake, just for kicks, though it isn't really crummy, it's just a little scummy with algae.) We went for a long swim and then rowed around the lake with our new friends in their inflatable life raft.

But a day later September 1st reared its ugly head. The day dawned overcast and cold, with gusty winds blowing out of the north. Fall, it seems, arrived right on schedule in der Faderland. It appeared as if ordered to do so by the ghost of der Fuhrer himself. And it is amazing how swiftly the whole weather pattern has changed since then. Even though we got a few nice days of Indian Summer, most of September was gray and chill, with frequent rain, crisp nights and dewy mornings. The leaves, even now, have begun to turn. And another phase of the great cycle begins.

The end of the month is nigh, and a new day dawns on the German capital. (Well, *dawn* if you can call this gray ooze of light in the east a dawn.) It appears as though another overcast day is in store for Berlin. *Mein Gott* in *Himmel* I am so tired of the color gray. I thought I had finally left it behind when we departed San Francisco after living there for ten years. But what followed was two years of "early morning low clouds and fog" in Marina Del Rey. Next came the master of gray, Seattle, for two more soggy years. When Berlin came down the pipe, I

287

thought, *wunderbar*, at last, a chance to get away from the gray. But I knew not of what I thought. That blasted color has followed me even here.

I guess I should try to be more positive. That's what my psychologist friend would say. I should look on the bright side. I should consider myself a connoisseur of gray. Lord knows I've seen enough of it. I've seen every shade there is – from dark gloom to dazzling bright, and all the shades in between. I've seen every tint of gray – from pink to golden to purple. I know every texture – from sticky to drizzling to dry rot. Every temperature – from frigid to middling to muggy. Every smell – from ocean crisp to sooty smog to tule swamp gas. Enough with the gray already. Give me some sun for Christ's sake!

I don't get any, but I roll out of bed anyway and walk into our gray kitchen. The kitchen is obviously somebody's idea of the industrial look. Gray tile, gray counters, stainless steel sink. I pour myself a cup of coffee from our matching gray German coffeepot. Whew, at least the coffee isn't gray. Black is a nice color, even if it isn't a color. Then I go to the gray fridge and get the milk and pour some in my cup. Ah, Jeez, now my coffee even looks gray.

I hear a scrabbling up on the roof. It's those birds again. Every morning and every evening eight full-grown crows have a family gathering on our roof. (Did you know that crow children stay with their parents well into adulthood? Also, related families team up and form a clan. They lay claim to a territory and defend it against other crows.) The crows on our roof talk over what's going on in the world six floors down and find out how each other are feeling. Sometimes they have a good laugh together and at other times they squabble. They have an amazing range of vocalizations. Everything from raucous caws to warblings to sputterings that sound like a motor scooter with dirty spark plugs.

After every rain there are some puddles up there on the flat roof where they like to have a drink and maybe splash around and wash up. Sometimes the crows bring along a snack, some little piece of garbage or maybe some dead thing. Then they like to try to steal it from one another. It turns into a riot.

There's also a couple of shallow planting beds up there. Somebody in the past must have had a little garden up there. I can see the remains of the beds from my back patio. This summer the beds sprouted a fine crop of scraggly weeds. The family of crows, and other birds as well, like to come and peck around for the weed seeds. They also like to dig around in the soil looking for grubs or worms or whatever. They have a fine time up there tossing gravel around and making plenty of racket. Sometimes I zip open the electric-powered skylights and make sounds like a ferocious, hungry cat. The crows listen alertly, and when I stop they laugh and go back to playing around up there.

The crows in Berlin don't look like the crows in the U.S. The ones here are a different variety I guess. They're about the same size, maybe a little bigger, but they look like they're wearing a gray vest. No kidding. Their bodies and their wings are black, but they have this gray coloring, just like they were wearing little gray vests. (There's that damn color again.) The crows here have pretty big beaks, which makes me suspect that they might even be ravens. *Shudder.*

So I go into my bedroom and pull on my faded Levis and my favorite faded shirt with its tiny black and white squares. Then I go into the bathroom to brush my hair and see if I need to shave. I pick up the brush, look at myself in the mirror, and freeze. Oh, my God. I can't believe this. I think I'm turning gray. No, not my hair, you turncoat. My face! My face looks gray! Oh, no! Maybe I'm sick or something.

I put the brush down and have a closer look. Maybe the light is funny in here, I think, or maybe my eyes are playing tricks on me. No. My face really does look gray. It looks about the same color as those bratwurst and fried onions I had for dinner last night. And yes, I do need a shave. But even the stubble on my chin is gray. And look, my messed up thinning hair is turning gray too. Drat. I look into my eyes in the mirror and notice that my baby-blues have faded, faded to gray. I look at my hands…gray. I quickly roll up my sleeves and look at my arms…gray. I unbutton my shirt and as I do so I notice that the little black and white squares of my shirt have blended to gray. I look at my chest...gray. Oh, Lordy, I'm afraid to look any more. I rush out of the bathroom and stick my gray Tam O'Shanter on my gray head and hurry into the bedroom again. I pull on my socks and my dirty white shoes that are starting to look gray too. As I'm tying the laces I notice that our rug is gray. Aaaaah! I gotta get outa here.

I ride the elevator down to the ground floor and it seems to take forever. I can't help noticing that the stainless steel interior of the elevator is gray. I rush outside, banging doors as I go. I screech to a halt on the gray cobblestones of the sidewalk. The sky is still gray. All the six-story buildings on my block are different shades of gray. The leaves of the trees along the street are beginning to turn kind of a dull gray-brown. The trunks are gray. The moldy dog turds around their bases are gray. Aieeeeee!

I run. I run like a mad man, wild-eyed, directionless. The whole world melts into a gray blur streaming past me. Gray cars, gray people, gray politicians winning elections, gray newspapers floating in an updraft of smoggy gray air. My ears hear nothing but the hum of gray noise. Hell, I'm gray too. I'm a gray blob of protoplasm rushing through a gray void.

After about ten blocks I stop running. You *Dummkopf*, I say to myself, gasping for breath. You really ought to get a grip on yourself. Maybe you should go see your psychologist friend and get your head shrunk. You're starting to think like that madman Poe writes about in his short story "The Black Cat." Do you  remember it? The guy in the story can't get his mind off the black cat and it drives him crazy. Now you can't get your mind off the color gray. I think you're fixating, old boy.

But even though I know I'm doing it, I don't seem to be able to shake it off. I'm standing on a corner in a daze of gray, when suddenly I hear the approach of an emergency vehicle. It's an ambulance. It is about the size and shape of a laundry truck and is painted a shockingly bright day-glow red. It has six large flashing blue lights on top and it screams past me going "ee-ah, ee-ah, ee-ah!"

"Look at all the colors!" I exclaim. "Oh, how beautiful! How stimulating!"

The ambulance's passing is like a much needed slap in the face. Ka-pow!

Thanks. I needed that.

I've snapped out of it. Now I'm O.K. I'm sane. I really am sane. I'm sane, I tell you... sane!

The Night of the Flies

1964

The winter storms that year were more powerful than anything even the oldest surfers could remember. They generated huge waves that pounded the entire coast of California. Massive swells swept through the Santa Barbara Channel, and high seas brought the local fishing industry to a standstill. Pilings were torn loose from the Ventura pier and sent crashing into others pilings, crippling the whole structure. Mammoth breakers ripped great strands of kelp loose and sent them adrift, and every high tide brought extensive erosion along the coast.

But we surfers loved every minute of it. The waves were monstrous, thrilling, scary, and we all got truly memorable rides that winter. By the time April rolled around the sea had returned to normal, but the high spring tides carried tons of kelp onto the beaches and deposited it there in vast, tangled messes. There was so much kelp that the authorities couldn't deal with it. So it sat there on the beach for months – steaming and noxious and smelling to high heaven. Great swarms of flies descended on the rotting kelp and made themselves at home.

I was nineteen at the time, and living in an old, dilapidated Victorian at the foot of Palm Street in Ventura. That old Victorian was in its last year of existence, having been condemned by the city and slated for demolition. About ten of us young surfers had managed, over time, and with no small amount of jockeying, to rent all four apartments of the house. For most of us it was our first time away from home, and we were living wild and free. Our unstated goal was to surf all day and party all night. We rode that poor old house pretty hard.

One Sunday evening, weary of our own excesses, we decided to leave the house to the mercy of the cockroaches and go out to a movie. There was a new film in town starring the Beatles. It was called "A Hard Day's Night." We were all big Beatle fans and were really stoked about seeing it. But shortly before we departed we were paid an unexpected and unwelcome visit by a couple of well-known local *Greasers*.

In the surfer terminology of the time, a Greaser was a tough guy with slick hair who spent an inordinate amount of time working on his car and as a result always had black grease under his fingernails. When Greasers weren't working on their cars they were cruising Main Street looking to impress everyone with what fine machines they drove. They spent their spare time drag racing other Greasers, drinking beer, crashing other people's parties, acting macho, and fighting with anyone who didn't sufficiently express admiration for them.

In Greaser terminology we were called *Surf Rats*. We were all wimps, according to the definition, who spent an inordinate amount of time in the ocean and as a result our noses were always sunburned and our bodies encrusted with salt. When we weren't surfing we were busy waxing our surfboards and looking to impress everyone with what blond, suntanned gods we were. We spent our spare time telling lies to other surfers about what great waves we'd caught, drinking cheap beer, throwing wild parties, and making love to any female who would have us.

I knew both the Greasers who visited us that Sunday evening. One of them happened to be the older brother of my sister's boyfriend. His name was Jim. He was a transplanted Texan and was everything you might expect: tall, lean, tough, and mean. Jim had a reputation as somebody you didn't mess with. You didn't even want to know why. His partner was a huge bull of a man named Warren who had a violent temper and a reputation for being both brutal and sadistic. Warren was so big he made us surfers look like boys.

The sun was just going down when Jim and Warren walked in the perpetually wide-open front door with not so much as a 'howdy do.' They both stood there in the entryway holding open bottles of Coors beer in their hands. Warren called out, "Hey! Where's the party?" He looked around licking his chops like a Grizzly bear that just stumbled onto somebody's picnic.

There was a Rolling Stones album playing in the front apartment – the rooms that faced the ocean. Inside, four of us surfers were sipping on half-quart cans of *Brew 102* watching the sunset while waiting for our friends in the other apartments to finish getting ready to go to the movies. We were sitting on the raised wooden platform in front of the wide window that looked out on the sea. The platform was covered with four or five old mattresses.

Jim and Warren sauntered into the apartment like they owned the place. Jim looked at us and his lip curled. "Hells bells," he said, "Where's all the chicks?" He and Warren must have been drinking beer all afternoon because they both looked about three sheets to the wind.

"There's no chicks here," said Dude, our most stalwart member.

"Shit," said Warren with obvious disappointment. "What are you punks doin'?"

"We're about to leave," explained Dude. "We're goin' to the flicks tonight."

"Shit," said Warren. "I heard you fuckin' Surf Rats had a party every night down here. And that's what we're here for – a party. Either that or maybe a little ass-kicking."

This was not good news to us. Even though we outnumbered them there wasn't one of us who wanted to tangle with them. Even if we ganged up on them, there was no guarantee we could take them. And we would probably pay a pretty stiff price for trying.

I noticed Jim was staring out the window with glazed eyes. I knew he was at least partly human. He was not completely immune to the beauty of the sunset over the ocean.

I'd had some prior contact with him through my sister and his brother. Taken alone and sober, he was not a bad guy.

"Hey, Jim," I piped up, "How ya doin'?"

He looked over and seemed to recognize me for the first time. He nodded, playing it cool.

"I hear there's a party down on Pierpont tonight," I said, "You guys might want to check it out."

Before he could respond, Warren says to me, "Who the hell asked ya, punk?"

"Take it easy, Warren," said Jim. "I know him. He's a good head." I figured Jim didn't want to hassle me because it might cause trouble between my sister and his brother. I guess he thought, for better or worse, I was almost family.

Warren said, "I don't give a damn what he is. I feel like kicking some ass."

"Aw, hell," said Jim, "Take it easy, man. There's nothing happening here. Let's go for a ride."

"Shit. I'm just getting warmed up here. I feel like maybe exterminating some Surf Rats tonight." He looked us over as if he were trying to decide which one of us was most worthy of being squashed.

Jim turned to me and winked. "Come on, Warren, we're leaving."

"Shit," said Warren for about the hundredth time. He tilted his head back and chugged the half a bottle of beer he had

left. Jim turned and started for the door. Warren looked over at us with an evil grin. Then he cocked his arm, and threw the empty beer bottle right through the front window. We all ducked as shards of glass went flying.

"Aw, Jesus, Warren," said Jim.

"'Sorry about that," said Warren, with a grin. Then the two of them left. They got in their car and burned rubber half way up the street.

The front window of the apartment was made up of panes of glass about 16" square held in place by narrow wood sashes. Luckily, Warren's empty bottle had only broken one of the panes. It wouldn't be that hard to fix.

While we were practicing calling those Greasers every dirty name we could think of, and describing in detail what we should have done to them, the guys from the other apartments finally showed up. After we clued them in on what happened we all trooped out of the house. We decided to walk since there were too many of us to fit in one car.

We locked up the house and left a light on in the front apartment. The light was an old plastic beer sign that looked like the planet Saturn. The planet was a blue sphere about the size of a tether ball and the ring around the outside was white and had *Hamms* spelled out in red letters. There was a light bulb burning inside. The light hung from the ceiling in the room with the big window across the front.

We had a blast at the movies. The Beatles were great. On the walk home we all decided to grow our hair long. We got home around 11 PM and clomped into the front apartment, which was more or less party-central because of its open floor plan. It seemed awfully dark in there for some reason.

My friend, Deuce, said to Dude, "Hey, wingnut, I thought you were going to leave the light on."

"I did leave it on, you dolt."

"Well, how come it's so dark in here then, ass-bite?"

"Hell, I don't know, renob." (That's boner spelled backwards.)

We could all just barely see the light burning. It was on, but it seemed so dim. As we walked towards the front window I felt a fly land on my forehead, and then another one landed, and another, and another. Suddenly there were flies all over my face. I brushed them aside, but more landed almost immediately.

"Jesus," said Deuce, "this place is full of flies." Everybody was swatting like crazy, trying to get the flies off of them.

"What are we gonna do?" asked a guy named Wiener from next door.

"Kill 'em," said Deuce. "I gotta a can of *Raid* under the sink. I've been spraying the goddamn cockroaches with it." Deuce went into the kitchen and turned on the light. It was then that we could really see for the first time just how many flies were in the apartment. There must have been a million of them.

"Holy shit," said Dude. "Look at that. They're kelp flies. They must 'a come in through the busted window."

Deuce came back with the can of *Raid* and climbed up on the wooden platform. He aimed it at the light and started spraying. Flies immediately started dropping like flies. It looked like it was raining flies. We all scattered away from the deluge. Deuce started waving the can of Raid back and forth, cutting great swaths of death through the teeming flies. We all started coughing like crazy because the spray was filling up the room. I ran and got a grimy dish towel and tied it around  my face like a bandana. Everybody ran and got tee-shirts or whatever they could and did the same.

"Holy Christ," said Dude, "the fuckin' flies are still coming in." We all looked at the hole in the window and saw hundreds of new flies streaming in. They were obviously attracted to the light.

"Cover up the hole," suggested some budding Einstein.

Dude grabbed a pillow from off the platform and stuffed it in the hole. It was probably somebody's sleeping pillow. Deuce continued to spray until all the flies were dead and the can was empty. When all the excitement was over, our so-called friends from the other apartments turned tail and went home. I guess the idea of cleaning up the mess grossed them out.

So Dude, Deuce, and I were stuck with the job. We tilted the mattresses up on the platform and pounded on the backs to shake off all the dead bodies. Every horizontal surface in the apartment was covered with dead flies. With rags and brooms we swished them off onto the floor. I found an old push broom in the hall closet and started sweeping them into a pile. When I was done, the pile was about four feet across and a foot deep.

Looking down at the disgusting mess, Deuce scratched his head and said, "What are we gonna do with all these dead flies?"

"I saw a cardboard box out in the hall closet," I said. "We can scoop 'em up and put 'em in the box. I think it's big enough. If not, we can just mash 'em down a little so they'll all fit. Then we can dump 'em out on the beach. That's where they came from."

"I got a better idea," said Dude. "Hand me that phone book."

"Oh, yeah? What's on your mind, nimrod?"

"Let's take 'em over to Warren's place and decorate his goddamn pickup truck."

Dear John Letter
1967

Dear John,

I hardly know where to begin; I have so very much to say that I never really had a chance to say before. John, I have often felt the clash between your way of life and my own. I've tried reasoning it out and telling myself that the difference really didn't matter. I have to admit it does matter. You're torn between a liberal and conservative life, and who am I to decide which is best for you. We never sat down and talked about it, but I think if we would have we'd have discovered how wrong we were for each other.

I truly love you with all I have to offer, but sometimes I feel that isn't enough for you. I would never tell you I approve of some things you do because I'd be lying. I love you, not because you're different or because you're a surfer. I love you because you are you.

It seems every time I admire you for being an individual, your friends drop by and you become a face in a crowd; doing as they do, speaking as they speak. You tell me that surfers are individuals, but in a group they're all the same. I believe you are different and very special. I think you are a wonderful person, but you are defeated before you begin if you don't let your own personality shine through.

I love you because you are something I'm not. I wish I had some of your gentleness and wisdom. I just couldn't bear to see you change or get into any sort of trouble (I would be too disappointed and hurt). I would feel I'd failed and my love for you had failed also. I don't ever want to take you away from your friends because I know you would someday resent me for it. Maybe I'm overly conservative, but John, you have so much more than you realize. I want to spend the rest of my life with you, but not with your friends. I don't feel I'm any better, but I feel I am different and have different interests. Maybe someday you'll realize that being secure and living a normal life has its benefits, darling. This has been bothering me for over two months and I was just afraid to talk it over with you. I know if I stayed I'd try to change you and rather than do that and hurt you, I'd rather let you live as you want to live. I swear there will always be a place in my heart for you.

This is so hard for me to do – but I know you will be much happier without someone from another world to confuse you.

All my love,
Colleen

The Tears of the Turtle
1978

The primitive reptilian mind of the sea turtle told her it was time to go ashore. Ninety million years of history had taught her species to know when the time was right for the laying of eggs. Gracefully, through warm tropic seas she swam, her front flippers working in unison like the wings of a bird. She felt calm in the darkness under a cloud-obscured moon. Darkness was her ally in this desperate enterprise.

High tide let her get in close to the sandy beach before her flat plastron began to drag along the bottom. She paused and surveyed the shore. She detected no movement, and her keen sense of smell caught only the scent of vegetation. Laboriously she pulled herself up out of the shallows and onto the sand. With a great effort she dragged herself up the steep beach, her flippers now  working alternately, like legs. She breathed heavily from the exertion of pulling her hundred pounds of shell-encased flesh across the soft sand.

Up near where the vegetation began – above the high-water mark – she found a good spot for her nest: the sand was moist and warm, and the digging would be easy. She set about her task. First, she dug herself a body pit by sweeping sand backwards with her front flippers, and then moving forward a little so that her hind flippers could push the sand further back and out of the pit. After about fifteen minutes of strenuous effort, her body lay nestled down in the shallow pit, her upper shell just sticking up above the surface.

She rested for a few minutes and then began to dig the egg chamber under the body pit, this time using only her rear flippers. With exquisite delicacy one of her rear flippers reached

301

down into the pit, scooped up a palm full of the moist sand, gently lifted it to the side, and dropped it. She repeated this maneuver with her other rear flipper, and continued alternating back and forth between them, slowly excavating the nest that would hold her eggs.

As she worked on in silence, the wind came up and swept the clouds away from the moon. The light shone down brightly then, and exposed her toiling there on the sandy, tree-lined shore of a small island. She did not like the light, but she could not stop now. The laying urge was strong upon her.

If humans had happened along that deserted beach under the ethereal light of the moon, they would have seen tears streaming down her ancient, craggy face, and would perhaps have wondered why she cried.

Science would inform them that tears are merely the turtle's way of secreting salt from its body. Science would tell them the tears are also helpful in keeping sand out of her eyes. It is Science's opinion that the tears have nothing to do with the dreadful exertion of crawling up a steep beach from her home in the sea, of the arduous and time-consuming excavation of a pit in a dangerous and alien world. Science would say the tears are unrelated to the withering fear of the terrible land-creatures, the agonizing pain of birthing, and the immense heart-ache of a mother who knows that most of her babies will be gobbled up by predators within minutes of emerging from their gritty nursery in the sand.

But then Science does not know everything.

Subject: Italy
Date: 3 December, 1998

Hannibal did it with elephants. So I saw no reason not to do it with a horse. An iron horse that is. I'm talking about crossing the Alps, of course. Gretchen and I departed on that remarkable trip on the 11th of November, after spending a couple of nights in medieval Munich. (Munich, so old and quaint it reminded me of a theme park, only Munich is real.) We picked a perfect day for crossing the Alps: a mix of sun and cloud, craggy peaks up ahead stabbing into great gray globs or standing in stark profile against the barren blue. There were flurries of snow in the shadowy passes, and everywhere the sun-dappled colors of fall mixed in with the evergreens. Pretty damn fine.

Clickety-clack, clickety-clack, the wheels were singing on the railroad tracks. Climbing. Oh man, we were climbing. Giddyup, ye faithful electric-powered iron horse. Up and up, into the Austrian Alps. Innsbruck came 'round the bend. Too early for much snow on the ski slopes. Onward, winding into the heart of stone, snow-capped mountains. For lunch we dipped into the roast chicken and German potato salad we bought in Munich that morning. Popped a couple of Pilsners in our private compartment to wash it down. Not bad. Burrrrp.

Clickety-clack, clickety-clack. High alpine villages off to the left and right. A twisting road first above us, then below, then above again. Passed through a long dark tunnel. Then through green and amber forests clinging to steep hillsides. Rivulets of icy water jumped off sheer rock faces. Along came another tunnel. Poof-fah. They sure do like 'em long in these parts. And then we ever so gradually found ourselves rolling downhill. It dawned on us that we'd bloody done it. We'd bloody well crossed over to the other side. Felt like crossing the equator or something. Coasting down towards Italy through the mountains! Mediterranean sun shining on the inclines!

We stopped at the border to switch train crews. Off with the uptight Germans and on with the spacey Italians. You could feel everything loosened up right away. Forget your ironclad schedules, your attention to detail, your safety inspections. Forget even the ritual of punching your ticket. Let's just ride, amici. Enjoy the scenery. Relax. This is *la dolce vita*.

A verdant valley opened up down below. As we wound through it, it widened. Broader, ever broader the valley spread, rock-clad mountains leaning back on either side. Fruit trees, already harvested, dropped their leaves in narrow orchards. Pruning was underway. Here and there spires of smoke signaled the burning of cuttings. Tiny villages dotted the sunny slopes. Hilltop monasteries looked down on misty canyons. A stream got bold and became a river. As we descended, the valley gradually leveled and we came upon a rolling countryside alive with olive orchards and vineyards. Now we really felt we were in Italy. The mountains melted into brown hills like those of Napa in the fall.

Clickety-clack, clickety-clack. Across the undulations of Tuscany we rolled, through the fields of wheat, corn, grape, olive and tobacco, on into the region's capital, Florence. Ah, Florence, beautiful Florence: birthplace of the Renaissance, home of great art, architecture, painting and sculpture. Home to Michelangelo, Rossini, Boticelli, Machiavelli, Raphael, Titian, Dante and the beneficent Medici. Home too to hordes of tourists like us. But what the heck, if you can't fight 'em, join 'em. Which is what we did for the next three days. Even in November the tourists were everywhere. I can't imagine what it's like in summer. Disneyland, I suppose.

We rented a rooftop hotel room in the Old City with a view over tiled roofs to the Piazza del Duomo. The Duomo was built by Brunelleschi in the 1300s and is the largest domed church in Europe. From our window we could look across at the Duomo and the tall Campanile next to it. When we first checked in we saw a cat sitting on the apex of the building next to us. The cat was licking its paws with the great dome rising up behind him. When the cat noticed us looking out the window it scampered over and jumped up on our windowsill to say hello and get petted.

Then we went out and got swallowed up by Florence. The next three days were a blur of twisting streets, magnificent architecture, churches, gardens, fountains, paintings and sculpture.

Clickety-clack, clickety-clack. With a belly full of culture and less-than-stellar cuisine, we blew town. Headed west through the land of the Etruscans. Made a beeline for the beach on the west coast, as any self-respecting former surfer would do. Took the better part of a day getting there by train. Ended up in an area known as Cinque Terre (Five Lands). It is named so for the group of five picturesque villages clinging to the cliffs that look south over the Ligurian Sea. It is an area noted for its impressive vistas, clear waters, great fishing, and sweet Sciacchetra wine. The five fishing villages are centuries old, each with its own labyrinth of stone houses molded to the hillsides and its own miniature boat haven. Above each town the hills are terraced with grape and olive orchards. Fantastic. Warm, sunny & calm. I was in Heaven. (The only downside I could see was that there wasn't much surf in *this* Heaven.)

Under sunny blue skies we hiked the goat-path trails that link the five villages. If you've ever driven the Big Sur coast in California you know the type of terrain we found in Cinque Terre. Only instead of pine and fir, the steep hills are terraced with ancient narrow orchards tended by the locals. Down below an azure sea calmly licked the rocks. Some of the stretches along the goat paths were really treacherous, very narrow and slippery from recent rains, with precipitous drops hundreds of feet down to the rocky shore. But all along the way you could see clear to the blue bend of the horizon, with miles of rugged coast to the left and right. The seaside villages of Monterosso, Vernazza, Corniglia, Manarola, and Riomaggiore winked in out of view as we traversed the slopes.

The southernmost village, Riomaggiore, is a place fit for any lonely aesthetic, artist, composer or writer seeking refuge from the modern world. The marine views from its pastel garrets are soul soothing and sublime, the fishing village is fascinating, quaint and quiet. A sleepy place isolated from a tempestuous world.

On several occasions as we hiked we came upon some of the locals among the terraced orchards. They worked in small groups tromping around on fine nets spread under the olive trees. Grandpa tickled the branches with a long pole. Grandma instructed little kids on how to raise the net to funnel the olives towards the sack. Blankets spread with wine, bread and cheese lay nearby. With a palpable pastoral calm they waved and called out *buon giorno* as we passed.

On several occasions too, we came upon cats. They sat by the trailside or wandered down out of steep vineyards. They mewed their hellos. They were very friendly, not in the least wary. They came to us happily and rubbed against our legs like long lost friends. What they were doing out miles from the nearest village I don't know. Maybe they followed the harvesters, or other hikers like us.

After three days of this bucolic paradise our two pair of sore feet got itchy again. Time to move on. Clickety-clack, clickety-clack, the wheels were singing on the railroad tracks. We mounted the iron horse and eased on down to Lucca. Lucca, sworn enemy of Pisa, still stands, a walled city, standing as it has for a thousand years. Spent an afternoon wandering its ancient streets, visiting its cathedrals. Had a great meal in Lucca and then moved on deep into the heart of Tuscany. Arrived in another age-old walled city, this one on a hilltop, San Gimignano. Checked into a wonderful hotel with a great view of the fertile Tuscan countryside. Spent two nights there, explored every nook and cranny, and then took aim at the glory that was supposed to be Rome. On the way we took time for a brief visit to Sienna. Now I know where the color got its name.

Our trip to Rome took us through Florence again. We stopped there only long enough to check the train schedule and to transfer to an express train for Rome. In the process I was relieved of my flight bag by a couple of enterprising, very professional and opportunistic Gypsies. A moment's inattentiveness on my part was all it took. In Florence, a treasure trove of great art, I must admit, their accomplishment was in itself a work of art. The flight bag they made off with was luckily bereft of anything of real value. (No money, passports, tickets, etc.) Just a couple of bottles of Chianti, my toiletries, postcards, some papers and receipts. The loss of the wine was regrettable, but hardly worth shedding a tear over. There's no shortage of wine in Italy. The toiletries were easily replaced as well. The biggest bummer was the loss of my diary. I have been keeping a diary for over twenty years. Every night before going to sleep I spend about ten minutes noting the events of my day in my little diary. I calculate that I had spent fifty hours writing in "this" year's diary. Not only was that time now wasted, but all the data from probably one of the most interesting years I have had was lost. Truly a bummer. I feel that an irreplaceable gap has opened up in my life.

Clickety-clack, clickety-clack. Rome was all I expected, and less. Ah, poor victimized Caesar. Woe to thee oh noble Augustus. Forsooth thou foolish, fiddling Nero. What have they done to thy fair city? Ravaged and plundered and dragged her down. Despoiled her with their machinations, with their poisonous airs and noxious ways. Oh for the glorious city of one million nobles, freemen and hapless slaves that once inhabited these seven hills. How vilely Rome has quadrupled itself and grown foul in this age of abominations. Nonetheless, one can still get a sense of your legendary past.

We spent three days pounding the paths of the ancients. The ruins would have seemed barren and lifeless had it not been for the cats. Fat felines were everywhere, adorning the ruins like ancient gods, languid, well fed, luxuriantly comfortable with their surroundings. There must have been either a lot of slow rats in the vicinity or a lot of friendly tourists like the one we saw opening a can of cat food and setting it out for the already bloated loungers.

Before we had left Berlin, weeks ago, we purchased train tickets that allowed us a month of almost unlimited first class travel in Italy and Germany. So once again we saddled up and prepared to move on. After three days out in the open in Rome our lungs were singed by smog, our nostrils fried by ozone, our nerves shredded by traffic and noise. Clickety-clack, clickety-clack the wheels went singing on the railroad tracks. South again along the coast. Two and a half hours to Naples. Pulling into that corrupt city of over one million Catholic hypocrites we saw off to the left, through a pall of smog, the towering presence of wrathful Mt. Vesuvius. (It is the only active volcano on the European continent.) We checked into a hotel, had lunch, and then took off on foot to explore Mafiaville.

If getting around Rome on foot was a crapshoot because of the gazillion hell-bent-for-leather motor scooters and crazed Alfa Romeos and streaking Ferraris, Naples was like playing Russian Roulette with a 44 Magnum. Scooters hummed along on the wrong side of the road, swooped onto the sidewalk, ran stop lights. Cars hauled ass, their drivers blissfully unaware of that funny thing down there on the floorboard called a brake pedal. Trucks and buses screamed by like Formula One racers. Exhaust billowed up it in great blue clouds that hung motionless over the twisting streets. Stop signs seemed to be taken as mere suggestions. Crossing an intersection on foot was like playing a 3-D computer game with Ninja assassins jumping out at you at every turn. You had to be careful where you darted or dodged or hopped to as well. (Doggy land mines, you know.) Daunting at first, the "Flatten Me If You Can" game actually became fun after a while.

That night we watched a story on TV about a 15-year old kid who had been found in nearby Sicily pumped full of bullets. We heard later that it was meant as a message to his father, who apparently had Mafia ties. The father, it seems, had done something wrong, but not wrong enough to get himself hit. That night we lay awake and listened to the hum of cigarette boats manned by Mafia soldiers making runs back and forth to the mainland from ships with doubtful registry anchored in the Bay of Naples. Everyone in Naples seemed to be some kind or hustler, con man, or quick-change artist, or to have some shadowy connection with the black market. Smugglers come into the restaurants in Naples and proffer their goods to the diners. Management and the cops look the other way. Cops on the street are oblivious to any shenanigans other than the mugging of tourists and the robbing of banks. (Activities that are bad for business.)

(Note: we never felt threatened anywhere we went in Italy. It may have been rife with corruption, but we never felt paranoid like we do in some American cities.)

The next morning we took a local train out along the great curve of the Bay of Naples and visited the ruins of Herculaneum and Pompeii. What a mind blower. Herculaneum was a beach town and spa of four or five thousand people when Mt. Vesuvius erupted and sent down a wall of mud forty feet high and buried it in 79 AD. Since then almost the entire town has been excavated. It was fascinating and spooky wandering around in that great hole in the ground. We got there early, right when it opened for the day, and it was very still and quiet. A ghost town. The houses were beautiful, the water system sophisticated, the streets paved with stone. Once again we came upon cats, cats that seemed right at home, like they lived there. I was beginning to wonder if these calm felines might be the embodiment of the lost Romans. Everywhere we went we found them in the ruins of a fallen empire.

The afternoon was spent in Pompeii, a much larger town than Herculaneum. It was a summer retreat for wealthy Romans. Pompeii, population ten thousand, was buried on the same day as its sister city (August 24, 79 AD). Whereas Herculaneum was buried in mud, Pompeii was overcome by ash and lapilli (volcano-ejected stones). Later rain on the fallen ash hermetically sealed Pompeii, preserving it in a timeless state for over 1,700 years. The first systematic excavations began in 1778. As of this year (1998), four-fifths of the city has been uncovered. When the walled city of Pompeii was a living entity, it was located five hundred meters from the Bay of Naples. Now it lies two kilometers from the shoreline. That gives you an idea of how much volcanic material was laid down over it. Of the possible ten thousand inhabitants of Pompeii it is estimated that only 2,000 diehards perished on that fateful day in August (and they did die hard). The other eight thousand probably split when Vesuvius began pelting them with stones. There is evidence that they made a hasty departure and took some of their valuables with them. But they left plenty behind. Much of the art, statuary, household items and other valuables have been recovered from the site and are now on display in the Museo Nationale in Naples. We went there and viewed them the day after visiting the ruins. But as we wandered the fascinating streets of tragic Pompeii, we once again came upon dreamy, friendly, apparently well-fed cats. They sat staring off into the distance, as if they saw or maybe heard something way off over there. Strange. The souls of the dead?

After three weeks on the road the comforts of home beckoned, as did the now familiar sound of iron wheels on iron tracks. We booked a sleeper car on a train out of Naples one evening and rode through the night up The Boot, over the Alps (now covered with snow), and on into Munich the following morning. Clickety-clack. From there it was an all day trip back to Berlin. It had snowed all over Germany in our absence. Fields of it. Forests full.

When we arrived at the Zoological Garden Station it was after nightfall with the temperature hovering right at freezing. We emerged onto the square at the Ku'damm and found an outdoor Christmas market in full swing. Lights twinkled, young lovers strolled, organ grinders cranked, bundled up vendors hawked their goods. After three weeks of pasta we eagerly sunk our chops into steaming roast bratwurst and bread rolls. We went home and fell into bed. As we snuggled under the blankets I felt the ghost residue of the rocking of the train and heard the phantom clickety-clack. It made me think of Robert Frost's poem 'After Apple-Picking' where the picker feels the sway of the ladder and the ache of the rungs under his feet as he lies abed. As I slowly drifted off to sleep I could have sworn I heard a faint mewing sound on the furry edges of my dreams.

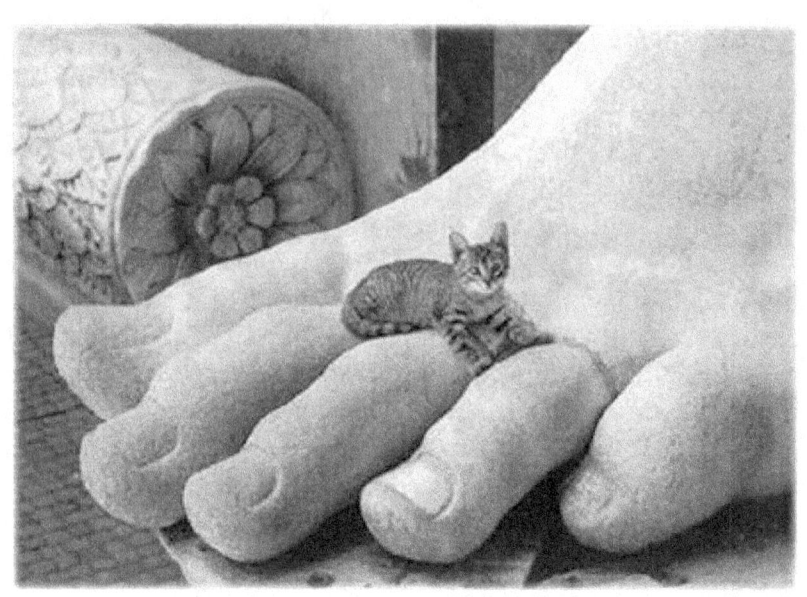

Acknowledgements

Many thanks to my family and friends who unwittingly provided me with so much grist for the writing mill. You would have fared better if this weren't a book of fiction. Thank you Edgar Allan Poe, O. Henry, W. Somerset Maugham, John Steinbeck, Raymond Chandler and all my other favorite authors for demonstrating how to tell a good story. Thanks to Chris Ritke for shooting the pool photos (including the cover), and to all the other photographers out there who so unselfishly allowed me to share their pictures as eye-candy in this book. Thank you Ojai and Ventura for nurturing me, and Chico State College for living up to your reputation. *Fa'a fetai* to the islands of Samoa for sharing your rugged beauty, your rich traditions, your toughness and your hospitality. Thanks also for helping me grow up a little. *Danke schön* to my German friend, Friedhelm Most, for having such excellent English skills and for showing me the ins and outs of Berlin and its night life. Thanks to my old friend Rabbit MacKay for sharing the Gila Monster story with me, and thank you T.L.K. for sending me that lovely Dear John Letter. It's the best one I ever got. I'm glad that despite your eloquent letter, we actually did get back together. And Jimmy O., where would I be without you? You came along when I needed a mentor. Thanks for the lifetime of reading, writing and poverty, you son of a bitch, wherever you are. And finally, many thanks to Vivian Sudhalter, my eagle-eyed editor and stalwart supporter on this book and on my previous one – the historical novel "Making the Reata."

TT

www.ingramcontent.com/pod-product-compliance
Lightning Source LLC
Chambersburg PA
CBHW060400260626
47160CB00006B/2379